WELCOME TO T...

New York Times Bestselling Author

JULIE JAMES

~A *Booklist* Top 10 Romance of the Year~
~American Library Association Reading List for Top Genre Novels~
~Best Contemporary Romance, *All About Romance* Reader Poll~
~National Readers' Choice Award Winner~
~RomCon Readers' Crown Award Winner~
~A *Cosmopolitan* Red-Hot Read~

continued . . .

About That Night

"Filled with fast quips and chemistry that heats up the pages. Readers will love the back-and-forth between the main characters . . . and the story is a fantastic romantic comedy. This one would be great on the big screen."
—*RT Book Reviews* (Top Pick)

"Julie James's best book to date! . . . It is utterly enchanting, sensual, and fabulous. Julie James gives a robust voice to contemporary courtships! Amusing and sexy, Julie James's books are flirtatious temptations for every reader."
—*Romance Junkies*

"The sexiest book of Julie James's yet . . . Smart [and] fun."
—*Smexy Books*

A Lot Like Love

"Julie James writes books I can't put down. *A Lot Like Love* kept me up way past midnight!"
—Nalini Singh, *New York Times* bestselling author

"Sexy fun. Romance fans will pop their corks over this one."
—*Library Journal*

"Fueled by equal measures of seductive wit, edge-of-the-seat suspense, and scorching-hot sexual chemistry, James's latest scintillating novel of romantic suspense is a rare treat."
—*Chicago Tribune*

"[James] exhibits her trademark sizzle and wit."
—*Booklist*

"You'll fall head over heels for *A Lot Like Love*."
—*USA Today*

"Julie James . . . is mastering the genre of romantic suspense." —*The News-Gazette* (East Central Illinois)

"James writes characters so real you can almost reach out and touch them. A delicious blend of romance and suspense."
—*RT Book Reviews*

"Just the right balance of charm, love, action, and touches of humor and suspense." —*Fresh Fiction*

"There's a whole lot to love about *A Lot Like Love* from Julie James. This is a superb read, plain and simple."
—*Babbling About Books, and More*

Something About You

"Smart, snappy, funny yet realistic. I can't count the number of times I laughed while reading the book . . . This is one book I can totally recommend." —*Dear Author*

"From first impressions to the last page, it's worth shaking your tail feather over . . . This is a contemporary romance well worth savoring, and laughing over, and reading all over again." —*Smart Bitches, Trashy Books*

"Just plain fun! James is a master of witty repartee."
—*RT Book Reviews*

Practice Makes Perfect

"A tantalizing dessert—a delicious, delightful read that all hopeless romantics will enjoy." —*Chicago Sun-Times*

continued . . .

It Happened
One Wedding

JULIE JAMES

JOVE BOOKS, NEW YORK

THE BERKLEY PUBLISHING GROUP
Published by the Penguin Group
Penguin Group (USA) LLC
375 Hudson Street, New York, New York 10014

USA • Canada • UK • Ireland • Australia • New Zealand • India • South Africa • China

penguin.com

A Penguin Random House Company

IT HAPPENED ONE WEDDING

A Jove Book / published by arrangement with the author

Jove Books are published by The Berkley Publishing Group.
JOVE® is a registered trademark of Penguin Group (USA) LLC.
The "J" design is a trademark of Penguin Group (USA) LLC.

For information, address: The Berkley Publishing Group,
a division of Penguin Group (USA) LLC,
375 Hudson Street, New York, New York 10014.

ISBN: 978-0-425-25127-0

PUBLISHING HISTORY
Jove mass-market edition / May 2014

PRINTED IN THE UNITED STATES OF AMERICA

10 9 8 7 6 5 4 3 2 1

Cover design by Rita Frangie.
Cover photograph of wedding shoes © Miljan Mladenovic / Getty Images.

To my parents

Acknowledgments

I'm indebted to several individuals who helped me make this book what it is today. First and foremost is Brent Dempsey, whose knowledge and insight were invaluable to the development of this story. I'm incredibly appreciative for all the assistance.

Thanks as well to Dave Scalzo for answering my many questions about the world of private equity and investment banking, and whose enthusiasm for the subject was key in the development stages of my heroine. I'm also particularly grateful to Pamela Clare for her knowledge of firearms and for going above and beyond in providing me with the technical expertise for a shooting range scene that, sadly, had to be cut from the book. Also thanks to Dr. Alex Lin for his obstetrics expertise.

I'm truly appreciative of my wonderful beta readers, Elyssa Papa and Kati Brown, two smart and thoughtful women who make my stories stronger and are a genuine pleasure to work with. Thanks to my editor, Wendy McCurdy, who always knows how to point me in the right direction with a story, and whose insight was instrumental in helping me through the early drafts of this book. Thanks to my publicist, Erin Galloway, and the entire team at Berkley, and also to my agent, Robin

Rue, for all her support and knowledge and encourage-
ment this past year.

Finally, to my husband, who married a lawyer and now
lives instead with a woman who wakes him up at 3 A.M.
saying she has no clue where to go with her book.
Thanks for always listening.

One

WELL-TRAINED IN THE art of reading the subtle cues of body language, FBI Special Agent Vaughn Roberts was quite certain this date was going down in flames.

On the upside, it wasn't *his* date that was crashing and burning. Rather, the unfortunate rendezvous was between the attractive auburn-haired woman who'd caught his eye when she'd walked into the coffee shop twenty minutes ago and some dude in a striped banker shirt who apparently was vying for the Guinness record for World's Longest Story Ever.

The woman nodded along with the story, trying to appear interested. She blinked, stifled a yawn, and then quickly grabbed her coffee and took a sip to cover.

Vaughn smiled. He guessed that this was either a blind date or an online match, given the way the woman had looked around the shop when she first arrived, paused, and then walked over to Striped Banker Shirt's table with a tentative smile. He also guessed, given the way things were going, that this would be the *only* date these two would ever have. But he gave the woman props for being polite while the guy continued to ramble on.

One of the most important first-date rules, Vaughn knew, was to ask *questions*. Women liked men who were curious about them—and, just as important, they liked men who paid attention to their answers. As a man who was trained to ask questions and pay careful attention to answers, he had something of an edge in this.

Striped Banker Shirt, on the other hand, obviously missed the memo.

Going back to his own business, Vaughn pulled out his cell phone and checked his e-mail. He had ten minutes to kill before meeting his younger brother, Simon, and Simon's new girlfriend at a restaurant around the corner for dinner—a dinner he was very curious about.

This was his first time meeting Isabelle since his brother had begun dating her three months earlier. But Simon had mentioned her on more than one occasion, and that spoke volumes. Like Vaughn, Simon avoided talking too much about any one particular woman around his family. Doing so inherently invited numerous questions from their very traditionally minded, very Catholic mother, who'd been hoping for one of her sons to settle down for some time now. Having written Vaughn off as a lost cause—the mere idea of a thirty-four-year-old committed bachelor being thoroughly "un-Irish"—she'd pinned all her hopes on Simon.

But now here they were, the first time Simon had specifically asked Vaughn to meet someone he was dating. Not unexpectedly, Vaughn was under strict instructions to call his mother with a full report as soon as dinner was over.

A masculine laugh cut across the coffee shop, interrupting Vaughn's thoughts. He glanced up from his phone, thinking perhaps the date he'd been observing had turned for the better.

No dice.

Striped Banker Shirt was still rambling away, now laughing at his *own* stories, because—obviously—not only was he a good-looking guy in an expensive suit with a knack for scintillating conversation, but he was *just so funny, too*!

Right.

Women liked confident men, no doubt. But as a guy who'd

never had any problems meeting women—quite the contrary, actually——Vaughn also knew that a woman wanted a guy who expressed interest in getting to know *her* specifically. And Striped Banker Shirt had failed woefully on that score.

Vaughn saw the woman make a deliberate gesture of checking her watch. Curious, he watched to see what would happen next. The next time Striped Banker Shirt came up for air, she quickly jumped into the conversation with a smile. The smile temporarily silenced Striped Banker Shirt, as well it should.

She had a gorgeous smile.

It was about this time that Vaughn really began paying attention to *her*, instead of the awkward but interesting-to-watch-and-pass-the-time circumstances of their date. Her auburn hair fell past her shoulders in a stylish, layered cut. In fact, everything about her looked stylish and put-together, from her ivory ruffled blouse to her sleek gray pencil skirt to the light summer scarf around her neck. He guessed her to be in her early thirties, and in some kind of professional occupation, given her well-tailored clothes and classic heels.

In other words, she was smart, attractive, and seemingly single.

He could work with this.

After a few moments, Striped Banker Shirt stood up from the table, gesturing emphatically as if to say, *No problem, I have somewhere to be, too.* And obviously he had places to go because not only was he good-looking and funny with a fancy job, *but he was important, too*!

Sure.

Now Auburn had a decision to make. She could take the easy way out—*E-mail me, let's do this again*, and then never write the guy back—or she could go for the more awkward, but honest, *This was nice, but I'm just not feeling a connection between us.*

Striped Banker Shirt pointed to his phone. *How about I call you sometime?* Then he waited to see if he was in.

Vaughn waited along with him.

The woman shook her head regretfully.

Vaughn's interest shot up fivefold. As a man who valued

honesty in his own relationships, he liked this woman's style. It took balls to go with the truth in these circumstances.

Striped Banker Shirt clearly had not expected the rejection, and, for that, Vaughn was sympathetic. He watched as the guy asked the woman a question, ironically choosing this moment to finally give her an opportunity to speak. She appeared to answer graciously, saying something that made him nod and, with a bit of a bewildered expression, head for the door.

As soon as he left, she let out a sigh of relief and took her cell phone out of her purse.

Vaughn watched as she crossed one long leg over the other, getting comfortable in her chair.

It would be a shame to let a woman like that end her Friday night on such a sour note.

WELL, THAT HAD been unfortunate.

Sidney Sinclair texted her best friend, Trish, who'd helped create her dating profile last Saturday night over a bottle of pinot noir. At the time, the idea of online dating had struck her as fun and exciting—and maybe it would still prove to be that—but thus far, she was batting 0 and 1.

BACHELOR NUMBER ONE IS A NO-GO, she texted Trish. HE TALKED TOO MUCH.

Within seconds, Trish texted back. ISN'T TALKING A GOOD THING ON A FIRST DATE?

Of course, Trish was trying to put a positive spin on things. As the happily-married-with-child best friend of a single, thirty-three-year-old woman, it was part of the job description.

AS IN, DONKEY FROM SHREK TOO MUCH, Sidney typed back.

OUCH. THAT'S NOT GOOD.

No kidding. William, aka Bachelor Number One, had seemed to have a lot of potential. As a trader, he was in the investment business. Right there, they'd had some common ground, something they—meaning her included—could talk about. And he'd said he liked to travel, go to the movies, and enjoyed trying new restaurants in the city. All of which fell solidly in the "plus" column.

What he hadn't mentioned in his profile was that he liked to talk about these things in mind-numbing detail.

Not that Sidney couldn't appreciate that people sometimes got nervous on first dates and might possibly talk a lot to compensate for that. But William hadn't seemed nervous so much as full of himself—and that definitely merited a big old pass in her book.

One of the things Sidney had decided, now that she was back in Chicago after eight years in New York, was that she needed to have a plan when it came to dating. It had been six months since she'd broken her engagement with her now ex-fiancé— plenty of time to mourn the loss of that relationship.

Moving back to Chicago, her hometown, was her chance to get a fresh start. And to make the most of the opportunity, Sidney had decided to draw on the skills she'd cultivated in her professional life. As a director at one of the most success-ful private equity firms in the country, she had great instincts when it came to determining whether a company was a good or bad investment. Those instincts, in fact, were the reason her new firm had approached her three months ago, at the Manhattan-based investment bank where she'd previously worked, and asked her to manage a four-billion-dollar fund they'd nearly finished raising.

Now she simply needed to apply those same instincts to her personal life. One had to be somewhat businesslike in order to survive the thirtysomething dating scene; to be suc-cessful, she needed to be open to new prospects, but also decisive and quick to move on when a candidate looked to be a less-than-stellar investment.

Maybe some would say her approach to dating was too pragmatic, perhaps even somewhat aloof. Maybe some people would say that she should follow her heart instead of her head when it came to falling in love.

She used to be one of those people.

"At least the coffee's good here."

The rich masculine voice had a hint of rough grit to it. Sidney looked up from her cell phone and—

Criminy.

It was him. The hot guy she'd noticed when she'd first walked into the coffee shop. He was tall and somehow managed to look ruggedly sexy, despite the rather conservative dark gray suit and blue tie he wore. Maybe it was the short cut of his thick, brown hair. Or his keen hazel eyes. Or his strong, chiseled jaw with that just-perfect amount of five-o'clock shadow.

Too bad she had no clue what he was talking about.

"The coffee?" she asked. "As opposed to . . . ?"

"The conversation," he said. "Your date looked like it could've gone better."

"You noticed that, did you?" She wasn't sure how she felt about the fact that a perfect stranger had been paying such close attention to her date.

"Yes. But only because I'm trained to notice things." He flashed her a smile. "It's not like I'm some creepy perv or something."

"Probably that's exactly what a creepy perv would say."

"True." There was a teasing gleam in his eyes. "I could show you my badge, if that'll make you feel better."

Sidney looked him over more closely. Presumably, this reference to a "badge" meant he was in some kind of law enforcement. She could see that—he had the bold air of someone accustomed to being in a position of authority. "Why do I get the feeling I'm not the first strange woman you've offered to show your badge to?"

"Trust me, in my line of work, a lot of strange women have seen my badge. Strange men, too." With that, he grabbed the chair on the opposite end of the table and sat down.

Um. . . hello? Sidney gestured to the chair he'd just helped himself to. "What are you doing?"

He looked at her as if this was obvious. "Starting a conversation."

"But I don't even know you."

"That's why I'm starting a conversation. Let's begin with the basics. Like your name."

Ah, right. Sidney knew exactly what was happening here. This guy had seen her on her failed date, had obviously deduced that she was single, and now thought she was easy pickings.

"I'm not giving you my name," she said.

"All right, then. 'Ms. Doe,' it is," he said, undeterred. "Why don't you tell me a little about yourself, Ms. Doe?"

She leveled him with her best "Scram, buddy" gaze, perfected after eight years of living in New York. "So we're going with the good-cop pickup routine now? How original."

His tone turned wicked. "I can easily switch to the bad-cop routine, if you like."

Sidney fought back a blush at the innuendo. "I'm betting those kinds of comments normally work really well for you, don't they?"

"The question is, are they working for you?"

"Not at all."

"Damn. Guess I'd better switch tactics, then."

"And I'd love to stick around for that. Really." Sidney checked her watch. "But, unfortunately, I have a dinner I need to get to."

He surprised her then.

His expression turned more earnest. "Okay, look. Maybe I'm coming on a little strong here. Normally I would've thought up some witty opening line, followed by this whole cute pickup routine in which I charm and impress you—yes, I see the skeptical look there, but you'll have to trust me on this: it's quality stuff. But like you, I have somewhere I need to be. So I'm under the gun.

"The simple truth is, you've had me intrigued from the moment you walked into this coffee shop. And I'd like to know more. You don't have to give me your number or even your name. Just meet me here tomorrow, same time. I'll buy you a cup of coffee, we'll talk, and then you can decide whether I really am the asshole you're thinking I might be." A smile curled at the edges of his mouth. "I might actually surprise you on that front."

Confident, flirty, and drop-dead gorgeous. It was a lethal combination that Sidney had no doubt typically played very well for this guy. She could easily say *Why not?*, meet him again tomorrow, and if he was as cocky as she thought he might be, that would be the end of that. She'd get a free cup of coffee out of it and the cheap thrill of having a guy who looked like him chasing after her.

But.

The problem was, she knew this guy. She'd dated this guy. Hell, she'd been *engaged* to this guy. Manhattan was crawling with guys just like him: confident, good-looking, and slick as all get-out. And she was plenty familiar with the way things would turn out because she'd once gone down this exact road with Brody: this guy wouldn't actually be an asshole tomorrow, instead he would be smooth and smart and witty, and coffee would turn into drinks and drinks into dinner, and she would have flutters of excitement in her stomach throughout every moment of it. Blah, blah, blah.

She was so *over* this guy.

Because, in truth, any woman who allowed herself to be swept up in the romantic fantasy of dating this kind of guy would be ignoring one crucial fact.

This guy was a bad investment.

And she knew that better than anyone.

Still, the logical part of her realized that the hazel-eyed, dark-scruff iteration of This Guy who sat across from her right then hadn't actually done anything wrong to her. Because of that, she smiled in an effort to be polite. "That's nice of you to ask. But, unfortunately, I'm going to have to say no."

"Great." He nodded, as if expecting this very answer. Then his brow furrowed, and he cocked his head. "Wait—what?"

Sidney bit her lip to hold back a laugh. Ah . . . when she told this story later to Trish, the perplexed look on this guy's face would be the highlight.

"I'm afraid I have to pass on meeting you tomorrow," she explained.

His confused expression turned to one of understanding. "Oh, sure. Because you have other plans, right?"

She shook her head. "Not really. It's more just a flat-out no."

"Huh." He folded his arms over his chest, taking a moment

to think that over. "I have to say, I was expecting a different answer."

Yes, she got that.

"Can I ask why?" he said.

"I just don't think you're my type," she said, for simplicity's sake.

"Interesting. You were able to determine 'my type' in the all of five minutes we've been talking?"

Now he was pushing her buttons a bit. "Yes."

"That's impressive. See, it's my job to size people up. So I'm intrigued to hear if you're as good as you obviously think you are."

Sidney threw him a look. "Honey, you know exactly what your type is. And so does every single woman in her thirties."

"I see." He leaned back in his chair and beckoned with this hand. "Now I really need to hear this."

Logically, Sidney knew this was not the kind of conversation one should have with a perfect stranger in a coffee shop. First of all, there was no point. Second, she had places to be, and allegedly so did he.

But his eyes dared her.

Despite her better judgment, she felt a spike of adrenaline course through her, a rush to rise to his challenge. Back when she'd first started working as an investment banker in Manhattan, she'd known plenty of men who'd assumed they could intimidate her with tactics just like these.

They'd assumed wrong.

So she, too, sat back in her chair and got comfortable. She'd tried to be as diplomatic as possible in her rejection, but, hey, if this guy insisted on answers, then answers he would get.

"All right." Her eyes raked over him in assessment. "You're thirty-four or thirty-five, gainfully employed, never been married. You think maybe you'll settle down one day, perhaps when you're forty, but for now you work hard at your job, so you want to play hard, too. You tend to skew more toward dating women in their midtwenties, because women in their early twenties seem just a little too young and women in their thirties frustrate you with the way they all want to talk about marriage and kids by the third date. You'll go out with a girl a few times, you'll have a lot of fun together, and then when she starts pushing for something more serious, you'll move on to someone else, wondering why it is that women can't be content to just *date* without needing a commitment. And why would you want to commit to one person right now? For men as attractive as you, this city is one big candy store, filled with so many shiny treats, you couldn't possibly choose just one. So instead, you run around with your obviously healthy ego, sampling as many of the goods as you can get your hands on—simply because you can."

When finished, Sidney took a deep breath and felt strangely . . . good. For the last six months, she'd been so determined to move forward after her breakup with Brody, and to keep a stiff upper lip around her friends, family, and work colleagues, that she'd barely vented at all to anyone. So it felt great to finally express her frustration.

To this guy, apparently.

Better him than anyone else, she figured. It wasn't as though she was ever going to see him again.

He rested his arms on the table. "Well. On behalf of the male population, let me be the first to apologize for whatever *he* did."

Sidney's eyes narrowed. He was being sarcastic—fair enough, given what she'd just said to him. But that hit a little too close to home. "We're done here, right?"

"I'd say so." He got up from his chair. "Enjoy your coffee, Ms. Doe." He walked out of the café without further word.

Sidney took a deep breath, shaking it off. She was meeting her sister, Isabelle, and her sister's boyfriend in a couple minutes and didn't want to show up for dinner in a crummy mood.

She noticed that the man at the table next to her, in his sixties, was watching her. Clearly, he'd caught the show.

"Well, he *asked* for my opinion," she said defensively.

"I'm just wondering what you're going to do to the next guy who walks in," the older man said. "They're gonna start taking them out of here in body bags."

Probably it was high time she left this coffee shop.

Two

SO, APPARENTLY, THAT was a *no* from Ms. Doe.

Vaughn cut across the street, dodging around a taxi in the intersection while trying to dislodge the self-righteous speech that was stuck in his head like an annoying earworm.

And why would you want to commit to one person right now? For men as attractive as you, this city is one big candy store, filled with so many shiny treats, you couldn't possibly choose just one.

Well, in a nutshell . . . yes.

He didn't deny it; he liked to have fun. He had a healthy dating life, he was free to go out with different women and have a good time, and he didn't see why he should feel guilty about any of that. There wasn't some big angsty reason he avoided commitment, he simply enjoyed his life as it was. He was a single man with a good job living in a vibrant city teeming with interesting people, a variety of things to do and see, new restaurants and bars to try. He didn't knock anyone else for wanting to settle down, but he, personally, didn't feel a compulsion to do so at this particular point in his life. Maybe when he was forty.

He could practically hear the snarky Ms. Doe smugly shouting *I knew it!* in his head.

Indeed, she'd pretty much described him to a tee—something that undoubtedly would have impressed him more if she hadn't been such a pill about it. He felt a little guilty about the sarcastic comment he'd made, but this was substantially mitigated by the fact that she'd so obviously relished busting his balls first. Not the way things typically went when he hit on a woman—not to toot his own horn, but women really dug the FBI thing—but, oh well. It wasn't like he was ever going to see her again.

Most thankfully.

Vaughn caught sight of The Boarding House, the restaurant where he was meeting Simon and Isabelle, and pushed all thoughts of the cantankerous Ms. Doe from his mind. Although he'd been to the bar several times, which was known for its massive chandelier made out of nine thousand wineglasses, he'd never eaten in the main dining room on the third floor. The space, he saw, had been designed with exposed beams, hardwood floors, large bay windows, and what appeared to be thousands of wine bottles artfully installed in the ceiling.

He saw Simon seated at a booth by one of the windows next to a pretty woman in her mid-to-late twenties with strawberry blond hair.

So this was the mysterious Isabelle.

He headed over to their table. Simon stood up, gripped his shoulder in hello, and immediately made the introductions.

"Isabelle, this is my brother, Vaughn. Vaughn . . . this is Isabelle."

"It's a pleasure, Isabelle," Vaughn said warmly, while shaking her hand. This was obviously a big deal for Simon, so he planned to be on his best behavior. Which meant he'd save all embarrassing anecdotes about his brother at least until the main course.

"It's nice to meet you," she said. "Simon's told me so much about you."

"I had to edit a few of the stories, but she gets the gist," Simon teased.

Chuckling, Vaughn sat down. He noticed the seat next to him had a place setting.

"Isabelle's sister is coming tonight, too," Simon explained.

"Meeting both families?" Vaughn raised an eyebrow. "This is getting serious."

"Actually, Simon has already met Sidney," Isabelle said. "But we thought it would be nice to have dinner with both of you tonight."

Vaughn thought that seemed a little . . . interesting. Perhaps something was up? "The more the merrier." He took a sip of water, checking out Simon's big goofy smile over the top of his glass.

Something was up, all right.

"Ah, perfect timing. There's Sidney now." Isabelle waved excitedly at someone across the restaurant.

Vaughn had his back to the entrance, so he turned around to look.

No.

Fucking.

Way.

It was the cantankerous Ms. Doe.

Catching sight of him in that very same moment, she stopped dead in her tracks. Vaughn was pretty sure she muttered *Oh shit* under her breath.

His sentiments exactly.

Sidney quickly recovered and headed over.

Isabelle got up from the table and hugged her. "I'm so glad you're here." She turned to Vaughn. "This is Simon's brother, Vaughn. Vaughn, my sister, Sidney."

Vaughn stood up and held out his hand. Given the circumstances, he had no intention of indicating that they'd previously met. "Nice to meet you, Sidney."

Locking eyes with him, she seemed to be on the same page. She slid her hand into his. "You, too."

"Sid," Simon said, as if they were old friends. He came around the table and pulled her in for a big hug.

Then they all took their seats, Vaughn next to Sidney. He folded his hands on the table. *Well, isn't this cozy?*

Isabelle looked at Simon. He shrugged, still with the goofy smile. She turned back to Sidney and Vaughn, speaking in a rush. "Okay, I know we should wait, so that you two can get to know each other a little better, but I can't help it. Simon and I have some news."

"In that case, Vaughn and I are happy to fast-forward through the getting-to-know-each-other part," Sidney said with a charming smile.

"Quite happy," he agreed, matching her charm with his own.

"Aw, you guys are so sweet. Well, then, I guess there's no sense beating around the bush . . . " Isabelle sneaked a look at Simon and then threw out her hands. "We're getting married!"

Vaughn's mouth fell open at the same time Sidney covered hers with her hands.

"Oh my god," Sidney said.

He wholeheartedly concurred with that sentiment. His brother had *proposed* after only knowing Isabelle for three months? He'd thought they were going to announce that they were moving in together, which would've been a significant milestone in its own right. But *marriage*?

Kind of a big deal, that.

"This is such wonderful news," Sidney said. With a huge grin, she stood up to hug her sister.

Vaughn looked across the table and saw his brother watching him with obvious hesitation.

Seeing that . . . got to him.

Okay, yes. In his mind, proposing to a woman after only knowing her for three months was utterly crazy. How could anyone be that certain, in such a short amount of time, about spending the rest of his or her life with just one person? His eye twitched at the mere thought. No more chase. No more fun one-night stands. No more thinking about that threesome you'd had with what's-her-name and her hot friend, and wondering if they might be up for it again some time. *Poof*—all of that gone, just like that.

But this was Simon's decision, not his. And while Vaughn

wasn't entirely sure he understood what had motivated his brother to propose this quickly, he *did* know that he wasn't going to be the asshole who spoiled such a big moment.

So he, too, got up from his chair. He grinned and slapped Simon on the back. "My little brother's getting married. Holy shit."

Simon laughed and pulled him in for a brotherly hug.

More congratulations followed—Sidney hugged Simon, Vaughn hugged Isabelle, Vaughn and Sidney kept a mutual safe distance from each other—and then they all took their seats.

"One of the reasons Isabelle and I wanted to tell you first is because we'd like you to be the best man and maid of honor at the wedding," Simon said.

Isabelle wagged her finger jokingly. "So no fast-forwarding over the getting-to-know-each-other part. As the two most important people in our lives"—she gestured between her and Simon—"you two are going to be stuck together a lot."

"How much fun is this going to be?" Simon asked enthusiastically.

Vaughn and Sidney eyed each other skeptically.

Right.

ALL THINGS CONSIDERED, dinner went fairly smoothly.

Vaughn had to hand it to Sidney—the woman had a stellar poker face. She wasn't overly chatty with him, but she didn't ignore him, either. Her tone, and the things she said, were perfectly polite.

It certainly helped that for the first hour of dinner, he and Sidney were barely required to speak to each other at all. Almost immediately after Simon and Isabelle dropped their engagement news, a swirling vortex of bridal shower/wedding reception/honeymoon talk descended upon the Roberts/Sinclair party, ensnaring all in its path. In response, Vaughn did what any special agent would do when finding himself in a situation in which he was thoroughly out of his comfort zone—he maintained as low a profile as possible and kept his mouth shut.

But when the desserts arrived, Isabelle and Simon tried to spark more of a dialogue between their siblings.

"Do you feel like you're settled in at your new office?" Simon asked Sidney. He turned to Vaughn to explain. "Sidney recently moved back here after living in New York for several years."

"I'm getting there," Sidney said. "We closed our fund last week, so now is the time when I really get to work."

"What is it you do?" Vaughn asked. *Other than bust the balls of men who innocently try to hit on you, that is.*

"I used to be an investment banker. But I switched over to the buy side—now I'm a director at a private equity firm."

"Sounds impressive." Actually, as an agent on the FBI's white-collar crime squad, Vaughn was familiar enough with Sidney's business to know two things: one, having landed a director position, she was very good at what she did, and, two, she made a ton of money for doing it. But *she* didn't need to know he was impressed from a professional standpoint. He could easily picture her in her high-powered job, in her fancy office, buying companies and figuring out how to turn them around and sell them at a profit.

Under different circumstances, he probably would've found that image rather sexy.

"Vaughn's a special agent with the FBI," Isabelle told Sidney, keeping the conversation going.

Sidney looked him over, likely remembering his teasing offer to show her his badge. "What kind of cases do you work on?"

"I'm on the white-collar crime squad. I mostly investigate public corruption crimes."

"Vaughn does a lot of undercover work," Simon said proudly. "He's one of the small percentage of agents who've gone through the FBI's undercover school at Quantico."

"I didn't realize you guys actually had a school for that," Sidney said.

"Me, either." Isabelle looked intrigued. "Are there classrooms and everything?"

"Yes, but most of the time we were off campus, using a nearby town to make the situations feel more authentic,"

Vaughn said. "It's basically three weeks of role-playing under-cover scenarios and learning how to react if things go wrong."

"How cool," Isabelle said. "Isn't that interesting, Sid?"

"Fascinating." Her tone a touch dry, Sidney took a long sip of her wine.

And so the dance continued.

Vaughn and Sidney navigated their way through the chit-chat, all politeness and congeniality, for the rest of the evening. The only time that façade broke was for a brief moment outside the restaurant, after they'd finished dinner. Isabelle hung back to use the restroom after saying her good-byes, and Simon stepped away to give his ticket to the valet.

Leaving Sidney and Vaughn alone.

She walked over to a waiting taxi. Vaughn followed and, being a gentleman, opened the door for her.

"I would offer to split a cab, but I'm afraid me and my 'obviously healthy ego' would crowd you too much." He added a smooth smile just in case Simon was watching.

"Been waiting to say that all night, have you?" she quipped.

"Trust me, it's by far the most polite of all the things I've been waiting to say all night." He gestured with his hand—*don't let the taxi door hit you on the way out*—then watched as she climbed into the car.

The slit of her pencil skirt parted mid-thigh as she scooted in.

She glanced up and caught him looking.

Yeah, whatever. Vaughn shut the door firmly.

Pill or not, the woman had some damn fine legs.

SIDNEY SHOOK HER head as the cab drove away from the restaurant, still in disbelief that the guy with whom she'd had her snarky run-in at the coffee shop was Simon's *brother.* Isabelle's future brother-in-law.

Apparently it was just one of those fluke coincidences. She, being efficient, had scheduled her date with William at a cof-fee shop close to the restaurant where she was later set to meet Simon and Isabelle. According to the conversation she'd overheard between Vaughn and Simon, Vaughn had left work later than expected, without enough time to fight traffic all the way home and change out of his suit, so he'd decided to kill a half-hour at the same café.

Fate undoubtedly was cracking herself up over this one.

She pulled out her phone to text Trish, and then saw it was after ten o'clock. Thinking it was a little late to be gossiping with anyone who had a four-month-old baby at home, she decided to hold off until the morning.

The cab pulled to a stop in front of her home, a turn-of-the-century brownstone town house that had been gut-rehabbed by the previous owners. Sidney paid the fare, cut across the street, and then let herself in through the front door. She set down her purse and kicked off her heels, her mind playing through Vaughn's last comment to her.

Trust me, it's by far the most polite of all the things I've been waiting to say all night.

He was so . . . smug. Annoying, too. And even more annoying was the fact that he just *had* to be good-looking, with his interesting undercover job—*Ooh, look at me, I'm a hot FBI agent, I went to school to be this bad-ass*—blah, blah, blah. And now her sister was marrying his brother, which meant that she would be stuck bumping into this guy for eternity.

Wonderful.

A knock at the front door jolted Sidney out of her reverie. Not expecting any company at ten thirty on a Friday night, she checked the security camera that linked to her television.

Surprisingly, it was Isabelle.

Sidney opened the front door and let her sister inside. "Hey, you. I didn't think I'd be seeing you again tonight."

"I asked Simon to drop me off so we could talk. You know, just the two of us."

Sidney smiled, less surprised now. Despite a five-year age gap, she and her sister had always been close. Having been raised by a mostly absentee father and a revolving door of nannies and stepmothers, they'd been the only constant in each other's lives. She and Isabelle had talked and Skyped constantly while she'd been living in New York, but she'd nevertheless missed this—being able to talk in person.

She led her sister into the living room and plunked down on the couch. She was eager for all the details she hadn't wanted to ask in front of Simon and his oh-so-special agent brother. "So? Were you totally surprised when Simon asked you to marry him? I mean, it has only been three months."

Sitting on the couch next to Sidney, Isabelle curled her feet underneath her. "Yes and no. The subject came up when we were having a conversation about something else."

"What sort of 'something else'?"

"I'd just told Simon that I was pregnant."

Wait—*what*? Sidney blinked. "Oh my god."

A smile peeked at the corners of Isabelle's mouth. "That was pretty much my first reaction. Simon's, too."

Wow. Her sister—her little sister—was *pregnant*. Sidney didn't know where to start, she had so many questions. "So this was obviously unplanned, then."

"Um, yeah. Three weeks ago, I'd decided to give Simon a drawer of his own in my bedroom. You know, so he could have a place to keep his things when he slept over. We'd opened a bottle of champagne to celebrate—because at that time, *that* was a big step in our relationship—and we got a little tipsy. The details are somewhat fuzzy, but I'm kind of thinking we didn't get the condom on fast enough."

Oops.

Sidney reached for her sister's hand, still getting up to speed. "How are you feeling about all this?"

Isabelle took a deep breath and exhaled. "It's been a bit of a whirlwind since I found out, and I'll obviously have to juggle some things around with my clients once the baby comes," she said, referring to her social work practice. "But I think Simon and I are starting to wrap our minds around it now."

"Is this why you want to get married so quickly? Because— not to sound all big sister here—you don't *have* to get married just because you're having a baby, Izz."

"I know." Isabelle looked at her earnestly. "But the thing is, I knew I wanted to marry Simon after our second date.

He's the one, Sid. And getting married before the baby comes is really important to him. So, sure—maybe things are happening faster than I'd envisioned, but we're rolling with it."

Sidney searched her sister's face for any sign of uncertainty. "You're sure this is what you want?"

Isabelle nodded, without any hesitation. "Positive."

Sidney's big-sister protective instincts relaxed a bit. "Okay, then. I guess we'd better get going on those wedding plans." She clapped her hands excitedly. "What do we have? Eight months to pull this off? Maybe seven, to be safe?"

Isabelle pursed her lips. "Well, see, here's the thing about that. Apparently, Simon's mother is a very traditional Catholic. He's worried she'll be disappointed if she knows that I'm pregnant before we get married, so we're kind of hoping to have the wedding before we tell her about the baby."

"Oh. So you're eloping?"

"I threw that out as a possibility, but Simon says his parents would be crushed if we did that. So, instead we're thinking about having a wedding here before I start to show."

"That's great, Izz. But I'm thinking Simon's mom is going to figure out the situation when—*hello*—a baby shows up five months after your wedding. Unless you're planning on telling her that the stork now offers expedited shipping?"

Isabelle threw her a look. *Ha, ha.* "Obviously, we'll have to tell her before that. I just don't want her to be upset before the wedding." She paused. "I mean, I've never met the woman, and I don't want her first impression of me to be that I'm the girl who trapped her son into marriage by getting pregnant after dating him for only three months. That's not how it's supposed to go the first time I meet my future mother-in-law. My in-laws are supposed to be happy that I'm marrying their son, and my mother-in-law is supposed to . . . I don't know . . . pass along family recipes to me, and maybe show me how to make a perfect piecrust, and help me pick out the baby's baptism gown, and just . . . do all those things that moms do."

Sidney's throat suddenly felt a little tight, knowing exactly where Isabelle was coming from. Both of them had missed out on so many of those kinds of moments, since their mother had passed away from breast cancer when Sidney was nine years old and Isabelle only four. And since their father was . . . well, their father, he hadn't provided much by way of a "typical" nuclear family experience.

"I just really want Simon's parents to like me." Isabelle smiled cheekily. "Once they see how adorable I am, and how perfect Simon and I are together, we'll spring the news on them. And, in fairness, it's not just Simon's parents. This pregnancy is something special, something personal between Simon and me. I don't want a bunch of people talking about how I got knocked up before getting married. They can say what they want after the wedding—but for now, Simon and I want to keep this between us. Well, and you."

Sidney squeezed her sister's hand. "You know what I think? I think it's nobody's business whether you're pregnant. You tell people when you're ready. When Trish was pregnant, she waited until she was out of the first trimester to tell anyone. You're just extending that a little."

"Exactly," Isabelle said emphatically.

"So, three months, huh? It's going to be tight, pulling that off." Sidney winked. "Lucky for you, you happen to have a kick-ass maid of honor to help."

Isabelle bit her lip, suddenly looking hesitant for the first time that evening. "So here's the part where you need to be totally honest with me. I looked everywhere in the city for availability in the next three months—but not surprisingly, things are booked. I did find one venue that happened to have an opening the Saturday before Labor Day. It's a beautiful place, too."

"Great. So what's the problem?"

"It's the Lakeshore Club."

Sidney paused, hearing that.

Oh.

"I knew it was a terrible idea," Isabelle said immediately. "Forget I even asked, Sid."

Terrible may have been a bit extreme. But admittedly, Sidney hadn't expected her sister to say she wanted to have her wedding at the Lakeshore Club—the place where Sidney had planned to have *her* wedding reception, just six months ago.

Given how that experience had turned out, with Sidney calling off the wedding two weeks before the big day, the idea of Isabelle having her wedding there was indeed a little . . . weird. But was she really going to let a little weirdness get in the way of her sister's plans? She knew how much Isabelle wanted to pull this off, and besides, the Lakeshore Club was indeed a great venue.

As she had many times in the last six months, Sidney took sentiment out of the equation and fell back on pragmatism.

And a pragmatist would say that her pregnant sister shouldn't be stopped from having the wedding of her dreams just because Sidney's ex-fiancé had been screwing his twenty-four-year-old personal trainer.

That decided, she answered Isabelle with a deliberately easy smile.

"Not a terrible idea at all. The Lakeshore Club it is."

Three

MONDAY MORNING, SIDNEY sat at the head of a sleek, gunmetal-gray granite table in one of the conference rooms at the downtown offices of Monroe Ellers. Six pairs of eyes stared back at her, belonging to men and women who were among the best and the brightest graduates of their MBA programs, who now had successful careers as associates and analysts at one of the finest private equity firms in the country.

Men and women she would now lead.

For the past few weeks, she'd been settling into her new role, acclimating herself to the company, and working with the other directors in closing the fund and bringing in the last of the investors. They'd raised four billion dollars, a good-sized fund, from a combination of clients that included corporate investors, university endowments, private investors, and teacher pension funds.

Now it was time to get the ball rolling. They had the money, so the next step was for her to find companies that her clients should invest in. It was time for her to step up to the plate and show that she was as good as the partners at Monroe Ellers believed she was.

"Who at this table has found me the next Dunkin' Donuts?" she asked the group.

Six pairs of eyes glanced worriedly at each other, undoubtedly not having expected this question. *Shit, she expects us to have an answer to* that*?* Dunkin' Donuts was one of the most successful consumer product private equity turnarounds in recent years. The company had been on the verge of being wiped out by Krispy Kreme until it was purchased by several private equity firms—who then stepped in and changed the marketing plan to focus on coffee and beverages instead of doughnuts. It turned out to be a brilliant strategy: six years later, the private equity funds nearly doubled their investment by selling Dunkin' Donuts for almost two billion dollars in profit.

But no director, no matter how good, should ever expect from her associates—nor guarantee to her clients—that kind of return on an investment. "I'm kidding, guys. You all looked so serious, I couldn't resist."

She saw them relax a bit in their chairs. This was their first team meeting, and she understood their nerves. They had no idea what to expect in terms of her management style and expectations. They'd probably heard some things about her, how she'd established herself as a consumer product specialist while vice president at her former investment bank, and likely assumed that she would be aggressive and eager—as many New York investment bankers were—to make her mark in her new role here. And they would be right about that.

But.

There was a difference, as she'd come to appreciate these last eight years, between being led by someone who was aggressive and eager, and someone who was simply a jerk. So this first team meeting was her chance to set the tone, right from the start, of what these associates and analysts could expect while working for her.

With that in mind, she folded her hands on the table. "Over the last few weeks, I've met with all of you individually, and we've had general conversations about some possibilities I want to explore with this fund. But, seeing how this is the first time we're all sitting down together, I thought we should discuss my specific vision for this project.

"When I first began talking to the partners about the possibility of coming to work for Monroe Ellers, they asked what my strategy would be in running a successful fund. My answer was simple: I told them that I like to grow companies. I look for businesses that have potential—maybe an established company that's struggling and needs a new direction, or perhaps a smaller business that has a marketable idea but doesn't have the resources to expand. That's where we come in—we find that potential and we cultivate it. And, hopefully, we make a lot of money for our clients in the process."

Sidney saw a few smiles at that. The room was nodding along and appeared to be responding well to her speech. Then again, five out of the six people at the table had huge coffee cups in front of them, so it could've just been the caffeine kicking in. "So the four-billion-dollar question becomes, which companies do we believe have that kind of potential? As it so happens, I have a few ideas on that front." She fired up the PowerPoint presentation she'd prepared on her laptop, which sat in front of her.

A photograph of a storefront popped onto the white screen in front of them. "Vitamin Boutique. Primarily a Midwest-based specialty retailer of, you guessed it, vitamins, with 125 stores across twelve states. I met last week with the investment bankers representing the company. They tell me that they're looking for an opportunity to grow beyond the Midwest, expand into other distribution channels, and significantly bolster their online presence. They made it clear that they're interested in a buyout."

Sidney saw that the associates and analysts around the table had begun diligently taking notes. "By the way, you'll be dividing into two teams and splitting this list, so start thinking about which companies you want to spend the next four weeks learning inside and out. Standard due diligence: all their financials, pending lawsuits, who their corporate lawyers are, and how big of a pain in the ass those lawyers are going to be if we do the deal."

One of the associates, Spencer, let out a bark of laughter. Then he stopped abruptly as if uncertain.

Sidney nodded encouragingly. "No, you were right, that was another joke. Let's not hold back here, people, we'll be working together on this project for the next five or six years. Feel free to chuckle away at these witty little comments of mine whenever it strikes your—hey, there we go, now the room's warming up . . ." Over their laughter, she clicked the touchpad on her computer and the logo for another company popped onto the screen. "All right. Next up, Evergreen Candles."

The meeting continued for another thirty minutes, after which the team members dispersed. Sidney hung around the conference room for a few minutes to talk with an associate who had some questions, then made her way back to her office.

She heard a knock on her door a few minutes later and looked up just as Michael Hannigan popped his head into her office. The youngest of the three partners on the firm's investment committee, he'd been the one who'd recruited her the most aggressively and had become a mentor to her since she'd started working at Monroe Ellers.

"I heard you killed it in your first team meeting," Michael said.

Sidney never ceased to be amazed by the rapidity with which information could spread through an office. "How could you know that already? I just finished the meeting about five minutes ago." She cocked her head. "Did they actually say 'killed it'?" Admittedly, she'd been trying hard to have a good vibe with the group, but she didn't want to *look* like she'd been trying hard. Kind of like a good first date. If memory served.

"Stacy has the desk right outside the conference room," he said, referring to his secretary. "She tells me that's what people were saying as they left your meeting." He winked before leaving. "Can't wait to hear your plans for the fund."

Sidney smiled after he left, thinking that she did indeed have plans. And not just with respect to work.

This upcoming wedding had given her clarity on a few things.

AT LUNCHTIME, SIDNEY met Trish at a restaurant between their offices, eager to share her plan with her best friend. But first things first.

"How's your first day back at work going?" she asked Trish, who'd just returned to her media relations job with United Airlines after a four-month maternity leave.

"I've already had three crises to deal with. I love it," Trish said with a laugh. With her blond hair newly cut in a stylish bob, and her navy power suit, she looked ready to take on the world. "But wait, I need to get my hourly fix." She pulled out her cell phone, and both she and Sidney *aw*-ed at the cute pictures of her son, Jonah, that the nanny had texted that morning.

"How was the rest of your weekend?" Trish asked, after putting her phone away.

"Quite interesting. I have some news. Isabelle is getting married."

Trish's expression conveyed her shock. "What? I didn't realize your sister was seeing anyone that seriously." Having been best friends with Sidney since the third grade, she'd known Isabelle for years.

"Actually, she and Simon haven't been dating that long. She met him three months ago," Sidney said.

"Three months? And they're already engaged?"

Sidney shrugged casually. Trish was her best friend, and she didn't like keeping secrets from her. The only thing that trumped that, however, was her loyalty to her sister—which meant keeping Isabelle's pregnancy news on the down-low. "She says she knows Simon is her Mr. Right. They're going to get married Labor Day weekend. At the Lakeshore Club."

"The Lakeshore Club?" Trish studied Sidney carefully. "That's a little odd, given your history with that place."

Well . . . yes. "Isabelle asked if I'd be okay with her having the reception there."

"And *are* you okay with her having the reception there?" Trish asked.

Yes. No. Sidney had waffled all weekend on this. But she'd given Isabelle her blessing, so now she would make the best of it. "Sure. In fact, this whole situation has given me extra incentive to get my personal life back on track. I'm kicking this plan to start dating again into high gear."

"Glad to hear it," Trish said enthusiastically.

"I knew you'd be on board."

"Assuming you're truly ready to be dating again, that is."

Sidney pulled back in surprise. "Me? Of course I'm ready. It's been six months. I'm thirty-three years old, I can't wait forever before throwing myself back out there. I've got plans, desires, biological clocks ticking."

Trish raised an eyebrow. "And that's all that's driving this new 'extra incentive' of yours?"

"Yes." Sidney saw Trish's look and conceded. "Okay, fine. Admittedly, given the circumstances, I would prefer *not* to show up dateless to my younger sister's wedding. If I do, somebody is going to give me the 'Poor Sidney' head-tilt. And you know how I feel about the head-tilt."

"That I do."

The "Poor Sidney" head-tilt was her nickname for the look her former New York colleagues had given her after she'd ended her engagement. Because she and Brody both had been investment bankers in Manhattan, the scintillating tale of how she'd discovered his cheating had spread like wildfire through their professional community. After that, she'd gotten a lot of sympathetic looks around the office; and several well-meaning people had called, e-mailed, or dropped by to ask how she was "hanging in." And while she'd known that her friends and co-workers had been simply trying to be nice, she'd found the whole thing incredibly embarrassing.

It was not an experience she wanted to repeat at her sister's wedding.

"I've got my dating profile up, and that's a start, but I real-ized this weekend that I need a more specific plan of attack. Brody's 'excuse' "—Sidney made mocking air quotes—"for cheating was that he panicked over the idea of getting married. That he freaked out at the idea of 'forever.'"

Trish snorted. "Have I ever mentioned how much I intensely despise the man?"

That made two of them. "So this time around, I'm not making the same mistake. No more commitment-phobic men, no more player types, no more guys with issues or drama or whatever. I knew about Brody's reputation before we started dating, but I let his charm cloud my judgment. That's not happening again. From now on, I'm taking the same approach that I do with work: no matter how good a candidate looks at first blush, if I spot any red flags, he's out."

"What kind of red flags?" Trish asked.

Sidney smiled, prepared for exactly that question. "I did some due diligence this weekend." She took her iPad out of her purse and pulled up the list she'd created. "This is a compilation of the various articles I researched."

Trish read out loud. "'Signs he's not ready for a commitment.'" She scrolled down. "Oh my gosh, there have to be thirty things on this list."

"Thirty-four. Although a few are somewhat redundant."

"'If he moves too fast into the relationship, he'll likely exit it fast, too. But if he moves too slow, he's likely either not sure about you or still hung up on a previous relationship.'" Trish continued reading. "'He's not available on weekends. He doesn't introduce you to his family or friends. He doesn't talk about the future. He doesn't talk about his past. He's not settled at work.'" She looked up. "What's that about?"

"According to my research, men need to feel confident and secure in their ability to provide before being ready to commit to a long-term relationship."

"I see." Trish moved farther down the list. "'He talks poorly about his ex, he won't talk at all about his ex, he's not on stable emotional footing with his parents, the majority of his friends aren't in committed relationships . . .'"

"Because men typically choose to spend their time with people whose values they share," Sidney explained.

"Uh-huh." Trish kept reading. "'He doesn't ask about your

day, he doesn't handle adversity or criticism well at work, he doesn't call when he says he will . . . ' " She trailed off, skimming through the other items. Then she set the iPad down on the table and paused for a moment, as if thinking carefully about her next words. "This is a very . . . extensive list. And no doubt, there's some good advice here." She reached over and squeezed Sidney's hand affectionately. "But Sid, sweetie, there's never any guarantee that you won't get hurt in a relationship. No matter how vigilant you are for red flags or how much due diligence you do."

Sidney thought about that. She thought about the day that her life had been turned upside-down, how she'd been blindsided, how the story had spread to virtually everyone she knew, and how for months she'd felt weak and foolish and gullible and not at all like herself. Because the Sidney Sinclair she'd always known was a strong, confident, savvy woman. But in one fell swoop, Brody had managed to make her doubt all of that.

With that in mind, she looked her friend in the eyes. "This list is the closest thing I've got to a guarantee, Trish. I have to believe that. Because I'm sure as hell not going through another Brody experience again."

She closed the iPad cover—as if to say the discussion was over—and then smiled. Over the last six months, she'd learned that the best way to handle any conversation that was getting a little too personal was to simply move on. "So. Is Jonah getting any teeth yet?"

ENJOYING THE WARM, early June weather, Sidney and Trish decided to walk back to their respective offices instead of taking cabs. As they strolled along one of the bridges that crossed the Chicago River, Sidney remembered something.

"Oh my gosh, with the conversation about Isabelle's wedding and everything else, I completely forgot to tell you about Vaughn."

"Who's Vaughn?" Trish asked.

"Simon's brother. And you are not going to believe this."

She filled Trish in on all the details about her and Vaughn's Meet So-Not-Cute at the coffee shop and their awkward reunion at dinner with Isabelle and Simon.

"An FBI agent, huh?" Trish's expression turned sly. "Is he foxy?"

"That whole story, about the strange coincidence, and my glorious Speech of Many Insults, and the fact that I'm going to be stuck running into this dude forever, and that's your first question? 'Is he foxy?' " Sidney shook her head. "Trishelle . . . on behalf of womankind, I was expecting a more enlightened discourse."

Trish simply waited.

"Totally foxy," Sidney said. Hell, Trish was going to see him at the wedding, there wasn't much sense in denying it. "When he walked up to my table, my first thought was *Criminy*. Unfortunately, then he spoke."

Trish threw her arm around Sidney. "Somewhere out there, waiting for you, is the total package. A *Criminy* guy who's just looking for his Ms. Right to settle down with."

Sidney smiled at that, not wanting to ruin the mood. But the pragmatist in her said not to pin her dreams on that. Actually, the pragmatist in her said not to pin her dreams on any man, *Criminy* or otherwise.

Such a skeptical bitch these days, her inner pragmatist. But not a fool.

Never again a fool.

Four

ACROSS TOWN AT the Chicago FBI building, Vaughn rode the elevator up to the twelfth floor with his partner, Special Agent Seth Huxley. They'd just returned from lunch and were on their way to meet their boss, the special agent in charge—or "SAC" as he was referred to around the office—about a new investigation.

"Who's it going to be this time? The mayor?" Huxley asked, being wry.

"Hope not. I like the guy," Vaughn said. Although in his line of work, he'd learned to never trust any politician's public persona.

In the past year, he and Huxley had developed something of a specialty in undercover sting operations involving dirty government officials—part of the U.S. Attorney's fight against corruption in the city of Chicago. Over the course of the last twelve months, they'd taken down a state senator, a state representative, and three aldermen, all for bribery. On top of that, they'd recently arrested an Illinois state prison guard who'd been selling assault rifles to ex-felons.

In his eight years with the FBI, Vaughn had worked on

several different squads before being transferred to white-collar crime. Nick McCall, Vaughn's boss, had been the most senior undercover agent on the squad before being promoted to special agent in charge two years ago, and the office had needed to fill Nick's former spot with an agent, like Vaughn, who had similar undercover experience.

All FBI special agents were qualified to handle brief "walk-on" roles—undercover jobs in which the agent had only a couple of interactions with the suspects. But as the only agent on the white-collar crime squad who'd gone through undercover school at Quantico, Vaughn was the go-to guy whenever an investigation required a more extensive UC role. Which was fine with him—he found the work to be interesting and challenging, and he also liked the behind-the-scenes planning that came with every investigation. Whenever he took on a new identity, he needed to think about how his character would act, what he would look like, what he would wear, the kind of car he would drive and, if necessary, the type of gun he would carry. By all outward appearances, he needed to *be* whatever bad-guy type he was playing—because without that attention to detail, he could blow the entire investigation. Or get himself killed.

Standing in the elevator, Vaughn fought back a smile while watching Huxley carefully adjust the pocket square in the breast pocket of his custom-tailored suit. Unlike his fastidious partner, Vaughn had neither a pocket square nor a custom-tailored suit. In fact, on many days he didn't even have a tie, having yanked it off in annoyance by ten A.M.

He'd been skeptical when Huxley had first been assigned as his partner two years ago. All he'd known at the time was that the younger agent had gone to Harvard Law School, joined the Chicago white-collar crime squad immediately after graduating from Quantico, and wore Ralph Lauren shower shoes in the FBI locker room.

Yep.

But he'd since come to see why the SAC had put them together. Vaughn's undercover assignments involved a lot of variables and unknowns, and the best way to handle those variables and unknowns was to plan for every possible contingency. That was where Huxley came in—undoubtedly, he was the most organized, efficient, and detail-oriented agent Vaughn had ever met. Because of that, surprisingly, their partnership actually . . . worked. Vaughn was the front man out in the field, assuming various undercover roles, while Huxley deftly micromanaged all the behind-the-scenes details.

"We start training today," Vaughn said.

The elevator arrived at the twelfth floor and they both stepped out.

"Morgan is going to meet us in the locker room?" Huxley asked.

Vaughn nodded. "Six o'clock." A week ago, he'd declared that he and his closest friend, Assistant U.S. Attorney Cade Morgan, were going to run in the Chicago triathlon. He'd made this decision for two reasons: one, he enjoyed pushing himself physically, and Cade, a former college football star, was of a similar mind-set; and two, he'd sensed that Cade had needed some sort of activity to distract him ever since his formerly estranged father had passed away after a tough eleven-month battle with brain cancer. Cade had jumped quickly on the triathlon idea, and then Huxley had come on board, and today the three of them would begin an eleven-week training program for the big day.

"I assume you've already ordered your monogrammed Ralph Lauren wetsuit?" Vaughn quipped.

"I checked. They don't make one," Huxley said.

"What's scary, Hux, is that I have no clue if you're being funny or dead serious." They rounded the corner and stopped at the desk outside the SAC's office.

"You can head on in. He's expecting you," said Nick's assistant.

As Vaughn headed to the door with Huxley, he saw that their boss was worked up about something. Nick paced in front of Jack Pallas, one of the agents from the Violent Crimes squad.

"The whole thing is outrageous," Nick was saying. "They corner you and suck you in with all their slick talk before draining every last penny out of you. I should haul every single one of them in here for price gouging and profiteering."

"He and Jordan went stroller shopping this weekend," Jack explained as Vaughn and Huxley walked in and sat down in front of Nick's desk.

"These things cost more than my first *car*," Nick said.

"Babies are not cheap." Jack cocked his head. "And remind me—how many are you having?"

Valuing his job—and not being quite as good friends with Nick as Jack—Vaughn held back a grin and carefully kept his face expressionless. A few weeks ago, Nick and his wife had discovered that she was pregnant with twins. For a couple days afterward, the agents of the Chicago FBI had watched with no small amount of amusement as their fearless leader had walked around the office in a daze, murmuring "There are *two*," to anyone who offered his or her congratulations.

Now fully recovered from the news, Nick chuckled at the joke. "Just the two. Assuming nobody hits us with any more surprises at the next ultrasound." He moved around his desk and took a seat.

He rested his arms on the desk. "All right, let's get down to business. As I mentioned earlier, I have a new investigation for you two. One that will involve some undercover work," he told Vaughn and Huxley. "On Friday afternoon, Jack received a call from one of his confidential informants, who relayed some information that certainly merits our attention." He turned to Jack. "Why don't you bring them up to speed?"

"The CI's name is Hector Batista," Jack began. "He works in an auto body shop on the South Side. I met him several years ago, while working undercover in the Martino case. He was a lower-level smuggler back then, mostly stolen cigarettes and slot machines, but that career came to a halt after the U.S. Attorney shut down Martino's organization. Batista still keeps an ear to the ground, and he's given us solid information in the past."

"He's a paid informant?" Vaughn asked.

"Yes. But he also owes me a favor," Jack said, indicating that he believed Batista was particularly trustworthy. "He called me on Friday morning and we met shortly after that. Batista started the conversation by telling me that he'd sought out a Chicago cop who supposedly could make traffic tickets disappear. The cop's name is Craig Pritchett. I've already looked him up; he's in the Fifteenth District. According to Batista, after they discussed the traffic tickets, Pritchett made a comment to the effect that he'd heard Batista was 'connected.' Batista sensed something was up, and encouraged the cop to keep talking. So he did.

"Pritchett told him about a smuggling business he has going with some other police officers," Jack continued. "He said he'd heard that Batista might know of people who would be interested in that kind of thing. Pritchett bragged that because he and his buddies are all cops, they could transport anything into the city without getting busted. He mentioned cigarettes, stolen merchandise—and guns."

Vaughn raised an eyebrow at this last part. Chicago had some of the strictest gun-control laws in the United States, and law enforcement was constantly trying to stem the flood of illegal firearms transported in from states with more lax gun laws. As police officers, Pritchett and his friends were supposed to be *helping* in the war on crime—not bringing in more guns that would go straight into the hands of criminals.

"Sounds like Pritchett's smuggling ring needs to be put out of business," Vaughn said.

"We'll send Batista back to Pritchett, and he can tell the cop that he does know of someone who would be interested in his services." Nick turned to Vaughn. "How do you feel about being a gun dealer for the next couple months?"

Vaughn felt pretty damn good about that, if it meant taking down a few corrupt police officers. "I'll start working up a legend this afternoon," he told Nick, referring to the various information details—ID, phone number, etc.—that would support his undercover identity.

Nick nodded. "Good. As a former police officer, I take allegations like this very seriously. Let's show these assholes what happens to dirty cops who smuggle guns into this city."

Ready to rock and roll, Vaughn answered for both Huxley and himself.

"Got it covered, boss."

AFTER THE MEETING adjourned, Jack followed Huxley and Vaughn down to the seventh floor, where the white-collar crime squad was located, and gave them more detailed background information on Batista.

"I'll set up a meet-and-greet between you and Batista for later this week," Jack told Vaughn before leaving.

"Sounds good." Settled in at his cubicle, Vaughn was about to begin working on his undercover legend when his cell phone rang. He checked and saw that it was Simon.

"I know it's short notice, but I was wondering if you're free Saturday night?" Simon asked.

Actually, Vaughn had a date scheduled that night, with an investigative reporter from the *Tribune* he'd met a few months ago. She was twenty-six, focused on her career, and had zero interest in a steady relationship at this point in her life. They got together occasionally for drinks, dinner, and good times.

"I had plans, but nothing too important," Vaughn said. "What's up?"

"Apparently Isabelle's father and stepmother are throwing their annual summer party on Saturday, and they've decided to 'announce' the engagement there."

"Sounds very upper-crusty."

"Oh, it'll definitely be upper-crusty. Isabelle's dad runs a hedge fund and has some big house on the North Shore. So break out your seersucker suit because they've extended an invitation to you, as well."

Seersucker suit? Sure, Vaughn had three of them stashed in his closet, for all the croquet tournaments and garden parties he got invited to. "On second thought, I really shouldn't cancel my Saturday plans. Because those plans involve me getting laid, while this party sounds . . . really boring."

Simon chuckled. "So I'll see you there at seven o'clock?"

"Yeah, yeah." Vaughn already had a pen out to write down the address.

"Hey, at least you know Sidney now," Simon said. "That's one person you can talk to."

Sure.

Because that was always such a hoot.

Five

VAUGHN STEPPED OUT onto the terrace that overlooked the grounds behind Ross Sinclair's Tudor-style mansion and saw immediately that Simon hadn't been joking about this being an upper-crust affair. Milling about the impeccably manicured lawn and sculpted gardens were what he guessed to be nearly two hundred guests in cocktail attire. Waiters in tuxedos carried trays of hors d'oeuvres, wine, and champagne as a string quartet played from the second-floor balcony of the house.

Safe to say this was a bit different from the "summer parties" he and Simon had attended while growing up in Apple Canyon, Wisconsin—population 3,468 at last count.

Vaughn spotted Simon and Isabelle on the opposite end of the terrace, chatting with several couples who appeared to be in their forties. He smiled at the sight of his brother—a graphic designer who typically wore T-shirts and jeans everywhere he could get away with it—wearing tailored tan pants and a pressed linen shirt, thinking how proud their mother would be to see her younger son so spiffed up.

Simon caught sight of Vaughn heading over and grinned. "There he is—we were just talking about you."

"Simon was telling everyone how he'd decided to move to Chicago after living with you the summer after he graduated college," Isabelle added.

"Actually, I was saying how I'd decided to move to Chicago *despite* the fact that you and I lived together for a summer," Simon deadpanned, as he clasped Vaughn's hand in greeting.

"My brother, always the comedian," Vaughn said to the group. He shook hands as introductions were made. Apparently the couples were friends of Isabelle's stepmother, Jenny. A few minutes into the conversation, another couple came over—a tall man in his sixties with salt-and-pepper hair and sharp blue-green eyes, and an attractive brunette probably twenty years his junior.

"Dad, Jenny, this is Simon's brother, Vaughn," Isabelle said. "Vaughn, this is my father, Ross Sinclair, and his wife, Jenny."

"The FBI agent," Ross said, looking Vaughn over as he shook his hand. "Were you one of the guys who arrested that nineteen-year-old who was planning to plant a bomb outside Wrigley Field?" he asked, referring to a case that had recently been in all the local media.

"No, sir. That credit goes to the agents on the terrorism squad."

"Oh." Ross suddenly looked bored with the conversation. "What squad are you on?"

"White-collar crime."

Ross raised an eyebrow. "Ever arrest any hedge fund managers?" he quipped, getting a chuckle from the crowd.

"Only the criminal ones."

Ross looked at Vaughn again—seemingly still sizing him up—and then left to greet some people who'd just walked in.

Simon leaned in so only Vaughn could hear. "Yep, that went about as well as my first conversation with him. And basically every conversation thereafter. The guy's a tough nut to crack."

Like father, like daughter, Vaughn thought.

A waiter stopped to offer him a glass of champagne, which

he declined. But while turned in that direction, his eyes landed on someone talking in a group out on the lawn.

Sidney.

Since she wasn't looking, Vaughn let his eyes linger for a moment. Admittedly, he didn't know a lot about women's fashion, but he assumed that her pink dress sported some sort of fancy designer label. And whatever she'd spent, it was worth every penny. The dress cut asymmetrically across her legs, and one ruffled sleeve draped teasingly off her right shoulder. Combined with the high heels she had on, the look was both classy and sexy as hell.

She had one hand on her hip as she chatted with a couple who appeared to be roughly her father's age. As if sensing Vaughn's gaze, she looked over and caught his eye.

Her eyes briefly took in his tie-less suit and open-necked shirt. Then, with a deliberately disinterested air, she turned away from him and focused once again on her conversation.

Ah . . . the cold shoulder. So that was how they were going to play this tonight. That was just fine with him.

FOR THE NEXT half hour, he did the rounds with Simon and Isabelle, making polite conversation about the wedding and entertaining the group with funny anecdotes about Simon, as was his duty as best man and older brother. Then there was a clinking of glasses as Ross Sinclair moved to the center of the terrace to make a toast. The people who'd been mingling out on the lawn gathered closer.

"Jenny and I want to thank all of you for coming tonight," Ross began, with the confident air of a man used to speaking in front of others. "It's wonderful that so many of you could join us on this happy occasion." He looked over at his younger daughter and future son-in-law. "As all of you may or may not know, Isabelle and Simon began dating not too long ago. So when she brought him over for dinner last weekend, and he pulled me aside to ask for my permission to marry her, my first question was"— he cocked his head in mock confusion—"What's your name again?"

The crowd broke out in laughter.

"Simon," called out Simon good-naturedly.

The crowd laughed more.

"*Simon*—right," Ross said, hamming it up. He continued when the crowd quieted. "But after getting that out of the way, my second question was to Isabelle. And that was, simply: 'Does he make you happy?'" He smiled at his daughter. "And without hesitation, she said yes."

He paused as the crowd *aw*-ed, and Simon and Isabelle exchanged an affectionate look.

"That was all I needed to hear." Ross lifted his glass. "So with that, I'd like you to raise your glasses in toast to the happy couple as they continue on their journey together. To Isabelle and . . ." He trailed off, making an *oops* face as though he'd forgotten again.

"*Simon*," the crowd responded in unison, laughing.

"I'll get it one day!" Ross said, over the din.

Everyone clapped at the toast and took a sip of champagne.

The crowd broke off into various groups, chatting and mingling. Simon and Isabelle were across the terrace, engaged in conversation. Seeing that he had no one else to talk to, Vaughn decided to check out the gardens.

He headed for the stairs. As luck would have it, he and Sidney met at the top.

"Vaughn, hello," she said, with a pleasant smile.

"Sidney . . . good to see you again," Vaughn replied ever-so-politely.

They walked down the steps together.

Leaning in, Sidney spoke so only he could hear. "We part ways at the bottom of the steps?"

"I'll go right, you go left."

Some woman passed them on the wide staircase, heading in the opposite direction. She grinned, seeing them side-by-side. "Well, won't you two look lovely walking down the aisle together?"

Vaughn's eye twitched. "Wrong siblings," he told the woman.

"She meant for the recessional," Sidney explained, as they hit the bottom of the stairs.

"Oh." That *definitely* made a lot more sense.

"You know, sometime in the next three months, you might want to Google what the best man actually does at a wedding. Just a suggestion," she said in parting, still with the feigned smile for the sake of anyone who might be watching.

Vaughn stopped her as she turned to leave. "Did you say three months?"

She rolled her eyes. "Fine. I guess it's technically eleven weeks now."

That wasn't what he'd meant. "My brother and your sister are getting *married* in eleven weeks?" Admittedly, he wasn't exactly an expert on weddings, but that seemed incredibly fast. Like . . . *oddly* fast.

Sidney paused. "I'd assumed they'd told you the date already. It's the Saturday before Labor Day."

"I hadn't heard."

"Oh." She shifted, as if uncertain what to say in response to that. "Well . . . now you have." She strode off, following the walkway that cut a path across the lawn to her left.

Eleven weeks.

Still chewing on that piece of information, Vaughn followed the walkway in the opposite direction from Sidney, wondering if, perhaps, there was some particular reason Isabelle and Simon wanted to get married so quickly. Having no one to talk to at the moment, he decided to do some light reconnaissance. While pretending to admire the gardens, he found a vantage point that allowed him to watch Isabelle and Simon, who stood on the terrace, talking with others.

A waiter came by, offering the group more champagne. Isabelle declined, and as the waiter moved on to the guests next to them, Simon gave his fiancée a subtle wink.

Interesting.

BY NINE O'CLOCK, Vaughn was ready to call it a night.

He was warm in his jacket—which, for logistical reasons, he couldn't take off—and he'd pretty much exhausted his ability to make polite chitchat with a bunch of people he didn't know.

Parched from all the conversation, he decided to grab something to drink before getting on the road for the forty-minute drive back to the city. He made his way to the bar that had been set up on one end of the terrace and ordered a club soda.

Drink in hand, he leaned against the terrace while people watching. Over the last hour, he'd continued his surveillance of his brother and future sister-in-law, noting that the latter hadn't drunk anything alcoholic all evening. Possibly, this meant nothing. Perhaps Isabelle was the designated driver for her and Simon tonight. Perhaps she simply didn't feel like drinking.

Or perhaps she was pregnant.

Having begun to suspect this, Vaughn had "offhandedly" mentioned to Simon and Isabelle that he'd heard he needed to mark his calendar for the Saturday before Labor Day. They'd both squirmed, their speech patterns a bit rushed as they told some long-winded story about the gorgeous view from the terrace at her father's country club, and how Isabelle had always wanted to have a partial outdoor wedding there, but this was the only available date before April, and *everyone* knew how the weather in Chicago was just so unpredictable in April, and besides, they didn't want to wait that long, because Isabelle was thinking about expanding her social work practice next year and combining that with a wedding simply would be too much to deal with.

Uh-huh.

Vaughn had nodded along with the whole speech, as if buying every word. But having interrogated many people over the last eight years, he could tell when a story was too perfectly thought out, too detailed. It was one of the more common mistakes people made when trying to cover up a lie.

What he couldn't figure out, however, was *why* Simon felt the need to lie to him about Isabelle's pregnancy.

Their mother? That, he understood. Kathleen Roberts came from a devout Irish Catholic family and had conservative views about the order in which marriage and sex were supposed to take place. Vaughn had no doubt that his mother would be upset if she learned that one of her sons had gotten a woman pregnant out of wedlock. Not angry, just . . . disappointed. And being good Irish boys—with a healthy dose of Catholic guilt complex—Vaughn and Simon hated to disappoint their mother.

But obviously, the situation was different between *him* and Simon. Of course, Simon could confide in him about things like this—they'd always been close as brothers. Or at least . . . he'd always assumed they were.

Vaughn mulled that question over in his mind while finishing his club soda. He was on his last sip when something caught his eye. A flash of pink and auburn to his left.

Truth be told, this wasn't the first time this particular flash of pink and auburn had caught his eye. Sidney had been everywhere at this party tonight, mingling and smiling and laughing and seemingly always in his line of sight with her sleek legs and that damn ruffle that fell off her shoulder. It was a very clever trick, this peekaboo sleeve of hers. It made a man think . . . things.

Things a man definitely had no business thinking about a woman he'd gone out of his way to avoid all night.

Brushing that aside, Vaughn set his empty glass on the tray next to the bar. Just then, his ear caught the conversation of the group standing behind him.

". . . heard that the reception is going to be at the Lakeshore Club," said a woman.

"Wasn't that the place where Sidney was going to have *her* reception?" asked a second woman.

"Yes. Maybe Isabelle can have her sister's wedding dress and veil, too. Somebody might as well use them," the first woman snickered.

"No way. That dress is a curse. You heard what happened, right? How she found out her fiancé was cheating?" said the second woman.

A third woman jumped in, shushing the first two. "*Shh*. Sidney's standing right *there*," she whispered.

Vaughn looked over his shoulder and saw Sidney midconversation with two men who, if he recalled correctly from

the whirlwind of introductions, worked at her father's hedge
fund. She stood closest to the gossiping women, so it was
certainly possible she'd heard them talking. But her expression gave nothing away as she carried on, business as usual.

Then Vaughn heard another voice. His own.

*Well. On behalf of the male population, let me be the first
to apologize for whatever* he *did.*

So he'd been a little . . . sarcastic at the coffee shop. Maybe
more than a little. Sidney certainly hadn't held back with her
self-righteous speech, which meant he'd been entitled to respond
in kind. Still, after hearing that her ex-fiancé had cheated on
her, he felt a touch guilty about his comment right then.

Definitely time to call it a night.

He found Isabelle and Simon, and had every intention of
saying a quick good-bye. But instead they introduced him to
yet more people—people who, as often was the case, were
fascinated to hear that he was an FBI agent and immediately
hit him with the standard litany of questions. *Do you carry
a gun?* (Yes.) *Do you have it on you right now?* (Yes.) *Can I
see it?* (No.) *How many people have you arrested?* (Probably
less than expected; undercover operations take time to carry
out.) *You work undercover? Cool! What's that like?*

And so on.

Finally, he made his getaway twenty minutes later. He
decided to walk around the house instead of going back inside,
thinking it would be his quickest escape route. He immediately
shucked his suit coat as he followed the paved walkway past
the swimming pool and guesthouse, and into a more secluded
garden with an elegant three-tiered fountain.

Sitting on a bench, tucked away from the rest of the party,
was Sidney.

She jumped and stood up, clearly startled by his arrival.
For a split second, he felt bad for intruding, thinking perhaps
she'd overheard the gossip and had come out here to get a
short break from the party.

But then she spoke.

"You again," she said.

"Me again," Vaughn drawled in return. As if it was *his*

fault they kept crossing paths at this party. If he had his druthers, he and The Cantankerous Miss Sidney Sinclair would go their separate ways and—*wow*, the V-neckline of that dress dipped enticingly lower than he'd realized.

Focus, Roberts.

"I was just leaving," he said.

"So I gathered." Her gaze fell on the jacket he'd thrown casually over his shoulder and held with one hand. "You must've been roasting in that thing."

"Occupational hazard."

She looked confused. "I'm sorry?"

"It's considered poor form for an FBI agent to have his gun exposed in public," he explained.

"Oh." Her eyes traveled down to his right hip, where he carried his Glock. "You must have to get creative when wearing a swimsuit."

With anyone else, Vaughn would've said that was a joke. But with Sidney, he couldn't quite tell. He cocked his head, trying to get a read on her, and looked her over.

It was that damn sleeve of her dress. Suddenly, he found himself fighting the urge to reach out and tug it up over her shoulder.

Or tug it lower, perhaps?

Their eyes met over the soft, ambient lights of the fountain.

"You said something about leaving?" she asked.

Right. "Enjoy the rest of your party, Sidney."

Then he turned on his heel and walked away, the sounds of the string quartet fading in the distance.

Six

AFTER WORK ON Monday, Vaughn met Huxley and Cade in the state-of-the-art gym located on the second floor of the FBI building. They were in the second week of their triathlon training program, which meant they'd added a fifty-minute run on the indoor track to their usual weight-lifting workout.

They fell into an easy groove during the run, talking mostly about Officer Pritchett and Co.'s smuggling ring. Because Cade was in the special prosecutions group at the U.S. Attorney's Office, the division that handled corruption cases, he often served as a consultant on any legal issues that arose during Vaughn and Huxley's investigations.

"We met with Batista last week," Vaughn said to Cade as they began their fourth lap around the track. "He agreed to set up a meeting with Pritchett and wear a wire. He'll tell Pritchett he knows a guy who needs a few things moved from point A to point B. That's where I come in."

"What's your name this month?" Cade joked, referring to the multitude of identities Vaughn had assumed over the years as part of his various undercover operations.

"Mark Sullivan. Gun buyer. Drives a Hummer H3, wears

expensive suits, and carries a Kimber 1911 handgun," Vaughn said.

"No clue what that is," Cade said.

"Let's just say, it's a gun with swagger." He took his tools very seriously when working undercover.

In the locker room after their workout, Cade and Huxley asked about the engagement party, both of them having met Simon on several occasions.

"You should've seen the place," Vaughn said, drying himself off after a quick shower. "Huge mansion on the lake, in-ground swimming pool, guesthouse, the whole works. Isabelle's father runs a hedge fund. Obviously quite successfully."

"And you approve of your future sister-in-law?" Cade asked.

"Sure. Isabelle seems great." *Her sister, on the other hand . . .*

Huxley studied him as he slid on his boxer briefs. "What's the 'but'?"

"No 'but,'" Vaughn said. "I like Simon's fiancée." *And, fortunately for him, she inherited all the good-natured genes in the family.*

Cade furrowed his brow. "There it is again—that look. Like you want to say more."

Vaughn scoffed at that as he pulled on his clothes. "There's no look."

Cade pointed. "Huxley just put on his underwear. Not once, in the two years that you two have been partners, have you ever missed an opportunity to smirk at the fact that the man *irons* his boxer briefs."

"Hey. They fold neater that way. It saves space in the drawer," Huxley said.

Cade gave Vaughn a look. *I rest my case.* "So? What gives?"

Vaughn took in the tenacious expression on his friend's face and knew that any further denials would only bring on more questions. He sighed. "Fine." He thought about where to begin. "Isabelle has a sister."

Huxley rolled his eyes. "Here we go."

"No, no. *Not* here we go. She and I are not going anywhere," Vaughn said emphatically. "The woman's a . . ." He paused, trying to think of the right word. He caught sight of another agent, Sam Wilkins, passing by their row of lockers. The man was a walking dictionary. "Hey, Wilkins—what's that word you used the other day, to describe the female witness who kept arguing with you?"

"Termagant," Wilkins called over. "Means 'quarrelsome woman.'"

Vaughn nodded at Cade and Huxley in satisfaction, thinking that definition perfectly captured Sidney Sinclair. "There. She's a termagant."

"It can also mean 'vixen,'" Wilkins shouted from the next aisle over.

"Thank you, Merriam-Webster," Vaughn called back, with a half growl. "I think we've got it."

Cade raised an eyebrow teasingly. "So. Does the *vixen* have a name?"

Yep, Vaughn had walked right into that one. "Sidney."

"You just met her this weekend," Huxley said. "What could you two possibly have to quarrel about?"

"Actually, we met the weekend before last. Simon and Isabelle invited us both to dinner to tell us about their engagement."

"And you and Sidney had some sort of falling out then?" Cade asked.

Vaughn hedged. "Technically, the falling out happened before dinner, at a coffee shop around the corner." He paused. "When I hit on her."

"You hit on your future sister-in-law's *sister*?" Huxley asked, his tone clearly indicating that this was a big no-no.

"I didn't know she was Isabelle's sister at the time," Vaughn said, in his defense. "I saw a hot single woman and I acted. That's what I *do*."

"How did you know she was single?" Huxley asked.

"I could tell that she was on a first date. Things didn't work out between her and the other guy, so I walked over and tried to pick her up," he said matter-of-factly.

"How'd that go?" Cade asked.

"Not well." Vaughn zipped up his fly, and saw his friends fighting back grins. "She profiled me."

Cade let out a bark of laughter. "Get out of here."

Vaughn grabbed his duffle bag and shut his locker with a resounding clang. "I'm serious. There was a speech and everything. She told me that I run around with my 'obviously healthy ego' and compared me to a kid in a candy store when it comes to women—trying to get my hands on as many 'shiny treats' as possible."

Cade's mouth twitched. "How dare she. That's just so . . ." He trailed off, as if thinking about how best to respond.

"Dead-on balls accurate," Huxley finished.

The two of them began laughing.

Vaughn glared. "I'm starting to get the impression that you guys are enjoying this."

"Oh, definitely," Huxley said, still chuckling.

"Why?" Vaughn asked, annoyed. They were his closest friends, which meant they were supposed to be on *his* side.

Cade answered that question with one of his own. "When's the last time a woman rejected you, Roberts?"

Vaughn paused, having to think that one over.

Cade grinned, his point made. "*That* is why we're enjoying this."

"I'M SURE SHE'LL be here any minute," Sidney said assuredly.

Jackie, the bridal shop sales associate who'd squeezed Isabelle into this appointment during her lunch hour as a favor to a friend, smiled politely. "Not a problem."

Given the bridal shop's location on Oak Street, home to many of the city's most upscale stores and boutiques, Sidney guessed that Jackie had perfected the art of saying "Not a problem" in response to a wide variety of comments, questions, and situations. Still, given the efforts the sales associate had gone through to accommodate them, Sidney felt bad that Isabelle was late—which was not like her. She checked the clock on her phone, and was about to send her sister a text

message, when the door to the shop flew open and Isabelle
hurtled inside.

"Oh my god, where's the bathroom—I need it *now*!" she
shouted at Jackie.

Mouth open, Jackie pointed to a corridor on her right.

Isabelle took off at lightning speed.

A moment later, a door slammed down the hallway. After
an awkward pause, Sidney turned and smiled at Jackie. "Well,
at least she's *in* the shop now. Yay, progress."

"Perhaps you have some idea of your sister's taste and
could begin looking over the dresses I've pulled?" Jackie suggested. "I'm afraid there aren't that many choices. Given the
extremely short time frame we have to work with, Isabelle's
only option is to go with a dress we already have here in the
shop in her size."

Five minutes later, Sidney found herself in a dressing
room, surrounded by yards of tulle, silk, charmeuse, duchess
satin, and organza. She flipped through the gowns that Jackie
had pulled for them and then paused when she came to a one-
shoulder silk gown with a draped bodice that looked remark-
ably like the wedding dress she'd ordered for herself back in
New York.

She fingered the delicate material as the memories washed
over her—the first time Brody had kissed her on the steps
outside her apartment in SoHo, his spontaneous proposal in
Central Park, the rush of excitement and happiness she'd felt
when trying on her wedding dress for a final fitting, just two
weeks before the big day.

Then came another memory, one of betrayal and hurt and
shock.

Sidney grabbed the hanger and emphatically slid the dress
to the other end of the rack, out of sight and out of mind. She'd
learned her lesson, and she had her plan now—never again
would silly, fanciful emotions cloud her judgment when it
came to men.

The dressing room door opened. Isabelle stepped in and
sank onto a love seat. "Well, that wasn't fun," she groaned.

Sidney had gathered that. "Morning sickness?" She took a seat next to her sister on the love seat.

"Afternoon and evening, too. The doctor says it can happen at any time. Yippee," Isabelle said, raising her fist mock cheerfully. "So far this week, I've had to run out of four client appointments."

"You had your first doctor's appointment? How did it go?" Sidney asked.

"I peed in a cup, they confirmed that I'm having a baby, then I puked into a bedpan while a nurse took four vials of blood from me."

"And who says pregnancy isn't a beautiful thing?"

Isabelle smiled weakly at that and pushed herself upright. She eyed the rack of gowns. "So. One of those is going to be my dream wedding dress."

Sidney got up from the couch. "I've gone through most of them. These dresses here are the ones you'll want to focus on."

Isabelle wrinkled her nose, pointing to the first one on the rack. "I'm not a big fan of empire waistlines."

"In three months, I'm thinking that's the only waistline that's going to work if the goal is to keep the peanut on the down-low."

Isabelle blinked. "Right. Duh." She took a deep breath and put on a smile. "Okay, empire waist, it is." She stood up and joined Sidney at the rack. She leafed through the dresses with somewhat lackluster interest at first, but then she stopped when she saw the last one. "Wait. This one's not so bad. Actually, I really like this one." With an enthusiastic flourish, she pulled the dress out to show Sidney. "What do you think?"

The gown was sleeveless, with straps that widened into a deep V. With a sweetheart neckline trimmed in lace, high waist, and full tulle skirt, it was sophisticated in a classic 1940s Hollywood kind of way. "It's perfect," Sidney said, completely genuine. "Let's see it on."

Giggling excitedly, Isabelle twirled with the dress in the direction of the private dressing area. She stopped mid-spin and put her hand over her stomach. "Oh, boy."

Jackie chose that moment to stick her head into the dressing room. "How's everything going so far? Is there anything I can get you?"

"I'd say a trash can," Sidney told her. "Quickly."

To her credit, Jackie didn't even bat an eye.

"Not a problem."

"OH MY GOSH, Izz. You've got to try at least one bite of this."

Isabelle, who'd insisted on treating Sidney as a thank-you for going dress shopping, held up a hand, refusing the forkful of red velvet cupcake. "Ugh. No thanks." She put a hand on her stomach. "Apparently, the peanut doesn't like the looks of that cream cheese frosting."

They walked along Oak Street as Sidney ate from the plastic container the woman behind the counter at Sprinkles bakery had hurriedly tossed at them, presumably after seeing Isabelle's face turn greener than the sugar topping on their key lime cupcakes. The original plan had been to eat in the bakery, but then Isabelle had covered her mouth with another "Oh, boy," muttered something about "strong smells," and they'd hightailed it out of the place ASAP.

"I will make a mental note not to serve anything with cream cheese frosting at your bridal shower," Sidney said. "I'm thinking it would put a slight damper on the festivities if the guest of honor throws up on the cake."

Isabelle half-smiled at the joke, seeming distracted. "True." She cocked her head, as if pondering something. "So what do you think about Vaughn?"

Sidney paused, mid-cupcake bite, as several responses immediately sprang to mind. *Irritating. Cocky. Player. Delicious.*

She gave herself a mental face slap for that last one.

"Vaughn? Why would I think anything about Vaughn?" she asked, going for a nonchalant air while trying not to think about the way he'd looked the last time she'd seen him, at the engagement party. She'd escaped to the garden by the fountain—her mother's favorite spot in the days before the cancer had left her bed-ridden—because she'd needed a moment to cool her temper after hearing the gossips talking about her broken engagement. There'd been a moment, when she and Vaughn had been standing by the fountain, alone, when she'd been struck by how effortlessly handsome he'd looked with his coat off and tossed over one shoulder.

Her first instinct, naturally, had been to be snarky. *You said something about leaving?* She didn't need to be noticing how handsome a man like Vaughn Roberts was.

"I get a vibe that you don't like him very much," Isabelle said.

Imagine that.

"I thought everything seemed fine between Vaughn and me when we met you and Simon for dinner the other night," Sidney said evasively. And technically, that wasn't a lie. She'd gone out of her way that night, and at the engagement party, to be polite to Vaughn—at least in the presence of others.

"Maybe I'm just not used to seeing you around single men since your breakup with Brody."

Sidney's head spun toward her sister. "What's that supposed to mean?"

"It means that you seemed a little tense around him. Like you were giving him back-off signals or something." Isabelle held up her hand, seeing Sidney open her mouth. "Which would be totally understandable, given what happened with The Asshole," she said, her nickname for Brody. "I would imagine that it's a little scary, thinking about putting yourself out there again."

Sidney resisted the urge to roll her eyes. First Trish, now her sister was trying to bait her into a discussion using her therapy techniques. "I'm doing *fine*," she said assuredly. "In fact, I just set up two dates for next week." She declined to mention that Isabelle's wedding was, in part, the driving force behind her determination to get her love life in order. As close as she was with her sister, that felt odd to admit.

"Oh." Isabelle seemed briefly surprised that she didn't already know about the dates, but then she smiled. "Well, that's great. I'm glad to hear you're moving on."

"Exactly." Sidney took a bite of her cupcake. "*Mmm.* No

offense to the peanut, but he or she is crazy to miss out on this frosting." Yes, she was changing the subject. She was truly happy that Isabelle and Simon were getting married and having a baby—she wouldn't begrudge her sister anything. But talking about her dating life emphasized the fact that *she* was now back at square one, single again at thirty-three and trying hard to quell her growing fears that all the non-weird, commitment-ready men in this city had already been snatched up.

They walked in silence for a few moments before Isabelle cleared her throat. "So, this weekend I'm supposed to drive up to Wisconsin with Simon and Vaughn. They have some project they need to help their dad with, and Simon's parents suggested that I come up, too, so we could meet."

"Ooh, your first chance to dazzle the future in-laws." Sidney winked while licking frosting off her fork.

"Um . . . right. See, here's the thing. Simon and I were talking about it last night, and he told me that his parents' house is a small ranch next to some woods or something. Three bedrooms, just one-and-a-half bathrooms."

Sidney was sure that this verbal blueprint of the Robertses' house was going somewhere, but so far . . . no clue. "A ranch in the woods sounds cozy. Isabelle Sinclair goes country."

"That's the problem—it is cozy. Too cozy. With this morning sickness, I'm constantly running to the bathroom. You think Vaughn the FBI agent isn't going to notice that? Or Simon's mother?"

That was indeed a tricky situation. Sidney thought for a moment. "Maybe you could pretend you came down with the stomach flu or something."

"Then in three months, after this whole thing comes out, she'll know I lied to her. I'm trying to avoid actual outright lying, if at all possible. So I've come up with another solution to the weekend problem."

"Oh, good. What's that?"

"You go on this trip, too."

Sidney laughed, thinking that was a joke. Then she saw Isabelle's expression. "Yeah . . . that's not happening. I don't do country." Her idea of rustic was having to walk more than three blocks to a Starbucks.

Isabelle clasped her hands together, ready to plead her case. "Come on, Sid. It's only for one night. We drive up Saturday morning, and we'll be back Sunday evening. You told me your work schedule was better now that you started this new position. Surely you can take a break for two days."

Absolutely she could. Since she had switched over to private equity, people accommodated *her* schedule, not the other way around. But that wasn't the point. "I don't see how it helps *you* if I go. What's the plan here? That I go to the bathroom with you, and we pretend that it's me getting sick? Hey, I know—maybe I'm the one with the secret baby."

"No, if you go, we can stay at a *hotel*. It was already going to be tight with me at the Robertses' house, but if I had said I wanted to sleep at a hotel instead of their place, I would've seemed like an uppity rich girl. But if you go, we can get around that, and the entire Roberts clan won't have to wake up to the sounds of me hurling in the bathroom."

"Okay, fine. Maybe the hotel thing would help you. But *why* would I randomly tag along this weekend?"

"Because you thought a weekend out of the city sounded relaxing?" Isabelle suggested.

Sidney gave her a look over the top of her sunglasses. *Try again.*

Isabelle remained undeterred. "Fine. You're there because it's the efficient thing to do. With less than three months to go, we have tons of stuff to talk about between the bridal shower, bachelorette party, and wedding. So we'll use the three-hour car ride each way to make a dent in that."

Sidney *hmphed* at that. The "efficient" angle at least made some sense.

Isabelle smiled hopefully. "Please, please, please? I just want this weekend to go smoothly. More than anything."

Sidney took a deep breath, and then sighed in resignation. Isabelle always had been the one person she could never say no to. "I'd better get a kick-ass maid of honor dress out of this."

Isabelle squealed and threw her arms around Sidney in a huge hug. "Thank you! It's going to be fun, you'll see. Simon says it's beautiful up by his parents, plus you and I can stay up late in the hotel room, watch a sappy romantic comedy, and look through wedding magazines."

One arm around her sister, Sidney tilted her head affectionately against Isabelle's as they began walking. "I suppose there are worse ways to spend a weekend."

"Even a weekend spent with Vaughn?" Isabelle asked, still fishing.

On second thought . . .

Sidney maintained her casual demeanor. "I told you, there's no bad vibe between him and me. I'm sure we'll get along just fine this weekend."

At least in the presence of others.

Seven

BEHIND THE WHEEL of his Dodge Charger, Vaughn watched as two long, slender legs stepped out of the driver's side of the Mercedes sedan parked a few feet away.

Out climbed Sidney, the warm breeze blowing her wrap dress an inch or two higher.

Vaughn unrolled his window, peering at her from behind dark sunglasses. "Maybe if you drank just a little less water?"

Sidney tipped her bottled water at him, her third so far this trip. "Need to stay hydrated. I'm a city girl—not used to all this fresh air." With a smile that said he could kiss-off if he didn't like the sound of that, she headed into the gas station.

The passenger door of the Mercedes opened, and Isabelle scrambled out. "As long as you stopped, I might as well stretch my legs, too." She leaned against the car and took a few deep breaths.

Next to Vaughn in the passenger seat, now it was Simon's turn to chime in. "Good idea. Might as well stretch a bit myself."

"Take your time," Vaughn said easily. He watched as Simon jogged over to Isabelle and put his arm around her, murmuring something in a low voice that Vaughn couldn't hear.

So, this was the story they were all going with. They'd stopped three times in just as many hours, and Vaughn had heard so much talk about "fresh air" and "stretching" that one would think his companions were partaking of some sort of traveling yoga class instead of road tripping.

It seemed fairly obvious that, in reality, Isabelle was feeling carsick and needed to make a few stops to break up the ride. For that reason, Vaughn was careful not to complain about the snail's pace they were making up to his parents' house—he felt bad that Isabelle was uncomfortable. Indeed, life would be so much easier on all of them if everyone just told him the damn truth. But since that apparently wasn't the plan, he would continue to play the role of a guy oblivious to all the shenanigans around him.

Luckily, they were less than twenty miles from his parents' house. The bad news was, however, that in about two miles they would be leaving the highway and the remainder of the drive would be slow, hilly, and winding. His parents lived in a small lakeside community, and in order to get to their house, one needed to traverse a complicated web of unmarked roads—not recognized by GPS—that passed through limestone bluffs, canyons, and deep ravines. For a first-time visitor, his parents' house was difficult to find—which was why he and Simon had insisted that the two cars stay together for the drive.

A few minutes later, Sidney came out of the gas station carrying a plastic bag. "Some snacks for the road," she said cheerfully.

Vaughn could see the contents through the plastic bag and doubted the bottle of ginger ale and small box of saltine crackers Sidney had purchased were for her. But still, he said nothing.

All part of the little dance they were all doing.

They hit the road again, with Sidney's sleek black Mercedes right behind him.

"What do you think Mom and Dad are going to think of

her?" Simon asked, as they cruised along the last stretch of highway before the turnoff.

Vaughn pictured the sophisticated knot Sidney had pulled her auburn hair into, and the summer dress, heels, and Gucci sunglasses she was wearing. He'd been wondering that same thing himself. "That she's very 'New York.'"

Simon cocked his head, as if confused. "Oh. No, I meant Isabelle. You know, the one I'm marrying?"

Right. "They'll think she's great, Simon." His mother had called him, and undoubtedly Simon, too, nearly every day this past week, wanting to know what time they planned to get on the road, what time they would be leaving on Sunday, and whether the "girls" were sure they wanted to stay at a hotel. His parents had been happy to hear that Isabelle was bringing her sister. His mother was Irish, after all—in her mind, when it came to family, the more the merrier.

Initially, Vaughn had found the last-minute addition of Sidney curious. But now, having observed the situation, he got it: Sidney was there to help Isabelle and Simon maintain their cover, to deflect attention from the fact that her sister wasn't feeling well. And while as a general rule he disliked being purposely deceived, as an older sibling himself, he found the protective nature of Sidney's actions rather . . . endearing. Perhaps underneath all that snark, there was a softer side to Sidney Sinclair.

At least when it came to some people.

"Mom told me she's planning to make shepherd's pie for lunch," Simon said, interrupting his thoughts.

"The specialty of the house." Seemingly, Simon and Isabelle weren't the only ones hoping to make a good first impression. His mother's shepherd's pie could make a grown man cry.

Simon cleared his throat as they passed by the rolling fields of a dairy farm about five miles out from his parents' place. "I need you to do something for me."

From Simon's serious tone, Vaughn could guess what might be coming. *Don't tell Mom and Dad, but Isabelle is pregnant.* Good, it was about time he was brought into the circle of trust. He was an FBI agent, for chrissakes. Isabelle and Simon needed help with a little undercover work? *Pfft.* That was his specialty.

"I want you to be nice to Sidney this weekend," Simon said.

Vaughn blinked in surprise. "Why would you think I wouldn't be nice to her?"

"Isabelle told me that she doesn't think Sidney cares for you much."

"If that's true, then maybe you and Isabelle should be having the 'be nice' conversation with Sidney instead of me."

"I'm being serious, Vaughn," Simon said. "Sidney means the world to Isabelle. So if you've done something to offend her, or piss her off, or annoy her, just fix it."

Vaughn grumbled under his breath. If he and Sidney were *not* being so clandestine about the origins of their meeting, he would've pointed out to his brother that all he'd done was hit on the woman. This was hardly a federal crime, in fact— *hello*—it was a *compliment.*

Simon wasn't letting go of the subject. "Look, I know Sidney can come off a little tough when you first meet her. But she and Isabelle are really close—their mother died when they were young, and the way Isabelle tells it, Sidney essentially took on the role of watching over her after that."

"What about their father?"

"I get the impression he wasn't around much between his job and personal life."

"Well, marriages take a lot of work. Especially four of them."

Simon chuckled. "So you'll play nice this weekend, then?"

"I'll play nice," Vaughn assured him. Because of his job, he was a pro at masking his thoughts. Certainly he could act civil toward Sidney for the next thirty-six hours, even if she was a termagant. With great legs.

"Good." Simon pointed, as if having just thought about something. "But not *too* nice."

"You know, you're getting to be kind of a pain in the ass with all these rules. You ever hear the term 'groomzilla'?"

Simon let out a bark of laughter at that. "There's no such thing."

Vaughn gave him a look that said the jury was still out on that one.

"IZZ, ARE YOU seeing this? We've got cows. And look—there's an actual farmhouse." Sidney peered through the windshield. "It's like we've stepped into a John Cougar Mellencamp song."

Sidney Sinclair had indeed gone country.

Isabelle, however, did not appear to be enjoying this slice of Americana quite as much. "Why do cows have to smell like cows?" she groaned.

Sidney glanced over. "So roll up your window if the smell is bothering you."

"I need the air or I'll throw up. Do you want me to throw up? Do you? Because I'll hurl all over this car, right now."

This had been how Sidney's last three hours had gone—trapped in a leather-interior hellhole with the crazy pregnant lady. She hoped the menfolk were having a nice, relaxing road trip in that souped-up man car they were riding in because as soon as they got to the Robertses' house, she was pawning the woman formerly known as her sister onto the dude whose sperm had apparently turned her into a she-devil. "I'll tell you what—let's save the *Exorcist*-like spewing for the ride back. We can't use up all the fun car games on the first day."

Isabelle threw her arm over her eyes, groaning again. "Don't make me laugh. My stomach hurts too much. Are we almost there yet?"

As if Sidney had any clue where they were going. She followed dutifully behind Vaughn's car, past the farm and open fields, until they turned off the two-lane highway onto an access road marked "Apple Canyon." There, the scenery became more heavily wooded, and the streets no longer were marked. Sidney saw a yellow hazard sign for deer crossing, and the city girl in her immediately slowed and gripped the steering wheel tight with two hands—images of Bambi leaping tragically to a death-by-Mercedes flashing across her eyes. Then they came around a hill, and her eyes widened at the scenery before her.

They entered a gorgeous valley, with rolling green hills on both sides, and drove over a bridge that crossed a winding, picturesque creek. There were a few houses scattered along the valley, but they kept going, up another hill and past a waterfall. "Izz, sit up. Check out the waterfall."

"Just tell me that means we're close and I can get out of this damn car."

Ah, her sweet sister, soaking in every moment of the journey. They drove for a few more minutes, then Vaughn's car slowed considerably and turned onto a one-lane gravel road. Rocks flew up, hitting the underside of the Mercedes in a staccato burst of *ping*s and *clang*s. They drove into a small subdivision of nine or ten houses, spaced apart by at least an acre or more of land. Sidney followed as Vaughn pulled into the driveway of a white ranch house with a welcoming front porch and a pretty, multihued cottage garden.

Sidney parked the car and turned to her sister. "Ready for this?"

Isabelle, who looked a little better now that the car had stopped, took several deep breaths. Then she nodded and even managed a smile. "Let's do it." She opened the door just as Simon walked up, and he helped her out of the car. Hand-in-hand, they walked up the cobblestone walkway to the house.

Vaughn walked over to Sidney's side of the car, looking inconveniently sexy in his dark sunglasses and day-old scruff, gray T-shirt, and jeans.

"Guess that leaves you and me," he said as she climbed out of the car.

Great, she thought sarcastically. But then her heel slipped on the gravel driveway, and Vaughn instantly put his hand on her waist to steady her. Sidney felt a quick flare of heat in her stomach.

Oh, brother.

Hi, Hormones. This guy? Yeah, that's still a no.

"Thanks," she said.

He peered down at her through his sunglasses. "You might want to lose the heels for the weekend, city girl. That is, unless you're trying to get my hands on you." With a cocky smile, he turned and headed toward the front door, all broad shoulders and lean muscles in his jeans and T-shirt.

Sidney glared at his back as she followed him up the cobblestone pathway.

It was going to be a long two days.

Ahead of her, a petite, sixtysomething woman with dark hair was greeting Isabelle with a warm hug. Seeing Sidney approach, Kathleen Roberts pulled back from Isabelle and smiled. Her hazel eyes were Vaughn's, and her voice carried a hint of an Irish brogue. "And this must be Sidney."

Sidney held out her hand. "It's a pleasure to meet you, Mrs. Roberts. Thank you for having us here."

"Of course!" She waved them all vigorously into the house. "Come inside, you must be starving after the drive." She paused in the doorway, two disapproving eyes falling on Vaughn.

He held up his hands. "I just got here. How can I be in trouble already?"

She pointed to his dark, stubbled jaw. "They don't have razors anywhere in the city of Chicago?"

Sidney decided then that she was going to like Kathleen Roberts just fine.

Eight

ONCE INSIDE, SIDNEY and Isabelle were introduced to Simon and Vaughn's dad, Adam Roberts, a tall, big bear of a man with a thick shock of silver hair. They all moved into the family room, and Sidney mostly hung on the sidelines of the conversation as Kathleen and Adam got acquainted with Isabelle. The Robertses' house was sunny and brightly decorated, with beautiful oak bookshelves in the family room that Sidney guessed were Adam's handiwork—Simon had mentioned once that his father used to be a carpenter.

The initial awkwardness of Simon and Isabelle's meet-the-parents moment quickly dissipated, and everyone fell into comfortable, easy conversation. Afterward, Kathleen moved into the adjoining kitchen to finish preparing lunch, while Simon gave Sidney and Isabelle a quick tour of the house.

"And this is my old room," Simon said, looking semi-embarrassed. "I keep telling my parents they should turn it into an exercise room or something, but my mom says she's too nostalgic for that."

Isabelle peeked in and covered her mouth in a half-hearted attempt to hide her giggle. "Oh. My. God. There's a poster of

Heidi Klum on the wall. And look at that glamour shot of you on your desk." She peered closer. "Are those laser beams in the background?"

"Yep. That would be my high school senior photo," Simon said.

Isabelle laughed and kissed his cheek. "It's adorable. Show me more." She eagerly stepped inside his room.

Simon gestured for Sidney to join them. "Care to join us?"

"As much as I hate to pass on the glamour shot, I'll let you two have this moment to yourselves." Truthfully, she felt a little like a third wheel right then. "I think I'll see if your mom needs any help getting lunch ready."

She headed down the hallway in the direction of the kitchen. She found Kathleen rinsing a carrot in the apron-front sink while chatting with Vaughn, who sat in one of the stools by the island.

Both of them looked over when Sidney walked in.

Kathleen smiled. "Sidney. We were just catching up. Come join us."

Sidney eyed the empty bar stool, which sat close to the one already occupied by Vaughn. Too close. "Is there anything I can do to help?" she asked Kathleen.

"How sweet of you to ask." Kathleen nodded toward two plump red tomatoes that sat on a cutting board on the island. "I still need to dice those tomatoes for the salad, if you'd like to help with that."

"I'd be happy to." Sidney headed over to the island, looking around for a knife.

"On the counter, by the refrigerator," Vaughn said.

Following his direction, Sidney spotted the knife block. "Thanks."

With a skeptical expression, he watched as she selected a long, large serrated knife and returned to the cutting board. "Watch those fingers," he said. "The nearest hospital is forty-five minutes away."

While his mother's back was to them, Sidney gave him dry look. "I'll do my best."

She picked up the first tomato, and began making slices

almost all the way through, a quarter of an inch apart. Then she turned the tomato and did the same thing, bisecting her original slices. When she'd finished that, she flipped the tomato on its side and diced through, the tomato falling onto the cutting board in perfect, ripe cubes.

She set down the knife, and looked at Vaughn with satisfaction as she wagged her fingers. "Still have all five of them." Then she popped one of the tomato cubes into her mouth.

Kathleen came around to check out Sidney's handiwork. "Somebody knows how to cook," she said, impressed.

"Only a little," Sidney said, with a conceding smile. "Back in New York, one of my friends roped me into taking a Knife Skills class. I thought it was a self-defense course."

Kathleen laughed at the joke, and then turned around to get something out of the refrigerator. Sidney grabbed the second tomato and saw Vaughn watching her.

She glared. *What?*

His hazel eyes crinkled at the corners as he kept right on looking.

Her scowl deepened. *Go away.*

He winked.

Clearly, the man lived to annoy her.

When Kathleen shut the refrigerator door and turned around, both Sidney and Vaughn resumed their normal expressions. Kathleen put a bottle of what appeared to be homemade salad dressing in the middle of the farm table that sat on the other side of the island.

As she passed by Vaughn, she gave her son's unshaven jaw another once-over. "So that's the look now, is it?"

With a mischievous smile that said he'd gotten more than a handful of lectures from his mother over the years, Vaughn got up from the stool and walked over to the sideboard across from the kitchen table. "It's only temporary, Mom." He opened one of the cabinets and pulled out a stack of plates.

"Sidney, is that what you girls go for these days?" Kathleen asked, pointing toward her oldest son. "All this scruffy whatnot?"

Well, nothing like putting her on the spot here. Personally,

Sidney thought that the dark hint of scruff along Vaughn's angular jaw looked fine. Better than fine, actually. She would, however, rather be trapped for the next thirty-six hours in a car with the crazy pregnant lady before admitting that in front of him.

"I generally prefer clean-shaven men." She shrugged—*sorry*—when Vaughn gave her the side-eye as he began setting the table.

"See? If you don't believe me, at least listen to her," Kathleen said, while peeling a carrot over a bowl at the island. "If you want to find a woman of quality, you can't be running around looking like you just rolled out of bed."

"I'll keep that in mind. But for now, the 'scruffy whatnot' stays. I need it for an undercover role," Vaughn said.

Surprised to hear that, Sidney looked over as she dumped the tomatoes into a large salad bowl filled with lettuce. "You're working undercover now?"

"Well, I'm not in the other identity right this second," Vaughn said. "I'm kind of guessing my mother would be able to ID me."

Thank you, yes, she got that. "I meant, how does that work?" Sidney asked him. "You just walk around like normal, being yourself, when you're not . . . the other you?"

"That's exactly how it works. At least, when we're talking about a case that involves only part-time undercover work."

"But what if I were to run into the other you somewhere? Say . . . at a coffee shop." A little inside reference there. "If I called you 'Vaughn' without realizing that you were working, wouldn't that blow your cover?"

"First of all, like all agents who regularly do undercover work, I tell my friends and family not to approach me if they happen to run into me somewhere—for that very reason. Second of all, in this case, the 'other me' doesn't hang out at coffee shops."

"Where does the other you hang out?" Sidney asked. Not to contribute to his already healthy ego, but this was pretty interesting stuff.

"In dark, sketchy alleys doing dark, sketchy things," Vaughn said as he set the table with salad bowls.

"So the other you is a bad guy, then." Sidney paused, realizing something. "Is what you're doing dangerous?"

"The joke around my office is that the agents on the white-collar crime squad never do anything dangerous."

Sidney noticed that wasn't an actual answer to her question.

When the room fell momentarily quiet, Kathleen looked between Sidney and Vaughn. "You know, Sidney, when you girls first came in, I spent so much time catching up with Isabelle, that I feel like we didn't get to talk much. Tell me more about yourself. What is it that you do for a living?"

"I'm a director at a private equity firm."

"Oh, that sounds impressive. Have you always worked in Chicago?" Finished with her peeling, Kathleen grabbed a shredder out of the cabinet in the base of the island.

Sidney rinsed off her knife at the sink. "Actually, I first worked in New York as an investment banker after finishing business school. I just moved back to Chicago two months ago."

"Your father must be so glad to have you back in town."

Sidney kept her expression nonchalant, not wanting to reveal the complexity of her relationship with her father. Professionally speaking, she had a great deal of respect for him. Coming from a middle-class background, he'd put himself through business school and now ran one of the most lucrative hedge funds in Chicago. He was a natural leader: sharp, decisive, and cool and collected when taking risks. Her father knew how to command a room; she remembered being in awe of him when she was younger, watching him at her parents' parties and noticing how he always seemed to be the center of attention no matter who he was talking to. But his devotion to his career, and the egotism that had sprung from his success, had put a distance between him and his daughters—and had undoubtedly contributed to the problems in his later marriages.

Clearly, their upbringing had been a lot different from that of Vaughn and Simon. This whole cozy scene, the sit-down family lunch on a Saturday afternoon, was something she hadn't experienced since she was a young girl, before her mom died. But for simplicity's sake, Sidney nodded and gave the expected response. "Yes, he is."

Over in the adjacent family room, whatever sporting event Adam had been watching must have ended. He shut off the television and stood up from the couch. "What time is lunch?" he called over.

"Now," Kathleen said.

"That's the best time," he said.

Vaughn was dispatched to alert Simon and Isabelle that lunch was ready, and within moments they were all seated around the knotted pine farm table. There was a bounty of food on the table: freshly baked soda bread, salad, and the main course, shepherd's pie. Kathleen led them in saying grace, and Sidney and Isabelle shot each other we're-such-heathens looks as they bowed their heads, not having done this in years. After a chorus of amens, Vaughn and the other Robertses all made the sign of the cross, and then everyone heartily reached for whatever dish was closest.

"Oh! I almost forgot." Kathleen momentarily left the table and came back with a bottle of wine. "Since this is a special occasion, our first time meeting our future daughter-in-law, I thought we should celebrate." She handed the bottle to Vaughn, along with a corkscrew. "I can never work those things." She turned back to the rest of the table, explaining. "One of Adam's clients gave him this bottle years ago. We've been saving it for the right moment."

"Rich family, big house just outside of Milwaukee," Adam added. "They wanted two walls of built-in bookshelves in their living room, and they asked me to do it in two weeks, before some big family party they were having. We got the job done in twelve days," he said proudly. He gestured to the bottle. "I don't know much about wine, but they said this is a good one."

"I think it's time we found out." Kathleen took the open bottle Vaughn set in front of her and poured each of them a glass. She then raised her glass in toast.

Next to Sidney, Isabelle shot her a silent plea. *Help.*

Sidney gave her a reassuring look that said she would take care of it.

"There's an Irish blessing that I think fits well here," Kathleen said. "May love and laughter light your days, and warm your heart and home."

After a round of "Cheers," Sidney took a sip of her wine. She waited as Isabelle faked a sip, then deliberately set her glass on the table right next to her sister's.

Isabelle glanced over and smiled, catching on. The Robertses' bringing out a special bottle of wine for a toast—that Isabelle obviously couldn't drink—was a small hiccup in the let's-pretend-nobody's-pregnant plan, but nothing that couldn't be resolved with a few stealth maneuvers. Sidney simply would drink a little of Isabelle's wine when nobody was looking.

People passed food every which way, and Sidney paused at the delicious aromas coming from the shepherd's pie, the hearty layers of mashed potatoes, sautéed lamb, carrots, peas, and onions. "This smells incredible, Kathleen."

"It's the boys' favorite," she said. "Isabelle, I'll have to give you the recipe."

"I'd like that. Thank you."

Sidney peeked over, expecting to see a big grin on her sister's face. After all, this was exactly what Isabelle had been hoping for—to bond with Kathleen this weekend.

But instead, she looked pale while staring at the shepherd's pie on her plate.

Isabelle exhaled slowly, speaking under her breath. "Oh, boy."

Sidney's hand froze. She knew that *Oh, boy*.

Seriously, they couldn't take the pregnant lady anywhere.

Nine

VAUGHN HAD TO give the Three Amigos credit: they worked well under pressure.

Next to him, Simon "stole" the last bite of Isabelle's shepherd's pie off her plate.

"Simon," she pretended to protest.

"Sorry," he said with an impish grin, gesturing to the empty casserole dish. "There's no more left, and I've waited months for that pie."

"Now how could I begrudge you that?" They smiled at each other, all schmoopey-like.

It took all of Vaughn's undercover skills to keep from rolling his eyes.

This performance had been going on for the past twenty minutes, in which Simon had managed to eat every bite of shepherd's pie on Isabelle's plate. There'd been a lot of coy looks between them, but Vaughn had pretended to be oblivious to the whole thing—just like he was pretending to be oblivious to Little Miss Sneaky Drinks across the table, on Isabelle's other side.

To be fair, Sidney at least managed to be subtler in the

charade, with the sleight-of-hand routine she had going on with Isabelle's wine. She'd taken a few sips from each of their glasses, seemingly with neither of his parents being the wiser. But, apparently, these three also believed they were fooling *him*, an FBI agent, and for that Vaughn didn't know whether to be amused or insulted. Perhaps a little of both.

After lunch, Sidney and Isabelle offered to help with the dishes, while the three men headed out to the backyard. Vaughn and Simon planned to re-shingle the shed roof that weekend, undoubtedly with a whole lot of micromanaging from their retired-carpenter father, who'd been strictly forbidden by their mother to undertake any strenuous labor after his heart attack six months ago.

"I called in all the supplies at McGovern's," their dad said, referring to the local hardware store. "You can take my truck to pick everything up."

Simon nodded. "Sidney and Isabelle can follow us into town so they can get settled in at the hotel."

"Assuming your mother will let you pry those girls from this house," Adam said. "You should have seen her these past two weeks. I think all of Apple Canyon has heard about her son and his *fiancée*." He looked proudly at Simon. "We're happy for you, son. Isabelle seems like a wonderful girl."

Simon answered without any hesitation. "She is, Dad."

For a moment, Vaughn caught himself wondering what it felt like to be *that* certain—to know, without a doubt, that he'd found the one person he wanted to spend the rest of his life with. Between Simon's getting married and suddenly having a baby on the way, Vaughn would've expected his brother to be in a mild-to-moderate state of panic. But instead, Simon seemed completely calm about the whole thing.

Vaughn watched as his dad pulled Simon in for a hug and patted him heartily on the back in congratulations. He smiled at that, then left them to their father-son moment while he headed back inside the house to grab the keys to his dad's truck.

Enough of the sentimentality—he, at least, had a shed to re-shingle.

*   *   *

A HALF HOUR later, Vaughn and Simon stood in the drive-way, leaning against their father's pickup truck and waiting as the women said their temporary good-byes in the doorway. Vaughn's gaze fell on the cute curve of Sidney's ass as she laughed at something his mother said.

"Mom really seems to like her," Simon said.

Vaughn grunted, having noticed this, too. Seemingly, the elder Sinclair sister was perfectly capable of piling on the charm for anyone except him. "I think she won Mom over the minute she diced that tomato."

"Talking about Isabelle again."

Obviously.

Vaughn tore his eyes away from the saucy auburn-haired woman who was here, in his parents' house, winning them over with her smiles and making them laugh with her self-deprecating, *I-thought-it-was-a-self-defense-course* jokes. It was a good thing she was heading to the hotel for a few hours, because he needed a break—a break from those legs, and the blue-green eyes, and the flirty wrap dress that tied at her waist, and could easily be undone with one sharp tug.

He was thinking things again.

A few minutes later, the four of them were finally on their way, with Sidney's car once again following behind him. Vaughn took the shortest route to town, a twenty-minute drive along hilly, winding roads.

They pulled into the driveway of Carter Mansion, a Victorian-style bed-and-breakfast where the Sinclair sisters would be spending the night. As soon as Sidney's car rolled to a stop behind the pickup truck, Isabelle scrambled out and hurried up the front steps of the inn, not bothering to wait for the rest of them.

"I guess she's eager to check in," Simon said, with an attempt at a casual laugh. Then he climbed out of the pickup, grabbed Isabelle's suitcase from the trunk of the Mercedes, and quickly followed his fiancée inside.

And then there were two.

Vaughn exited the truck and walked around to Sidney's car. He found her standing next to the sedan's open trunk, taking in the picturesque town before them—a quaint cobble-stone street flanked by brightly colored historical buildings.

"So this is 'town.' " She cocked her head, as if surprised. "It's so cute and charming." She turned and raised an eyebrow. "You really grew up here?"

Ha, ha. "What were you expecting? A tavern, a gas sta-tion, and some diner named Flo's, advertising the $5.99 meat-loaf special?"

"Of course not."

He gave her an unwavering I-can-wait-for-the-truth-all-day FBI stare.

She rolled her eyes. "Fine. Maybe that's something along the lines of what I'd pictured."

Satisfied with the admission, Vaughn reached for the han-dle of her suitcase. He grunted as he lifted it out of the trunk. "Christ, what did you pack in here?"

"An espresso machine. There's no Starbucks for miles, so I had to improvise."

He was about to respond—*You've got to be kidding me*—when he caught the sparkle of amusement in her eyes and realized she was messing with him. "Cute. What's really in the suitcase?"

She grabbed her laptop bag and threw the strap over her shoulder. "Bridal magazines for Isabelle. Lots of them." She shut the trunk of her car and they began walking up the drive-way to the mansion.

"Ah. You mean the ones filled with articles like, 'How to Dazzle Your Guests with Ridiculously Overpriced Center-pieces,' and 'Where to Register for Obnoxiously Expensive China You'll Never Use'?"

"And here I thought I was snarky."

"Come on. You have to admit, the whole thing is a racket," he said. "The wedding industry preys on stressed-out brides, convincing them that they have to spend crazy amounts of money to create some romanticized idea of the perfect day."

"And when you're forty-five, and your twenty-four-year-old fiancée wants to create wonderful memories that you two will remember for the rest of your life, I'm sure that's the exact speech you'll use to rein her in," Sidney quipped, not missing a beat.

Ooh, she sounded *irritated* with him again. Vaughn turned around, walking backward so he could face her. Strangely, seeing her aggravated expression made him grin—and want to goad her on even more. "I like this scenario. Tell me more about this twenty-four-year-old wife of mine. Is she hot? Smoking body?"

Sidney smiled sweetly. "Remember that thing you said to me at the coffee shop? That we could meet the next day, so you could surprise me by *not* turning out to be the ass I thought you might be? I think we've officially established that you would not have been successful in that endeavor."

He stopped at the base of the steps. "But I haven't shown you my best moves."

"Honey, I already know your best moves," she said, tilting her head back to meet his gaze. "And five years ago, I might've been tempted. But now I'm looking for more . . . serious contenders."

Personally, he thought it wouldn't kill her to have a little fun—she had her whole life to be bored by serious contenders. "That's the second time you called me 'honey.' I can't decide if I like it or if I'm starting to feel objectified," he teased.

She sighed. "I seriously don't think I can walk down an aisle with you."

His voice dipped lower, a slow drawl. "Careful, Sinclair. Those are very heady words to a guy like me."

She left him standing there, by himself, at the base of the steps.

With a grin, he turned and watched her go. *Yep, still cantankerous.*

But that didn't mean he couldn't enjoy the view from behind.

Vaughn followed her to the inn's front door, catching sight of the placard that said the mansion had been built in 1849.

Stepping inside, he saw that careful attention had been paid to preserve the historical character of the house. To his left was a parlor with a wood-burning fireplace and antique furnishings. Across the foyer was a living room with a small reception area.

A woman in her mid-fifties, dressed in jeans and a floral top, sat behind an ornate wooden check-in desk. She greeted them with a warm smile. "Welcome to Carter Mansion."

Sidney looked around. "My sister, Isabelle, came in here a few minutes ago. At least, I thought she did."

"She and Simon just headed upstairs. They said you were right behind them. Sidney, right?" The woman introduced herself as Lauren, one of the co-owners of the inn. She gave them an overview of the amenities as she checked Sidney in. "You'll be staying in the Jocelyn Room. Your sister's room is right next door." She slid a small metal key ring with the inn's logo across the desk.

Sidney's eyes widened, seeing that. "Oh, wow. You have actual *keys*, not a key card." She took out her cell phone and snapped a photo.

"She's from the city," Vaughn explained to the innkeeper.

Sidney nudged him with her shoulder. "You're from the city now, too."

"But I blend in anywhere. It's an FBI thing."

She snorted at that. "Blend? There had to be thirty people in that coffee shop that day, yet you were the one I noticed as soon I walked in."

Interesting admission. "Checking me out, were you?"

Sidney blushed, then turned to Lauren—clearly not about to answer that. "What time is check-out?"

"Noon. A full gourmet breakfast will be served in your room at any time of your choosing between seven thirty and nine thirty A.M." Lauren turned amiably to Vaughn. "I'm in the church gardening group with your mother. Be sure to tell her I said hello."

"I'll do that," Vaughn said.

"She's talked a lot about Simon's engagement, but didn't

say anything about you." The innkeeper pointed between Vaughn and Sidney. "Have you two been together long?"

Sidney blinked, then gestured at Vaughn. "Him and me?" She laughed. "Oh, no. Noooo, no, no."

Vaughn smiled at Lauren, nonplussed. "In case you missed it, that would be a no."

Ten

AFTER UNPACKING, SIDNEY and Isabelle curled up on Isabelle's bed with a stack of bridal magazines and got down to work.

Over the next couple of hours, they decided on the color of the bridesmaids' dresses, finalized the guest lists for the bridal shower and bachelorette party, and pulled together several magazine clippings with photos of table centerpieces to show the florist. Sidney was about to move on to the next item on the agenda—potential locations for the rehearsal dinner because that needed to be booked ASAP—when she looked over and saw that Isabelle had fallen asleep, her head tucked into the crook of her arm.

Quietly, Sidney got up and grabbed the throw blanket that had been folded across the bottom of the bed. She laid it over Isabelle, whose expression was one of serene contentment as she napped with a bridal magazine lying open on the bed in front of her. Seeing that, Sidney felt a pang of something bittersweet. She, too, had once felt that happy and hopeful about her own wedding—before she'd been unexpectedly yanked out of the fantasy by the appearance of her fiancé's *lover*.

Shoving the unwelcome memory aside, she tiptoed out of the room.

Once inside her own room, Sidney caught up on e-mail and texted Trish the photo of the *actual key* the innkeeper had given her.

I THINK I'M IN MAYBERRY, she typed.

A few seconds later, she received Trish's reply. I HEAR SMALL TOWNS HAVE HOT SHERIFFS. GO SPEED THAT MERCEDES DOWN MAIN STREET AND GET YOURSELF A DATE.

Sidney smiled. If only it were that easy.

Deciding that a more casual look would be appropriate for dinner, she changed into jeans, flat sandals, and a flowy, white embroidered camisole top. She let her hair down from the twist she'd pinned it into that morning, let it fall into messy waves, and used a curling iron to touch up the ends. She was just finishing up when she heard a knock at her door.

Isabelle shuffled in, yawning. "Simon just texted me. He said he'll pick us up in twenty minutes." She looked Sidney over. "Wow. That's the most non-businesslike I've seen you look in years."

Sidney scrutinized her reflection in the mirror on the back of the closet door. "It's missing something. Do you think they sell cowboy boots in town?"

"Not ones that are made by Manolo Blahnik," Isabelle said teasingly.

Well, that was indeed a crime.

FOR DINNER, KATHLEEN diverted from the traditional Irish traditions and instead made chicken with lemon, green olives, and couscous—which seemed to agree much better with both Isabelle and the peanut. Sidney sat with her sister to her right, and Kathleen, at the foot of the table, on her other side. The mood was boisterous, with everyone talking every which way, and Sidney found herself chatting quite a bit with Kathleen.

Over coffee and dessert, a delicious pistachio chocolate chip cake that was another favorite of "the boys," the conversation took a turn that Sidney supposed was inevitable.

"I noticed you haven't mentioned anything about a boyfriend," Kathleen said to her. "Does that mean you're single?"

The din around the table suddenly quieted, and five pairs of eyes focused on Sidney.

Well. Nothing like putting her on the spot again.

"Yes, I'm single," she said.

"I don't understand that." Kathleen gestured to her. "How is it that a smart, pretty girl like you hasn't been snatched up by some good man?"

"Mom," Vaughn said. "I'm sure Sidney doesn't want to be interrogated about her personal life."

Deep down, Sidney knew that Vaughn—who'd obviously deduced that she'd been burned in the past—was only trying to be polite. But that was the problem, she didn't *want* him to be polite, as if she needed to be shielded from such questions. That wasn't any better than the damn "Poor Sidney" head-tilt.

"It's okay, I don't mind answering." She turned to Kathleen. "I was seeing someone in New York, but that relationship ended shortly before I moved to Chicago."

"So now that you're single again, what kind of man are you looking for? Vaughn?" Kathleen pointed. "Could you pass the creamer?"

He did so, then turned to look once again at Sidney. His lips curved at the corners, the barest hint of a smile. He was daring her, she knew, waiting for her to back away from his mother's questions.

She never had been very good at resisting his dares.

"Actually, I have a list of things I'm looking for." Sidney took a sip of her coffee.

Vaughn raised an eyebrow. "You have a list?"

"Yep."

"Of course you do."

Isabelle looked over, surprised. "You never told me about this."

"What kind of list?" Kathleen asked interestedly.

"It's a test, really," Sidney said. "A list of characteristics that indicate whether a man is ready for a serious relationship. It helps weed out the commitment-phobic guys, the womanizers, and any other bad apples, so a woman can focus on the candidates with more long-term potential."

Vaughn rolled his eyes. "And now I've heard it all."

"Where did you find this list?" Simon asked. "Is this something all women know about?"

"Why? Worried you won't pass muster?" Isabelle winked at him.

"I did some research," Sidney said. "Pulled it together after reading several articles online."

"Lists, tests, research, online dating, speed dating—I can't keep up with all these things you kids are doing," Adam said, from the head of the table. "Whatever happened to the days when you'd see a girl at a restaurant or a coffee shop and just walk over and say hello?"

Vaughn turned to Sidney, his smile devilish. "Yes, whatever happened to those days, Sidney?"

She threw him a look. *Don't be cute.* "You know what they say—it's a jungle out there. Nowadays a woman has to make quick decisions about whether a man is up to par." She shook her head mock reluctantly. "Sadly, some guys just won't make the cut."

"But all it takes is one," Isabelle said, with a loving smile at her fiancé.

Simon slid his hand across the table, covering hers affectionately. "The right one."

Until he nails his personal trainer. Sidney took another sip of her coffee, holding back the cynical comment. She didn't want to spoil Isabelle and Simon's idyllic all-you-need-is-love glow.

Vaughn cocked his head, looking at the happy couple. "Aw, aren't you two just so . . . cheesy."

Kathleen shushed him. "Don't tease your brother."

"What? Any moment, I'm expecting birds and little woodland animals to come in here and start singing songs about true love, they're so adorable."

Sidney laughed out loud. Quickly, she bit her lip to cover.

When Vaughn's eyes met hers across the table, she realized that for one brief moment, they were on the same page.

"So," Kathleen said, picking up the cake cutter. "Who wants seconds?"

AFTER THE DINNER dishes were cleared away, Kathleen disappeared for a few minutes, then came back into the kitchen carrying a stack of photo albums.

"Oh, crap, no," Vaughn groaned.

"No way, Mom," Simon said definitively. "Not the photo albums."

"What? I'm sure the girls would love to see these. You boys were so cute when you were younger." She shooed them away. "Go work on the shed while we talk."

The three women moved into the family room, and Kathleen walked Isabelle and Sidney through the photo albums. She shared funny anecdotes about the family, and turned nostalgic when she opened Simon's baby book. "I wrote everything down, knowing he was going to be my last. Adam and I had planned to have a bigger family, but there were complications when Simon was born. I'd always wanted to have a daughter." She looked up from the baby book and smiled at Isabelle. "At least now I get to have a daughter-in-law. Finally."

Isabelle returned the smile. "I realize that Simon and I have only known each other a few months, but I hope you know that my feelings for him are completely sincere. I think he's just . . . wonderful. He's funny and sweet and caring, and such a *good* man. I can't wait to marry him and start a family, and begin building memories of our own, just like these." She gestured to the photo albums on the coffee table in front of them.

Kathleen's eyes were misty. "Well. I think that's just about the sweetest thing I've ever heard." She laughed, wiping her eyes. "I'd say this calls for a hug." She pulled Isabelle in and squeezed her.

Sidney felt a tightening in her chest, watching the two women embrace. Isabelle had missed out on so many moments like this, both of them had. But happy though she was for Isabelle, seeing her sister bond with her future mother-in-law served as yet another reminder of the place she had always assumed she, too, would be in at this point in her life.

Careful, warned the pragmatic voice in her head. *That's starting to sound a bit like jealousy.*

Sidney stood up from the armchair. "I'm going to grab a glass of water. Anyone else need anything?"

"Actually, Sidney, if you don't mind, grab a couple bottled waters from the refrigerator and bring them out to the boys," Kathleen said. "And find out how much longer they plan to be."

Thinking that some air would do her good, Sidney nodded. "Sure, no problem." She grabbed three bottled waters from the fridge, then headed out to the backyard and followed a row of colorful flowers to the white painted shed. She could see Simon working on a section of the roof close to the ladder, so she called his name and held up the bottled water. "Your mom wants to know when you guys are wrapping up."

He climbed down the ladder and took one of the bottled waters. "I think we'll probably call it a day. It'll be dark soon, anyway." He shouted up to Vaughn, who poked his head around the peaked part of the roof. "I'm heading in."

Vaughn nodded and went back to his hammering.

Not about to stand around all night waiting for him, Sidney set his bottled water on the grass next to the ladder. She turned to follow Simon, but then hesitated.

Perhaps she could use just a teeny tiny break before heading back inside to the most adorably-in-love couple this side of Chicago.

She noticed a path to the left of the shed. Seeing that it led into the woods adjacent to the Robertses' house, she decided to check it out. Closer to the trees, the path split in two. Mindful of the approaching darkness, she ignored the path that led deeper into the woods and chose the other one, which took her to a small clearing. She slowed her stride as she neared the top, struck by the picturesque view. The Robertses' property was at the top of a hill, and from the clearing she could see down into the valley. The deep blue of the sky was streaked with brilliant hues of red, burnt orange, and yellow as the sun began its descent behind the hills.

Seeing that she still had time while it was light outside, she took a seat in the grass. She tucked her knees and rested her chin on her forearms, soaking in both the view and these few brief moments when she was blissfully free of all wedding talk.

Eleven

DON'T EVEN THINK about following her.

Vaughn repeated this mantra in his head as he pounded away with the hammer. When he finished the row of shingles he'd been working on, he decided to call it quits for the evening. He and Simon had more work to do tomorrow, but they were making good progress—over half the roof was done.

He wiped his brow with his arm, then climbed down the ladder and cracked open the bottled water Sidney had left him.

She had a new look tonight, he'd noticed. Hair down, jeans that molded to her every curve, and some summery top that hugged tight to her chest and draped loose around her waist. He could practically feel his fingers tracing along her soft skin, trailing a slow path over the curve of her waist and up to the tantalizing swell of her breasts.

Christ.

Taking a frustrated swig of water, Vaughn swallowed and looked over at the path that led to the clearing. She'd been gone only a few minutes now, and he knew she couldn't go far. Although . . . there *was* always the possibility that she could stumble into some poison ivy. Or an angry badger. Or she could slip in those strappy designer sandals and tumble headfirst down the hill and into an entire *nest* of angry badgers.

Probably, he should check on her. Just to be safe.

That decided, he followed the path through the short stretch of woods that he knew like the back of his hand, and spotted her sitting near the edge of the clearing. She looked over her shoulder, eying him warily as he approached.

He stopped beside her. "So. How many things are on this list of yours?"

She watched as he helped himself to a seat in the grass next to her. "Thirty-four."

"*Thirty-four?* You can't be serious." Vaughn doubted any man could pass such a test.

Perhaps that was the point.

She sat up straighter, going on the defensive. "A few things are redundant, maybe, but overall it seems like a pretty solid list to me."

Well, now he was curious. He beckoned with his hand. "All right, lay it on me. Let's hear this list of so-called signs that say whether a man is ready for a commitment."

She cocked her head, feigning confusion. "And remind me—why is it that I care what you think?"

He raised an eyebrow challengingly. "Afraid I'll tell you the list is complete BS?"

She held his gaze defiantly, and then began ticking off her fingers. "He can't be hung up on a prior relationship. Must be available on weekends. Settled in his career. On stable emotional footing with his parents. Have friends who are in committed relationships." She paused, as if trying to remember the other things on her list.

Vaughn frowned. "I hope you've got more than that. Because you just described *me*."

Her eyes widened, her expression akin to abject horror.

Then after a moment's pause, she smiled. "Ah. But you fail the number one rule, the most important one of all: he *tells* you he's not looking for a serious relationship."

Vaughn exhaled. Thank god for the number one rule.

Stupid test or not, he didn't need to be giving off any signs of "commitment-readiness." That was fine for other guys, but he enjoyed his life the way it was, thank you very much.

Sidney sighed in relief. "Whew. That freaked me out for a moment there." She gestured at him. "I can't be having any of your type sneaking in undetected."

Now that remark got under his skin a little. "For the record, my type doesn't try to 'sneak in.' I'm always upfront about the fact that I'm not looking for a long-term commitment."

Her smile was sweet, her tone dry. "Aw, and that makes you such a good guy. Because you're *honest* about being a womanizer."

And . . . now she was getting under his skin *a lot*. "So you'd rather I lie?" He angled his body to face hers. "That I date a woman for a couple months, string her along, and *then* tell her that I don't want anything serious? Would that make me a good guy?" He leaned in closer to her. "See, this is why I don't date women in their thirties. You're jaded. And ornery. And you have a checklist with thirty-four goddamn things on it!"

She turned toward him, her cheeks flushed pink as she, too, raised her voice. "Don't put this on me. There's a reason women like me need a thirty-four-item checklist—to protect ourselves from all the guys like *you* out there."

"What's so terrible about a guy like me? Here's the way I see it: if you're looking for happily-ever-after, there are a lot better guys out there for the job. But if you want a good time, then I'm your man, baby."

"I'll say this, you're nothing if not confident."

Hell, yes, he was—and for good reason. He peered down into her eyes. "I would rock your world, Sinclair, and you know it."

It was about right then that he noticed they were sitting just inches apart on the grass. But she didn't move, and neither did he.

"Ah, yes. Your supposed 'moves.' " She emphasized the word with a saucy tilt of her head. "That certain . . . something that puts the 'special' in Special Agent Vaughn Roberts."

That *mouth*. Her sarcastic words pushed all his buttons,

but he nevertheless couldn't stop staring at her full, tempting lips. He lowered his head, his voice dipping lower. "Want to know what I think?"

She paused for a moment, as if taking in his proximity. He could hear the quickening of her breath.

"Not especially," she said.

The words were quintessential snarky Sidney Sinclair, but the husky tone of her voice was something new. Something that drew him in even more. "I think you're worried that if I kiss you right now, you might actually like it."

Her eyes flashed—with anger, no doubt, but also with a heat that came from somewhere else.

And before Vaughn even thought about what he was doing, he kissed her.

He pressed her lips open as his mouth moved demandingly over hers, all his frustration, his irritation, and his aggravation pouring into this one kiss. His tongue swept roughly around hers—not bothering with either sweetness or sophistication—and he felt her hands press against his chest. He braced himself for the shove, for her to push him away, but instead she gripped his T-shirt and pulled him closer and *oh sweet lord* she was kissing him back.

All of his restraint just . . . broke.

He grabbed her and pulled her into his lap, her denim-clad legs straddling his thighs. He tangled his hand in her hair as their mouths furiously melded together. She bit his lower lip, then sucked on the spot and licked her tongue over it in a way that had his cock straining against the zipper of his jeans.

He growled low in his throat and pushed her to the ground.

She moaned when he settled between her legs, and the sound only incited him more. He took her mouth possessively, voraciously, one hand gripping the nape of her neck as she battled him kiss for kiss. Needing to taste more of her, he angled his head and trailed his lips along the smooth skin of her neck, tugging her hair back to expose more. She dug her nails into his back, through his T-shirt, so he nipped her with his teeth, right at the base of her neck. She gasped and arched her back, then bent one knee, settling him deeper between her legs, and slowly she began rocking her hips against his throbbing erection.

Fuck.

His breath was a ragged hiss, his mouth claiming hers once more. She pushed her breasts eagerly against his chest, and all he could think about was sucking one of them into his mouth as he shoved her jeans down, yanked open his fly, and took her hard against the ground, making her scream his name as he—

"Vaughn!"

The voice—Simon's, coming from the backyard—made them both jump and pull apart.

They stared at each other, panting and wide-eyed.

"Oh, no," Sidney said. "You and I can't . . . I mean, we so, *so* couldn't . . . you know." She gestured between them, her lips swollen from his kisses, her cheeks flushed, and her glorious auburn hair spilling wildly over her shoulders.

Vaughn touched his mouth, still trying to wrap his mind around whatever the hell had just happened.

Simon called his name again, sounding closer this time.

Instantly, he moved into undercover mode. "Just act natural," he told Sidney. He reached over and picked a few wildflower petals out of her hair, speaking calmly. "We're two people looking at a nice view. That's all. You and I fell into a conversation about the wedding, and we started talking about the possibility of coordinating the dates for the bachelor and bachelorette parties. We thought that Isabelle and Simon might want to have them on the same night, given the time crunch."

"Right. Bachelorette party. Got it." Sidney exhaled, gathering herself.

Vaughn's gaze fell to the curve of her neck. "You have a red mark." He fixed her hair, moving it forward over her shoulders. "You might have to keep your hair down for the rest of the weekend."

He caught Sidney's glare as they resumed their positions. "Save the look, Sinclair. You bit me first."

She blushed as Simon stepped into the clearing.

Vaughn grinned. "Hey, bro. We were just talking about you."

FOR THE REST of the weekend, Sidney made sure she was never, ever alone again with Vaughn.

It wasn't as difficult a task as she'd feared: between Isabelle, Simon, and Mr. and Mrs. Roberts, there were lots of people around, and with a little bit of finessing, Sidney made sure one of them was always around *her*. She and Isabelle went back to the hotel shortly after Simon found her and Vaughn in the clearing, and they didn't return the next day until late morning, after the worst of Isabelle's morning sickness had passed.

By the time they arrived at the house on Sunday, Vaughn was already up on the shed roof, hammering away. Simon joined his brother on the roof, the menfolk finished their project, and then they cleaned up.

During lunch, Sidney and Vaughn exchanged all of about two words—although she did catch him looking at her at one point when she brushed her hair off her shoulders. Luckily, the red mark on her neck had already disappeared—and with it, all traces of her strange, hot tryst with Vaughn in the woods.

A tryst, she vowed, that was never to be repeated.

After lunch, it was time to say good-bye and hit the road.

"I'm so glad you joined us this weekend," Kathleen said, pulling Sidney in for a hug as they said their farewells on the driveway. Then she joined her husband on the front porch, and the two of them waved good-bye as Vaughn and Sidney's cars pulled out of the driveway.

"And . . . scene," Isabelle said, as the pretty white ranch grew smaller in Sidney's rearview mirror. She exhaled in relief. "I think we pulled it off. Not to get all Sally Fields here, but I think they liked me." She looked over gratefully at Sidney. "I hope the weekend wasn't too boring for you."

For a split second, Sidney was tempted to tell her sister everything. *So here's a funny thing: I kissed Vaughn.* But then

Isabelle would want to know whether the kiss had meant anything—and since it absolutely, one-hundred percent had *not*, Sidney figured it was best not to mention it at all.

"Not at all. It was fun," she assured Isabelle.

Isabelle reclined her seat and closed her eyes, mumbling something about taking a nap. With the radio on low, Sidney followed Vaughn's car through the now semi-familiar maze of woods, hills, and valleys that eventually led to the highway.

After they'd driven for about fifteen minutes, Isabelle sat up. "I think I'm going to be sick."

Sidney looked over. "Do you need me to pull over?"

"Yes—hurry."

Sidney came to a stop at the side of the road, and Isabelle scrambled out of the car and ran for some trees. Ahead of them, Vaughn's car slowed down, did a U-Turn, and came to a stop parallel to Sidney's, on the other side of the road.

Simon got out, with a sheepish smile. "She sometimes gets a little carsick," he said to Vaughn.

"Mmm-hmm," Vaughn said through the open driver's side window.

Simon trotted off toward the trees to tend to Isabelle, who was bent over and doing her thing.

Sitting in their cars on opposite sides of the road, Sidney and Vaughn looked at each other, neither of them making any move to get out.

Then they both turned away, the gray concrete highway a comforting gap between them.

Twelve

TWO WEEKS LATER, Vaughn made his debut appearance as "Mark Sullivan," a gun buyer who was eager to make the acquaintance of Officer Pritchett and his gang of corrupt cops.

Per his instructions, Batista had set up the meeting for that Friday afternoon at a diner in West Town. As Mark Sullivan, a man who made a pretty penny doing shady things, Vaughn looked like a guy who spent his free time hanging out at upscale strip clubs. He sported dark scruff along his jaw, a designer suit and Italian loafers, and a flashy Rolex on his wrist.

Pritchett showed up right on time, with two beefy twenty-something guys in tow. Unbeknownst to the three police officers, Vaughn also had brought guests to this party—a whole slew of them.

Crooked cops were considered dangerous targets. In addition to being armed, they had everything to lose if caught. For some criminals, going to prison was simply part of life on the streets, practically a rite of passage. But for government and law enforcement officials, being investigated by the FBI meant the end of the world—and if someone thought his

world was ending, there was no end to the foolish or dangerous things he could do.

Because of that, Vaughn and Huxley had taken no chances
with this meeting. Huxley and three of their squad mates
stood by in cars parked close to the bar, and all agents would
be listening to every word of Vaughn's conversation via the
pin-sized microphone he had attached to one of the buttons
on his shirt. Also joining them was a special operations group,
a team of eight agents armed with heavier weapons, who had
followed Pritchett and his two cohorts—already identified as
Officers James Mahoney and Ali Ortiz—to this meeting, and
had confirmed that the three police officers were armed only
with standard firearms and didn't have any further backup
waiting in the wings.

Pritchett spotted Vaughn at his table and walked over with
officers Ortiz and Mahoney in tow. After a few minutes of
posturing and feeling each other out, Vaughn and Pritchett
got down to business.

He told Pritchett that he'd had a few problems transporting
guns into the Chicago city limits, and that he'd been intrigued
when Batista had told him about the smuggling business the
cop was running on the side.

"It's fucking genius," Pritchett bragged to Vaughn. "I've
got a good group here. Whatever you want, we can get it done.
We rent vans or trucks, depending on the size of the job. If
anybody ever stops us, we'll just show them our badges and
say we're working off-duty to deliver items that somebody
bought at an auction. Nobody's gonna question that."

"You get stopped a lot?" Vaughn asked, looking skeptical.

"Not once. I'm just telling you that we have a backup plan,
if necessary," Pritchett said, quick to reassure him. "This isn't
some amateur thing I'm running here. We're *cops*. That's the
beauty of it. We know the way cops think."

"Such as?" Vaughn asked.

"Like, we know to split up when driving a route because
a large caravan of vans driving along Lake Shore Drive in
the middle of the night might arouse suspicions. We know
the neighborhoods and streets that cops patrol the most. We

know all kinds of tricks like that." Pritchett took a sip of coffee. "But it's not just the police you gotta worry about. Maybe somebody else gets word that you're moving guns and decides he wants in on the action. Maybe he thinks it'd be easy to take out a smuggler or two and steal your merchandise for himself." He nodded to the two beefy police officers on each side of him. "We're ready for that kind of thing. We're like the goddamn Boy Scouts. Right, Ortiz?"

" 'Always be prepared,' " the beefy cop on Pritchett's right answered with a sly grin.

Vaughn betrayed no reaction to that, but in his head he was thinking that the jury, and the press, was going to *love* that little exchange. Corrupt cops comparing themselves to Boy Scouts—it was sound bites like these that got blasted all over the media once a case went public.

"We have tasers, guns, and bulletproof vests," Pritchett boasted. "Whatever you need smuggled into the city, we got it covered. No one will mess with us."

Vaughn leaned back in his chair and studied Pritchett, as if thinking all this through. "I have a job out of Indianapolis," he finally said. "Maybe we could consider it a tryout."

Pritchett's eyes lit up greedily. "What's the cargo?"

"Firearms—a mix of assault rifles and handguns," Vaughn said.

Pritchett shrugged. "No problem."

"Guns are heavy. How many guys are in your crew?"

"Four, plus me."

"All of them come with those handy badges you talked about?"

Pritchett grinned at that. "Every one."

So they were looking at a smuggling ring with five active cops. "How do you know you can trust them? They're cops. What if they suddenly get a guilty conscience?" Vaughn pointed emphatically. "You fuck me on this, Pritchett, and it'll be the last fuckup you ever make."

Pritchett was quick to ease his concerns. "Don't worry. I handpicked all these guys myself. It took me almost a year to put this group together. These guys are solid—they know a good business opportunity when they see one."

Vaughn pulled a piece of paper out of his pants pocket and slid it across the table to Pritchett. Enough of the chitchat—it was time for them to seal this deal. "The top address is the warehouse in Indianapolis where you'll pick up the guns. Be there a week from Monday at midnight. Park on the south side of the lot—a guy named Masso will be waiting for you. You'll bring the guns to me at the other address."

"What's our cut?" Pritchett asked.

"Fifteen grand," Vaughn said, his tone an indication that this was not open for negotiation.

Pritchett exchanged another look with the police officers at his side, then turned back to Vaughn with a nod.

"Done."

LATER THAT EVENING, after Vaughn had changed out of his swanky clothes and ditched the Rolex, he and Huxley filled Cade in on the progress of the Pritchett investigation at a pub located around the corner from the U.S. Attorney's Office.

"So who's Masso?" Cade asked. Eventually, after any arrests had been made, the agents would turn over the case to the U.S. Attorney's Office for prosecution—but until that point, Vaughn, the senior agent assigned to the matter, was running the show.

"Masso is Special Agent Brent Lyons in the Indianapolis office," Vaughn said. "On Monday night, he'll be waiting for Pritchett's crew with several duffle bags of guns that, unbeknownst to them, we've rendered inoperable." He paused when the waitress brought their burgers, and didn't waste any time in digging in. Undercover work always made him ravenous—perhaps it was the extra kick of adrenaline.

He continued after swallowing. "So, if everything goes as planned, in a month or so, Hux and I should have enough evidence for you to—" He stopped, seeing Cade and Huxley exchanging bemused looks. "What?"

"You really aren't going to say anything about the situation at your three o'clock?" Huxley asked. "They've been looking over here since we sat down."

Vaughn glanced out of the corner of his eye and spotted a table with three women in their midtwenties, all dressed up for a night on the town in jeans, heels, and skin-revealing tops. The brunette facing him caught his eye and boldly held it for a long moment before returning back to her conversation with her friends.

He shrugged. "Eh. They all have that fake too-tan look."

Cade stared at him, speaking slowly. "It's Friday night. There are three attractive women checking you out, and this is the entirety of your response? That they're too *tan*?" He looked Vaughn over with sharp eyes. "What's going on with you? Are you sick? Bleeding internally in the head?"

Huxley rubbed his jaw, musing. "A similar thing happened the other day," he told Cade. "The new cute barista at Starbucks was flirting with him, and he didn't even notice."

"What new cute barista at Starbucks?" Vaughn asked indignantly.

Huxley gestured to Vaughn. "See? It's like his radar is broken or something."

"Hmm." Cade looked Vaughn over, folding his arms across his chest. "How long has he been like this?"

Vaughn glared at them while grabbing a couple of French fries. "Any time you two want to stop talking about me like I'm not here, that'd be cool. Really."

"Two weeks," Huxley said to Cade, ignoring Vaughn. "Ever since he came back from that weekend at his parents' house."

Hearing that, Cade raised an eyebrow. "How curious. Correct me if I'm wrong, Agent Roberts, but wasn't that the last time you saw a certain vixen maid of honor?"

"Still with the vixen jokes?" Vaughn asked him.

"Remember how much shit you gave me when I first started dating Brooke?" Cade threw back in response.

Vaughn smiled fondly. No doubt, he'd been all up in his friend's business over that for weeks.

Crap.

"And me, when I first got together with Addison?" Huxley added, referring to his fiancée, another agent in the white-collar crime group.

"A happenstance that still remains a bigger FBI mystery than who shot JFK," Vaughn quipped.

Both Cade and Huxley stared at him unwaveringly.

Tough crowd.

"Whatever. This is completely different," Vaughn said definitively. "I don't even like Sidney. She's everything I'm *not* looking for: argumentative, not remotely easygoing, and completely open about the fact that she wants a long-term commitment. I haven't seen her for two weeks, and trust me— it's been two of the most peaceful weeks of my life." In fact, it had been a relief to throw himself into work since he'd been back from his parents' house, and to be free of a certain red-head whose kiss was *way* hotter than it should've been for someone so cranky and difficult.

"You're doing that thing again," Huxley observed. "Like you want to say more."

"I really don't."

"You know we're not letting you leave until you give us something, right?" Cade asked.

Unfortunately, Vaughn did know this. His friends would fixate on the situation with Sidney and thoroughly annoy him until they got whatever answers they thought they were look-ing for. "Fine," he said, figuring he might as well rip off the Band-Aid and get it over with. "I kissed her."

"You kissed the maid of honor?" Huxley asked incredu-lously.

"No, I figured I'd plant one on the woman my brother's going to marry," Vaughn said dryly. "Yes, the maid of honor." He held up his hand, seeing Huxley open his mouth. "And whatever you're going to say, don't. It was just an angry, impulsive thing."

"An angry kiss, huh?" Cade asked. "How'd that go?"

Vaughn's lips nearly curved in a smile. *She bit me.* An image flashed into his head, of him and Sidney kissing heatedly in the grass—an image that was quickly replaced by her wide-eyed reaction afterward.

Oh, no. You and I can't . . . I mean, we so, so couldn't . . . you know.

"Let's just say, we agreed that it was a mistake," Vaughn said.

With that settled, he steered the conversation away from his not-to-be-repeated dalliance with Sidney and back to the topic of his undercover operation into a group of corrupt cops transporting illegal firearms into the city.

Kind of a big deal, that.

Thirteen

TUESDAY MORNING, SIDNEY sat once again at a sleek gunmetal-gray granite table in one of the conference rooms at Monroe Ellers. This time, however, there were only three pairs of eyes staring back at her, belonging to the partners who made up the firm's investment committee.

She and her team had done their research. She'd considered all the financials, she'd weighed the pro and cons, and she believed she'd found a company that would be a great investment for her private equity fund.

Now she just had to get her firm's most senior partners on board.

This pitch signified her first real test since she'd joined Monroe Ellers. If the investment committee approved her idea, it would be a demonstration of their confidence in her. *Not* approving her idea, on the other hand, would mean they had doubts—which most certainly would be a shaky start to her career in private equity.

"So. Tell us about Vitamin Boutique," said Michael, one of the investment committee's three members. He gestured to the report Sidney had prepared, which sat on the table in front of him.

"Certainly," Sidney said, with a confident nod. She felt comfortable being in the hot seat, and trusted her instincts. She'd been a little unsettled after her trip to Wisconsin and that wild kiss with Vaughn, but that feeling had since passed. Here, she was in control and in charge—and ready to do her thing.

"A few months ago, I read an article in the *Journal* about the retail industries that had performed best during the recession. The vitamin and supplement industry was included on that list," she began. "It's a twenty-five-billion-dollar industry, and one of the few areas of retail that actually thrived during the economic downturn. Currently Vitamin Boutique is primarily a Midwest retailer, but I think there's a real opportunity to grow the company into a national chain."

She started the PowerPoint presentation she'd prepared on her laptop. On the screen in front of them, a color-coded graphic of the United States popped up. "The blue dots indicate the existing locations of Vitamin Boutique stores. But with the right strategies and management, this is where I think the company can be in five years." She clicked the touchpad of her computer, and the screen changed, indicating a significant increase in the number of stores, spread throughout the entire country. "I think we can add roughly 400 stores in five years time."

"And how are we going to do that?" asked Rick, the most senior of the investment committee's members.

Sidney answered without hesitation. "First, we would expand into California and Florida, where the company already receives a significant number of mail orders through its catalog. After that, we'd use site-selection models to help us identify potential additional store locations." After explaining the need to choose sites with high visibility—primarily endcap locations in suburban strip malls and corner stores in urban areas—she went on to discuss the need to bolster the company's online presence and expand direct sales through its Web site. She explained how she intended to recruit top talent for Vitamin Boutique's executive team, the need for the company to increase customer loyalty by implementing a rewards card program, and how they should employ an aggressive pricing strategy, perhaps discounting as much as twenty-five to forty percent every day.

Then she put up the final screen of her presentation, which contained the bottom line. "In five years we'd take the company public via an IPO, and I estimate that we'll exit at ten times earnings. If that happens, I think we'll have a group of very happy investors."

"That's what I like to hear," Michael said, which got a chuckle out of everyone.

Sidney folded her hands on the table, preparing to be grilled. "I'd be happy to answer any questions you might have."

Bring it on.

THE FOLLOWING SATURDAY, Sidney watched from the back of her living room as twenty-five women *ooh*ed and *ahh*ed over the serving platter Isabelle unveiled from its gift box.

The bridal shower was a success.

This was no small feat, considering she'd had all of three weeks to pull it together, *and* had to work within the guidelines set by both Isabelle the excited bride-to-be and the crazy pregnant lady.

We should have flowers for centerpieces on the tables. That would be so pretty! Just no roses, lilies, lavender, or anything else with a strong scent. Flowery smells make me puke.

Sid, I saw the most adorable three-tiered minicakes in Martha Stewart Weddings. They'd be perfect for dessert! But tell the bakery that they have to use buttercream—the thought of that pasty, sugary fondant makes me puke.

Ooh, let's have fun drinks!

No alcohol.

Simon's mom will be driving back to Wisconsin after the shower, so it can't start too late.

*We'd better not start too early, unless you want me to
throw up all over the egg salad finger sandwiches.*

*Actually, nix the egg salad finger sandwiches. Yellow food
makes me puke.*

And so on.

From her post in the back of the room, Sidney took a sip
of her ginger ale and orange juice, glad to finally have a break
now that the guests had been served lunch and dessert. Mary-
ann, one of Isabelle's bridesmaids, was writing down the gifts
brought by each guest, and the other two bridesmaids were
in charge of passing Isabelle the presents and reboxing them
once they'd been opened.

Trish came in from the courtyard, where the catering company had set up a bar, and walked over to Sidney.

"You planned a lovely party, dar-ling" she said, mock
extravagantly, while tipping her champagne flute to Sidney's
in cheers. Then she took a sip and made a face. "Except what's
up with the virgin mimosas?"

"Half of Isabelle's friends are either pregnant or breast-
feeding," Sidney said, going with the tiny white lie she'd prepared in response to this very question. "It seemed like the
alcohol would go to waste." Indeed, a sizable portion of the
women surrounding Isabelle were wearing cute summery
maternity dresses. "But I did tell the bartender to stash one
bottle of champagne off to the side, if you're interested."

"Reid is watching Jonah, which means I have a weekend
afternoon all to myself for the first time in nearly five months.
Hell yes, I'm interested," Trish said.

They sneaked out to the courtyard, giggling surreptitiously
as the bartender poured them champagne. He then added a
splash of orange juice to each glass so no one would realize
what they were drinking.

"It'll be our little secret," he said, with a wink at Sidney.

Drinks in hand, Sidney and Trish returned to the back of
the living room just in time to see Isabelle open a set of crystal water goblets.

Trish leaned in, whispering. "He's cute."

"Who?"

"The bartender. You look great in that dress—you totally should chat him up."

Sidney glanced over her shoulder and took a second look at the bartender. Sure, he was cute, but he was also *young*. "He's, like, twelve."

Trish grinned wickedly. "If he's serving alcohol, he's legal."

"Come on. I'm probably ten years older than that guy." Sidney blinked as the truth of that sunk in. "Oh my god, when did I get to be ten years older than that guy?"

Trish tipped her champagne glass. "Welcome to your thirties."

Trapped in a sea of married and/or pregnant twentysome-things, and standing next to her best friend who, while thirty-three like her, had the husband, the child, and the whole kit and caboodle, Sidney could practically hear the alarm going off on her biological clock, shrilly blaring away as she searched frantically for a snooze button.

"I've been meaning to ask. How's your dating plan coming along?" Trish asked.

"I've gone on eight first dates in two weeks," Sidney said.

Trish blinked. "Eight? Why didn't you tell me about any of them?"

"I was waiting to text you with the good news that I was on a *second* date."

"None of them worked out?" Trish asked, looking disappointed.

Sidney shook her head. "Not a one."

"The guys you're meeting online are that bad?"

"Actually, I've been pleasantly surprised by how cute some of them are. But they didn't pass the commitment-readiness test. Something was always off."

"Such as?"

"Well, let's see." Sidney ticked off the list with her fingers. "Leo from last Tuesday was obviously still hung up on his ex. Felix from last Thursday says he's up for partner at his law firm this December, but isn't sure he'll make it." She pointed at Trish. "Remember, a good candidate should be settled in his career. Then there was Jesse, who I met last Friday for dinner and asked me to go back to his place for a 'drink' afterward. That's moving too fast—it means he'll exit the relationship just as quickly as he jumped into it. As opposed to Jayden, Saturday's dinner date, who was off to a promising start and then asked if we could get together again in two weeks, when his work schedule 'settles down.' The rules say that's a big red flag that he's married to his job." She paused, trying to remember the rest. "Hmm, who else? Ah, Santiago on Monday. None of his friends are in committed relationships—he says they're all still in the playing-the-field phase." She threw Trish a knowing look. "How long before he decides what they're doing sounds more fun than a relationship? Am I right?" She moved to her other hand, needing more fingers. "Then Wednesday, drinks with Mason. Still lives with his parents. Um, no. Then there was Vince, who I met for dinner last night. The guy stared at my boobs the whole time. Seriously, you would've thought I'd sewn eyeballs to my nipples."

Trish laughed. "Wait—that's only seven. I thought you said you went on eight dates."

"I left out Karl the fireman. We had coffee last Wednesday."

"What was wrong with him?" Trish asked.

"Nothing. Actually, he was the one guy I liked. But he, uh . . . didn't e-mail me back after our date."

"Oh." Trish thought about that. "Well, obviously he's a moron then."

"Obviously." The quip rolled off Sidney's tongue, as expected.

Then, out of the blue, it happened.

Hot tears pricked at her eyes.

Mortified, she stepped around the corner and into the dining room.

Trish followed, her expression concerned. "Sid . . ."

"Don't let Isabelle see," Sidney said, using the wall to block them. She took a deep breath, shaking her head. "It's so stupid." Then she smiled at her friend, embarrassed. "It's not about the fireman. It's just . . . everything. Isabelle's wedding, all these pregnant women, the fact that I can't even get a second date." She brushed away her tears. "Three years of my life wasted because I was dumb enough to fall for Brody's I'm-a-changed-man routine."

"Dumb enough?" Trish looked her in the eyes. "Sid, you do realize that *you* didn't do anything wrong in picking Brody, right? He's the one who screwed up."

Sidney said nothing for a moment. Then the doorbell rang, sparing her from having to answer.

Quickly gathering herself, she stepped around the corner and saw Isabelle heading to the front door.

In walked Simon, with Vaughn right behind him.

Sidney rolled her eyes. Just what she needed—this guy.

Simon smiled at the group as Isabelle led him and his brother into the living room. "Ladies, I hope we're not interrupting."

"I asked Simon and Vaughn to help transport the gifts to my apartment," Isabelle explained.

"I don't mind being used for my muscles. As long as there's cake in return." Simon kissed her affectionately on the cheek.

At mention of the word *muscles*, twenty pairs of female eyes shot to the tall and broad-shouldered Vaughn, who, naturally, looked devilishly gorgeous again, in jeans that hung perfectly on his lean hips and a white collared shirt with the sleeves rolled up around his strong, corded forearms.

Arms that once had pinned Sidney to the grass, as he kissed her senseless.

Ignoring the slightly . . . flustered feeling brought on by the image, she purged the memory from her mind. No point in going there.

Trish turned to Sidney, pointing subtly at Vaughn. "*That* is Simon's brother? The one who hit on you?" She went back for a second look. "Criminy is right."

"Trust me, the glow fades once he speaks," Sidney grumbled.

As if sensing that she was talking about him, Vaughn's gaze met hers across the room. He looked her over, taking in her dress and heels. Then he clenched his jaw and turned away to greet his mother.

"What was that?" Trish demanded to know, in a hushed tone.

Sidney tried to play innocent. "What was what?"

"That look between you and Vaughn," Trish said. "I can't decide if you two should box a few rounds or go screw each other brainless in the pantry."

"My god, Trish—his mother is standing right over there."

"In that case, I'd strongly suggest locking the pantry door should you choose option B."

Very funny. Then Sidney spotted Amanda, Isabelle's other single bridesmaid, noticeably eying Vaughn.

Something about that compelled her to lean in toward Trish. "If I tell you something, you can't tell Isabelle or anyone else."

Trish's voice was hushed. "Ooh, I like this lead-in."

"I just don't want anyone to get the wrong idea," Sidney said.

"Obviously."

"It meant nothing."

"Of course it didn't."

Sidney lowered her voice more. "That weekend I went to Wisconsin with Isabelle, I kissed Vaughn."

"Shut *up*. Why are you just telling me this now?" Trish whispered demandingly.

"Because it shouldn't have happened."

Trish cocked her head. "Why not?"

"Because I don't even like him. He's . . . irritating. And smug. He's too confident, too in-shape, too good-looking— and far too aware of all those things."

"No one's telling you to marry the guy," Trish said. "You've got your plan. Rock on. But why should you feel guilty about having a little fun with Mr. Right Now until Mr. Right comes along?"

Sidney opened her mouth, then paused, not having an immediate answer to that. "What am I going to do with a Mr. Right Now?" she asked skeptically.

"Anything you want." Trish grinned slyly. "You want my advice?"

Sidney thought about that. "I don't think so."

Trish marched ahead anyway. "Forget about whether he's irritating, Sid. *Embrace* the fact that he's too in-shape and too good-looking. I know you'd envisioned yourself being on a different track at thirty-three, but there is one really awesome thing about being single." She pointed across the room. "You can have meaningless, mind-blowing sex with a guy like that."

Sidney stole a peek over her shoulder and saw Vaughn teasingly *aw*-ing as Simon pulled a dainty floral teacup out of one of the opened gift boxes.

Definitely not a Mr. Right.

With an easy grin, he folded his arms across his chest, which pulled his shirt up just enough to reveal the FBI badge and the gun holster at his right hip.

"Any ideas coming to you yet, about what you might do with a Mr. Right Now?" Trish asked teasingly.

Sidney stared at those broad shoulders and at the chest that had felt incredibly solid in those moments they'd been pressed together in the clearing.

It *had* been a while since she'd seen any action . . .

But then reality set in. This was *Vaughn* they were talking about. Even if she could get past the irritation and the smugness—and that was a big *if*—he was still her sister's future brother-in-law. She turned to Trish, to explain. "It's just not a good—"

Trish grabbed her arm, cutting her off. "Wow, he totally checked out your ass as soon as you turned around." She pulled back to get a better look. "Mmm-hmm, I bet he's a dirty talker. I bet he knows tricks. Seriously, Sid, you so need to get on this."

A woman's voice interrupted them. "What are you two gossiping about so intently over here?"

Sidney spun around, and smiled at the short, dark-haired woman walking over. "Kathleen—hello," she said, with a nervous laugh as Vaughn's mother approached. She scrambled to think of something to cover. *Gossip? Nah, just having a few impure thoughts about your oldest son.* "Trish and I were just saying how much we liked the china pattern Isabelle and Simon picked out."

"Oh. From the looks on your faces, I thought it was something juicier than that," Kathleen said, with a wink.

Awkward.

"Did you enjoy the lunch? Is there anything I can get you?" Sidney said, eager to move off that topic.

"That's sweet of you to ask. But I'm good, thank you. Everything was delicious."

They chatted amiably for a few minutes before Kathleen said she needed to get on the road for the drive back to Wisconsin. "But before I go, I have something for you." She pulled something out of her purse, an ivory note card with a blue and orange floral border, and handed it to Sidney.

At the top, it said, "From the kitchen of Kathleen Roberts." Sidney smiled, reading the line below it. "It's your shepherd's pie recipe." It was such a simple thing, but she found herself quite touched by the gesture.

"You seemed to really enjoy it," Kathleen said. "I figured maybe you'd want to make it yourself someday."

"Thank you. I'll do that." Impulsively, Sidney hugged her before saying good-bye.

Trish raised an eyebrow after Kathleen had left. "When did you become a hugger?"

Good question. Sidney shrugged this off. "She's sweet. Isabelle struck mother-in-law gold with that one."

Neither of them said anything for a moment. Then Isabelle turned to Sidney. "Should we sneak another glass of champagne from the cute bartender?"

With a smile, Sidney nodded. "I'm in."

WHIRLWIND-STYLE, THE PEOPLE from the catering company swept through Sidney's first floor and began packing up all the food, drinks, glasses, and dishes as soon as the last guest left. Wanting to stay out of the way, Vaughn headed outside to Sidney's private courtyard and took a seat in one of the cushioned lounge chairs. Either she or the previous owners had transformed the yard into a cozy urban garden, complete with shrubs, brightly hued flowers, brick pavers, and a small stone water fountain.

Apparently the Sinclairs liked their water fountains.

Vaughn caught sight of the lady of the house as she breezed by the French doors while answering some question posed by one of the catering crew. She was wearing another one of her trendy dresses, he'd noticed. This one was a white, billowy mini-dress belted at the waist with a thin gold band—which she'd paired with gold strappy heels that made her legs look sky-high.

One of the reasons he'd come out to the courtyard was to stay out of *her* way. He'd found it nearly impossible to be around her and that dress without remembering the moments in the clearing when she'd straddled him with those spectacular legs as they kissed feverishly. And since he was pretty sure it would be poor form to walk around with a raging hard-on in front of her sister and his brother, he'd figured it was best to keep his distance.

As if determined to thwart him, Sidney opened the French doors and stepped out into the courtyard.

She ignored him at first, looking around the yard, and then put her hand on her hip. "Have you seen Isabelle?" she finally asked him.

"I saw her and Simon go upstairs about ten minutes ago."

"Oh." She looked him over with cool blue-green eyes. "We still have half the presents to load up, if you want to make yourself useful."

"Nah, I'm good. Being useful is overrated." Seeing the spark in her eyes, he fought back a grin. "I'm kidding, Sinclair. I need the keys to Simon's car in order to load up the rest of the gifts, but I was thinking it might not be a good idea to follow him and Isabelle upstairs. I don't want to see anything involving the two of them that can't be unseen."

That got a slight smile out of her. "I doubt they're fooling around up there."

He shrugged his broad shoulders. "What do I know? Maybe the sight of tiny teacups gets engaged couples all worked up."

She considered this, then made a face, as if getting a visual. "If they're not back down in a couple minutes, I'll brave it and go looking for them."

Not seeming to know what else to do—he was the one remaining guest in her house—she took a seat in the chair across from him. She crossed her legs, her dress hiking a few extra inches up her thighs.

Vaughn looked, then returned his eyes to her.

There was a slight pink flush to her cheeks, as if she'd noticed him checking her out, but her tone remained casual. "So. How's your investigation going? Has the 'other you' been hanging out in any dark, sketchy alleys doing dark, sketchy things?"

"Actually, that's exactly what the other me will be doing on Monday night." Vaughn said.

"Really?" Sidney cocked her head, studying him. "I can't picture this other you."

"You wouldn't like the guy. In addition to being a criminal, he's got this continuous five-o'clock shadow problem."

In response to his comment, her gaze held on the stubble along his jawline.

She shifted in her chair.

"I saw my mother give you her shepherd's pie recipe," Vaughn said. "That's a big stamp of approval, coming from her."

"Your mother obviously is an excellent judge of character," she said.

"And you say that *I'm* confident."

The words fell between them, both of them fully aware that she'd made the comment just before they'd gotten all tangled up in each other in the clearing.

Vaughn couldn't help it. Alone with her like this, he could practically feel the nip of her teeth on his lip, the erotic sensation of her fingers digging into his back. It was that damn minidress. He envisioned himself kneeling in front of her, pushing that dress the rest of the way up her thighs and making her scream with his mouth.

Her chest moved up and down, her breath a little quicker. "You shouldn't look at me that way."

His voice was a low growl. "Believe me, baby, I'm trying not to."

The creamy skin along her neckline turned pink, and he could see her nipples tighten through the thin material of her dress.

Christ.

She opened her mouth to answer and—

"There you are."

Vaughn forced himself not to react to the interruption. Simon, again.

Then he turned his head and knew instantly from his brother's expression that something was up. "What's wrong?"

"It's Isabelle." Simon looked over at Sidney. "I think we might need to get her to the hospital."

Fourteen

SIDNEY WAS UP out of her chair in an instant. "Where is she?"

"In the guest bathroom upstairs," Simon said.

Nodding, she hurried into the house, climbing the stairs with him right on her heels. The guest bathroom was the first door on the left; Sidney pushed it open and found Isabelle sitting on floor, clutching her abdomen.

"Sid. I think something might be wrong with the baby."

Sidney knelt down beside her sister, struck by how pale she looked. "Are you bleeding?"

"No, I checked. But it hurts a lot." Isabelle winced, breathing shakily. "The pain started this morning. At first I thought it was just a bad stomach cramp because I felt nauseous, too. But it's getting worse." She clutched Sidney's hand.

"It's okay, Izz," she said, her tone more reassuring than she felt. "Let's just get you to the hospital and find out what's happening."

When Isabelle nodded, Simon stepped in and scooped her into his arms. "I've got you," he murmured soothingly as he stood up. "Everything going's to be fine."

They found Vaughn waiting at the bottom of the stairs. His eyes filled with concern when he saw Simon carrying Isabelle.

"We need to get her to the emergency room," Sidney told him.

"I'll drive," he said, already moving toward the door.

A few moments later, Vaughn skillfully—and hastily—zipped his car through the heavy traffic on Michigan Avenue. Sidney looked over her shoulder and saw Simon tenderly stroking Isabelle's arm in the backseat. She lay curled against his chest, one hand over her abdomen, her mouth set tight in pain.

"Hang in there, Izz. We're almost there." As she turned back, her eyes met Vaughn's.

"We're just a few blocks away," he told her. "I'm going to drop you guys at the door. Then I'll park the car and meet you inside."

"I think the hospital has valet." Sidney bounced her leg nervously, stealing another look at the backseat.

"It's my work vehicle. I can't let anyone else drive it." Vaughn grabbed his cell phone from the console between them and handed it to her. "Add your phone number to my contacts in case I need to text you."

Sidney took a deep breath. "Right." She finished typing just as they pulled up to the entrance to Northwestern Memorial's emergency room.

Vaughn threw the car into park and took the phone that Sidney gave back to him. His hand brushed against hers.

"I'll find you," he said.

She nodded.

Then they both got out of the car. Vaughn held the door as Simon eased Isabelle out, and then Sidney followed behind Simon as he carried her sister into the emergency room. Moments after he explained to the nurse behind the intake desk that Isabelle was pregnant and in a lot of pain, another nurse came out with a wheelchair. That nurse wheeled Isabelle through a set of double doors, with Simon walking alongside them and filling in the details as Isabelle gritted her teeth and told the nurse her symptoms.

They turned a corner, and the nurse took Isabelle into a small private room. She and Simon helped Isabelle get onto the bed, and then the nurse stepped toward the door, gesturing for Sidney to follow.

"If I could ask you to wait out in the hall," she said, with a reassuring smile. "The doctor will be in right away to examine her."

But that's my little sister. Sidney nodded. "Of course." As she left the room, she spotted a doctor wearing a white coat and scrubs heading down the corridor toward them. Sidney moved off to the side as the doctor breezed by. She heard him introduce himself to Isabelle and Simon and then—

The door shut behind him.

Sidney stood there for a moment, in the middle of the hallway. Then she spotted an alcove nearby, walked over, and took a seat on the bench.

All those times she'd been so snarky, calling Isabelle the crazy pregnant lady in her head. And now . . .

She bit her lip, fighting back a wave of emotions.

Vaughn turned into the hallway just then. Seeing Sidney, he headed over and sat down next to her on the bench. "How is Isabelle?"

Sidney shook her head. *No clue.* "I don't understand what happened. She was fine during the shower, and then this came out of nowhere." She fought back the sting in her eyes, her voice trembling a little. "She's just in so much pain. I've never seen Isabelle look that scared before."

Vaughn put his arm around her. "She'll be okay," he said soothingly. "She's in good hands, Sidney. They'll take care of her."

Sidney rested her head against his shoulder. They stayed that way for several moments, the warmth of his body seeping into hers. When she finally pulled back, he peered down into her eyes.

He reached up and gently tucked a lock of hair behind her ear.

The sound of approaching footsteps interrupted them.

Sidney blinked and slid over on the bench as a nurse led a patient into the room next to Isabelle's.

"Thanks," she said to Vaughn, managing a slight smile. "I'm okay now."

Fortunately, they only had to wait a few minutes. The ER doctor stepped out of the room and hurried down the hallway, and then Simon came out to give them an update.

"It's not the baby," he said, first thing. "They did an ultrasound—Isabelle has a twisted ovary. The ER doctor wants to bring in an OB/GYN specialist for a consult, but he said that she needs to have surgery right away. He says that if they act quickly, they have a good chance of saving the ovary."

Sidney exhaled, digesting that. "How is Isabelle? Can I see her?"

Simon nodded. "She's asking for you. The nurse gave her some medicine for the pain, which helped."

Thank god. Not wasting another moment, Sidney got up and walked into her sister's room.

WHEN IT WAS just Simon and Vaughn out in the hallway, Simon blew out a ragged breath of air and sat down on the bench. He ran his fingers through his hair and took a moment to decompress.

Finally, he looked sideways at Vaughn. "So. I guess this is probably a good time to mention that Isabelle is pregnant."

That got a small chuckle out of Vaughn. "I kind of figured that already. I've had my suspicions for a few weeks."

Simon nodded. "Isabelle wondered if you knew."

"You could've told me, Simon," Vaughn said, not unkindly. "I get why you might not want Mom to know yet, but why not talk to me about it?"

Simon leaned forward, resting his elbows on his knees. "I guess I didn't think you'd understand."

"I wouldn't understand that you want to marry the woman who's pregnant with your child? I think that's a concept I can grasp."

"See, that's just it." Simon gestured emphatically. "I knew that's how you would see it. That I'm marrying Isabelle because I got her pregnant. And I don't want you, or Mom, or anyone else to think about Isabelle that way—that she's the woman I *had* to marry, because it was the right thing to do. Because the truth is, I knew I wanted to marry Isabelle on our second date. She invited me up to her apartment that night, and I saw that she had the entire James Bond collection on Blu-ray. Naturally, being the Bond aficionado that I am, I threw out a little test question for her: 'Who's the best Bond?' "

Vaughn scoffed. "Like there's more than one possible answer to that."

"Exactly. Sean Connery's a no-brainer, right? But get this—she says *Daniel Craig.*" Simon caught Vaughn's horrified expression. "I know, right? So I'm thinking the date is over because clearly she's either crazy or has seriously questionable taste, but then she starts going on and on about how *Casino Royale* is the first movie where Bond is touchable and human, and then we get into this big debate that lasts for nearly an hour. And as I'm sitting there on her couch, I keep thinking that I don't know a single other person who would relentlessly argue, for an *hour*, that Daniel Craig is a better Bond than Sean Connery. She pulled out the DVDs and showed me movie clips and everything." He smiled, as if remembering the moment. "And somewhere in there, it hit me. I thought to myself, I'm going to marry this woman."

Vaughn smiled, thinking he might have to work that into his best man speech. "Why haven't you told me that story before?"

Simon paused, as if trying to decide how best to explain. "I don't know . . . maybe because you and I don't talk about those kinds of things. You're the guy I talk to about a fun, random hookup. Or about some hot girl whose number I got while waiting in line at the deli on my lunch break. I guess I just didn't think you'd understand something that's not so, you know, shallow."

Vaughn blinked. *No offense taken.*

Simon quickly backtracked. "I mean, not that I think *you*

are shallow. Just that, well, lately, none of your relationships with women have had much substance, you know? And that's cool; that's your perspective—hey, I used to be in that place myself."

"Before you left and went to the deeper place." Vaughn pretended to think about that. "Question: can I still hang out with you, now that you're in this deeper place? Obviously, I'm used to the shallower stuff, but maybe I can wear a pair of water wings, or hold onto one of those pool noodles or something."

"I'm going to be getting shit for the 'shallow' comment for a while, aren't I?"

Before Vaughn could answer, the ER doctor came around the corner with a woman in her early forties wearing blue scrubs and Crocs. "Mr. Roberts, this is Dr. Takacs from our obstetrics and gynecology department," he said to Simon. "She'll be taking over your fiancée's case."

After a brief hello, Dr. Takacs and the ER doctor stepped into Isabelle's room. They waited expectantly in the doorway for Simon.

Simon looked uncertainly at Vaughn. "Um . . . are we okay?"

While the unfinished conversation still lingered in the air, Vaughn knew his brother had a lot more important things to worry about right then. "Simon?"

"Yeah?"

"Go be with your fiancée." Vaughn nodded in the direction of Isabelle's room, with a smile that said everything was cool between them.

Simon grinned in relief. "Right." He got up from the bench and hurried into the room.

When his brother was gone, Vaughn leaned forward on the bench and rested his elbows on his knees.

I didn't think you'd understand something that's not so shallow.

Well. That certainly was an interesting insight into his brother's view of him. Sure, he took a casual approach to dating, and yes, he often was the guy talking about a hot hookup. But he hadn't realized this was something that had created some kind of gulf between him and this new version of Simon, who suddenly was ready for marriage, the two-point-five kids, and the minivan in the suburbs.

Not sure what to make of all that, Vaughn ducked his head and briefly closed his eyes.

He heard the soft click of heels against the hospital's tiled floor and opened his eyes to find a pair of gold strappy heels directly in his line of vision.

He looked up.

Sidney stared down at him, taking in his uncharacteristically serious demeanor. Vaughn braced himself for the inevitable quip or saucy comment.

Instead, she simply took a seat on the bench next to him.

"Some day," she said.

Vaughn looked sideways at her, and then nodded.

Indeed it was.

Fifteen

PACING IN THE waiting room of the surgical floor, Sidney impatiently checked her watch again. "They said the surgery would take about an hour, right?"

Sitting in one of the chairs that bordered the path she had cut umpteen times since they'd wheeled Isabelle out of the emergency room on a gurney, Vaughn answered her with maddening calmness. "I don't think that included all the prep and post-op time. That takes a while."

What was he, a surgeon now? Of course *he* could remain calm. *He* didn't have ovaries, let alone twisted ones—Sidney's uterus cramped just imagining what that must've felt like. Nor did he have an eleven-week-old baby growing inside him.

Men. Clueless lummoxes, the whole lot of 'em.

"I can see your lips moving as you mutter about me, you know," he said.

Figured. All the lummoxes in the world and she had to be trapped in this waiting room with the one who had superpowers of observation.

She looked over and saw him watching her with amusement, his long legs stretched out comfortably in front of him.

Oh . . . whatever. Fine. So maybe her nervousness was making her a touch cranky right then. In her defense, that was her sister they'd wheeled out on that gurney, her younger sister, her only sibling, for whom she'd felt semi-responsible since they were kids. A sister who she could still remember as a sweet five-year-old, waiting on the front porch of their house on the day Sidney had returned from sleepaway camp the summer after their mother had died. She could picture the huge smile on Isabelle's face as the car had pulled into the driveway, the way she'd bounded down the stairs and had hugged Sidney tight and declared that she was never, ever allowed to leave again for that long. *Not like Mommy,* she'd said.

And now Sidney was teary-eyed and sniffing.

Vaughn got to his feet, as if that settled it. "Okay, Sinclair. Let's go."

"Go where?"

"Out of this waiting room," he declared. "You need a break. There's a Starbucks in the lobby with a grande Frappucino with your name on it."

She scoffed. "I can't leave. What if they finish the surgery and Simon is looking for us?"

"Well, lucky for you, you're traveling with an FBI agent. And I just so happen to be in possession of a cutting-edge device that allows a person to track anyone down, anywhere in this city." Vaughn pulled something out of his pocket and held it up: his cell phone. He looked around furtively, and put his finger to his lips. "*Shh.* Don't tell anyone. We're talking supersecret FBI technology here."

She threw him a look. "Are we through with the comedy routine now?"

He held out his hand to her, not saying anything further. He simply waited with that infuriatingly confident look.

With a sigh—it wasn't worth the argument—Sidney let him lead her out of the waiting room. They walked to the elevators and waited. She could see the satisfied gleam in Vaughn's eyes, and she was about to comment when an elderly woman stepped out of the waiting room and joined them at the elevator bank.

The woman smiled at the two of them just as the elevator doors opened and they stepped inside. As the elevator doors closed, Sidney noticed that the woman kept looking at them.

"It's okay, I'm a little emotional, too," she said to Sidney, with a kind expression. "My husband is having his third heart surgery in two years. Sitting in those waiting rooms . . . it gets you thinking." She gestured at Vaughn, smiling fondly. "I was watching you two. You remind me of my husband and me thirty years ago. Oh, the arguments we used to have. We could go back and forth, all day long." She winked. "My husband called it foreplay."

Alrighty, then. Nothing like a little too much information from a perfect stranger. But Sidney was distracted by something else the woman had said. She pointed between herself and Vaughn. Sure, maybe, for a split second she'd contemplated the idea of having meaningless sex with the guy, but a relationship? *Hell to the no, sister.* "Oh, we're not a couple."

"Definitely not a couple," Vaughn added emphatically.

"He doesn't do couples," Sidney explained.

"She has a checklist," Vaughn said. "With thirty-four things on it."

The elderly woman eyed them carefully, as if she wasn't buying it. "Uh-huh."

"See, her sister is marrying my brother," Vaughn continued. Like Sidney, he seemed to feel the need for further explanations.

"He's the best man. I'm the maid of honor," Sidney said. "And we keep getting stuck together because of this whole big wedding and secret baby drama with our siblings."

"Probably, it's not so much a 'secret' baby if you tell everyone about it," Vaughn said under his breath.

"She doesn't know us and it gives context to the story," Sidney muttered back. Then she smiled at the elderly woman. "See? Clearly not a couple."

The woman smiled as the elevator stopped at the third floor. "Well. Obviously, I was mistaken. Carry on as you were." With a friendly nod in good-bye, she stepped out of the elevator.

Once she was gone, Sidney and Vaughn shared an incredulous look.

"Why does that keep happening to us?" Sidney asked.

"She's just thinking about her husband," Vaughn said. "She wants to see happy couples everywhere."

The elevator doors sprung open at the first floor, and Vaughn put his hand on the door to keep it open for Sidney. She took a step forward and suddenly felt a tug of resistance. She looked down and then realized something.

She and Vaughn had been holding hands the entire time since he'd led her out of the waiting room.

Vaughn stared down at their joined hands, seemingly just catching on to this fact himself. Then he looked back up to meet her gaze.

They dropped hands instantly.

"You said something about coffee?" Sidney asked, a tad overbrightly.

"Yep, I think the Starbucks is right this way," Vaughn said, his tone cheerfully nonchalant.

They scurried off, maintaining a good two feet of space between them.

ABOUT A HALF hour after Vaughn and Sidney returned from their coffee run, a relieved Simon came to the waiting room with the news that Isabelle was out of surgery and that both she and the baby were doing fine. He led them up to the fourteenth floor of the hospital, where Isabelle was recovering from the surgery in a private room.

Vaughn fought back a smile as Sidney fussed over Isabelle's blanket and pillow, wanting to make sure she was comfortable. These brief glimpses into the softer side of the oft-prickly elder Sinclair sister were rather . . . cute.

"Did they say how long you'll be in the hospital?" Sidney asked.

"Only twenty-four hours, since it was laparoscopic surgery," Isabelle answered drowsily, obviously still feeling the effects of the anesthesia. "And then I need to take it easy for a week."

"A week or *two*, depending on how quickly you recover," Simon corrected her.

Isabelle frowned. "I'll have to call all my clients and cancel their appointments this week. And then we have our tasting at the Lakeshore Club next Sunday. If we have to reschedule that, I'm not sure when we'll be able to get it in. We're running out of time."

Sitting on the opposite side of the bed from Sidney, Simon stroked Isabelle's forehead. "Don't worry about the wedding stuff. I told you, all that will come together. For now, let's just stay focused on getting you and the baby the rest you need."

"Do you want me to call Dad?" Sidney asked.

Isabelle and Simon exchanged looks, as if they'd discussed exactly that. "We'd still like to keep the fact that I'm pregnant on the down-low, if we can. That is, if you two don't mind keeping up the charade a little longer." Isabelle looked tentatively at Vaughn, who sat a little farther from the bed, in the chair next to the window.

Vaughn was surprised she even had to ask. Yes, fine, maybe he wasn't "the guy" people typically talked to about love and weddings and babies, but he hoped there at least wasn't any doubt that he could keep his mouth shut. This was Simon and Isabelle's business, and their news to share when they were ready. "I'm okay with that," he assured Isabelle. "In fact, I volunteer if you ever again need someone to take a piece of shepherd's pie off your hands. The last time, poor Simon here nearly broke out in a sweat trying to finish that thing."

Isabelle and Sidney laughed as Simon shook his head good-naturedly. "I won't lie, those last couple bites weren't easy." He nodded at Sidney. "Next time, I want to be the one who gets to drink the wine."

"Next time, maybe someone should just get the condom on fast enough," Isabelle said, with a cheeky smile.

"That wasn't entirely my fault, sweetie." Simon turned to Sidney and Vaughn. "See, what happened is—"

Both Sidney and Vaughn held up their hands.

"Don't need to know," Vaughn said.

"Yes, let's just keep that one of life's little mysteries," Sidney concurred.

Isabelle's chuckle morphed into a yawn, her eyes tiredly drooping closed.

"I think we should get going," Sidney said quietly to Vaughn.

Realizing that he was Sidney's ride home, he nodded and stood up. "Is there anything you need me to bring you?" he asked Simon, assuming his brother was spending the night.

"I'm good. The nurses said I could pick up toothpaste and stuff in the gift shop downstairs. My car is still parked in front of your place," Simon said to Sidney. "Is it okay if I leave it there for now? I'll cab over and pick it up in the morning."

A half-asleep Isabelle mumbled something incoherent from the bed.

Vaughn, Sidney, and Simon all looked at each other cluelessly.

"I can't be positive, but that sounded like 'thank-you notes,'" Vaughn guessed.

Simon looked both amused and exasperated. "She was talking about that before her surgery. She asked me to bring her thank-you notes for the shower gifts, so she can write them in the hospital tomorrow during her 'downtime.' I keep telling her all that stuff can wait, but she has this timeline she says we need to stick to." He held up his hand, his thumb and forefinger close to touching. "We're just a tiny bit busy these days, planning for a wedding and a baby at the same time."

Vaughn and Sidney exchanged looks. Hell, the thought of planning either one made Vaughn's eye twitch, let alone both at the same time.

"Is there anything we can do to help?" Sidney asked.

"Yes." Simon pointed at the two of them. "Go home. You two have been awesome today—thank you for everything."

Sidney treaded softly on her way out, and Vaughn followed behind.

In the doorway, he looked back and saw Simon tenderly

stroke Isabelle's cheek. She opened her eyes for a moment and smiled, and the two of them shared a look so intimate that Vaughn felt like an intruder just standing there.

He had no idea what it felt like, having that deep of a connection with another person. But seeing his brother look so content in spite of all the chaos of the day, he suddenly found himself wondering.

"Everything okay?"

Vaughn turned back and saw Sidney waiting for him in the hallway. Shaking off the unsettled feeling that had crept over him, he nodded. "Yes."

"DID SIMON SEEM a little stressed out to you?" Sidney asked, as they drove back to her place.

"I'd say more than a little," Vaughn said.

"Isabelle, too. She hired a wedding planner to help out, but there's still so much that she has to do on her own. I'm worried she's going to push herself too hard after this surgery." Her big-sister protective instincts were kicking in more than ever after today's scare with Isabelle. "I'll talk to her about delegating a few things to me."

"Maybe I could help with some of the wedding stuff, too."

Sidney laughed, then saw Vaughn frown. "Wait—you're being serious?"

He shrugged. "Sure, why not?"

"No offense, but you don't exactly exude a 'wedding planning' vibe."

"And thank God for that. But I think I can manage a few tasks. How hard could it be to pick out a photographer? Or a band? Just ask them if they plan to play 'Y.M.C.A.' or that annoying Kool and the Gang song. If they say no, they're hired."

"A little more goes into planning a wedding than that," Sidney said dryly. Then she bit her lip, not having meant to lead into that topic.

Vaughn glanced over, but said nothing further. They drove for a few moments in silence, and Sidney couldn't help herself from sneaking a few peeks.

He really was just so . . . attractive. With his shirtsleeves rolled up around his forearms, and that strong, sexy jawline, and that body, and those striking hazel eyes, Special Agent Vaughn Roberts was the kind of man a woman noticed—even across a crowded coffee shop when she was supposed to be meeting someone else for a date.

I know you'd envisioned yourself being on a different track at thirty-three, but there is one really awesome thing about being single. You can have meaningless, mind-blowing sex with a guy like that.

"You shouldn't look at me like that," Vaughn said, in a low voice.

"Sorry. I was just . . . thinking about something my friend Trish said."

He studied her. "When's the last time you had anything to eat?"

Sidney checked the clock on the dashboard and saw that it was after ten o'clock. "Probably the same time that you had anything to eat."

"We could stop somewhere."

Sidney thought about that for a moment. "Actually, I'd really like to go home and get out of this dress and heels." Then she looked at him. "I have a refrigerator stocked with finger sandwiches and minicakes, if you're interested."

He held her gaze, his eyes a molten dark green-gold. "I just so happen to love minicakes."

Sixteen

AFTER LETTING VAUGHN inside, Sidney excused herself to change out of her dress and heels. Sadly, she did *not* invite him upstairs to join her.

So instead, Vaughn settled for watching the sway of her hips as she walked up the steps. Sometimes he didn't know whether he was coming or going with this woman. In the car, he'd thought there'd been a little flirtation going on between them, but for all he knew "fingers sandwiches and minicakes" really meant . . . finger sandwiches and minicakes.

Hands tucked in his pockets, he checked out the living room and adjacent dining room, able to get a better look now that the space wasn't crammed with twenty-five bodies. What struck him immediately about the townhome was that it had been decorated in an intriguing blend of modern and antique furniture pieces.

A few minutes later, Sidney rejoined him downstairs just as he was eying a rustic African statue that set atop a contemporary sleek lacquer chest.

"Your style is more eclectic than I would've guessed." He turned and saw that she'd changed into black yoga pants and a pink tank top that scooped low enough to reveal the top curves of her breasts.

"I sort of fell into that style out of necessity," she said. "I left New York with only half of the furniture I'd collected while there. It wasn't enough to fill this space, so instead of trying to find pieces that semi-matched what I had, I figured I'd go with something completely different." She looked around the room. "Actually, I kind of like the way it turned out."

"I take it your ex-fiancé got the other half of your furniture?"

She tilted her head. "So you've heard the story, then."

"Bits and pieces."

"Hmm." Clapping her hands together, she changed the subject. "So. About those finger sandwiches."

Apparently, they really had been talking about actual finger sandwiches.

Damn.

A few minutes later, Vaughn found himself seated at the butcher block island in her kitchen, watching as Sidney pulled trays out of the refrigerator that were piled high with tiny sandwiches and minicakes.

"Any chance you're going to pull something out of there that comes in an extra large?" He picked up one of the miniature cakes, a small dainty replica of a three-tiered wedding cake, and held it between his fingers. "I feel like a giant."

She laughed—not a wry snicker or a bemused chuckle, but an actual full-out laugh that lit up her whole face. "I'll be sure to pass along your complaints to the Lilliputian chefs."

She took a seat on the barstool next to him and plucked a cucumber sandwich off the top of the pile. Vaughn scanned the stack, on the off chance there was a bacon-double-cheese or hot-Italian-beef finger sandwich stuck in there somewhere. No such luck. Instead, he settled for ham, brie, and apple.

"So how's life in private equity treating you these days?" He reached over to the pitcher of orange punch that she'd set out on the counter and poured a glass for her, and then one for himself.

"Good." She smiled proudly. "In fact, the investment

committee at my firm just approved of the first deal I put together."

Vaughn reached for his glass. "How big a fund are we talking about here?" He took a sip of the orange punch and grimaced. "What is *that*?"

"That is a virgin mimosa, and we're talking about a four-billion-dollar fund."

He was genuinely impressed, hearing that. "Look at you, Ms. Thing. That's a lot of money you're in charge of there."

"This is true."

"Are you nervous?"

She shook her head. "No."

"All those people counting on you to deliver, and you're telling me you're not the slightest bit anxious?" Spotting a dry bar she'd set up on the built-in butler's pantry that joined the kitchen to the dining room, he walked over and checked out the selection of liquor.

She turned on the barstool, facing him as he strode across the room. "That's what I'm telling you."

"Come on." He grabbed a bottle and headed back into the kitchen.

"No, really. I do all my due diligence before committing to an investment, I evaluate the pros and cons, and then I spend weeks thinking about the ways we can develop and grow a company beyond what others might see. But once I've done my research and I've made up my mind, I'm all in."

"Ah, yes. You and your research." Vaughn opened her refrigerator and found what he was looking for—tonic water.

"Yep, me and my research. Hey, don't knock the system—it works. If you do your homework up front, there's less risk of encountering any unexpected surprises down the road."

"Sounds like your approach to men."

"It's a sound theory. I see no reason why it shouldn't apply to men, too." She watched as he grabbed two rocks glasses and poured them each a drink. "What's this?"

"Grey Goose and tonic. After the day we've had, I'm thinking we could use something with more bite than a virgin mimosa."

Seemingly in agreement, she took a sip.

Vaughn took a seat on a barstool, resting his hand on the counter close to Sidney's. "So."

"So," she said back.

He reached out and touched his thumb just above her upper lip. "You have a little smudge of cream cheese here." He wiped gently, focusing on her full, very kissable lips. Then his gaze traveled up, to those gorgeous blue-green eyes.

Eyes that, oddly, were regarding him with amusement.

"Are you actually using the there's-something-on-your-lip move on me?" Sidney asked. "That has to be the oldest move in the book."

Seriously, this woman *reveled* in busting his balls.

He scoffed at her question. "Give me a little credit, Sinclair. Next time, I'll let you walk around with food on your mouth." Actually, there'd been no cream cheese—it *had* been a move.

One that obviously needed to be struck from the playbook ASAP.

From the way her eyes sparkled, she still wasn't buying it. "I'm a little disappointed, Special Agent Roberts. Here I'd thought that a pro like you would—"

Fuck it. Vaughn hooked his finger around one strap of her tank top and pulled her in for a kiss.

That was one move, at least, he knew she liked just fine.

WITH A SOFT moan, Sidney's lips parted eagerly for Vaughn. He slid his hand to the nape of her neck, holding her firmly as his mouth took control, his tongue sweeping around hers in a hot, demanding circle.

She reached up and sank her fingers into the back of his dark hair, and before she realized what was happening, he lifted her up and settled her on his lap. She shifted, moving so that the thick ridge of his erection was right between her legs.

He groaned and broke away from her mouth, sliding his hands to her bottom. "Tell me to leave right now if you don't want this to go all the way tonight."

She closed her eyes, giving in to the flood of sensations as his mouth burned a path along her throat. "Take me upstairs," she said raggedly.

He scooped her up, and she hooked her legs around his waist. She cupped his face between her hands, the kiss never stopping as he carried her to the staircase and up.

"Where's your bedroom?" he growled.

"To the right." Her lust-addled brain tried to focus as they moved through the hallway. "This doesn't change anything between us. No one can know." *Wow*, the sexy scruff along his jaw felt good and rough against her skin when he nuzzled her neck.

"Are you using me for sex, Miss Sinclair?" he said wickedly.

"Yes. So, yes," she said. It had been a long time—too long—since she'd been this turned on. As long as they both understood that this was a no-strings-attached deal—and of course, *he* understood that—damn straight, she was going for this. Mr. Right may not yet have waltzed into her life, but Mr. Right Now was currently doing a fine job of getting her hot and bothered in the interim.

He set her down on the floor next to the bed. Not wasting another moment, he gripped the bottom of her tank top and yanked it over her head. Then his fingers skillfully undid the front clasp of her bra and let it slide off her shoulders to the floor.

Her nipples puckered in the cool air-conditioned room.

"Now there's a pretty sight." Vaughn cupped her breasts and rolled her nipples between his thumbs. "Do you want my mouth here?"

Her breath caught. "Yes."

"Then get on the bed."

Somebody, it seemed, liked being a little bossy in the bedroom. But, seeing how this particular order aligned with *her* agenda, Sidney acquiesced. She climbed onto the covers, sliding back to watch as Vaughn toed off his shoes and socks, then unclipped his FBI badge from the waistband of his jeans and removed his gun. He set both on the nightstand.

His eyes glinted in the moonlight as he moved over her on the bed, trapping her underneath his long, muscular frame. He lowered his head, until their mouths were just inches apart. "Kiss me."

With a coy look, she reached up and ran her thumb over his bottom lip. Then she pressed her lips to the same spot, right where she'd once bit him, before opening her mouth to his in a slow, steamy kiss.

She heard a low rumble in his chest. His hands slid over her body, trailing lightly over her sensitized skin. He caressed a long lock of hair that had spilled over her shoulder, letting it run through his fingers.

"So beautiful." His fingers continued to trail downward, over the peaked tips of her breasts. Then he followed with his mouth.

Sidney arched off the bed when he sucked the tip of one breast between his teeth. She smoothed her hands down his back, frustrated by the feel of cotton. "This shirt has to go."

He pulled back long enough to undo the buttons and yank off his shirt. After tossing it to the floor, he reached for her again.

"Hold on." She stared at him, shirtless before her. "I'm going to need a moment here."

Holy crap, he was perfect.

It was like looking at a sculpture cast in moonlight, every muscle exquisitely solid and defined. She touched his chest, just to confirm he was actually real, then trailed her fingers down his six-pack abs.

He sucked in a breath when she did that.

"My god, how much do you work out?" she asked.

"About an hour and a half every day. I'm training for the triathlon with some friends."

Of course he was.

"Um, my mouth was on a breast a minute ago. Any chance we can cut the ogling short and get back to that?" he asked.

"Smart a—" She gasped when he pinned her underneath him and picked up where he'd left off. Within moments she was writhing beneath him, the ache between her legs nearly unbearable.

"Vaughn," she moaned.

"What do you want?" he asked huskily.

So many hot, naughty things sprang to mind. "Touch me."

He gripped the waist of her yoga pants and eased them down her legs. "With my mouth or my fingers?"

Oh, god. "Either. Both." Her body trembled as he ran a finger over her ivory silk underwear, right between her legs.

"You're so wet, Sidney. So damn hot." He peeled the silky underwear off, then cupped his hand between her legs and parted her soft folds with his fingers.

She tightened her grip on the back of his hair. "If you don't get inside me soon, I'll bite you again."

"Feeling a bit prickly, are we?" he asked. "I'm going to make this real good for you, I promise." He eased a finger inside her and began to stroke in a slow, smooth rhythm.

She bit her lip to keep from crying out. It was all just so good—*he* was so good. He added a second finger, moving in and out as he lowered his head and flicked his tongue over the tip of one of her breasts. That pushed her over the edge and she came, hard and fast.

She opened her eyes and watched as Vaughn got up and stood at the edge of the bed. His gaze burned into hers as he reached into the back pocket of his jeans and pulled a condom out of his wallet. He tossed it on the bed, then shed his jeans and boxer briefs.

Sidney's eyes widened at the sight of him. Granted, she'd only seen one other penis in the last three years, but this particular model seemed quite . . . impressive.

He grinned devilishly. "Need another moment?"

She crooked her finger at him and he climbed back onto the bed.

"Let me touch you," she murmured. She stroked her hands over his chest, planting soft kisses along his neck. He closed his eyes, his breath quickening as her hands drifted lower. Teasingly, she brushed her fingertips along the length of his erection.

"Wrap your hand around me," he said.

She did so, stroking him slowly and getting incredibly

turned on by the feel of his hard, smooth cock. She felt his hand tangle in her hair.

"I want to fuck you. Now," he said in a guttural voice.

Liquid heat curled low in her stomach as he settled between her legs and grabbed the condom. He rolled it on, then grabbed her wrists and pinned them against the bed with one hand.

Their eyes met and held as he slowly thrust into her, inch by exquisite inch.

She moaned, overwhelmed by the fullness of him.

He clenched his jaw. "Christ, you feel so damn good."

He let her get used to him with several long, smooth, strokes, then he began to thrust faster. His eyes seared into hers as he pounded into her, taking her hard. Their bodies slapped together, their moans tangled in the air, and in those moments there was no checklist, no biological clock, no cheating ex-fiancé. Instead, there was only the delicious wave of pleasure building up in her as she let go and let Vaughn take her over the edge again. She cried out, digging her nails into his back and squeezing her legs tighter around his hips. He thrust hard, and again, and then groaned as he shuddered and buried his face in her neck, slowing down and finally collapsing on top of her.

A few moments later, he got up to dispose of the condom in the bathroom. When he strode naked back into the bedroom, Sidney tucked one arm under her head, watching him appreciatively. "Mmm-hmm."

He climbed back into bed and slid one arm around her waist as she curled onto her side, facing him. "Look at you, all satiated and de-snarked for once."

She poked him in the chest.

He swatted her ass in return.

And then together, they drifted off to sleep.

Seventeen

AT SEVEN THIRTY A.M., the ring of Vaughn's telephone yanked him out of a deep sleep. His head jerked up off the pillow and he blinked, quickly getting his bearings.

Sidney's bed.

Gun on the nightstand.

Sexy redhead curled up against his chest, who rolled off him with a grumpy mutter and covered her head with a pillow. A few waves of red hair escaped, cascading over her bare shoulders and back.

Apparently, somebody wasn't much of morning person.

In fairness, on this particular occasion, Vaughn wasn't much of a morning person, either. Normally, he had no problem getting up at seven thirty A.M., but, as demonstrated by the nakedness of the sexy redhead next to him, he'd had a long night.

He grabbed his phone off the nightstand and saw that it was Cade calling. Given the early hour, he mentally scrolled through the list of cases he and Cade were working on, assuming there had to be some kind of emergency.

"Yeah," Vaughn answered, his voice gritty with sleep.

His friend's tone sounded distinctly sly. "So, Huxley and I are standing outside your place, wondering where you are."

"That sounds a little stalker-ish." Vaughn's attention was immediately diverted when Sidney shifted next to him, pushing the sheet down to expose the top curves of her very cute ass.

Hmm.

His best friend's voice in his ear interrupted that line of thought. "If by 'stalker-ish' you mean picking up your absentee ass for the workout we'd scheduled, then sure. Huxley and I are stalking you."

Workout.

Shit.

Vaughn got out of bed, realizing he'd forgotten that he, Cade, and Huxley had bumped up their regular Sunday training session because Cade had plans to go to the beach with his girlfriend later that morning. "Sorry, man—I completely forgot about the time change. I'll be there in ten minutes." He hung up as Sidney rolled over and gave him a lazy Sunday morning smile.

On second thought . . .

Vaughn pushed the errant thought from his head. He had plans, his friends were waiting for him, and besides—he didn't do lazy Sunday mornings after a hookup. That was too couple-ish.

"Some sort of FBI emergency?" she asked, tucking her hand under the pillow as he yanked his clothes on.

He shook his head. "I forgot I'm supposed to meet my friends. We're doing an hourlong swim and a thirty-minute run today."

"Have fun with that. *I*, on the other hand, will be tackling an hourlong nap this morning, possibly followed by a thirty-minute bath." She smiled contentedly, and then froze, as if thinking of something. "Wait—Simon's car is still out front, right? I wasn't thinking about that last night. If he picked the car up early, he would've seen yours out front and realized that you're still here."

Vaughn had a feeling that, in those circumstances, he would've received a call from his younger brother—*Hey bro, I'm outside Sidney's house and you're apparently inside. Something you want to tell me?*—but strode down the hallway to the guest bedroom to check, anyway.

He looked out the front windows and saw Simon's car still parked out front.

All clear.

Vaughn headed back to bedroom, where Sidney was sitting up, with the sheet wrapped around her. "His car is still out front. We're safe."

She exhaled. "Whew. I wouldn't have wanted to explain, you know . . . this." She gestured between them.

"I hate to break it to you, but I think your sister and my brother probably already realize that you and I do 'this.'"

"Not together." She watched as he grabbed his gun, holster, and badge off the nightstand and put them on.

"I notice that you check out my gun a lot," he said teasingly.

She gave him a look. "I don't 'check out' your gun. I've just never been around anyone who carried one before." The sheet dipped at her chest, exposing one tantalizing breast and rosy nipple.

It's an eleven-week training program, Vaughn mused. Really, missing one swim wouldn't make *that* big of a difference.

"So, you said something about leaving?" Sidney asked.

Vaughn blinked, snapping out of it. He stepped over to the bed, unsure whether he was amused or insulted by her bluntness. Maybe a little of both. "Don't get all sentimental on me now, Sinclair." He leaned down and kissed her forehead, then turned to head out.

Her voice stopped him in the doorway. "Vaughn."

He looked back over his shoulder.

"Tell the 'other you' to be careful on Monday night, when he's hanging out in those dark, sketchy alleys."

Something in Vaughn's chest tugged tight that she'd remembered. "I will."

* * *

VAUGHN FOUND A spot on the street a half block down
from his apartment, parked, and braced himself for the inevitable. Cade and Huxley sat on the front stoop to his building,
their bikes parked on the sidewalk out front since the plan
was to ride together to the gym at the FBI building for extra
exercise.

The two men took in the sight of Vaughn walking up in
his clothes that were rumpled after a night spent on Sidney's
floor, and his hair that undoubtedly was sticking up in every
direction.

"At least you've moved on from the maid of honor," Cade
said, with a grin.

"Well, not exactly . . ." Vaughn hedged.

Cade's eyes widened. "You slept with the maid of honor?"

"Sidney." Vaughn unlocked the main door to his loft condo
building.

Alongside Cade, Huxley followed Vaughn up the steps to
his unit on the second floor. "Oh, boy. I'd been hoping it was
just the cute hostess at that Mexican restaurant we ate at last
week."

Vaughn looked over his shoulder quizzically. "What cute
hostess?"

Huxley shot Cade a knowing look. "This is getting
serious."

"*Nothing* is getting serious," Vaughn said emphatically, as
he let them into his apartment. He tossed the keys on his
counter. "And why are you riding me about this, Hux?" Sure,
his partner was a little on the uptight side—actually, a lot on
the uptight side—and seemingly had come out of the womb
ready to propose to a woman, given how quickly he'd put a
ring on Addison's finger. But Huxley usually just responded
to his myriad dating adventures with a roll of his eyes and a
few sarcastic remarks.

"Because I think it's a bad idea for you to get involved with
the sister of your brother's future wife," Huxley said bluntly.

Vaughn scoffed at that. "We're not 'involved.' " Both Cade

and Huxley raised an eyebrow. "Okay, so maybe we got involved for one night. We're adults. We can handle it."

"Your families are connected. You're going to be running into this woman for the rest of your life. When this goes south"—Huxley gestured to Vaughn's disheveled, post-hookup appearance—"and with you, it inevitably will, the situation could get complicated."

Vaughn grabbed a PowerBar out of his pantry. "Last night, a sexy, smart woman told me that she wanted to use me for sex. That's not a complicated situation, that's an *awesome* situation."

"Sexy and smart? Sounds like someone has a crush," Cade said.

Christ, these guys were all up in his business over this. "Was I really this annoying when you two were single?"

"Worse," Huxley and Cade said simultaneously, without hesitation.

Well, still. The circumstances were completely different between him and Sidney. Vaughn cracked open a bottled water to wash down the PowerBar. "Look, I get that you guys are all settled in your perfect relationships, and as part of that, you've shut down the part of your brain that used to actually have some game." He paused. "Except for you, Hux. It's pretty much always been lights-out in that department for you."

His partner glared.

"The point is, I think I'm good here," Vaughn said. "Sidney made it perfectly clear that last night was a no-strings-attached deal. That's my wheelhouse, gentlemen."

That having been established, he headed down the hallway, toward his bedroom, to change into his workout clothes.

"Checking to see if she texted you yet?" Cade called out.

Vaughn shook his head.

Yep. All up in his business.

LATER THAT DAY, after Sidney had caught up on some much-needed sleep, showered, and had breakfast, she drove to the hospital to visit Isabelle. On her way out, she noticed

that Simon had picked up his car. For the second time that
day, she breathed a sigh of relief that he hadn't come by in
the wee hours of the morning and spotted Vaughn's car out
front. That would've been . . . not good.

As far as she was concerned, Isabelle and Simon never
needed to know that anything had ever happened between
her and Vaughn. Last night had been fun, and hot, but that
was *all* it had been—a one-night stand. Sure, she was attracted
to Vaughn, and she had no regrets that they'd slept together,
but it wasn't like anything serious would ever happen between
them. As Trish had said, he was a Mr. Right Now.

And a *fantastic* Mr. Right Now, at that.

Sidney parked the car in the hospital garage, thinking she
should probably erase all traces of her suspiciously glowing
I-just-got-laid grin before she got to her sister's room. She
didn't normally keep secrets from her sister, but obviously,
this was different. It would be awkward for all of them if
Simon and Isabelle knew that she and Vaughn had slept
together—especially when neither she nor Vaughn planned
to take things any further than that.

Just act normal, she told herself as she exited the elevator
at Isabelle's floor. *Like nothing happened.* As far as her sister
and Simon were concerned, Vaughn had driven her home
from the hospital last night, and then they'd gone their separate ways. That was her cover story, and she, being the confident woman she was, would have no problem sticking to—

She stopped in her tracks just outside Isabelle's room, hearing a familiar low masculine voice with that distinctive sexy,
gritty edge.

Shit—Vaughn.

Sidney was grateful that the drawn privacy curtain prevented
everyone from knowing she was there. She needed a little space
from Vaughn right then, especially while the hot memories of
the things they'd done were so fresh in her mind. She turned to
go, thinking she would run a few errands on Michigan Avenue
and come back in an hour or so. But then she caught a snippet
of Vaughn's conversation with Isabelle and Simon.

"I'd been thinking," Vaughn was saying, "given all you

two have on your plate, that maybe there are some things I could do to help out with this wedding."

Dead silence followed.

"You know, you all can stop staring at me like my eyebrows fell off for throwing out the suggestion," Vaughn said dryly.

Out in the hallway, Sidney fought back a grin as Simon and Isabelle laughed.

Vaughn continued. "Look, I know I might not be the first person everyone thinks of when it comes to weddings. But I would very much like to be a part of *this* particular wedding."

Out in the hallway, Sidney couldn't help but smile.

Well. That was actually kind of sweet.

"We'd like that a lot, Vaughn. Thank you," Simon said. There was the sound of some hearty man-type backslaps—*aw*, the Roberts brothers were hugging—and then Isabelle spoke.

"Actually, if you're interested, we have our tasting at the Lakeshore Club scheduled for next Sunday, so we can finalize the menu for the reception," she said. "They said we could bring two guests, so we plan to invite Sidney. Maybe you'd want to come, too?"

"I'd like that," Vaughn said.

Sidney stepped away from the doorway as they finished their conversation. While walking back to the elevator, she thought about Isabelle's remark.

Our tasting at the Lakeshore Club . . . We plan to invite Sidney.

The last contact she'd had with anyone at the Lakeshore Club had been seven months ago, when Douglas, the club's events manager, had regretfully informed her that he couldn't refund any of the deposit she'd paid for the wedding, given how close to the date she and Brody had canceled. And now, on Sunday, she would return no longer as the bride-to-be, but as the dutiful maid of honor and the bride-who-never-was.

She was bracing herself for a lot of damn head-tilts.

Eighteen

VAUGHN PULLED HIS car up to the ornate wrought-iron gates at the end of the Lakeshore Club's private driveway and gave his name to the security guard. "Vaughn Roberts. I'm here for a tasting for the Roberts-Sinclair wedding."

The guard consulted his guest list and nodded. "You'll be in the reception hall. Follow the driveway until you get to the end. It's the white building with columns overlooking the lake."

Vaughn thanked the guard and proceeded onto the club's grounds. He passed by tennis courts, an indoor and outdoor pool, an indoor ice-skating rink, and a picturesque nine-hole golf course before arriving at his destination: a stately white Georgian-style mansion.

Nice digs.

When he pulled into the lot for the reception hall, he spotted Sidney's black Mercedes. It had been a week since he'd seen her, both of them keeping their distance after their hot night together—as was expected. In order to avoid emotional entanglements, he had a strict rule against seeing the same woman twice in one week.

Technically, as of 7:35 this morning, he was free and clear of that rule as far as Sidney Sinclair was concerned. Not that he was anticipating anything, he'd just . . . made a mental note of that fact.

He followed the walkway to the open front doors of the mansion. He stepped inside and took in the lobby's elegant crystal chandelier and wide, grand curving staircase. The doors to his left led to a large ballroom, presumably where the reception would take place.

Vaughn walked into the oak-paneled ballroom and saw French doors that led out onto a terrace. He stepped outside and took in the sight of the sparkling blue water of Lake Michigan that stretched before him. He smiled slightly, having a proud big brother moment, as he thought about Simon dancing with Isabelle out here, or his parents, who he was pretty sure had never attended a wedding anywhere this upscale before.

The Robertses of Apple Canyon, Wisconsin, had indeed arrived.

"You must be Simon's brother."

Hearing the voice, Vaughn turned to face the neatly dressed fortysomething man who stepped out onto the terrace. "Guilty as charged. Vaughn Roberts." He extended his hand in introduction.

The other man, who wore a crisp linen summer suit and blue shirt, smiled as they shook hands. "Douglas Slater, events manager for the Lakeshore Club. Isabelle called just a minute ago, saying that she and Simon got held up at their appointment with the florist earlier this afternoon. She said they would be a few minutes late. I saw you out here and thought I'd see if I could get you something to drink while you wait."

Vaughn's phone buzzed just then. He pulled the phone out of his suit jacket and saw that he had a text message from Isabelle, letting him know about the delay. "Thanks, but I'm good for now," he said in response to Douglas's drink offer. He tucked the phone back into his jacket. "Have you seen Isabelle's sister, Sidney?"

"Not yet. You're the first to arrive," Douglas said.

Having seen the Mercedes, Vaughn knew that wasn't the case. The Mysteriously Absent Miss Sidney Sinclair was here somewhere.

Douglas cocked his head, his tone softening. "Speaking of Sidney . . . how is she doing these days? I've thought about her a lot since, well, you know."

Actually, Vaughn didn't know all that much, although he'd gathered the gist of what had happened between Sidney and her ex. "She's doing great," he told Douglas. And he left it at that.

Then he looked around. "Maybe I'll walk around for a bit while I'm waiting."

"Of course." Douglas pointed to their left, where the terrace wrapped around the ballroom. "I don't know if you're a golf man, but if you walk down the steps around the corner and follow the path to the left, you'll come to a gazebo that has some nice views of our nine-hole course."

Perhaps Sidney had decided to check out the view herself while they waited. "Thanks for the tip." Vaughn followed Douglas's directions and quickly found the path the events manager had referred to. The walkway led him away from the lake, to a wide green lawn not visible from the road and parking lot. The lawn sloped up, and at the top of the hill, nestled next to a weeping willow tree, was the gazebo. Spotting a splash of auburn red inside the white gazebo, he headed over.

Sidney had her back to him as she leaned against the gazebo's railing, the sunlight playing with the copper and gold highlights of her hair. Vaughn slowed down as he approached. Part of his interest, admittedly, was because she wore killer red heels and another one of her summery dresses—this time, some red, yellow, and blue dress that looked both arty and New York chic with its blowsy top and short flare shirt. But he also paused because there was something about the way she looked out at the golf course that struck him as somber.

His footsteps were soft against the wood as he climbed the two steps into the gazebo. Sidney looked over her shoulder as he approached.

Vaughn joined her at the railing. "Are you hiding out here?" he asked bluntly.

She looked surprised. "No." But after a moment she conceded. "Maybe a little. I got Isabelle's message that they were running late, and I didn't feel like hanging around inside."

"Douglas the events manager asked about you. He wanted to know if you're doing okay."

"Did he say it like this?" She cocked her head in imitation. 'How *is* Sidney doing?' " She smiled slightly. "I get that sort of thing a lot."

Vaughn waited to see if she continued.

"You obviously know there's a story," she said.

"I do."

"I suppose you expect me to tell it to you now."

"Nope. No expectation."

A long silence fell between them.

"Well . . . as long as you're twisting my arm with all these questions, Agent Roberts," she quipped. "Look, I think it's inevitable that you'll find out sometime before Simon and Isabelle's wedding. I suppose I'd rather you hear the story straight from me." She gestured to the mansion on their right. "I was supposed to get married here this past October. But I broke things off with my fiancé a month before the wedding."

"Name?"

"Brody. And you're not going to do your FBI interrogator thing through this whole story, are you? That kind of ruins the flow."

He fought back a smile. "Sorry."

"It was a Sunday, and I was at the bridal salon for my final dress fitting. The people who worked at the salon were making a big deal out of it, so they had me try on the shoes, and the veil, because it was all about creating the moment. They had me come out of the dressing room, to the three-way mirrors in the middle of the shop, and everyone was *ooh*-ing and *ahh*-ing over the dress and the whole effect. But then this woman walked into the store." Sidney paused at that part, remembering. "She stood there for a moment, staring at me in my dress, until she said, 'You're Sidney Sinclair, right?'

So I'm thinking maybe she's one of my friends' younger sisters, because I can't place her but she seems to know me. So I said, 'I'm sorry. Do we know each other?' To which she replied, 'You should know me. I'm the woman who's been fucking your fiancé for the last three months.'"

"Sidney," he said, his voice softer than usual.

"You're doing the head-tilt."

Right. He wanted to say that she didn't need to be glib about this, but he sensed she needed to tell the story her own way. "So what did you do?"

"Well, seeing how we were standing in front of all the bridal salon employees, not to mention the other customers who'd gathered around for my big dress moment, there wasn't much I could do. I excused myself and followed the woman outside the bridal shop. When we were standing on the street, I just looked at her and said, 'All right. Let's hear it, then.'" Sidney shrugged. "And she proceeded to tell me everything. How she and Brody met at the gym, the things he'd told her about me and about how he was freaking out about getting married, and all the ways they'd had sex—including in our apartment, in our bed, when I was traveling. Apparently, she'd been trying to convince Brody to break it off with me for some time. When he didn't, she decided to follow me from our apartment to the bridal shop, thinking she could catch me alone and take care of things herself."

She looked out at the golf course. "After hearing everything she said, I just . . . started walking. All the way home, twenty blocks. By the time I got to our apartment, I had blisters on my feet, so I took off the shoes to walk up the two flights of stairs. When I opened the front door, Brody was sitting on the couch, reading the *Wall Street Journal* like it was just a regular Sunday afternoon. His mouth fell open when he saw me standing there, barefoot and in my wedding dress. But then he smiled and said, 'Isn't this supposed to be bad luck?'"

"Please tell me you chucked the shoes right at the dickhead."

That got a small smile out of her. "Believe me, I was tempted. But at that point, I was just *done*. So I simply told him to pack a suitcase and get out."

There were lots of things Vaughn wanted to say in response to that story. But in the end, it boiled down to one thing. "Your ex is an asshole."

"Yep. And I'm the fool who somehow missed that."

He cocked his head, thinking that was an interesting thing to say. "In the FBI, we have this mantra: 'Trust but verify.' It means always corroborate what someone is telling you, no matter how believable they seem."

" 'Trust but verify.' I like that," she said. "Too bad I hadn't heard that mantra three years ago."

Vaughn turned to face her. "The point is, we're trained professionals. Every agent brags about his instincts, his ability to read people and know when someone is lying. Yet, still, we get that corroboration whenever possible. Because we're only human—sometimes, we put our faith in the wrong person. And you're only human, too, Sidney." He gave her a nudge. "Even if it kills you to admit it."

"Just a little." She cocked her head, studying him. "What's going on? You're suddenly being so . . . nice."

"It's really sweet, Sinclair, how you manage to say that with such surprise."

She laughed. "Sorry." Then her cell phone chimed from inside her purse. She checked it. "Isabelle says they're pulling into the driveway now."

A FEW MINUTES later, the group was seated in the main ballroom, at a rectangular table that had been set up for the tasting. Vaughn sat on Sidney's left, to her right was Douglas, the events manager.

On the opposite side of the table, Isabelle mulled over the appetizer options spread before them. "Okay, so far we've got the caprese cups, sage-and-sausage-stuffed mushrooms, mini crab cakes, and coconut shrimp—which means we need two more appetizers. What do you think about the bacon-wrapped scallops?" She turned to Simon, who sat next to her.

"If it was up to me, I'd wrap this entire dinner in bacon." Simon looked at Vaughn. "Back me up here, best man."

"Absolutely. Nothing says 'party' like cured meat."

As the rest of the group chattered away, Sidney found herself tuning them out, their voices fading. Being here, in this room, brought back memories of her own tasting, for which she and Brody had flown in from New York. It had been a whirlwind of a weekend, and she'd noticed at the time that Brody had seemed somewhat stressed and anxious to get back home. He'd told her he was just overwhelmed at work, but knowing what she did now, she realized that he'd likely been hurrying to get back to *her*.

I'm the woman who's been fucking your fiancé.

We did it in your shower, on your kitchen counter—in your bed, too.

"Sid, what do you think about the butternut squash croustades? Do you like those or the spring rolls better?"

But the best was the time we did it against the wall in the alley outside your apartment, while you were upstairs making dinner for him on his birthday.

"Sid?"

She blinked and saw everyone looking at her. "Sorry. I just was . . ." She took a breath, gathering herself. "I vote for the croustades." Across the table, Isabelle looked at her with concern, and Sidney could also feel Vaughn's eyes on her.

She ignored both of them.

"So? What's next?" she asked, eagerly rubbing her hands together. "Salad course, right?"

Determined not to let any more unwelcome memories slip in, Sidney made sure she was on top of her game for the rest of the tasting—even remaining unfazed when there was an awkward moment during the entrée course.

"So that's the beef tenderloin and the salmon for the meateaters, and the potato tikki cakes as a vegetarian alternative." Douglas jotted down the selections. He smiled, pointing the pen between Isabelle and Sidney. "Funny, you two chose the exact same entrees."

As soon as the words came out, he looked at Sidney with a chagrined expression. "I shouldn't have said—"

"Great minds think alike," Sidney said, cutting him off and tipping her wineglass to Isabelle.

Later, in the parking lot as they said their good-byes, Isabelle pulled Sidney aside. "I'm so sorry that was awkward for you, Sidney." She looked contrite. "I shouldn't have asked you to come."

Sidney was a big girl—if she hadn't wanted to come today, she would've simply said no. "How many times do you plan to get married, Isabelle?"

"Um . . . just once, I hope."

"Exactly. And I don't want to miss any of it." With their father only tangentially involved in their lives, it was basically just the two of them—the way it had been for a long time.

Isabelle squeezed her tight in a big hug. "Have I ever told you how glad I am that you're back from New York?" Then the two of them headed back over to join the men, who were talking by Simon's car.

"I heard a rumor that an e-mail went out to people about the bachelor party," Simon was saying.

"Sure did," Vaughn said.

"On a scale of one to ten, how worried do I need to be about whatever you have planned?"

Vaughn dismissed this with a wave. "*Pfft*. Like a two."

Simon raised an eyebrow. "Your idea of a two or mine?"

"I guess you'll find out."

Seeing Isabelle and Sidney approaching, Simon smiled. "Everything okay?"

"Yep, we're good," Isabelle said. Both she and Simon said their good-byes, climbed into his car, and the two of them were off.

Sidney leaned against her own car, watching as Simon and her sister pulled away. When they were gone, she exhaled and looked around at the picturesque wide green lawn and the elegant white mansion.

"Is it tough being here?" Vaughn asked, moving to stand next to her against the car.

She debated whether to answer that. "It brings back some memories I'd rather not think about."

He nodded. They stood there for a moment, and then he looked at her. "How many of those dresses do you have, anyway?"

"Why? What's wrong with my dresses?"

"I didn't say there was anything wrong with them." His eyes traveled over her. "Not at all." He seemed to debate something for a moment, then he moved and put his hands on each side of Sidney, trapping her against the car.

She eyed her position. "What are you doing?"

He bent his head, his words low and smooth. "Let's just say, I know a really good way to get you thinking about something other than those unwanted memories."

"You're shameless," Sidney said. Although her pulse had already begun to quicken, having him this close.

His devilish smile was his answer.

TWENTY MINUTES LATER, Sidney dug her fingers into the smooth gray suede of Vaughn's sectional couch as he pumped hard into her from behind.

"Tilt your hips back. Take me deeper," he said in a guttural voice.

She angled her hips toward him, and moaned at the exquisite feel of having him so hard and thick inside her.

"Good . . . just like that, baby. Christ, I could fuck you forever," he rasped.

Bracing her hands against the couch, she thrust back against him. *Yes*, she needed this after today. Right then, there was no thinking about the past, no worrying about the future—just wild, raw sex that made her feel *good*. She and Vaughn had started kissing in the stairwell of his apartment building, and by the time they'd gotten inside his loft, they'd both been so turned on they'd hadn't even bothered to remove their clothes. Instead, he'd just bent her forward over the couch, pushed up her skirt and yanked down her underwear, and thrust deep into her with his own jeans unzipped around his hips.

She closed her eyes and gave into the sinfully erotic sensations washing over her. "Touch me," she murmured, needing his hands on her.

"Stand up," he said huskily, pausing to help guide her up. When she was partially upright, with his cock still buried inside her, he reached around and shoved down the sleeves of her dress. Next, he pulled down the cups of her bra. "Let me see those gorgeous breasts."

Her nipples tightened instantly in anticipation as she clenched between her legs. He slid one hand lower, to her clit. She gasped as he began to tease her, using his fingers to spread her open. When he slowly began thrusting inside her once again, she moaned so loud she feared the neighbors would hear. The feeling was so exquisitely incredible, all she could do was grip the back of the couch and hold on for the ride.

"Give me your mouth," he said, in a grit-edged growl.

She turned her head, her lips parting as his mouth took hers in a searing kiss, his tongue swirling around hers. She rocked her hips and started coming, a slow build that peaked so hard she cried out against him. Her legs quivered, but he held her, supporting her until she was steady on her feet once again.

She opened her eyes and saw that he was looking at her with a warm, wicked gaze.

"Again?" he asked.

Criminy.

Nineteen

VAUGHN CAME OUT of the bathroom and found Sidney propped up against the pillows on his bed, looking at something on her phone.

"Already checking e-mail?" he teased. Not that it bothered him—the woman ran a four-billion-dollar private equity fund. Safe to say she was going to have to check her messages on weekends.

"Mmm," she said distractedly.

Vaughn pulled on his boxer briefs and jeans. "Everything okay?"

She peered up at him, frowning. "What does it mean if a guy e-mails you four times in one day, and then waits a week before e-mailing again? Is he busy at work, or is he playing games?"

Vaughn stared at her. "You're e-mailing another *guy*? My God, woman, the condom's still warm in the wastebasket."

She gave him a look. *Ha, ha.* "I wasn't e-mailing another guy, I was checking for work messages. I just happened to see this other e-mail, too." She got out of bed and strutted by him, to where her underwear lay on the floor. "And don't act as though you're offended. Remember, you're"—she dropped her voice, imitating him—" 'always upfront about not looking for a long-term commitment. But if you want a good time, then I'm your man, baby.' "

He grabbed her dress off the corner of the television, where it had landed after he'd impatiently tossed it over his shoulder during round two. "Still, there's an etiquette to these things, Sinclair. Try to respect that." He held out her dress, then playfully moved it away when she reached for it. When she glared, he grinned and handed it over for real.

She looked around for her bra and spotted it on the nightstand, laying under his pistol.

"So who's the guy?" he asked, folding his arms across his chest.

"What guy? Oh, right. Actually, he's someone I went to high school with. He found me on Facebook, saw that I'd moved back to Chicago, and started e-mailing me," she said.

Vaughn watched as she grabbed the strap of her bra and slowly, very cautiously, tried to slide it out without having to touch any part of his gun. He went over to the nightstand, picked up his gun and badge, and handed her the bra. "To answer your question, he's not busy with work. He's playing games."

Letting her stew on that one, he headed out into the kitchen.

She came out of the bedroom a minute later, dress on and with her high heels dangling casually from one hand, her phone in the other. "You don't know for sure that he's playing games."

Vaughn finished drinking the glass of water he'd poured himself. "Trust me, I know how guys think." He poured a second glass of water for her. "When a guy e-mails or texts a bunch of times in a row and then goes radio silent for a few days, it's a ploy to make you wonder whether he's into you. Then, just when you're starting to feel a little insecure about things, he makes contact, knowing that *now* you'll be extra glad to hear from him."

Sidney looked disgusted. "That's so lame. And sneaky." She looked at him, frowning. "Do you use these tricks?"

Please. "I don't have to use tricks." Starving from all the bedroom—and living room—activity, he pulled out a bag of tortilla chips and a jar of salsa.

"Ah, right. Because you're the extra-Special Agent Vaughn Roberts." She took a seat in the bar stool next to him.

He winked. "Special enough to get you naked. Twice."

She considered this, while helping herself to a chip. "All right, tell me more."

"More what?"

"About how single men think. How to spot the good guys from the players."

Vaughn scoffed. "I'm not giving you tips on dating other guys."

"Why not?"

"Because we just slept together. It's . . . weird."

She reached out and touched his hand, smiling ever-so-sweetly. "Aw, baby, don't be like that. We're friends, right?" Her eyes danced mischievously. "Isn't that what you guys always say?"

Probably he'd best take the Fifth Amendment on that one. So he answered instead with a question of his own. "Don't you think you're being a little intense about all this dating stuff? I thought all you happily-ever-after types believe that when the time is right, Fate will send 'the one' your way."

"Well, Fate needs to get a move on," she said, dipping another chip into the jar of salsa. "I'm up against the clock here."

"Please don't start telling me about how your eggs have an expiration date." He pointed to her abdomen. "I don't need to be thinking about how there are fertile eggs in there right after we had sex."

"You used condoms and I'm on the pill. You might be studly, Roberts, but even your guys can't make it past all that. Besides, I wasn't talking about my *biological* clock, I meant that I'm up against the clock with this wedding here. I promised myself I'd have a date by then." She pointed with her tortilla chip. "So come on. Give me the straight skinny on the single, urban, thirtysomething man. How do I know if a guy's in it for the sex?"

"That's easy—*all* guys are in it for the sex. The real question is whether he's open to something on top of the sex."

"And that's where my checklist comes in." She took a bite of her chip, looking quite confident in this.

"I hate to break it to you, but any guy trying to play you will know how to get around that checklist. Players know all the right things to say. They'll send you sweet text messages wishing you good-night or saying they just want to see how your day went—because they know those kinds of things make women think they're good guys."

"Wait—pause right there." Sidney grabbed her phone and began typing.

Vaughn stared at her. "Are you taking notes?"

"Hell, yes. This is good stuff." She read out loud as she typed. " 'No texts good-night.' Got it." She looked up. "What else?"

"Seriously, Sinclair. I was just *inside* you ten minutes ago."

She reached out and touched his hand, her smile sweet once again. "Aw, baby. And you know how special that was to me."

Yep. *Reveled* in busting his balls.

Twenty

EARLY WEDNESDAY AFTERNOON, Sidney paced in her office, using a Bluetooth headset so she could stretch her legs. For over an hour, she'd been on a call with Gabe Ramos, the headhunter she'd brought in to help find a new CEO for Vitamin Boutique—someone who would be aggressive about growth without sacrificing profits and earnings.

She turned to the final candidate on the list of three executives she'd forwarded earlier to Gabe for discussion. "What about Karen Wetzel?" she asked. Wetzel was the executive vice president and chief merchandising officer of Toys "R" Us, and, according to Gabe's intel, was looking to spread her wings beyond a VP position.

"I heard PetSmart has been talking to her about their open CEO position," Gabe said.

Sidney mused over that. Wetzel had more experience in the specialty retail industry than any of the other candidates and, on paper, had been her top choice. "Do we know if that's a done deal?"

"I can find out," Gabe said.

She nodded. "See if you can reach her today. Tell her I'd

like to fly her out to Chicago if she's still considering other opportunities."

"I'll see what I can do," Gabe promised.

After she wrapped up her call, Sidney headed out to grab a quick lunch with Isabelle, who was downtown for a post-surgical follow-up with her OB-GYN.

"How'd it go at your doctor's appointment?" Sidney asked over their salads at Corner Bakery.

"He said everything looks great with both me and the peanut," Isabelle said. "He took a few ultrasound photos. Want to see?" She took the strip of black-and-white pictures out of her purse and handed it over.

"Oh my gosh." Sidney pointed. "Look, there's its nose. And a little hand."

"The doctor joked that the baby was waving 'Hi, Mom.'"

The alarm on Sidney's biological clock suddenly blared so loud it sounded more like a fire drill. She hit the mental snooze button and smiled at her sister. "Are you going to find out the gender?"

Isabelle shook her head. "Simon and I decided that we want to stick with the theme of this pregnancy and be surprised." She took a bite of her salad. "But enough about me—what's going on with you? Anything happening on the guy front?"

Not much. Just Vaughn and I having crazy-hot sex after your pre-wedding tasting. "Actually, I have a date tomorrow." Sidney cocked her head. "Come to think of it, you might remember the guy—Chad Bailey. He was a year younger than me in high school—he would've been a senior when you were a freshman?"

Isabelle set down her fork. "No way. I had a huge crush on Chad Bailey back then. And I wasn't the only one. I think half the cheerleading squad lost their virginity in the back of his Mustang GT."

"Please tell me you weren't one of them, because—*eww*—I'm not going on a date with someone you slept with."

"You're in the clear." Isabelle cracked open the water bottle, looking eager for the details. "How did you two reconnect, anyway? By the way, you definitely need to call me after the date and let me know if he's still as hot as he was in high school."

"He found me on Facebook. We've e-mailed back and forth a few times, and he asked if I'd meet him for a drink." Not that Sidney didn't have doubts, particularly after Vaughn's comments about what it meant when a guy rapid-fire e-mailed a woman and then fell quiet for a few days. But this was what single thirty-three-year-old women with blaring biological clocks did—they kept an open mind.

And apparently, they went on a *lot* of first dates.

THURSDAY EVENING, SIDNEY'S date with Chad started off better than expected. They met for drinks at a wine bar not far from her office and fell into a fun, easy conversation as they reminisced about high school.

"I had a crush on you back then, you know," he said, his brown eyes warm and friendly. "It broke my heart when you went off to college."

This provided her just the opportunity she'd been looking for. "From what I hear, you survived just fine," she said teasingly. "My sister told me some rumor about your Mustang GT and half the cheerleading squad?"

Chad laughed, looking embarrassed. "Oh . . . that. Well, I couldn't wait around for you forever, could I?" Then he leaned in, speaking more earnestly. "But all jokes aside, I've grown up a lot since high school. That's not who I am anymore."

That sounded potentially promising. Sidney took a sip of her wine and set down her glass. "All right, then. Tell me who you are now, Chad Bailey."

As they drank their wine, he told her all about his job as a consultant, his dog, and how he'd just bought a new condo in the Bucktown neighborhood. In return, he asked a lot of questions about her, and seemed genuinely interested in wanting to know more.

But there was just one thing.

During the date, he received several text messages—in fact, his phone chimed so often that he finally shut it off. "Sorry," he said, glancing at the screen. "Just some co-workers getting together after work." A few moments later, he excused himself to go to the restroom.

Sidney watched him go, thinking that this seemed a little . . . suspicious. Then again, it was possible that she was being too paranoid about such things. So far, Chad had sailed through her thirty-four-item checklist. Hell, he even had a dog—which, according to her research, was a big sign of commitment-readiness.

I hate to break it to you, but any guy trying to play you will know how to get around that checklist.

Deciding to go straight to the source, she pulled out her phone and texted Vaughn.

WHAT DOES IT MEAN IF A GUY GETS A BUNCH OF TEXTS WHILE ON A DATE, BUT DOESN'T WANT TO ANSWER THEM IN FRONT OF ME? SHADY, OR JUST BEING POLITE?

Moments later, she received Vaughn's reply.

YOU'RE ON A DATE RIGHT NOW?

Clearly, this was self-evident. YES, WITH HIGH SCHOOL GUY.

I THOUGHT YOU NIXED HIGH SCHOOL GUY.

I'M BEING OPENMINDED, she shot back.

SAYS THE WOMAN WITH THE THIRTY-FOUR-ITEM CHECKLIST.

Okay, so they were getting a little off topic here. JUST ANSWER THE QUESTION. CHAD WILL BE BACK ANY MINUTE.

OF COURSE HIS NAME IS CHAD.

She was tempted to take her phone and shake it. But seeing how she genuinely wanted Vaughn's opinion, she took a deep breath and counted to ten. ANY HELP? I'M GETTING MIXED SIGNALS HERE.

There was a long pause.

COME ON . . . YOU WOULDN'T WANT ME TO GET BURNED AGAIN, WOULD YOU? she cajoled.

After a moment, he answered.

JUST BE DIRECT. ASK HIM STRAIGHT-OUT IF HE'S SEEING ANYONE.

She rolled her eyes. That was his advice? DID THAT ALREADY. HE SAID HE'S NOT DATING ANYONE RIGHT NOW.

Vaughn's reply was quick. TIME TO CUT BAIT, SINCLAIR. HE'S PLAYING YOU.

She frowned. HOW DO YOU KNOW?

THAT'S MAN-SPEAK. WHEN A GUY SAYS HE'S NOT DATING ANYONE ELSE "RIGHT NOW," HE MEANS LITERALLY RIGHT AT THAT MOMENT. LAST NIGHT? ANOTHER STORY.

She scoffed at that. GET OUT OF HERE.

ASK HIM YOURSELF.

Chad's voice interrupted them. "Texting a friend to say how the date's going?"

Sidney tucked her phone back into her purse as Chad took his seat. "Maybe."

He winked at her. "So? How am I doing?"

"Time will tell," she said jokingly. She toyed with the stem of her wineglass, keeping her tone casual. "Here's a funny thing, going back to something we talked about earlier. My friend has this theory that when a guy says he's not dating anyone else *right now*, he's being tricky and just means right at that moment."

Chad opened his mouth, as if to defend himself. Then, perhaps seeing something in her gaze, he stopped.

He reached for his glass and took a sip of his drink, his playful expression now replaced by a smug, busted smirk. "So I'm a little precise with my answers."

And . . . another one bit the dust.

LATER THAT NIGHT, Vaughn, aka Mark Sullivan, watched as Officer Pritchett brought his rented van to a stop. They were in their usual meeting place, an alley behind an abandoned warehouse on the south side of the city. Vaughn had arrived twenty minutes ago, in the Hummer H3 he drove while undercover as Sullivan, and had ensured that the location was secure. As always, Huxley, the backup team from the white-collar squad, and the team from the special operations group were all parked in various locations surrounding the alley, listening in on their encrypted radios via the live transmission wires.

Tonight's meeting would be a turning point in Vaughn's investigation. Having tested the waters with the prior run—in which Pritchett's gang had smuggled several suitcases of handguns—he had decided to up the ante.

"Nice touch," he said when Pritchett stepped out of the driver's side of the van. He nodded at the police jacket the cop had displayed in the passenger window, with the letters *CPD* plainly visible.

Pritchett grinned smugly as another cop stepped out of the van—Officer Ortiz. "I thought so, too. Who's gonna pull us over when we've got that in the window?"

Vaughn saw the headlights of a second vehicle approaching. He stepped back as another van pulled up, this one with Officers Mahoney, Cross, and Howard, all from the Sixteenth District.

After the second group of cops exited their vehicle, Vaughn told Pritchett and Mahoney, who'd been driving the second van, to pop the trunks. He headed over to Pritchett's trunk first. Inside the back of the van were two large duffle bags. As he unzipped one of them, the cops all gathered around to watch.

Vaughn pulled out an M-16 assault rifle.

This was where the shit got very real. In his hands was an untraceable military rifle, which the police officers believed to be fully functional. Given what they knew about "Mark Sullivan," there could be no doubt in any of their minds that the weapon would end up in the hands of some thug who would use it against other thugs, civilians, or possibly even police officers.

Vaughn scanned their faces, waiting for any sign of doubt or hesitation among any of them.

Instead, Pritchett nodded at the M-16 and grinned. "And he's got some friends."

The rest of the cops laughed.

So much for doubt or hesitation.

Vaughn pulled out the other rifles and examined them. They'd been rendered inoperable by the agents in Indiana, although none of these assholes knew that. When finished with his "check" of both duffle bags, he zipped them up and then walked over to Mahoney's vehicle.

In the back of the second van were two more duffle bags. Vaughn unzipped them and saw that each contained twenty handguns, a mix of Ruger, Glock, and S&W pistols. All the guns were nine millimeter or larger calibers and had altered serial numbers. After ensuring that the guns he'd "purchased" were all accounted for, he zipped the duffle bags back up.

"All right, let's load them up," he said.

He and three of the cops, including Pritchett, carried the duffle bags over to the Hummer and loaded them into the back of the SUV. Then Vaughn grabbed a large envelope from the passenger seat.

He handed the envelope, which was filled with cash, to Pritchett. "Fifteen thousand for another job well done. My seller in Indiana says he can have shipments ready every two or three weeks. Think you guys can handle that?"

"I told you, Sullivan. This isn't fucking amateur hour here," Pritchett bragged. He held up the envelope. "As long as you keep paying, we'll bring as many guns as you want into this city."

Vaughn smiled, glad to hear it.

When this whole thing blew up, that answer was going to bite these dickheads right in the ass.

VAUGHN LET HIMSELF into his loft and peeled off yet another of Mark Sullivan's designer suits. Famished, as usual, from the undercover work, he threw a frozen pizza in the oven, poured himself a vodka tonic, and settled in at the counter to check his messages. He'd had to leave his phone at home for the undercover op—obviously, Mark Sullivan couldn't walk around with Special Agent Vaughn Roberts's cell.

He saw that he had a couple of texts, one from Simon asking how it went with the groomsmen's tuxes—*shit*, he'd forgotten about that—and another one from Mollie, the investigative reporter from the *Trib*, asking if he wanted to get together that weekend.

Shelving that question, he went back to his messages screen and saw Sidney's texts from earlier that evening, when she'd been on her date. She'd never responded to his last message, he'd noticed.

Ask him yourself, he'd said.

He wondered what High School Guy had said, and whether she'd finally nixed him for good.

So . . . ? he typed, and almost hit send. But then he realized it was after midnight. Probably best not to text her right then, as if he was ruminating about her date in the wee hours of the night. Which he wasn't, obviously.

He was just . . . curious.

Nothing more.

Twenty-one

FRIDAY MORNING, SIDNEY got some good news from her headhunter.

"I talked to Karen—she has an offer from PetSmart, but she hasn't accepted it yet," Gabe said. "She'd love to fly out to talk to you about the Vitamin Boutique position, but we need to move fast."

Sidney turned in her desk chair and pulled up the calendar on her computer. "Can she do an interview Tuesday? Wednesday? Find out what works best with her schedule, and I'll make it happen."

"Will do."

She spent the rest of the morning on the phone, first with Vitamin Boutique's board of directors, making sure that at least two of them would be available to meet with Karen the following week. After that, she had a lengthy discussion with the consulting firm she typically worked with in these situations so that they could begin figuring out what kind of compensation package PetSmart had likely offered Karen—and more important, the kind of compensation package *she* would need to convince the VP to come work for Vitamin Boutique instead.

Sidney hung up the phone shortly before noon and rolled her head, stretching her neck. She was just thinking she should send an e-mail to her team, updating them on these newest developments, when her secretary buzzed.

"I didn't want to interrupt your call, so I was about to bring you a note," Darnell said, speaking in a hushed voice. "A Special Agent Roberts is waiting in the reception area. He says he'd like to speak with you."

Vaughn? Here? Sidney didn't know whether to smile or roll her eyes at her secretary's whispered tone, having no doubt that a certain special agent had used his job title to get exactly that kind of reaction. "Tell reception that I'll be right out."

WHILE WAITING IN the sleek, sophisticated lobby, Vaughn studied the contemporary artwork on the walnut-panel walls. After a couple of minutes, he heard the sound of high heels clicking confidently against the pearl marble floor.

He knew that walk.

He turned around and watched as Sidney approached. With a smile, he took in her effortlessly stylish outfit—gray pants, ivory silk blouse, and a light peach scarf wrapped loosely around her neck.

She was just the woman he needed.

"Special Agent Roberts," Sidney said as she approached. "To what do I owe this pleasure?"

"I need your help."

That caught her off guard. She stepped closer and lowered her voice, her expression turning concerned. "Is everything all right? It's not Isabelle, is it?"

"Nothing like that. I need your fashion advice."

"Oh. Okay." She looked him over. "Well, with that suit, I think your tie could be a little skinnier."

Vaughn threw her a look. And made a mental note about

the tie. "I need to pick out the groomsmen tuxedos for the wedding."

"Ah. That's an important job. The tuxes help set the tone for the entire wedding."

"So I've just been told," he said dryly.

She cocked her head, her blue-green eyes sparkling. "Are you having some difficulty with your assignment, Agent Roberts?"

He could already tell he was going to regret this. "Here's the deal. Simon bought his tux, so he told me to pick out whatever I want for myself and the other groomsmen. No problem. Then I get to the store and the salesman starts asking all these questions. Bow tie or necktie? How wide would I like the lapel to be? Pleated pants or flat front? How many buttons on the jacket? Do I want a vest? A cummerbund? How formal are the bridesmaids' dresses? Because, as I recently learned, it's very important that the groomsmen's attire *complement* what the bridesmaids are wearing," he said, imitating the salesman's serious tone.

"This is true."

"So? What are you wearing?" he asked.

"A dark champagne strapless dress with a sash across the hip."

He raised an eyebrow. "Is it sexy?"

She raised an eyebrow back. "Should that really be your focus right now?"

It certainly was a far more interesting topic than what *he* was wearing to this superposh shindig. "Look, I wear suits every day—I can pick out a damn tux. And if this was a tux for my wedding, I'd be in and out of the shop in five minutes." He caught her looking at him strangely. "What?"

"I'm just waiting for your eye to start twitching after the reference to *your* wedding."

And there it went, right on schedule. "The point is, this is your sister and Simon's big day. And since I'm pretty sure that hell hath no fury like a pregnant woman whose dream wedding is ruined because the best man decided to go with vests instead of cummerbunds, I'm thinking I should get this right."

"Skip the vest, then. Isabelle can't stand them."

"Good to know. A cummerbund, it is."

"No cummerbund either."

Vaughn frowned. "Don't I need something that's going to coordinate with the color of your dress?"

"Why yes, you do. If this is 1998, and you're taking me to *prom*."

And . . . there was the snark again. "You're enjoying this, aren't you?"

"Quite a bit, actually."

He took a step closer. "Think about it this way, Sidney. You have to walk down the aisle next to me at this wedding. We'll be in numerous photos together—photos that the entire Sinclair family will look at for years to come. If my job as a groomsman is to complement *you*, do you really want to put your faith in whatever I might come up with?"

She considered this for a moment.

"Let me just grab my purse."

WHEN THEY STEPPED through the door of the tuxedo shop, the salesman who'd been helping Vaughn earlier came out of backroom.

He smiled when he saw them. "Special Agent Roberts. I see you've returned with backup."

"This is Sidney, our illustrious maid of honor."

She said hello, and then gestured to Vaughn. "Ignore everything this man told you during his previous visit."

"She tends to be a little sarcastic," Vaughn told the salesman, without batting an eye. "I'm told it's a New York thing. Which is really weird, considering she's from Chicago."

Sidney nudged Vaughn as she walked by him and eyed one of the tuxedos on display. "Did Simon tell you anything about the tux he's wearing?"

"He said it didn't have tails." From her expression, Vaughn gathered this was not a lot of help. He shrugged. "We're guys. We don't have long, drawn-out conversations about clothing. Actually, we don't have long, drawn-out conversations about anything if we can help it."

Sidney turned back to the salesman. "We'll go with something classic. Black, two-button jacket. Flat-front pants, no cummerbund, and—" She looked Vaughn over with a scrutinizing air. "A bow tie. Definitely."

"Excellent choice," the salesman said approvingly. "Let me grab my tape measure." He took Vaughn's measurements, and then asked his height, weight, and shoe size. He went into the back room and returned with a sample tuxedo and shoes. "The changing room is right there. Just holler if you need anything." He pointed to a private room behind the three-way mirror in the center of the store.

Vaughn changed out of his clothes and put on the tux. He checked himself out in the mirror, was satisfied that the tux fit well enough, and stepped out of the dressing room.

Sidney stood with her back to him as she chatted with the salesman. When she turned around and saw him in the tuxedo, she blinked. "You look so . . ." She trailed off and just kept looking at him.

Then she cleared her throat and regrouped. "It's nice." She walked over, scrutinizing him as he stood in front of the mirror. "It seems to fit well enough. What do you think?"

Her phone suddenly rang in her purse, which sat on a chair across from the mirrors. "Sorry. I should grab that in case it's work-related."

While Sidney took her call, the salesman walked over to Vaughn. "Would you like to try on something else? We have several different styles, in case you want to get a comparison."

Vaughn glanced over at Sidney, who laughed at something while talking on the phone. He thought back to her reaction when she saw him in the tux.

"You know, I think I'm good with this one," he said.

With a smile, the salesman nodded. "Of course, sir."

SIDNEY TOOK A bite of her risotto and thought for a moment about her next question. "Okay, I've got one. Most likely to get drunk and make an awkward impromptu toast at the reception."

To thank her for helping out with the tuxes, Vaughn had taken her to lunch at an Italian bistro nearby, one that had al fresco dining so they could enjoy the nice weather. Their current conversation had started with a bet—the person most likely to ask Isabelle at the wedding if she was pregnant—and that had led to all sorts of predictions about the big day.

Twirling his spaghetti gamberoni around his fork, Vaughn didn't pause a moment before answering. "My uncle Finn. Here's a tip: half my family is Irish. So any 'most likely to' distinctions pertaining to this wedding that involve drinking, we've got covered."

Sidney chuckled and grabbed another breadstick. "Now your turn."

He poured more olive oil onto the plate between them. "All right. How about . . . most likely to tackle another woman to the ground in order to catch the bouquet." He gave Sidney the side-eye.

"Who, me?" she asked.

Vaughn laughed as part of a breadstick came flying his way. "What? Not your style?"

"Definitely not my style. Not to mention, Isabelle has another bridesmaid, Amanda, who already declared that she's taking anyone out who gets between her and that bouquet at the wedding." Her turn again. "Most likely to photobomb the pictures of Isabelle and Simon cutting the cake."

"Also my uncle Finn."

"This Uncle Finn sounds like quite a character. I can't wait to meet him."

"I'm going to remind you of that when he's drunk and trying to grab all the bridesmaids' asses," Vaughn said.

"Gross."

His turn. "Most likely to get obnoxious with that annoying tradition of clinking glasses to get the bride and groom to kiss."

Sidney pointed. "Oh, I've got that one. My cousin Anna. She did that nonstop at my other cousin's wedding last summer. And if she tries pulling that crap at Isabelle's reception, she's going to find herself drinking out of a red Solo cup."

"At a Sinclair function? Are these ruby-crusted red Solo cups?" Vaughn asked.

Cute. Her turn. "Most likely to be the first one to cry during the ceremony."

He sat back in his chair. "Hmm. . . that's a tough one. Isabelle's got the hormones going for her, but lately Simon's been getting very sentimental and schmaltzy. Then there's *you*, another contender—don't make that face at me, I see the softer side that comes out when you think no one's looking—but, nevertheless, I think I have to go with my mom. She's so excited this is finally happening, I think we may need a whole box of Kleenex at the ceremony just for her." He cocked his head, as if curious about something. "What about your dad?"

"My dad? Ah, no. I think the idea of getting sentimental and schmaltzy at weddings wore off for him sometime around his third marriage." She took another bite of her risotto.

"You don't talk about him much," Vaughn said.

When Sidney had finished chewing, she shrugged. "Not much to say, I guess. We're not really that close."

"Has it always been that way?"

She fingered the stem of her water glass. "Not always. It was different when I was younger. He used to take me to work and show me around the office and tell everyone that I was going to be an investment banker someday, just like him. Obviously, the idea stuck with me," she said with a slight smile, before turning more serious. "But things changed after my mom died. My dad threw himself into work, and for a while, my sister and I barely saw him. And then he started dating Cecilia, his second wife, only six months after my mom died, and I resented that. Maybe that wasn't fair, but I was eleven years old at the time. I felt like he had moved on and forgotten about my mother, and I . . . still very much wanted to remember her."

She cleared her throat, not having meant to reveal something so personal. "Then, three years later, when I'd finally come to accept Cecilia, they got divorced. I found out later that my father cheated on her with Liza, Wife Number Three. Liza lasted ten years, until *she* divorced him, also for cheating, this time with a twenty-five-year-old tennis instructor at his club," she said, not bothering to hide her scornful tone. "Then he met Jenny at some party, and married her six months after that. They've been married nine years now and I guess it seems to be working. I don't ask. Frankly, I'm not sure I want to know."

"Do you think things might get better between you and your dad now that you're back in Chicago?" Vaughn asked.

"I don't know. Not really, judging from the way things have gone so far. When we talk about work things are okay, but when it comes to anything personal, I feel like there's this chasm of things we don't say to each other. I mean, obviously I've known for a while that my dad has a problem with the fidelity part of marriage." *To put it mildly.* "And while before, that was something I disapproved of, it's different now after what happened to me with Brody. I can't look at my dad the same way. I just . . . respect him less, because of the decisions he's made in his personal life." She paused. "And that's a hard thing to admit, especially since I used to idolize him so much when I was younger." She fell silent at that, and then took a deep breath and cocked her head. "How did we get on this subject, anyway?" She pointed, mock suspiciously. "Did you good-cop me, Roberts?"

He laughed, grabbing the carafe of ice water. He refreshed her glass, and then his. "It's so different with my family. No one gets divorced—as my mother would say, that's not the 'Irish way.' I guess people just stick it out if they're miserable."

"I don't know about the rest of your family, but your parents definitely aren't miserable. They're adorable."

He smiled at that, his affection for his parents unmistakable. "They are great. But don't let my mom fool you—she can be tough when she wants to be."

Sidney studied him, musing over something. "I'm curious. How is it that someone who grew up with such a nice, loving family ends up being so anti-marriage?"

"First of all, I'm not 'anti-marriage.' I think people who want to settle down should do exactly that. It's just not something I, personally, am looking for right now."

"Fine. Maybe you're not anti-marriage in that sense. But this playing the field attitude of yours . . . is that the way it's always been? Have you ever been in a serious relationship?"

"As a matter of fact, I have," he said, taking a bite of his breadstick.

Sidney blinked. *Wait—what?* Then she raised a skeptical brow. "By 'serious' I don't just mean that you actually called the same girl more than once."

"Actually, Little Miss Snarky, I dated someone for over a year."

Well, this was a surprise. "You did? When? What's her name?"

"Six years ago, and her name is Cassidy," he said.

"Why did you two break up?" Sidney gave him a withering look. "Do *not* say you cheated."

"I don't cheat. In fact, I like to think I'm honest to a fault with women."

Sidney rolled her eyes—*whatever*—but let that one slide so she could get to the juicy stuff. "So, Cassidy. Tell me more."

He shrugged. "We dated, we decided we wanted other things, and then we split up."

"But ever since, you haven't been in another serious relationship. Why is that?" She studied him, trying to figure out this puzzle. "Maybe . . . Cassidy broke your heart and you've never been able to recover, so you became this rakish man-about-town to hide your pain."

He cocked his head in amusement. "Man-about-town? Do we still use that term?"

"We do when we're trying to be polite and not say 'man whore.'"

"Tell me how you really feel, Sinclair. Don't hold back."

"Come on," she said, with a grin. "You've heard the story about my ex. Heck, I even told you the part about walking up the stairs with no shoes."

"And I still say you should've chucked them at the asshole." Vaughn sat forward, resting his arms on the table. "All right, so here's the story. When Cassidy and I dated, I was only a couple years into my career with the FBI. They assigned me to the squad that investigates violent crimes against children: kidnappings, sexual abuse, and online predators. It's typical to assign guys like me to that area: meaning, guys who don't have kids themselves. And, generally, they only keep you in that squad for a couple years because it gets to you.

"Don't get me wrong. Out of my entire career, I'm most proud of the work I did on that squad. Whenever you tell someone you're an FBI agent, they ask you about terrorism or organized crime or serial killers—but sometimes it's the smaller cases, the ones that don't get any media attention, that make you realize you really are making a difference in people's lives. I once carried a seven-year-old girl out of a basement where her stepfather had locked her up and had been abusing her for nearly two years. That's something I'll never forget."

He paused there. "But on the flip side, seeing that kind of stuff day in and day out is tough. It wears on you. About six months in, after seeing the sort of sick bastards that are out there, it got to the point where I didn't think I'd ever want to bring kids into this world. Cassidy, however, really wanted a family. And since I wasn't in a place to give her that, we decided to go our separate ways."

Sidney sat there, not sure what to say for a moment. "I didn't realize you'd done that kind of work with the FBI. I can see why that would scare you off of having kids. Wow."

He nodded. "The good thing is, once they moved me to a different squad, and I got some distance from those cases, things eventually got back to normal. I started doing undercover work, and that's been a really good fit for me."

"That's great." And Sidney was glad to hear it. But . . . she was missing something. "And when things got back to normal, and you once again were in a position to have a committed relationship, you decided to keep playing the field because . . . ?"

"Because . . . I realized it's fun to date lots and lots of women?"

She did a mental head-thunk. Of course that was his answer.

He held out his hands. "Look, I'm sorry if I don't have

some deeper, darker reason. I fell into this lifestyle because of my job, and then I realized I like it. What else can I say?"

She shook her head. "You know, I was with you as you were telling the FBI story. Hell, I even started to feel a little bad for the things I said at the coffee shop. And then—*poof*—we're right back where we started."

"You're irritated with me again."

Sidney thought about that for a moment. Then she sighed. "No, not irritated. You're right—at least you're honest. You're a known commodity, Vaughn. I guess there is some merit in that."

A long silence fell between them.

"So how did your date go yesterday?" he asked, changing the subject. "You never texted me back."

Great. Another fun topic—her as-of-yet-fruitless quest to find Mr. Right. "You were right about High School Guy. As soon as I busted him on the 'not dating anyone *right now*' thing, the date went completely downhill." She ran her hands through her hair and sighed. "Is it too late for me to realize that I'm a lesbian? Sure, I like penises, but I'm a smart girl—I could figure out what to do with the lady bits if need be."

"As hot as it is to imagine you figuring out what to do with the 'lady bits,' I don't think you need to worry. You're the total package, Sidney: smart, gorgeous, successful . . . dynamite in bed, too," he added, with a knowing grin. "It's not going to be long before some really lucky guy figures that out."

She rested her hand in her chin, and smiled genuinely at him. "That may be the nicest thing you've ever said to me, Vaughn Roberts."

She waited for him to make a joke or say something dry or sarcastic, but instead he just looked at her with the strangest expression. "What?"

He blinked. "Uh, nothing." Immediately, whatever that look had been, it was gone.

"So I'm dynamite in bed, huh?" Sidney preened a little, hearing that—especially coming from such an expert. After Brody had cheated, there'd been a small part of her that had wondered if perhaps she hadn't been sexy enough compared to his twenty-four-year-old lover.

Vaughn looked her over, his eyes suddenly a warm dark green-gold. "Baby, you are as fiery as that tiny landing strip of red hair between your—"

"Okay, got the picture. Thank you." She took a sip of ice water, then set down her glass. "Stop looking at me like that. I know what you're thinking."

There was that devilish smile. "What am I thinking?"

"That I'm going to sleep with you again because I'm feeling dejected about men and you"—she took in his broad shoulders, lean muscles, and ruggedly handsome face—"are a pleasant enough distraction."

"Pleasant enough distraction?" He gave her a get-real look. "And for the record, you're wrong. I couldn't sleep with you today even if I am thinking about it. I have a seven-day rule."

"What's a seven-day rule?"

"I don't have sex with the same woman twice in one week. That starts to get too couple-y." He saw her roll her eyes. "Oh, you can have a checklist with thirty-four items, and I can't have one rule?"

Touché.

THEY PARTED WAYS on the sidewalk outside the restaurant.

"You're heading back to the office, then?" Vaughn asked.

She nodded. "As much as I would love to play hooky on a Friday afternoon like this, I need to get back. I'm trying to steal a CEO away from PetSmart."

"If I had a dime every time a woman used that old excuse to ditch me."

She smiled. "So tomorrow's the big day, huh?" she said, referring to Simon's bachelor party.

"Yep. For you, as well. Do you have some crazy girl's night out planned for the bachelorette party?"

"Maybe," she said, being cryptic.

Vaughn thought about Sidney being out on the town,

drinking, wearing another one of her sexy dresses, getting wild with the rest of the girls, and probably flirting with guys. He felt a stab of something oddly possessive—which he quickly brushed aside. Sure, perhaps he felt a little protective toward her. That was only natural; they'd gotten close over the last few weeks. In fact, the stuff he'd told her about the dark phase he'd gone through after working on the child victims squad was something he almost never spoke about. He liked talking to her, and hanging out with her, and he sure as hell enjoyed sleeping with her. But that was *all* it was—they were just having fun together. They wanted completely opposite things, and they both knew that.

"Just don't do anything tomorrow night that I wouldn't do," he told her.

"Well, that doesn't eliminate much, does it?" She winked and turned confidently on her heel, long auburn swinging.

Probably he should've phrased that a different way.

Twenty-two

FIFTEEN WOMEN, INCLUDING Isabelle, let out a collective cheer when the waiter arrived at their table carrying a tray of lemon drop shots.

He served Isabelle first, setting one of the shot glasses in front of her. "For the bride-to-be."

Isabelle took a tiny sip and her eyes widened. "Wow, that's strong."

When the other women had been served their glasses, Amanda, who'd bought the round, raised hers in toast. "To Isabelle and her romantic whirlwind courtship with Simon. I think I speak for everyone at this table when I say . . . girl, I thought for sure you were pregnant."

The group burst into laughter.

Isabelle lifted her glass. "Bottom's up to that." She polished off the shot in one gulp. While everyone else was drinking, she winked at Sidney, who sat at the opposite end of the table.

Unbeknownst to all, Sidney had promised their waiter an extra twenty percent in gratuity if he served Isabelle virgin versions of whatever drinks everyone ordered for her. The plan had similarly worked like a charm earlier that evening at RPM Italian, where they'd had dinner. By now, Isabelle had drunk two virgin cosmopolitans, a virgin French martini, and three nonalcoholic lemon drop shots, and likely was flying high on a sugar rush from all the cranberry, lemon, and pineapple juice.

Sidney shared a conspiratorial smile with her sister, and was struck by a sudden bout of nostalgia. To cover, she looked out at the striking view to her right. They had a VIP table on the terrace of theWit Hotel's rooftop lounge, which, at twenty-seven stories up, looked out over the city's impressive night-time skyline.

She'd wanted to go all out for this bachelorette party because she knew that Isabelle had been stressed with the wedding planning and because things likely weren't going to get any *less* busy for her sister anytime soon. After the wedding, Isabelle would move into baby-prep mode, and five months later she would be a mom. Thus, in some ways, this bachelorette party felt like a final hurrah to the old days, the many years when it was basically just the two of them, the Sinclair sisters.

"Man, your sister can drink," said Trish, seated on Sidney's left. "I've only had half of what she's had, and I'm already feeling it." A breeze blew through her blond hair and she sighed contentedly. "It's so good to be out." She looked at Sidney. "Don't tell the other moms in my play group that I said that."

Sidney smiled. Trish had joined a neighborhood "new moms" group and, as the only woman who worked full-time, had been feeling a little like an outsider. "Your secret's safe with me."

Trish took a sip of her drink and then sat back in her chair. "So, catch me up. Tell me how things are going with your dating plan."

"I had drinks with Chad Bailey the other night. Remember him, from high school?"

"Ooh, I remember him being very cute. What's he like now?" Trish asked eagerly.

"Pretty much a jerk." Sidney filled her friend in on all the details of her date.

"Huh. So these tips about men that Vaughn is giving you. What's in it for him?" Trish asked.

"Unfortunately, so far, the satisfaction of being completely right," Sidney said dryly.

Trish cocked. "Is there . . . any chance he's trying to steer you away from other guys because he's jealous?"

Sidney snorted. "Ah, no. Guys like Vaughn don't get jealous. He won't even sleep with the same woman twice in the same week because he doesn't want any 'emotional entanglements.' As for why he's giving me these tips, I guess it's because we've kind of become . . . friends."

Trish stared at her in disbelief.

"I know," Sidney said. "I heard the word come out of my mouth and I'm just as shocked as you."

They both started laughing—an amusement undoubtedly aided by the drinks they'd already consumed that night.

"Do you have bend-me-over-the-couch sex with a lot of your friends?" Trish asked.

"Heck, maybe I should, after this." Still giggling, they clinked their glasses together.

"It's that good, huh?"

Sidney leaned in conspiratorially. "Oh my gosh, Trish. You should see the shape he's in. When he takes his shirt off, it's like . . ." She paused, trying to come up with a good analogy for naked Vaughn Roberts. "Remember when we went to Vegas, the dessert bar at the Bellagio buffet? It's like that. So much I want to try, I don't even know where to start."

"I told you that you needed this."

"You were definitely right."

"And I don't need to be concerned that you're starting to actually like the guy? Normally, you don't *befriend* the Mr. Right Now, I don't think."

"That's just because of this whole wedding thing. And actually, I think it's good that the two of us can have a conversation now without me ending up thoroughly annoyed." Some of the time. "I'm going to be running into the guy forever, you know." She looked at her friend without any hesitation. "You don't have to worry. I've got this, Trish."

"Got what?" said a voice, coming from behind Sidney.

She looked over as Isabelle took a seat in the open chair on her right. "We were . . . just discussing who's going to buy the next round of drinks."

"Cool. Guess what? I have some good news," Isabelle said excitedly. "Simon's coming here with the guys."

"He is?" Sidney asked, surprised.

Isabelle was doing her dreamy, glowing thing again. "He's been texting me all night, asking how things are going." She threw Sidney a secret look that suggested Simon was, once again, feeling protective of his pregnant fiancée. "He says he pitched the idea of coming here to the other guys, and once he told them that I had a cute, single sister, they were all on board. I think he must be pretty drunk."

"Thanks," Sidney said.

Isabelle laughed and squeezed her hand. "Not because he said you're cute. I meant that over the course of the evening, his text messages have gotten increasingly . . . sentimental. He says he misses me, just being away from me for one day." She looked at Sidney, beaming over this. "You don't mind that they're coming, do you?"

"Not at all. It's your bachelorette party, Izz."

Isabelle left to tell the other women the news, practically dancing around the table along the way.

Sidney and Trish exchanged looks. Both of them started giggling.

"My God, it's like she's in a Disney movie," Trish said. "Please tell me I was not that giddy when it was my turn."

"Giddy? No. But I do seem to recall somebody getting a little choked up when Reid's best man told that story about your first date during his toast."

"So my eyes were a little watery. It was allergy season."

"Sure it was." With a knowing smile, Sidney took a sip of her martini.

DESPITE HOLDING A firm belief that seeing one's fiancée on the night of one's bachelor party went against the natural order of things, Vaughn found himself crammed in an elevator with Simon and thirteen other guys, headed up to the rooftop terrace at theWit Hotel.

After an afternoon spent gambling on a riverboat casino, and then dinner at Zed451—an upscale steakhouse in the city's River North neighborhood—the original plan had been to stop next for drinks at the rooftop bar at EPIC. But then Simon, who'd sailed over the line between good-and-buzzed to outright drunk about an hour ago, had started texting his bride-to-be, messages that were undoubtedly even more schmaltzy than usual, given his inebriated state. And just like that, the plan switched.

They'd encountered one near obstacle: the bouncer in the lobby, who hadn't been particularly enthused about admitting such a large party of guys all at one time. Fortunately, a quick flash of Vaughn's FBI badge, accompanied by a generous tip, had taken care of that problem.

After the group got off at the twenty-seventh floor, Vaughn held back to wait for Cade and Huxley, who'd taken a separate elevator. He'd invited his friends, both of whom knew Simon fairly well, to tag along for the night.

The two men exited the elevator and checked out the place as they walked over to the railing, where Vaughn waited. It was a large bar, divided into multiple indoor/outdoor sections, with enough people to make the space feel crowded but not packed.

"If you like it, Morgan, we might want to book now for your bachelor party," Vaughn said, only half-joking.

Cade casually tucked his hands into his pants pockets. "I don't believe I've announced anything."

"Yet," Huxley said, as the three of them walked toward the bar on the patio. It wasn't exactly a secret, they both knew Cade planned to propose to Brooke soon.

"Hmm," was Cade's only response.

Vaughn and Huxley exchanged looks, letting that non-answer sit for a moment. When they got to the bar, Vaughn ordered three glasses of Macallan 18.

Then he studied Cade. Now that he thought about it, his

friend had been acting a little squirrelly all evening. "Something's up."

"What makes you think that?" Cade said.

"Instinct." Vaughn glanced at his partner. "What do you think, Agent Huxley?"

Huxley sized Cade up. "He's holding out on us."

Cade threw his hands in the air in disbelief. "I swear, I don't know how you two do it. From the moment I first got together with Brooke, you've had an eerie sixth sense about these things."

"First of all, the reason Hux and I have a sixth sense about these things is because we're bad-ass FBI agents who know everything."

"Word," Huxley nodded.

"But more important"—Vaughn grinned at his best friend—"Holy shit, Morgan. Did you ask Brooke to marry you?"

Cade smiled. "Yesterday."

"And . . . what did *she* say?"

Cade laughed at that. "She said yes."

Vaughn grabbed Cade's shoulder. "Hell, yeah, she said yes."

"Congratulations," Huxley said, raising a glass. "Ah, it seems like just yesterday that you were threatening her with obstruction of justice charges and she told you to kiss her ass."

They toasted, drank, and reminisced for a while, until Cade switched subjects. "So how long are you going to keep us in suspense here?" he asked Vaughn.

"Keep you in suspense about what?"

"Which one is Sidney?" Cade nodded in the direction of Isabelle's bachelorette party, which Simon and the rest of the guys had quickly infiltrated.

Auburn hair at two o'clock, smoking-hot black dress, holding a half-finished pink martini in her right hand. "Sidney . . . who's Sidney?"

Huxley snorted. "I'll go out on a limb and guess that she's the redhead by the railing who you can't stop checking out."

Realizing that the gig was up, Vaughn allowed himself a good, long look. With her hair falling past her shoulders in sleek waves, smoky eyes, red lipstick, and a black dress that dipped to a V in front, she looked every inch the vixen right then. She was talking to a blond woman—Trish, if memory served from the bridal shower—and they seemed to be . . .

His mind went blank when Sidney moved, giving him a glimpse of the slit in her dress that parted all the way up to her midthigh.

Sweet Jesus.

Vaughn cleared his throat and turned back to his friends. "Anyhow."

Cade laughed. "Anyhow? Huxley and I just went and played two rounds of pool during the time you were ogling her."

"So I checked her out." Vaughn shrugged. "She's an attractive woman."

"Please. We've been here for twenty minutes, and you haven't said one word about the brunette in the blue dress who's been eye-fucking you this whole time," Huxley said.

"What brun—" Looking across the bar, Vaughn spotted her now. Wow, Hux was right, she really was eye-fucking him. "Well, that's not happening."

"Because you're smitten with the maid of honor. Just admit it," Cade said.

"I don't do smitten, my friend."

"So if some guy walked up to Sidney right now and started hitting on her, you'd have no problem with that?" Cade asked.

Vaughn felt another one of those annoying twinges— which, like the other one, he promptly shoved aside. "If some guy walks up to her, I give it all of about five minutes before she sends him packing. Her checklist is like a fortress— nobody's getting through."

"Are you willing to bet on that? Because I think we have a situation here." Huxley leaned in toward Vaughn, his eyes trained on something across the room. "Your ten o'clock. Light brown hair, black shirt, about six feet tall."

Vaughn quickly identified the suspect. He watched as the other guy stared appreciatively at Sidney from across the room.

"Think he's going to make a move?" Huxley asked.

Vaughn's jaw tightened. "I'd say that's very likely, Agent Huxley."

Cade peered over his shoulder. "What are you two talking about? Is something happening?"

His eyes trained on the suspect, Vaughn watched as Black Shirt grabbed hold of his drink and turned around, leaning against the bar while fully checking out Sidney.

"Some guy is about to approach Sidney," Huxley said.

Cade looked at Vaughn. "You're not going to stand here and watch while another dude hits on her, are you?"

Vaughn thought about that. "That guy looks like a douchebag—she won't want to talk to him. I mean, really . . . I suppose I'd be doing her a favor by going over there and intercepting this guy."

Cade and Huxley exchanged looks.

"You do that," Cade said, his lips twitching in a smile. "Be a hero."

"Yes. Right." Vaughn nodded. "Just so we're all clear that I'm doing this for *her*." Right then, he saw Black Shirt push away from the bar and head into the crowd in Sidney's direction.

Enough of the chitchat—he had a douchebag to intercept.

Twenty-three

TRISH NUDGED SIDNEY, her tone sly. "Your *friend* is coming this way."

Yes, Sidney was aware of this. Actually, she'd been plenty aware of Vaughn ever since he'd walked into the bar. And she wasn't the only one: looking rakishly handsome in his suit jacket, pants, and open-necked shirt, he'd caught the eye of many a woman on that terrace—including Amanda, who'd been openly checking him out this whole time.

"Miss Sinclair," he said as he approached.

Then he surprised her by stepping closer and kissing her on the cheek.

"Uh . . . hi," she said, not exactly sure when they'd moved into the public kiss-hello phase.

"Hi, yourself," he said with a charming smile, standing very close to her.

When he didn't move away, Sidney lowered her voice. "What are you doing?" Her sister and his brother were standing close by. Yet here he was, quite obviously *leaning* in toward her.

He seemed amused by her question. "You're always

asking me that. I'm starting a conversation. Again." He winked.

Okay . . . "And how much have *you* had to drink tonight, Agent Roberts?"

He laughed as if this was the funniest thing, and touched her chin. "Always busting my balls, Sinclair."

Then he looked to his right, watching as some guy in a black shirt passed by them.

He waited until the guy was gone, then stepped back to an acceptable "just friends" distance. "So. Having fun tonight?" he asked both women, seeming normal now.

Sidney exchanged a look with Trish, who shrugged. No clue what any of that was all about. "You remember my friend Trish, from the shower?"

Trish shook Vaughn's hand. "We met briefly outside, when you and Simon were saying good-bye to your mother."

"Speaking of Simon, how is he holding up?" Sidney asked Vaughn.

"He's in that phase where he's telling everyone how much he loves them. And half the people, he actually knows."

She laughed. "Simon, a happy drunk? No way."

"How about Isabelle? Is she having a good time?" Vaughn asked.

"A great time, from what I can tell," Sidney said.

"She's been partying it up all night," Trish said. "Honestly, I had no idea she could hold her liquor so well." She finished off the last sip of her martini. "Which reminds me—it's my turn to buy her a shot. I'll be back in a few minutes. Or so," she added, giving Sidney a pointed smile.

"Make sure you ask Dwayne to get it for you," Sidney reminded her. "He's giving us a discount on all of our drinks."

"Got it." Trish headed off to track down the waiter.

Vaughn moved next to Sidney along the railing. Not surprisingly, he raised a brow. "Your sister is doing shots?"

"I tipped the waiter an extra twenty percent to give her nonalcoholic versions of all her drinks."

"Very sneaky," he said approvingly. Then his look turned more familiar. "You look incredible tonight."

She felt herself go warm at the compliment. "Thanks. We had a spa day earlier that included hair and makeup. I'm not sure about the lipstick, though. Too red?"

Belatedly, she realized that this question brought his attention to her mouth.

His eyes lingered as he gazed down at her lips. "I like the red."

Drawn in by his look, she tried to think of something that could steer them back to normal ground. "I have another Man-Speak question for you."

He frowned. "I just saw you *yesterday*. You've already been on another date?"

"Not another date. Just some guy who e-mailed me through the online dating service I signed up with," she said. "And don't act so scandalized. Do I even want to know how many women you've been texting and e-mailing as of late?"

He furrowed his brow, as if needing to think about that.

She'd take that as a no, she did *not* want to know. "So here's my question: what does it mean when a guy says he's 'pretty much single'?"

"That's easy. It means, 'I have a girlfriend, but I've kept my dating profile active anyway, and you're hot.'"

She shook her head. "I swear, Roberts, the more I learn about your gender, the more I think a sperm donor, a good handyman, and a great vibrator is the better way to go."

He let out a bark of laughter. "In defense of my gender, we're not all dogs. As a matter of fact, I happen to be friends and work with a lot of good guys."

"Ooh. Anyone you can set me up with?"

He gave her a long, dark scowl.

She'd take that as a no.

"I just breeched the sex-buddy etiquette again, didn't I?" she asked.

"Quite."

Sidney fought back a laugh, thinking that Special Agent Vaughn Roberts was rather cute when irritated.

Another person joined the group next to them, pushing her closer to Vaughn. Seeing her getting crowded, he took her elbow and slid them farther along the railing, where a concrete pillar blocked them from the rest of the bachelor and bachelorette party.

"So, I'm wondering something," she said.

"Yes, he's a player. Next question."

She poked him in the chest. "That wasn't the question. What I'm wondering is how you think your mother will react when she finds out that Isabelle is pregnant. Obviously, that's one of the main reasons they're going through this whole secret-baby charade."

"Funny, Simon and I were just talking about this the other day." He contemplated her question. "Look, my mother is very traditional in her beliefs. But does she truly believe that her two unmarried adult sons have never had sex? I doubt it. Still, as long as she has no specific evidence to the contrary, she's got plausible deniability." He shrugged. "Once she finds out that Isabelle is pregnant after the wedding, what's she going to say? They'll already be married by then. Plus, she loves Isabelle. Actually, she loves both of you."

Sidney perked up, hearing that. "Really?"

Vaughn nodded. "Every time I talk to her, she wants to know if I've seen you and how you're doing."

"That's so sweet. It's great how close you are with her—you're very lucky to have that kind of relationship."

Vaughn studied her for a moment. "What was your mother like?"

Sidney smiled fondly. "She had a wicked sense of humor. Before she got sick, she and my father used to tease each other all the time. She was a little hot-tempered—I know, the stereotypical redhead—but also very passionate and loving. Isabelle looks just like her. At times, it's almost uncanny."

"And what did you inherit from her?"

She'd never been asked that before. "My mother could be quite sarcastic when she wanted to be."

Vaughn's hand brushed against her cheek. "I think she'd be proud to see how her legacy has been carried out."

It was partially a joke, partially a compliment—or at least, she thought it was—and part something sweet that suddenly made Sidney's chest pull tight. "Thank you."

"You're welcome," he said huskily.

For a moment, he just looked at her.

"*There* you are!"

The voice—Simon's—came from their left. Sidney instantly took a step back, just as an inebriated Simon nearly tackled Vaughn.

"I've been lookin' all over for you," Simon said, red-faced and slurring his words. "I need to tell you somethin'." He threw his arm around Vaughn and squeezed. "I love you, man. This has been the best night ever. I got my friends, I've got my brother, I got my gir—" He blinked and then grinned as he teetered to the right. "Sidney—hey! How are you?"

Sidney smiled. Yep, definitely a happy drunk. "Probably not quite as good as you, but no complaints."

Simon pointed his beer bottle at her. "Isabelle told me about the trick you set up with her drinks. *Genius.*" He threw out his arms and narrowly missed shattering the beer bottle against the concrete pillar. "Best future sister-in-law ever, folks. Right here."

"Aw, thank you."

Vaughn subtly shifted his brother away from the column and out of harm's way.

Simon, still on a roll, gestured between them. "And I gotta say somethin' else. I know, in the beginning, there was some kind of . . . friction between you two."

Vaughn and Sidney exchanged a look.

Simon shook his head emphatically. "Don't know why, and it doesn't matter. What matters is that you put whatever it was aside for Izz and me. And *that* is truly cool." He looked at Vaughn and tapped his bottle to his chest, spilling beer all over his shirt. "You feeling me, bro?"

"I'm feeling you, man."

Simon turned next to Sidney, tapping his chest again. "You feeling me, Sid?"

"I'm feeling you."

"*Awesome.*" He caught sight of someone across the bar. "Dude! You made it!" With a grin, he walked over and threw his arm around a guy wearing a dark blue shirt.

"He is so going to be hurting tomorrow," Vaughn said.

"Eh, Isabelle will take care of him. Knowing those two, she'll probably think he's just *so adorable* when hungover and hurling in her toilet."

Vaughn laughed, and then looked at her for a moment.

"What?" Sidney asked.

He cocked his head. "Come with me."

She raised an eyebrow. "Oh, really?"

"Well, look how fast somebody's dirty little mind goes into the gutter." He took her hand. "Come on. There are some people I'd like you to meet."

Vaughn led her across the terrace toward the main bar, where the two men with whom he'd walked in earlier were having drinks. The taller man with brown hair nudged the blond one with glasses as she and Vaughn approached.

Vaughn stopped in front of them, giving them each a stern look. "Don't make me regret this."

The taller man laughed. "Who? Us?"

Vaughn made the introductions. "Sidney Sinclair, this is Cade Morgan and—"

The blond man jumped in. "Seth Huxley, Vaughn's partner." He shook her hand.

Cade was quick to follow. "It's nice to meet you, Sidney. Vaughn has told us"—he paused, glancing over Sidney's head at Vaughn—"nothing. Nothing at all about you. Who are you, again? Yeah, I don't think she's going to buy that one, Roberts."

"You'll have to excuse us if we seem a little excited," Huxley explained to her. "Vaughn doesn't introduce us to a lot of women." He thought about that. "Or any, really."

Vaughn clapped his hands. "Okay . . . clearly, some people have been drinking and getting loopy while I've been gone." He turned to Sidney. "Ignore them. They don't get out much. Sad, really." He leaned down, speaking in a low tone only she could hear. "And before you ask, they're both taken so, no, I can't set you up with them."

She snapped her fingers. "Damn."

"Just so I know: if I buy you a drink, is that likely to increase or decrease the sassiness?"

"Oh, increase, for sure."

"Good." His voice was low and flirty in her ear. "I look forward to it."

Delicious sparks of heat curled low in her stomach.

He flagged down the bartender and ordered them both drinks. While chatting with his friends, she learned that Cade had just gotten engaged. The vibe among them quickly took on a celebratory tone, heightened by the fact that tonight, apparently, was one of the rare nights that Vaughn and Huxley were unarmed, having left their guns at home—per FBI policy—since they'd known they would be drinking. Then Trish joined them, and this seemed to be even more of a cause for celebration, and suddenly they were all toasting to girls' nights out, and moms' nights out, and special agents' nights out, and the drinks really started flowing.

Somewhere along the way, Sidney felt Vaughn's hand brush against hers, and then he ran his thumb lightly over her fingers and drew teasing circles against her palm. Feeling a little warm, she stepped away from the group and headed off to the restrooms, all private, unisex rooms. She found one that was unoccupied and was just opening the door when she felt Vaughn's hand grab hers, tugging her the rest of the way inside.

He locked the door and instantly was on her, pinning her against the wall as his mouth hungrily claimed hers. She wrapped her arms around his neck and he settled against her, the hard ridge of his erection pressing between her legs.

"Are you drunk?" he asked, his voice thick with desire.

A little, yes, and so was he. "I feel good." When his hand found the slit of her dress and slid up her bare thigh, she moaned. "Keep going."

He slid his hand into her lace underwear and cupped her. "You're wet, Sidney. What have you been thinking about?"

She curled her hands around the lapels of his jacket and gave him a hot, open-mouth kiss in answer.

When he pulled back, his eyes burned into hers. "I'm taking you home tonight."

"What about your seven-day rule?"

His answer was low and gritty.

"It's after midnight. You're mine now."

IN SIDNEY'S BEDROOM, Vaughn watched as she slowly unzipped her dress and let it fall to the floor. She stood before him in her black lace bra, underwear, and heels. He had no doubt that many men at that bar tonight had fantasized about this very image, and now she was all his.

"Lie down on the bed," he said. He was definitely feeling the effects of the alcohol, and he could tell that she was, too. But her eyes still had that saucy, confident gleam that always seemed to be challenging him.

She lay on top of the bed and crossed one high-heeled leg over the other. She gave him a coy look, as if to say she was waiting.

He took off his jacket, uncuffed the buttons on his sleeves, and walked around to the foot of the bed. He grabbed her by the ankles and pulled her toward him, then leaned down to take her mouth in a slow, deep kiss. When he pulled back, he guided her up to a sitting position and knelt between her legs.

"After I take these off," he said, hooking his fingers into her lacy underwear and sliding them down, "you're going to spread your legs. Then you'll put your hands on your knees and hold yourself open for me."

"Will I now?" she asked.

"You will if you want what comes next."

Her eyes flashed, but she did what he asked.

His cock began to throb at the sight of her on the bed, legs spread and naked except for her bra and heels. "You are the hottest thing I've ever seen."

"Vaughn," she said in a husky voice. "Touch me."

He was all too happy to comply. He slid his hands underneath her ass and tilted her hips upward, then gave her a long, teasing lick between her legs.

She moaned, her hands tangling in his hair. He took her hands and put them back on her knees. "Keep yourself spread for me. Show me how much you want my mouth on you."

Then he lowered his head and set about the business of driving her absolutely fucking crazy.

Only when her entire body was shaking, when she was moaning almost nonstop, did he finally relent. "Do you want to come?" He circled his tongue teasingly around her clit.

"*Yes*. Please, yes," she breathed.

He slid a finger inside of her, holding her right along the razor's edge of an orgasm. "I love it when you're like this. So turned on. So sweet." He sucked her clit into his mouth again, knowing that would push her over.

When she cried out and her body clenched tight around his fingers, his cock strained against his zipper from the need to be inside her. He stroked her until she came down, then he stood up and undressed.

"My turn," she said, as he climbed onto the bed.

When he'd gotten settled against the pillows, she straddled him. She smoothed her hands over his chest, and then down his stomach, her fingernails scraping lightly across his skin.

"So it occurs to me . . . that a man like yourself probably has a particular way"—she took his erection in her hand—"he likes his cock sucked."

Sweet Jesus, Mary, and Joseph.

"You can start by wrapping those red lips around me," he said in a guttural voice. "I've been thinking about that all night."

"Hmm. And then what?" she asked, still stroking him. "Should I lick and tease you for a while? Or would you prefer I just take you as deep into my mouth as I can?"

Vaughn suddenly found his throat a little dry. "I vote for all of the above."

"Of course that's what you'd say." She bent down and licked a drop of precum from the tip of his shaft, then ran her tongue along the length. True to her word, she teased him with her lips and tongue, then finally slid him all the way in.

He groaned. "That's so damn good, Sidney . . . suck me

just like that." He tangled his hand in her hair as she used her tongue to caress the underside of his throbbing cock. With one arm tucked behind his head, he watched her, and when she brought him close to the breaking point, he gave into the possessive feeling that had been clawing at him all night. "Look at me, baby. I want to see your eyes."

She looked up, holding his gaze while she continued to slide her mouth over him.

The moment was so goddamn hot, he nearly came right there. "You drive me so fucking wild." He saw the flare of heat in her eyes and touched her cheek. "I need to be inside you. Now."

She slid him out of her mouth and sat up, grabbed his pants off the floor, and tossed him his wallet. Breathing heavily, he rolled the condom on and then watched as she guided the head between her legs and lowered herself all the way onto him.

"Put your hands on my chest." He grabbed her hips and began gliding her forward in time with his thrusts. He started slow at first, until her body adjusted to him. Then he picked up the pace, the two of them moving together as she rode him hard. "You fit me so good," he rasped as he hurtled toward the edge. "Come for me, baby. Let me feel it."

She said his name, her body squeezing tight and milking his cock. His jaw clenched from the force of his orgasm, and he shuddered as wave after wave hit him, until she collapsed on top of his chest and his arms wrapped tight around her, holding her close.

Twenty-four

VAUGHN WOKE UP to the sound of water running.

His head jerked up off the pillow and he blinked, quickly getting his bearings.

Sidney's bed.

No gun on the nightstand.

Sexy, naked redhead missing. Damn.

That covered, he fell back onto the pillow with a groan, feeling as though someone had taken a hammer to his skull.

As his eyes adjusted to the daylight, he noticed something that *was* on the nightstand, presumably set out for his benefit. A bottle of extra-strength Tylenol.

He smiled, thinking it was cute that Sidney had thought of him, then popped two of the pain relievers into his mouth. Slowly, the events of the night came back to him: the things said, the fun times had by all, the even better time had by him and Sidney when they'd gotten back to her place and—hold the phone—had Huxley actually said the words *eye-fucking*?

Clearer evidence that they'd all been good and toasted, there could not be.

The bathroom door opened, and Sidney stepped out with

her hair in a bun and a towel wrapped around her. She smiled when she saw he was awake. "How are you feeling?"

"Like I've been wrung out and hung up to dry." Vaughn watched as she pulled a pair of cream lace underwear out of one of her drawers and let the towel drop to the floor.

He was quickly getting better.

Sidney slid on her underwear and a bra, then pulled her hair out of the bun and let it tumble over her shoulders in auburn waves. He tucked his hands behind his head, thinking he could watch that move all day.

"I'm making a Starbucks run," she said. "What do you want?"

"You are a *goddess*. I'll take a venti of their dark roast."

She pulled on a pair of jeans and winced.

"Everything okay?" he asked.

"Let's just say, I woke up with scruff burn in some very interesting places."

He laughed, rubbing his unshaven jaw as he got out of bed. "Oops." He came up behind her and kissed her on the neck. "Mind if I use your shower while you're gone?"

"Uh . . . no. Not at all."

Thinking maybe he'd heard her hesitate, he tilted his head and saw that she was looking at their reflection in the mirror over the dresser.

A split second after their eyes met in the glass, she smiled. "So. Starbucks." She slid out from his arms. "I'll be back." She headed for the bedroom door.

"A shirt might be good."

"Right." She turned around. Wasting no time, she grabbed a shirt out of her closet—not even pausing to see which one— and walked out of the room, shoving the shirt over her head as she nearly flew toward the stairs.

Vaughn watched her go, thinking that was the fastest he'd ever seen Sidney Sinclair move.

Apparently somebody really needed her Starbucks.

AS SIDNEY HURRIED down the stairs, she told herself to chill out.

So, for one teeny tiny moment while looking at her and Vaughn's reflection in the mirror, she'd thought they looked cute together. So what? He was a very attractive man; he'd look cute standing next to a toaster. That didn't mean she was having relationship-type thoughts about the guy—because she definitely knew better than that.

Vaughn was the guy who picked up random women in coffee shops. The guy who had a seven-day rule in order to avoid emotional entanglements, the guy who hadn't had a serious relationship in years.

He was *not* a Mr. Right.

She'd made her pledge, and she was sticking to it. No more commitment-phobic men, no more player types, no more guys with issues or drama or whatever. She wanted someone who was solid and steady, someone who knew without any doubt that he was ready to go the distance.

Someone nice like Trish's husband, Sidney mused, while grabbing her keys off the console table for the three-block walk to Starbucks. She opened her front door. *Or Simon.*

Simon.

As in, the man who was walking up her front steps with Isabelle.

Sidney's stomach dropped as her mind actually processed that.

Isabelle and Simon—here.

Vaughn in the shower.

Oh.

Shit.

"Perfect timing—I'm about to explode," Isabelle said, her words as rushed as her footsteps. "I've had to pee since we left Starbucks."

Before Sidney knew what was happening, her sister barreled right past her and ran into the house toward the first-floor powder room.

No.

Simon, who wore sunglasses, gestured with the tray of drinks and paper bag he carried. "Isabelle and I wanted to say thank you for last night." He smiled. "We brought coffee and apple fritters."

"That's so sweet of you," Sidney managed.

This couldn't be happening. If Isabelle and Simon discovered Vaughn inside her house—in her *shower*, no less—it would look like the two of them were . . . doing exactly what they were, in fact, doing.

With that in mind, she held out a hand as Simon tried to step inside her place. "Hey, I know—it's such a nice day, why don't we stay out here and enjoy our coffee and apple fritters al fresco?"

Simon made a face. "Too much sunlight." He brushed past her, entering the house. "I don't think I've been this hungover since college." He headed in the direction of her kitchen.

Shit, shit, shit.

Sidney followed, wondering if there was any way she could at least hustle them onto her back terrace if she promised Simon a spot in the shade—or hell, a damn parasol. Anything to get them *out*.

Isabelle stepped out of the powder room and joined them in the kitchen. "Much better. Apparently, I've moved out of the nausea-and-vomiting phase of this pregnancy and into the peeing-every-half-hour phase."

"It could just be all the juice you drank last night," Simon said, grabbing an apple fritter out of the bag and taking a bite.

"Hey, those are for Sidney." Isabelle came over and gave her a hug. "I didn't get a chance to talk to you before we left the bar, since somebody"—she looked pointedly at Simon—"felt sick after deciding it would be a good idea to smoke a cigar for the first time last night."

"Word to the wise. Don't inhale, just taste," Simon told Sidney.

Out of the corner of her eye, Sidney noticed Vaughn's suit jacket hanging over the back of one of the barstools. "You know, actually, I was just on my way ou—"

Simon spoke at the same time, teasing Isabelle. "Besides, I figured that I needed to start practicing for when the baby comes. Isn't that what I'm supposed to do: hang out in the delivery room smoking cigars, while you do all the womanly stuff?"

"I hate to break it to you, buddy, but you are going to be right next to me for every moment of *all* the stuff—womanly, or otherwise," Isabelle said.

Sidney clapped her hands. "So. I can see you two are

raring up for some sort of cute play-fight. And it would be totes adorbs to watch, I'm sure. But there's this appointment that I'm very late for, so maybe I could call you later, Izz?"

"Huh. I don't think you can pull off a totes adorbs," Simon said, studying her.

Seriously.

"Is your shower running?" Isabelle suddenly asked. She looked up at the ceiling, which was directly below the master bathroom.

Think, Sinclair.

Sidney thunked her head. "Look at that. That's how late I am for this appointment. I was rushing around so much I even forgot to turn the shower off."

Of course, that had to be the moment Isabelle noticed Vaughn's jacket.

She gasped and stalked around the counter. "There's someone here." She picked up the jacket and held it up. "A *male* someone." Isabelle paused, looking a little hurt. "You didn't tell me you were dating anyone."

"Well, well, well, Miss Sneaky," Simon said, with a grin. "You were trying to rush us out of here before we could meet the guy, weren't you?"

"Who is he?" Isabelle wanted to know. "How come I don't know anything about him?"

Simon cocked his head, staring at the jacket. "What's really funny is that jacket looks a lot like the one—" He stopped, his mouth falling open. "Oh. My. God." He looked at Sidney, and then peered up at the ceiling.

He stormed out of the kitchen and up the stairs.

Sidney closed her eyes, bracing herself for the inevitable.

Seconds later, they heard the bathroom door open. Simon's voice thundered down the stairs. "Oh. My. God."

"Um, did he just walk in on a complete stranger taking a shower?" Isabelle asked.

"Not . . . exactly."

Simon strode back into the kitchen. "Yep. It's my brother."

Isabelle blinked. "What?" She turned to Sidney. "Vaughn's here? You slept with *Vaughn*?"

"By any chance would you believe we just went for a morning run together?" Sidney asked, going for a smile.

Judging from their expressions, they would not.

"It's not a big deal," she told them.

Isabelle pointed accusingly. "Amanda told me she thought you two were acting flirty last night."

Sidney scoffed. "*Pfft*. Amanda. What does she know?" Aside from the fact that she was, in this instance, dead-on-balls correct.

Simon pointed, too. "I remember now! You guys were huddled in that alcove when I came over to talk to Vaughn."

"And that didn't strike you as suspicious?" Isabelle asked him.

"Did you see me last night? I couldn't even *say* 'suspicious,'" Simon told her.

They both fell silent when the shower turned off upstairs. There was the sound of footsteps against the hardwood floors, and then everything went briefly quiet until there were more footsteps—this time heading down the stairs.

With damp hair, Vaughn walked into the kitchen while pulling on his shirt. Thankfully, he at least had pants on. "Apparently we have visitors this morning," he said, looking slightly amused.

"We? You two are a *we*?" Isabelle asked.

"We are definitely *not* a 'we,'" Sidney said.

"Can I have a word with you outside, *brother*?" Simon asked Vaughn.

Vaughn turned to Sidney. "That's Man-Speak for 'You're in some seriously deep shit.'"

AFTER VAUGHN AND Simon stepped out into the courtyard, Sidney took a seat next to Isabelle at the counter. "You probably have a few questions."

"You think?" Isabelle asked. "How long has this been going on?"

It was just a drunken one-night stand. The lie hovered on

the tip of Sidney's tongue for several moments. "The first time we hooked up was the night you had surgery."

"I see. And how many times have you hooked up since then?"

"In our defense, you and Simon keep finding ways to throw us together. This wedding is like a damn pressure cooker." Sidney saw her sister waiting. "Two more times. Oh, and we kissed up in Wisconsin. But that's it."

Isabelle blinked. "At their parents' house? Where was I?"

"I don't know, probably throwing up somewhere." When Sidney saw Isabelle make a face, she decided to come clean. "You were looking at photo albums with Mrs. Roberts. I went outside to give Simon and Vaughn some bottled waters, and I just . . . needed a break from all the wedding stuff. And also from seeing you bond with Kathleen and being in that place that *I* was supposed to be in. So I took a walk and Vaughn followed me and we started arguing and, I don't know . . . somehow we ended up kissing."

Isabelle cocked her head with a concerned expression, momentarily ignoring the part about Vaughn. "Why didn't you tell me that all the wedding stuff was bothering you?"

"You're doing the head-tilt."

"Come on, Sid. It's me."

Sidney sighed. "I didn't say anything because I don't want to spoil this for you. This wedding isn't about me, Izz, it's about you. And I guess I also didn't say anything, because I don't *want* to be bothered by this stuff. Brody and I split up over eight months ago. I need to move on with things—which is exactly what I'm trying to do."

"I just wish you'd told me about all this." Isabelle nodded in the direction of the yard. "Including Vaughn."

"I thought it would be weird for you and Simon to know that we'd hooked up, especially since it's just a casual thing." Sidney could hear the men talking outside but ignored it, focusing instead on what was happening between her and her sister. "I really hope this doesn't make things weird between us. You know I would never want that, Izz."

"I know." Isabelle reached over and squeezed Sidney's

hand. "And I know that lately I've been swept up in all the wedding and baby chaos. Everything's changing, but one thing will always stay the same, Sid: you and me."

Sidney smiled, repeating their mantra from when they were younger. "Sinclair Sisters forever, right?"

Isabelle smiled back, her eyes misty. "Always." She reached forward and hugged Sidney tight, then pulled back and wiped her eyes. "Now. About this thing with Vaughn."

"Shoot. I was really hoping you'd forgotten about that part."

"Apparently I have a lot of catching up to do. The last time you and I talked about Vaughn, I was worried you didn't even like him," Isabelle said.

"Okay, so here's the part where I have to come clean about something," Sidney said. "Vaughn and I had actually met before we had dinner with you and Simon. It was completely random: that evening, we both went to the same coffee shop beforehand. I was there on a blind date and when the other guy left, Vaughn hit on me."

"You're kidding." Isabelle thought about that, then folded her arms across her chest. "So basically, what you're telling me is that you and Vaughn have been lying to me and Simon from day one."

" 'Lying' is such a strong word. I'd prefer to say, 'omitting the truth.' " She saw Isabelle open her mouth to respond. "Kind of like what you and Simon are doing with this pregnancy."

Isabelle closed her mouth. Point taken. "Okay. But is there anything else you're 'omitting,' Sid? You say you've slept with Vaughn a few times now. He spent the night, he uses your shower . . . is it possible, maybe, this is turning into something more than a casual fling?"

Sidney paused for a split second, then cycled through Vaughn's greatest hits in her head.

I'm always upfront about the fact that I'm not looking for a long-term commitment.

I don't have sex with the same woman twice in one week. That starts to get too couple-y.

I realized it's fun to date lots and lots of women.

The pragmatic woman in her knew there could only be one answer to Isabelle's question.

MEANWHILE, OUT IN the courtyard, Simon laid into Vaughn the moment the patio door closed.

He threw out his hands. "Sidney? Really?"

"Come on," Vaughn said. "It's not *that* big of a deal."

"Not that big of a deal? You slept with my fiancée's sister. So now, when you do what you always do after sleeping with a woman—meaning nothing—and things get awkward between you and Sidney, *next* they'll get awkward between you and Isabelle. And then awkward between you and me, and maybe even me and Isabelle. There'll be this whole chain of awkwardness that *I* will have to deal with because you couldn't keep your goddamn dick in your pants."

"A little louder, Simon. I'm not sure the people one block over could hear you." He led Simon away from the patio door, around the side of the townhome where Sidney and Isabelle couldn't see them.

"Look, maybe I should've said something," Vaughn said. "But the reason I didn't was because I didn't want you freaking out about this. Everything is fine with Sidney. Nothing is going to get awkward."

"How could you possibly know that?" Simon demanded.

"Well, because I've been sleeping with her for the past three weeks and it hasn't gotten awkward yet. Far from it."

"What?" Simon threw his hands out again. "Three weeks?"

"Oh . . . right. You'd probably been thinking this was just a drunk one-night-stand thing." Vaughn pretended to muse over this. "Yeah, that definitely would've played off a little better. I'll have to remember that for the next future sister-in-law of yours that I sleep with."

Simon just stared at him.

Tough crowd.

"Come on, Simon, don't you think—"

"*Shh.*" Standing closer to the house, Simon shushed him. He pointed to the chest-high window about a foot behind them, which Vaughn realized was the window above Sidney's kitchen sink.

"I can hear the girls talking," Simon whispered. He took a step closer to listen.

"You know, if it'll help, I could always sneak a bug into Sidney's sugar jar," Vaughn said dryly.

Simon gave him a look—*ha, ha*—then pointed to the window, still whispering. "I want to see how much trouble you're in with my future wife, asshole." He crept a few inches closer, then waited. He looked at Vaughn. "They're talking about you."

"No, really?"

Simon listened for another moment, then narrowed his eyes at Vaughn. "You met Sidney at a coffee shop?" he whispered. "*This* is how I find that out?"

So, apparently, they were coming clean about that now. Vaughn ducked and moved to the opposite side of the window, wondering what other secrets Sidney was spilling.

He heard Isabelle speaking.

"So basically, what you're telling me is that you and Vaughn have been lying to me and Simon from day one."

Across the window, Simon nodded emphatically in agreement. *Exactly.*

"'Lying' is such a strong word," Sidney said. "I'd prefer to say, 'omitting the truth.' Kind of like what you and Simon are doing with this pregnancy."

Vaughn smirked at Simon. *Take that.*

"Okay. But is there anything else you're 'omitting,' Sid? You say you've slept with Vaughn a few times now. He spent the night, he uses your shower . . . is it possible, maybe, this is turning into something more than a casual fling?"

Vaughn went still, waiting for Sidney's answer.

"Give me some credit, Izz. You know I'm smart enough not to fall for a guy like *Vaughn*."

Vaughn stared at the window for a moment.

Very aware that his brother's eyes were on him, he looked over and shrugged. "See? Told you there was nothing to worry about."

Twenty-five

MONDAY AFTERNOON, VAUGHN stormed into the FBI office with an ax to grind.

While out grabbing a quick sandwich for lunch, he'd received an e-mail from Cade who, apparently, had dropped by the FBI building for a witness interview in another case and wanted to "talk" to Vaughn while there.

After getting off the elevator, Vaughn strode through the hallway and rounded the corner where his cubicle was located. He spotted Cade, chatting with Huxley at the cubicle across from Vaughn's.

"Hey, we were just talking about you," Cade said.

Vaughn folded his arms across his chest, getting right down to it. "Entrapment? We really need to have a conversation about this?"

Cade looked him over, as if sensing his mood. "You're pissed about my e-mail? I just said I wanted to talk."

"*Pritchett* approached Batista," Vaughn emphasized. "He told Batista about his group of cops who can transport anything into the city without getting busted. He asked Batista if he could hook him up with anyone who might be interested. How is that entrapment?"

"I didn't say it was," Cade answered calmly. "What I said was that in a case where the FBI is acting undercover as both the buyer and the seller of the illegal goods, we need to make sure that we have strong evidence of predisposition."

Vaughn scoffed. Generally, he liked working with the prosecutors at the U.S. Attorney's Office. He really did. And on a personal note, he and Cade had been good friends for years and he respected the hell out of the guy. But sometimes, occasionally, the prosecutors got so wrapped up in being lawyers and worrying about the big picture that they forgot that it was the *agents* working in the field everyday, putting their asses on the line to get the prosecutors the evidence they needed to do their jobs. "And how is Batista's testimony not strong first-hand evidence of that?"

"I'm just looking at this through my trial lens," Cade said. "Batista is a convicted felon. I'd rather not hang my entire rebuttal to any possible entrapment defense solely on his testimony. So, the more we can get Pritchett talking on the record about the other jobs they've done, the better."

Huxley jumped in here. "Which, as I was just explaining to Cade, I believe we have covered," he said to Vaughn. "I told him how chatty Pritchett's been and how much you've been able to draw out of him during your meetings."

"That's all I needed to hear," Cade said. "I'm just making sure we have our *i*'s dotted and our *t*'s crossed at this point so that we don't have a bigger problem later."

Well . . . fine. Vaughn supposed that didn't sound entirely irrational. "Good. Glad we got that straight," he said grumpily.

Now that the dust had settled, Cade looked him over. "Sounds like somebody skipped his skinny vanilla latte this afternoon. Everything okay?"

Vaughn shrugged this off. "Sure, everything's fine." He took a seat in his desk chair.

"So I shared with Addison the intel Sidney gave us about this charming, Mayberry-like small town you're from," Huxley said. "She was as shocked as Cade and I."

On Saturday night, when they'd all been buzzed, Sidney had entertained the group with stories about Apple Canyon—even getting several *oohs* and *ahhs* when she'd produced photographic evidence of the *actual key* she'd been given at the bed-and-breakfast. Though his memory was a little fuzzy about a few things, Vaughn distinctly remembered how much they'd all laughed that night. And also how some warm, unfamiliar feeling had settled deep in his chest, seeing her getting along so well with his friends.

"I told Brooke the same story," Cade said. "She suggested that the six of us get together for dinner some t—"

Vaughn held up his hand, cutting him off. "I think we all need to slow down. Sidney and I aren't doing a couples dinner or whatever with you guys. For starters, we're not a couple."

Huxley looked surprised by this. "You two sure seemed pretty friendly on Saturday night."

Vaughn shrugged. "I'm not saying I don't like her. She's great. We have a lot of fun together. But this is just a short-term deal between us—and believe me, if she were here right now, she would tell you the exact same thing."

Having nothing else to say about that, he turned around to face his computer and got back to work.

TUESDAY MORNING, SIDNEY had just finished a conference call with the consulting firm, wrapping up a few last-minute details regarding the compensation package she planned to offer Karen if the interview went well, when her secretary buzzed her.

"Your father called while you were on the other line," Darnell said.

Ah, good—Sidney had been waiting for him to call her back. She'd left him a message yesterday, saying that she'd like to drop by the house to go through her mother's wedding dress and accessories, which her father had been keeping in the attic. She wanted to do something special for Isabelle's "something old," and thought that incorporating something their mother had worn on her wedding day would be perfect.

She quickly called him back on his cell phone, wanting to check this item off her to-do list before her interview with Karen.

"I'm afraid I'm not going to be much help," her father said when he answered, immediately getting right down to it.

She knew her father was out of town, having taken a couple days off work to go golfing with some friends in Pebble Beach. Presumably, he'd misunderstood the nature of her request. "Oh, I don't need you to go through the stuff. I just wanted to check when it would be convenient for me to come by the house. If I drop by tomorrow evening, will Jenny be around to let me in?"

"Sidney . . . I don't have any of your mother's wedding things."

"Sure, you do." When she was a kid, she had often sneaked up into the attic to play dress up in her mother's wedding gown, veil, and shoes. "Her dress and everything else she wore is in the attic, in that old wardrobe we inherited from Grandma."

"The wardrobe's gone, along with everything inside. Back when Liza redecorated the house, she cleared everything out of the attic to make room for the furniture we were no longer using. I asked Jenny to check yesterday after you called and, well, it looks like your mother's old stuff got lost in the shuffle." Her father sounded contrite. "I'm sorry."

Sidney stared out her office window, focusing on a tour boat gliding along the Chicago River as she processed this information.

Her mother's wedding dress had gotten "lost in the shuffle" when Wife Number Three had gone on some stupid shabby-chic design overhaul, undoubtedly to scour the house of all signs of Wife Number Two. It was so exactly the kind of response she expected from her father, she didn't know why she was surprised.

Yet still, she had to fight back the burning in her eyes. And something in her snapped. "Of course that's what happened. Thanks, Dad."

He paused, as if surprised by her comment. "It's not my fault, Sidney. I didn't even—"

Yeah, yeah. She cut off the excuses. "Don't worry about it, Dad. I'll come up with something else for Isabelle. I have to get going—I need to finish preparing for an interview."

She said a quick good-bye, then stared at the phone after hanging up. Drawing on her three years of expensive New York therapy, she reminded herself that not everyone had a close relationship with their parents—and that she was *okay* with that.

Sure.

She took a deep breath, collecting herself and quelling her disappointment. Then she straightened up in her chair and returned to the task at hand.

BY THE TIME they got to the pasta course at Vivere, a contemporary Italian restaurant in the heart of downtown, Sidney felt confident that she'd found Vitamin Boutique's new CEO.

"I have to admit, I was really excited to get Gabe's call," Karen said. "Ever since I heard that your firm bought Vitamin Boutique, I've been eager to see who you'd bring on board."

Sidney eased back in her chair, curious about something. "Here's my question: with the offer from PetSmart already in your pocket, what is it about this opportunity that has you interested enough to interview with us on such short notice?"

The fifty-two-year-old executive nodded at the question, looking polished and confident in her gray skirt suit. "The PetSmart position would be great, don't get me wrong. But with Vitamin Boutique, I see a potential for expansion that's just . . . exciting," she said, speaking animatedly. "The company has a strong brand and loyal customer base here in the Midwest. To achieve the kind of growth your fund will want to see in five to seven years, you need someone who will lead the way in expanding and capitalizing on that base. I'm completely sold on your vision for the company, Sidney. I think Vitamin Boutique can be a nationwide retailer, and I'd be thrilled to be part of the team that makes that happen."

Sidney smiled, liking Karen's enthusiasm. They got down to brass tacks and outlined the terms of the compensation package she and the consultants had come up with. As expected, there were a few minor points that needed to be negotiated, but by the time dessert had arrived, they'd reached a deal.

"Welcome aboard," Sidney said as she shook her new CEO's hand.

They left the restaurant and began walking back to her office, which was only a few blocks away. It was a gorgeous summer afternoon, the type of day when Chicagoans flocked outside and enjoyed living in such a vibrant, charismatic city. Having been focused on the business side of things all morning, she and Karen chatted amiably about more personal topics.

"It's actually a perfect time for me to move," Karen said. "My youngest—my son—just went off to college, so my husband and I are officially empty nesters." They stopped at a street corner and waited for the light to change. "Do you have children?"

"No," Sidney said, ignoring the ticking sound coming from her biological clock. "Where does your son go to school?"

As Karen answered, Sidney noticed that a man waiting with them at the street corner—tall and attractive with sandy-blond hair, probably in his early thirties—was looking over at her. He seemed familiar, but she couldn't quite place him.

He smiled. "Sidney, right?" He stepped around the people between them and held out his hand. "Tyler Roland. We met briefly a few months ago, at Morton's. You were having lunch with Michael Hannigan, and I stopped by the table to say hello."

Now she remembered. "That's right. That was the day I flew in for my interview. Good memory," she said, impressed that he'd recalled her name.

He gestured. "So you're obviously here in Chicago. I take it that means your interview with Michael's firm went well? And . . . if it didn't, I'm going to feel real awkward for having just asked that question."

She laughed. "You're safe. I'm a director there now. Speaking of which," she turned, to make the introductions. "Karen Wetzel, Tyler Roland."

Karen and Tyler exchanged hellos. The light turned and the three of them crossed the street.

"So if I remember correctly, you and Michael are family friends?" Sidney asked him.

He nodded. "Our parents have known each other for years. Plus, he and I play squash together—even though he's terrible."

"Really?"

He grinned. "No. But tell him I said it, anyway. He's so competitive—it'll drive him nuts."

They slowed down after reaching the corner. "I'm heading this way. Off to court," Tyler said, pointing south. "You?"

Sidney pointed north. "This way."

"Well, then, it was really nice running into you again. Sidney . . . ?" Tyler cocked his head questioningly.

"Sinclair."

"Sidney Sinclair. I like that." He held her gaze for a moment, then said good-bye to her and Karen.

"He seems nice," Karen said, as they walked in the opposite direction.

Sidney nodded. "Yes, he does."

THURSDAY MORNING, SIDNEY heard a knock at her office door. She looked over and saw Michael standing in the doorway, holding a newspaper.

"I see we made the *Journal* this morning," he said, stepping inside and taking a seat at her desk. There'd been an article discussing the installation of Karen Wetzel as the new CEO of Vitamin Boutique, in which they'd described the firm's acquisition of the company to be "a deal to watch."

"I think Karen's going to be a great fit," Sidney said. They talked shop for a while, and she shared with Michael the next steps she planned to take with Vitamin Boutique, as well as a new company she was eying as a potential acquisition.

"I know I speak for the entire investment committee when I say how impressed we've been with your leadership and direction of this fund. Of course, I've been taking full credit for this as the person who recruited you," Michael joked.

Sidney chuckled. "I bet you have."

Michael tapped the arms of the chair with his hands. "There's another reason I dropped by this morning. Apparently you ran into my friend Tyler the other day?"

In the flurry of hiring Karen, Sidney had completely forgotten about that. "Oh, yes. He wanted me to tell you that you're terrible at squash."

"That's interesting, considering I just wiped the floor with him yesterday." Michael pulled something out of the pocket of his suit jacket. "When we were leaving the gym, he asked me to give you this."

He handed her a business card.

"I guess you made something of an impression on him. He said he wanted to give you his card the other day, but he sensed you might be in the middle of a business lunch and didn't think it was appropriate." Before she could say anything, Michael held up his hand. "Look, I don't know if you're single, and, frankly, I don't need to know. Call him, e-mail him, or don't. I'm just a messenger here—the rest is up to you."

Michael stood up to head out, but paused in the doorway. "He also said I'm supposed to tell you that he's a good guy." He held up his hands. "That's it. I swear, I'm out of this now."

Sidney liked working with Michael, and respected his opinion quite a bit. "And what do you say? *Is* he a good guy?"

Michael gave her a slight smile, as if to say that this was self-evident. "I wouldn't have given you the card if he wasn't."

Sidney stared down at the card after he left. She flipped it over and saw that Tyler had written her a message.

Maybe next time we can meet for more than two minutes?

Well, this was . . . unexpected. A quick Google search showed that he was a partner at Kendall & Jameson, a successful boutique labor and employment law firm. Which meant she could check off that box already: he was settled in his career. But beyond that, this Tyler guy came with a "recommended" label; he'd been referred by someone she trusted.

Perhaps she'd just been handed her first real lead in the search for Mr. Right.

Twenty-six

WITH FRIDAY CAME the end of a long workweek for Vaughn.

He and Huxley had picked up a new assignment, after receiving a tip from a Chicago nightclub owner who claimed that the head of the city code compliance department had demanded from him a cash payoff in exchange for not enforcing a large fine for what the club owner insisted was a bogus code violation. As part of the investigation, the plan was that an undercover agent would pose as the club's manager, and together he and the owner would make the payoff to the head inspector. Unfortunately, Vaughn was already working undercover in the Pritchett investigation, and since agents worked hard not to be involved in multiple UC roles at the same time, they had decided that Huxley would pose as the nightclub's manager—the younger agent's first time taking on a speaking undercover role after a botched attempt three years ago that had been stymied by a poorly timed case of the stomach flu.

To put it mildly, Huxley was stoked.

The investigation had gotten a little more intense this afternoon, when two different code inspectors had showed up at the nightclub to "remind" the owner of his (bogus) violation and also to reiterate that they had the authority to shut down his club at any time. That had put everything on fast-forward, and Vaughn had spent the rest of his day assisting Huxley in pulling together his undercover legend and getting everything set up with the tech team and the backup squad so that they could meet with the city inspector tomorrow for the payoff.

After that, he and Huxley had met Cade for their workout. With the triathlon only three weeks away, their workouts had intensified—today they'd swum for thirty minutes, had run for forty-five, and then had lifted weights for an hour. Vaughn had walked out of the FBI gym tired and ready to call it a night.

Admittedly, he'd been feeling a little off all week. He couldn't quite put his finger on what was bothering him, he just felt . . . irritated. Unsettled. He looked forward to an evening alone, so he could shake off whatever his problem was, reset, and get back on his game.

But when he was driving home, he received a text message that changed all that.

One word from Sidney.

HELP.

SIDNEY OPENED HER front door and found six-foot-one, nearly two hundred pounds of pissed-off FBI agent glaring at her.

"Never, *ever* do that again," Vaughn said.

"Okay, okay. I told you—I'm sleep-deprived. I wasn't thinking. Sheesh," And, point of fact, she'd already apologized after his first lecture.

Yes, she'd screwed up. She'd texted Vaughn *Help*, and then had heard her teakettle whistling on the stove. She'd left her phone in the bedroom and had headed downstairs into the kitchen—admittedly, in hindsight this was absentminded, but, *hello*, she was operating on about an hour's worth of sleep here—and by the time she'd sliced her fresh lemon for the tea, then had noticed her wilting flowers outside and had gone out to water them, and *then* had returned upstairs, she'd discovered that her text message had caused a bit of a hullabaloo with Vaughn, who had been trying to reach her.

"I'd already called in your number to the command room, so I could track you down by your cell phone," he said, stepping inside her house.

"Is that even legal?"

He glared again.

Sidney smiled sweetly. "What I meant to say was, thank you, Agent Roberts. I'm so appreciative of your concern for my well-being."

Vaughn stepped closer, putting one hand on the small of her back as he stared down into her eyes. "Just don't scare me like that again, Sinclair. Understood?"

Something about the seriousness on his face—such an uncharacteristic look for him—put a warm feeling in her stomach. "Understood," she said, her voice suddenly husky.

Then there it was, a loud double *beep* at the top of the stairs, right outside her bedroom.

She rested her forehead against Vaughn's chest and groaned. "Please. Just make it stop."

Her upstairs smoke alarm had started chirping last night around midnight, going off about every ten minutes. She assumed that it needed a new battery, so she'd thrown on a pair of jeans and had walked to a 24-hour convenience store a few blocks away. She'd bought a couple of 9V batteries, then had come home and pulled out her handy-dandy stepladder. The problem was, she couldn't get the damn casing off. Granted, she didn't have the best grip, because the ceilings in her turn-of-the-century brownstone were high and she'd had to stand on her tiptoes, but the stupid thing wouldn't budge. Then it had stopped around five A.M., apparently just to mock her, and she'd gone off to work thinking maybe she was in the clear. But nope—the *beep-beep* had started up again this evening, after she'd changed out of her work clothes and had just been getting ready to settle in with her parents' wedding albums and a nice cup of chamomile tea.

In her hour of need, she'd texted Vaughn.

"You know, those cases pretty much just pop right off," he told her.

Yes, thank you, she was aware that this was *supposed* to be how things worked. She'd been up at two A.M. last night, Googling the problem and watching umpteen videos with stupid smiling men on stepladders who'd explained how to change the battery on a smoke detector. But none of the stupid smiling men—not a one—had said what to do in the apparently unlikely event that the case did not, in fact, "just pop right off."

"It's stuck," she said.

"Did you turn it the correct way?" he asked. "A good way to remember is—"

"—if you 'righty-tighty, lefty-loosey' me right now, Roberts, I swear I will bite you again. The thing is *stuck*."

Grinning, he chucked her under the chin. "All right. I'll check it out."

Vaughn followed her upstairs, where her stepladder sat underneath the smoke detector outside her bedroom. He climbed up, reached for the smoke detector, and gave it a twist.

Nothing.

"It's stuck," he said, frowning.

She snorted. "Not exactly a newsflash, buddy." When he stared down at her, she smiled and touched his knee. "And what I meant by that was, thank you *so* much for rushing over here to help me figure out this mystery."

"So saucy," he said, shaking his head. He turned back to the smoke detector and scrutinized it for a moment. "Ah. There's the problem. Whoever painted your ceiling was sloppy—they painted over the rim of this thing and that probably sealed it shut."

He reached up and twisted again, harder—Sidney was satisfied to see that even Captain America here had to put some effort into the task—and then it popped off.

"Thank. God." She hurried into her bedroom and grabbed one of the new 9V batteries off her dresser. She handed it to Vaughn, who changed it out for the old battery, twisted the casing back on, and then climbed down the ladder.

"That should do it, but I'll stick around to make sure," he

said. "We might as well do the downstairs smoke detector, too. Who knows the last time the previous owners changed it."

He grabbed her stepladder and carried it downstairs, providing Sidney a nice opportunity to admire the way his tall, leanly muscular frame filled out his suit. It wasn't even that well-cut of a suit—*mmm*, the things she could do with this man in the men's department at Barneys—but it didn't matter. Knowing what was underneath the clothes, and just seeing him be so . . . capable, was enough to have her giving him a long once-over.

Downstairs, they discovered that the smoke detector there was sealed with paint, too. With a hard twist, Vaughn got it open.

"I was planning to order a pizza tonight," Sidney said, while throwing away the old batteries. "If you don't have any plans, you're welcome to stay—my treat as a thank-you." She smiled innocently. "I even promise to keep my hands to myself if you're worried about your seven-day rule."

"I've realized the seven-day rule is superfluous with you," he said, sounding wry.

She wasn't sure what to make of that answer. "So that's a . . . yes?"

"As long as you don't mind me getting comfortable. Long day at work." He took off his jacket and threw it over the back of one of her counter stools, yanked off his tie, and then loosened the buttons at his neck.

Keep going.

Sidney cleared her throat. "What do you like on your pizza?"

She placed their order and then opened a bottle of chianti. "You said you had a long day at work? How so?" She poured them each a glass.

"Huxley and I picked up a new investigation. We have to move fast with this one, so there was a lot of hustling to make sure everything is set."

"You can work undercover in two different cases at the same time?"

As they moved into the living room, he explained that his partner would be handling the undercover work this time.

That led to an amusing story about how Huxley and his fian-cée, also a special agent, had first gotten together after pretending to be a couple during a sting operation that had taken place at a restaurant.

He took a seat on the couch and set his wineglass on the table. "What are these?"

"Oh. My parents' wedding albums." She'd forgotten she'd left them out. "I was planning to look through them tonight. I've been thinking about what to do for Isabelle's 'something old.' You know, because brides are supposed to have 'something old, something new, something borrowed, something blue.' I thought it would be nice if she could have something that our mother wore on *her* wedding day. Unfortunately, I found out this week that one of my father's ex-wives pitched all my mom's wedding things. Supposedly, it was an accident—I guess with the high turnover of wives in that house, something was bound to get lost in the shuffle." She shook her head in both frustration and disappointment. Then she managed a half-smile at Vaughn. "I'm just a little ticked off about that, if you can't tell."

"Understandably so."

She sighed. "Anyway . . . now I'm thinking that I'll put an old photo of our mom in a locket, and Isabelle can wear that instead. Or carry it in her purse." She shrugged. "It's not the best idea, but it's all I could come up with."

"I'm sure your sister will think it's great." Vaughn pointed to the albums. "Can I take a look?"

The question surprised her. "Of course."

He picked up one of the albums and leaned back against the couch. Sidney scooted closer to him as he opened it to the first page, a photograph of her mother standing in front of a window while looking down at her bouquet.

Sidney smiled nostalgically. "I used to look at these albums all the time when I was younger, but I haven't seen them for years."

Vaughn turned the page to a candid shot of her mother laughing with one of her bridesmaids. "You're right. Isabelle does look a lot like her. But you have her smile." He pointed.

"I can practically hear her making some dry quip to this woman here as the photographer snapped the shot."

"That was her best friend, Ginny Gastel," Sidney said. "And you're probably right. I remember her and my mother laughing a lot whenever they were together."

Vaughn turned the page to a photograph of Sidney's father lined up with his groomsmen. He grinned at the sight of the men dressed in '70s gray tuxedoes with ruffled shirts. "Looking slick, Mr. Sinclair."

"Now *that* outfit I could handle being accidentally misplaced," Sidney said.

Vaughn pointed to the photo on the next page. "I'm guessing these are your grandparents? Will I be meeting any of them at the wedding?"

They went through both albums, with Sidney next to him on the couch, legs tucked underneath her. The pizza came just as they were winding down, and they decided to eat in the living room while watching some action movie that made Vaughn roll his eyes at the portrayal of the FBI characters.

"Come on. Where is his backup squad?" he said to the TV.

Sidney was curled up on the couch, feeling quite cozy after those two glasses of wine. Her lack of sleep the previous night was definitely catching up with her. "Do you always have backup?" she asked, leaning her head against him.

He moved his arm so that she could rest against his chest. "All the time. The FBI loves overwhelming people with manpower and firepower."

"Good." In her drowsy state, this suddenly was very important to her, knowing that he was as safe as possible while doing his extraspecial agent thing.

Her eyes felt heavy, so she decided to shut them for just a teeny tiny moment. The last thing she remembered was feeling Vaughn's fingers stroking up and down on her arm in a light, soothing caress.

A FEW MINUTES after Vaughn felt Sidney's body relax against his chest, she shifted and got even more comfortable, using his thigh as a pillow. He brushed her hair off her face, smoothing his fingers over the long, coppery strands.

The movie only had about ten minutes left. When it was over, Vaughn turned off the television, which caused Sidney to stir. She turned onto her back, her head still resting on his leg, and looked up at him.

She reached up and sunk her fingers into the back of his hair. "Stay tonight."

Looking down at her, Vaughn couldn't think of one reason why he shouldn't. Being with her tonight had eased that irritated, unsettled feeling he'd had all week. "As long as you promise that your crazy future brother-in-law isn't going to show up and start yelling at me again tomorrow morning."

She laughed at that, and then they both laughed even harder when Vaughn did his *Oh-My-God* impression of Simon walking in on him in the shower. And when they made it to the bedroom and he pulled Sidney into his arms, he couldn't help but think just how *good* it always was with her.

Something felt different between them as she led him to the bed. Instead of the impatient need to have her naked that he'd always felt before, tonight he took his time undressing her. He noticed little things he hadn't before, like the scattering of freckles across the top of her shoulders, which he kissed as he slid the straps of her bra down her arms.

Under the covers, his hands and mouth moved slowly over her. By now, he knew what she liked, knew all the things that had her moaning his name softly in the darkness, and when he finally eased into her, he kept his lower body still for several moments as they kissed, wanting to simply savor the feeling of being inside her.

And in that moment, he was pretty sure that nothing else had ever felt quite so right.

VAUGHN WOKE UP first in the morning and decided to take the initiative this time with the coffee. He got dressed quietly, not wanting to wake Sidney, and headed downstairs. He'd noticed her keys on the kitchen counter the night before, so he grabbed them and walked the three blocks to Starbucks. There, he realized he didn't know her coffee order, so he ordered a grande of the medium roast, thinking that was the safest bet.

He let himself back into her town house, and put the keys back in the same spot. Sidney's laptop set on the counter nearby, open but in sleep mode.

And that's when he saw it.

A small white card—seemingly a business card—lay upside down next to the laptop, with the handwritten words: *Maybe next time we can meet for more than two minutes?*

Vaughn flipped the card over and saw it was from some lawyer named Tyler Roland. He put the card back where he'd found it, then headed upstairs.

Sidney peeked one eye open as he took a seat on the edge of the bed closest to her. "You are a god," she said, spotting the coffee cups in his hands. She sat up, took one of the cups from him, and had a sip. "*Mmm.* Thank you."

He took a sip, as well. "Looks like somebody has another hot date coming up," he said conversationally. When she paused and looked at him, he explained. "His business card was on the counter next to your keys. 'Maybe next time we can meet for more than two minutes?'"

"Oh. Tyler." She stared at her coffee cup for a moment, twisting the sleeve. "He and I are supposed to have dinner this Wednesday."

Vaughn felt something gnawing in his gut, but he shook it off. Of course she had a date—she'd been going on dates this whole time. That was how these things worked; they were simply two people having a good time together. Sure, they'd gotten closer, and, yes, it was easy being around her, but that's what made the situation so ideal. There was no awkwardness between them—just a perfect no-strings-attached arrangement.

Exactly the way things were supposed to be.

"Ah. Another contender seeking to test his luck against the thirty-four-item checklist," he said, his tone deliberately teasing. "How did you meet this one?"

She looked at him. "You really want to talk about this?"

"You've been telling me about your dates all along. Why would it be any different now?"

Something flickered in her eyes, but in the next moment it was gone. "Right. Of course. Um, so . . . I met Tyler briefly a few months ago, then we ran into each other on the street the other day."

How fortuitous. "And he went straight for the dinner invite? No drinks or coffee first? Huh. That seems a little forward."

"Actually, we have a mutual acquaintance," she said. "He's friends with a partner at my firm who says that Tyler's a good guy. With that kind of endorsement, I figured he was dinner-worthy. Plus, I've been wanting to try Sogna ever since I moved back to Chicago."

"He's taking you to Sogna?" Vaughn was familiar with the restaurant, one of the most exclusive in the city. Not because he'd dined there himself—with a $210 prix fixe menu, it wasn't exactly in his budget. But last year, he'd coordinated a sting operation out of the place and he'd seen firsthand that it was nice. Really nice. "Sounds to me like somebody's trying to show off."

Sidney cocked her head, considering this. "I don't think so. Maybe he's just a foodie. He seemed really interested in hearing about the restaurants I'd eaten at in New York." She gestured with her coffee cup. "Oh. I just realized—I should start thinking about what I'll wear, in case I need to drop something off at the dry cleaners today. Maybe that pink dress I wore to my father and Jenny's garden party."

Vaughn's hand tightened around his coffee cup. He remembered that dress well. "I don't know . . . I thought I noticed something wrong with one of the sleeves on that dress. It kept slipping down your shoulder." Obviously, he was . . . just trying to help her avoid any fashion faux pas on her big date.

She smiled. "No, it's supposed to do that. Gives me *allure*."

Right.

LATER THAT AFTERNOON, Vaughn parked his car in the FBI lot, arriving just moments after Huxley. Seeing him,

Huxley waited in front of the security building, which all agents and visitors were required to pass through.

Vaughn slammed his car door—probably a little harder than necessary—and then strode over to his partner.

Huxley raised an eyebrow. "I think you left your side-view mirror on the pavement there."

"The door slipped," Vaughn said, with a nonchalant shrug.

Ignoring Huxley's skeptical look, he breezed into the security building and flashed his badge at the guards.

He, for one, had a corrupt city code inspector to take down tonight.

Twenty-seven

ON WEDNESDAY EVENING, Sidney walked into Sogna restaurant and smiled at the hostess. "I'm meeting someone here. I believe the reservation is under Roland?"

The hostess checked her reservation list and nodded. "Of course. Mr. Roland is already here. I'll show you to your table."

She led Sidney up the glass-and-steel staircase to the second floor of the restaurant's split-level dining room. At the top of the steps, Sidney could see Tyler waiting at a table next to the floor-to-ceiling windows that overlooked a romantic view of vibrant Michigan Avenue. Smiling when he spotted her, he looked classically handsome in his tailored sport coat and blue button-down shirt.

She felt a moment's hesitation before walking over, a slight jittery feeling in her stomach—which she immediately wrote off as butterflies of anticipation. *This could be it,* she told herself. This could be her last first date, her Mr. Right, the man she was meant to spend the rest of her life with.

The jitters in her stomach kicked it up a notch.

Ignoring that, she put forth her most charming smile as

she approached the table, determined to have the best damn first date ever.

"DO YOU MISS New York at all?"

Sidney rested her fork against her plate, thinking about Tyler's question. As it turned out, he *was* a foodie—for over a half hour they'd talked about their favorite restaurants, which had led to his current question. "I do, at times. But kind of the way you miss a cool place you went on vacation, or the city where you spent a summer abroad during college. As much as I enjoyed living in Manhattan, I don't think I ever fully settled in to thinking it was home." She turned the question around. "How about you? Do you ever think about living someplace other than Chicago?"

So far, Tyler was doing well against her checklist. In addition to their conversation about favorite restaurants, during the appetizer course, they'd covered a lot of the first-date basics. She knew he had a younger sister with whom he was close—something they obviously had in common; that he'd attended Harvard for both undergrad and law school; and that he liked to golf and play squash. Typically, however, this was the point in the date—when the questions became more substantive—that the contenders began to falter.

"No, not really," he said. "I mean, I like to travel and visit different places, and, obviously, there were the seven years I lived in Boston for school, but both my family and my job are here in Chicago. So I'm pretty set where I am."

This gave Sidney an opportunity to segue into the subject of his career. "How long have you been at your firm?"

"Two years, after lateraling in as a partner. We're a relatively new firm—we've only been open for three years."

Sidney's radar began to beep, hearing that. As a businesswoman, she knew how unstable start-up ventures could be—and if things weren't settled with Tyler's career, her research said he had to be nixed. "How's business going?" she asked, trying to sound casual.

"Great," he said, without any hesitation. "The two partners

who started the firm—friends of mine, actually—brought a huge client with them when they left our old firm. We've acquired a lot of new clients since then, so we've brought on five more associates and two other lateral partners. And I think we still might need to add to that number, given how much new business is coming in."

Great. So he's a workaholic. "Sounds like you guys are really busy."

"We're busy, sure—as a lawyer, you never want to be *not* busy. But one of the commitments my friends made when starting the firm was to staff cases so that no one works the insane amount of hours you see at large law firms." He smiled. "And if you knew the kind of lifestyle J.D. and Payton had at our old firm—basically meaning, no life at all—you'd understand why this is important to them. That's one of the main reasons I joined their firm . . . well, after waiting a year to see if they actually got the place off the ground," he chuckled. "Having a healthy work-life balance is important to me, too."

Well, isn't he just knocking these answers out of the park? Sidney's inner pragmatist gave her a sharp nudge.

I mean, yay!—he's knocking these answers out of the park!

"It is to me, too." Then she smiled, in concession. "At least now it is. Admittedly, when I was in New York, my scale was far more heavily tipped on the 'work' side of the work-life balance. But now I have this new job, with much better hours, and I feel a lot more settled. It's like, that piece of my life is good, that's set—I've got the career thing figured out. So now I'm in a position to start thinking about things beyond my career."

She waited to see how Tyler would respond. She was putting it all out there, making it clear that she was thinking big picture, not just looking for someone to have fun with. Every other Mr. Right contender—if they hadn't already failed her checklist—had crashed and burned at this part. They equivocated about what they were looking for in a relationship, they hemmed and hawed, or they said some platitude that, at best, could be read as ambivalent.

Tyler looked her dead in the eyes. "I feel exactly the same way."

Hearing that, Sidney took a deep breath.

Well, that was . . . fantastic. Awesome. She smiled at Tyler, not quite sure why she had that annoying, hesitant feeling in her stomach again—but it didn't matter. Fate had finally thrown her a bone. Tyler was good-looking, smart, successful, and had an easygoing nature that balanced well against her tendency to be, well . . . a little snarky and *not* so easygoing. And when, during dessert, he talked about being in a place in his life where he was ready to settle down, something he'd realized after seeing how happy his friends, J.D. and Payton, were after the birth of their first child, Sidney could practically see the bright neon arrow blinking in the air over his head. *Him! This one! Yes!*

So, at the end of the date, when they said good-bye in front of the taxi that would take her home, and he leaned in and huskily asked if his two minutes were up, or if he could see her again, the pragmatist in her knew there was only one answer to that.

She told him yes.

ACROSS TOWN IN his loft, Vaughn made himself a dinner of steak fajitas and settled onto his couch to watch television. He had his cell phone ready at his side, knowing what was coming.

It was Wednesday. Date night for Sidney. Which meant that any moment, the text messages would start rolling in with whatever issues—real or imagined—she identified with this new guy, this rich Tyler tool who clearly had a dick so small he needed to compensate by taking women to expensive five-star restaurants on first dates.

Sad, really.

But it didn't matter how nice the restaurant was, or whether Sidney's mentor claimed Tyler was a "good" guy. As Vaughn had told Cade and Huxley, her checklist was like a fortress: No man was getting through.

Speaking of which . . .

He looked down at his silent phone. He checked to make sure it was on, and then turned back to his fajitas.

Admittedly, he was curious to know how things were going on her date. Not because he was jealous or anything—*pfft*, he didn't do jealous—but because of the practicalities of their situation. He *liked* having sex with Sidney. But obviously, that would come to an end as soon as she started dating someone. And now that he thought about it . . . everything else would come to an end, too. Like the cute text messages. And all their conversations. And he no longer would be the guy she texted *Help* to when needing someone to pop the casing off her smoke detector. Or the guy she rested her head against when snuggled up on her couch on a Friday night. Some nameless, faceless new guy was going to horn in on all of that.

Vaughn looked down at his phone.

He shook off the thoughts—that wasn't anything he needed to worry about tonight. Any second now, he was going to hear the chime of a new text message, the chime that signaled the demise of rich, slick *Maybe-next-time-we-can-meet-for-more-than-two-minutes-which-also-happens-to-be-how-long-I-last-during-sex* Tyler Roland, Attorney-at-Law.

Vaughn picked up his phone to check that it had a signal.

Yep, any second now.

Twenty-eight

A WEEK AND a half later, Vaughn met with his boss, Special Agent in Charge Nick McCall, to give him an update on the Pritchett investigation.

"The cops did another gun run last night," Vaughn said. "We have one more scheduled for two weeks from yesterday, and after that, I think we'll have enough evidence to make our arrests."

"Let me know when that's going to go down," Nick said. "I want to make sure you have all the backup you need. These guys are cops. When they realize they're going to prison, who knows what they might try to pull."

Vaughn nodded in agreement. "If everything goes as planned, we'll make the arrests the following Monday. In addition to the backup squad and the SOG team, I'd like to bring in a SWAT unit." That would mean he'd have eight more fully armed guys in two big SUVs on hand, just in case.

He thought of the comment he'd made to Sidney the last time he'd seen her. *The FBI loves overwhelming people with manpower and firepower.*

An image of her popped into his head, curled against him

on her couch. Not wanting to go there, he shoved the memory aside and focused on the task at hand.

"That's one of the things I miss most about being in the field and working undercover in these corruption cases," Nick said. "That 'Oh, shit,' look on these assholes' faces when you show up on their doorstep with your FBI badge."

No disagreement there. "Speaking of working undercover, there's something else I wanted to discuss," Vaughn said. "With these public corruption cases being a top priority, things are getting busy in my squad. In order to manage the caseload, I think it would be helpful to have another agent who's been to undercover school."

Nick considered this. "Do you have anyone in mind?"

"I recommend sending Huxley." Vaughn saw his boss's look of surprise and acknowledged this with a nod. "I know. Two years ago, if you'd told me we'd be having this conversation, I never would've believed it. But Huxley's really come into his own these past couple years. He's thorough, decisive, ridiculously organized, and he gets the job done every time. Just last week, he needed to go undercover with barely any notice, and I was really impressed with the way he handled that."

Nick rocked back in his chair. "All right. I'll take your recommendation under advisement. If I decide to go forward with this, the first step would be for me to talk to Huxley and see if this is even something he wants to do."

"One thing: when you talk to him, don't tell him the thing I said about being impressed. I'll never hear the end of it."

The SAC chuckled. "Understood." Then he looked Vaughn over with sharp green eyes, taking in his navy pinstripe suit, new silk tie, and light-blue shirt—which, for once, was buttoned all the way. "You're looking spiffier than usual. Big plans tonight?"

"My parents are in town and we're having dinner." Vaughn rubbed his jaw. "My mom's not exactly thrilled with the scruff. I figured I'd tried to appease her by at least wearing a good suit."

Obviously, that was the only reason he'd gotten all dressed up for this dinner.

Or so he kept telling himself.

* * *

VAUGHN WAS THE first to arrive at Rosebud Steakhouse, the one restaurant at which his father insisted upon eating every time he visited Chicago. His parents were in town to run some errands—apparently his mother was going shoe shopping with Isabelle to find a pair that matched the dress she planned to wear at the wedding—and they'd driven in today so they could get an early start in the morning. Naturally they'd wanted to have dinner with him, Simon, and Isabelle.

And they'd invited Sidney to join them, too.

It would be Vaughn's first time having any contact with her since her date with Tyler, the night he'd stayed up far later than he would ever admit while waiting for a text message that had never come.

But that was cool. Sure, he was a little disappointed that he was losing out on some really hot sex, and, fine, maybe he also missed just . . . talking to her, but they'd both known the score. Of course, *he* knew the score. So when Sidney walked into the restaurant tonight, he was going to smile and be his usual friendly, smooth self because that was what he did. And this funk or whatever he'd been in for the last week could just fuck off and go find some emo, angsty guy to plague— because it was starting to seriously cramp his style.

That decided, he ordered a drink at the bar and took a seat. His parents had called to say they'd hit some traffic on the highway, so they were running a few minutes late. Sidney was the first to arrive. Dressed for work, she walked in wearing a sleek black pantsuit and had her hair pulled back in a sophisticated twist.

Eh. She looked . . . all right, he supposed.

Nice try, asshole.

Spotting him at the bar, she headed over. "Hey, you."

"Miss Sinclair," he said charmingly, totally on his game. But then he noticed something. "What's wrong?" He could see it in her eyes; something was bothering her.

She took a deep breath, waving this off as she took the seat next to him at the bar. "It's nothing. I just picked up the locket

I ordered to hold the photograph of my mother for Isabelle's 'something old.' It's nice, but it's not the same thing as having something that actually belonged to my mom. I still can't believe all of her wedding stuff got thrown away." She sighed, then shook it off. "Anyway . . . how are you?" She looked at him and smiled. "Hey, you took my advice about the skinnier tie." She reached up and tugged it playfully. "It looks good."

Vaughn looked down into her teasing eyes, thinking that it was just . . . really good to see her again. "Thanks," he said huskily. Then, clearing his throat, he added in a more glib tone, "You should probably soak it in while you can, because this is as stylish as I get."

"No pocket square for you?"

"Not even if I was standing buck naked in the middle of Wrigley Field on a sold-out game day and someone threw me one from the crowd to cover my junk."

She laughed hard at that. "So that's a no, then?"

He smiled. "That's a no."

The bartender came by to ask if she wanted anything to drink, and she ordered a glass of cabernet.

"I've been meaning to ask," she said, turning back to Vaughn. "What's the 'other you' been up to these days? I see you still have the scruff."

Let's just say I woke up with scruff burn in some very interesting places.

"The 'other me' has had a busy week. Just had a big meeting last night," he said.

"Everything go okay?"

"Yep."

"Ever been on a case where everything *didn't* go okay?" she asked.

"Actually, yes. Two years ago, I was working undercover as a gun buyer, and I drove this flashy Cadillac Escalade. I parked it in a garage and, randomly, some asshole stole it while I was meeting with the suspects."

"No way." She started laughing again. "What did you do?"

"I had to call a cab to drive me back to the FBI office." He held out his hands when she laughed harder. "Well, I couldn't have my backup team give me a ride, in case anyone was watching the garage." He shook his head, smiling ruefully at the memory. "Believe me—I caught shit for that one for a *long* time."

"I bet." Her eyes sparkling, she took a sip of her wine.

Vaughn was very aware that everyone else was going to show up at any moment, and there was something he wanted to know. "So, I haven't seen you since your date with the 'two-minutes' guy." He feigned cluelessness. "What was his name again?"

"Tyler."

"That's it. How did things go with you two?"

She looked at him, and at first he thought she wasn't going to answer. "The date went really well." She smiled. "No Man-Speak. He seems like a good guy. I'm seeing him again tomorrow, in fact. We were going to have dinner earlier this week, but he had to go out of town to cover some depositions for another lawyer at his firm. If all goes well tomorrow, I'm thinking I'll probably ask him to go to the wedding." She wiped her brow jokingly. "Phew. With only two weeks left, I was starting to cut it close there."

Vaughn sat there for a moment, feeling a pang of something sharp in his chest. But then he shoved the feelings down deep, blocking them out and putting them in a place where he could pretend they didn't even exist.

Well, that was just . . . great. Sidney had been wanting to meet her Mr. Right, and now perhaps she finally had. She and Vaughn had become friends over the past couple months, and as her friend, he knew this was a good development for her. Of course he wanted her to be happy.

In fact, looking into those blue-green eyes and seeing her smile right then, he realized he wanted that more than anything.

So he raised his glass in toast. And if the words tasted a little bitter coming out, he ignored that, too. "Well, cheers to that," he said smoothly. "You have found that most mythical of creatures in the urban dating jungle: the single, normal, commitment-ready, thirtysomething man. The checklist has prevailed."

He held out his glass. She paused, then clinked her glass to his. "To the checklist."

"Ooh . . . what are we toasting to?" said a familiar female voice.

Vaughn turned and saw Isabelle heading over to the bar, with Simon in tow.

"It's nothing," Sidney said quickly. She got off the barstool and hugged her sister in greeting.

His parents arrived shortly behind them, his mother giving both Sidney and Isabelle a warm hug. The hostess showed the six of them to their table, and the mood quickly became like their previous dinner together at his parents' house, everyone laughing, lots of cross-conversations. Vaughn sat across from Sidney, and from time to time he felt a tightening in his chest, watching her laugh with his parents or joke around with Simon, but he never once faltered in his charming, I'm-just-a-good-time-guy demeanor, the role he'd been in for the last several years, the role that was his comfort zone.

And when dinner was over, and everyone was saying their good-byes, he acted as though he didn't notice when Isabelle pulled Sidney off to the side.

"Call me Sunday morning and let me know how your date went," Isabelle said in a low voice. "If it goes well, I want to meet this guy." She winked at Sidney, then turned back to rejoin the rest of the group.

While Vaughn did a bang-up job of pretending not to watch as Sidney walked away.

ON SATURDAY NIGHT, Tyler walked Sidney back to her townhome. They'd had a nice, enjoyable dinner at Le Colonial, a French Vietnamese restaurant just a few blocks from her place. It had been her turn to pick the restaurant, and she'd deliberately chosen Le Colonial for its exotic, romantic décor. They'd even scored an outdoor table on the mezzanine level, with a view of the bustling street below. There'd been good conversation, good wine, and great food—all the makings of a perfect second date.

And it *had* been perfect. Well, mostly. Sure, Sidney still had that nagging, hesitant feeling, but she assumed that was simply because this was her first second date since her breakup with Brody. Of course she had trepidations; the last time she'd started down this road she'd been cheated on and had ended up with a broken heart. A few cautionary jitters were to be expected.

"I really liked that restaurant. Good choice," Tyler said, taking her hand as they walked along the sidewalk.

Oh. They were holding hands now. Because that was what people did on a date. "I've never had a lychee mimosa before," Sidney said. "It was different—in a good way."

"We'll have to go back there again," Tyler said.

Right. Sure. Maybe it would even become "their spot." They would be a couple and have a spot and everything would be lovely.

Say something about the wedding, her inner pragmatist nudged her as they headed up the steps to her front door.

Yes, the wedding. This was the perfect opportunity. The subject had even briefly come up during dinner, when she'd told Tyler that her sister was getting married in two weeks. She turned to face him when they got to the top of the stairs . . . but for whatever reason, the words got stuck.

He bent his head and kissed her.

Well . . . huh. At first, she wasn't feeling it, but then something changed. Assuming that her hesitations and trepidations were holding her back, she decided to say *screw it* to all of that. For once, she forgot about her checklist and the wedding and decided to get out of her head and simply let her heart lead the way. And after pouring all that into her kiss, she pulled back and peered up at him with a smile.

Then she blinked, because his eyes were the wrong color—blue instead of hazel.

And she realized, in that moment when she'd said *screw it* to her hesitations and trepidations and had let her heart lead the way, she'd imagined herself kissing Vaughn.

"Oh, boy," she said, with a ragged, panicky exhale.

"I know. I felt that, too," Tyler said.

She was officially screwed.

* * *

ON THE UPSIDE, Tyler handled the situation well.

Sidney let herself into her townhome, feeling bad and regretful about the conversation she'd just had—but she also knew that it had been the right thing to do. For one thing, Tyler deserved to be with a woman who wasn't imagining another guy while she kissed him. To spare his feelings, she'd told a small fib and had said she realized now that she wasn't over her ex-fiancé. He was gracious about that, and as he'd walked down the steps and out of her life, her one consolation was that a guy like Tyler wasn't going to remain single for long— some lucky woman was going to snatch him up real soon.

Unfortunately, that woman wasn't her.

She headed straight upstairs and changed out of her date clothes. After pulling on a T-shirt and pair of shorts, she curled up on her bed and thought about her next move. The checklist was irrelevant, at least for now. She most certainly wasn't going to have a date for Isabelle and Simon's wedding, and she'd just realized she had some sort of "feelings" or whatever for a man who—just last night—had been toasting her for having a date with another guy.

You know I'm smart enough not to fall for a guy like Vaughn.

Now more than ever, she needed to remember that.

Which meant her next move was clear. She would avoid Vaughn at all costs for the next couple of weeks—no more joking, flirty conversations; no more sexy scruff; no more talking to him about personal stuff or cozying up with him on the couch while looking at her parents' wedding albums. That was all *done*. She needed to get through this wedding, and then she and Vaughn could go their separate ways. Yes, they would still run into each other occasionally via Isabelle and Simon, but she could handle that. She just needed some space right now, some time away from him, so that these "feelings" or whatever could abate.

And abate, they would. She'd make sure of it.

Twenty-nine

AFTER BREEZING PAST the Shedd Aquarium, Vaughn ran through the Lake Shore Drive underpass and followed the sidewalk to Columbus Drive. One more turn, and then it would be a straight shot to the finish line.

A large crowd cheered from both sides of the street—over a quarter million spectators had gathered to watch nearly 11,000 athletes race in the Chicago Triathlon. Shortly after seven thirty A.M., Vaughn, Cade, Huxley, and the other 150 people in their wave had started out with a brisk 1.5 kilometer swim in Lake Michigan. After exiting the water at the Chicago Yacht Club, they'd hightailed it barefoot and in their wetsuits along a carpeted path to the first transition area, where they'd stripped down to their bike shorts and had thrown on jerseys, helmets, and shoes. Spirits had been high as Vaughn and Huxley had mounted their bikes for the forty-kilometer course, and even higher as they'd caught up with Cade, who had been swimming for years to help with a college football shoulder injury and had garnered a slight lead in the first leg.

Now they were in the homestretch, nearly about to finish the 10K run. Huxley had dropped back a little, but Vaughn was still fighting it out for the lead with Cade. They'd been pushing each other hard throughout the race, which was exactly what Vaughn needed: something to keep his mind focused. Being on the course and pushing his body to its limits gave him a place to channel the restlessness he'd felt all week.

"Second place buys lunch?" he huffed.

"You're on," Cade panted, matching him stride for stride.

They'd been far more loquacious with the trash talk earlier in the race, but after swimming, biking, and running thirty-two miles, they were out of breath and keeping it short and sweet. They rounded the corner onto Columbus, and the finish line at Hutchinson Field in Grant Park came into view. They heard a female voice cheering them on from the left.

"Whoo-hoo! Go Cade! Go Vaughn!"

Cade grinned. "That's Brooke." Suddenly spurred on, he picked up the pace even more.

Then a second female voice called out. "Come on, Roberts! Keep going!"

Vaughn's head whipped to the left, his heart pounding as he saw a red-haired woman cheering alongside Brooke, and for a split-second he thought—

Oh. Of course—it was just Huxley's fiancée, Addison.

He paid the price for the momentary distraction. He looked ahead and saw Cade cross the finish line a few feet in front of him. They both trotted to a stop amid the cheers of the energized crowd.

Breathing hard, Vaughn walked over and stuck out his hand to Cade for a job well done. "Show off," he said with a grin.

They moved off to the sidelines and grabbed some water, just as Brooke made her way through the crowd. Dressed in jeans and a T-shirt, and with her blond hair pulled back in a ponytail, she walked over to Cade and threw her arms around his neck in congratulations. He scooped her up as she kissed him.

"How's the shoulder holding up?" she asked.

"Shoulder? Oh, *shit*." Cade feigned dropping her, then caught her with a grin.

"Still, with that?"

He winked at her. "That move once helped me get very lucky." He pulled her closer, kissing her again.

Vaughn stepped away to give them some space. He looked over at the finish line just as Huxley ran through. He made his way over and congratulated his partner, then once again had to give space to a happily-in-love couple after Addison showed up and planted a kiss on Huxley that undoubtedly would've fogged his glasses had he been wearing them.

Feeling a bit like a fifth wheel, Vaughn took another swig of water while catching his breath. He stood in the grass along the sidelines, alone, as thousands of people hugged, kissed, and high-fived their loves ones all around him.

Then he felt a hand on his shoulder.

"I'd give you a hug in congratulations, but, *man*, you are sweaty and kind of funky-looking right now."

Vaughn grinned at the sound of the voice. Turning around, he was touched to see Simon. "Aren't you supposed to be in wedding-planning lockdown right now?" Although he'd told his brother that he was training for the Chicago Triathlon, he hadn't asked him to come watch the race. Frankly, he'd assumed that Simon would be too busy since the wedding was only six days away.

"Well, apparently, one can apply for a brief furlough from wedding-planning lockdown when one's brother is racing in a triathlon," Simon said. "How are you feeling?"

"A little pissed that I owe Morgan lunch, but otherwise pretty good."

"Mind if I join you guys?" Simon asked.

"That'd be great," Vaughn said. "Brooke and Addison are coming, too—the more the merrier."

Simon followed him back to his place, where Vaughn quickly showered and changed. When they arrived at O'Malley's, Brooke and Cade were already seated at a table for six.

"Let's see . . . what's the most expensive item here?" Cade mused, perusing the menu. "I need to make the most of my free lunch."

Vaughn ignored the jab. He introduced Brooke to Simon,

and then gestured to the ring on her finger. "I hear you're finally going to make an honest man out of Morgan."

She looked at Cade, feigning surprise. "Oh, is that what I agreed to? I just saw a diamond and shouted 'Yes!' to having a new piece of jewelry." She turned back to Vaughn. "Oops."

"That's cute," Cade told her.

"So what's your version of the story, Morgan? You never said how you popped the question," Vaughn said.

"Nothing too crazy. I just made Brooke breakfast that morning." Cade looked at his fiancée, and they shared an inside smile. "A Denver omelette."

"He had everything all set out when I walked into the kitchen—the omelette, coffee, and orange juice," Brooke explained. "And when I flipped over my coffee cup, there was the ring box, sitting on the saucer."

From the private way the couple was looking at each other, Vaughn gathered there was more to this Denver omelette story. But neither of them said anything further.

Huxley and Addison arrived shortly thereafter. Simon asked Vaughn, Cade, and Huxley which part of the race had been the toughest, and that spawned a long, testosterone-fueled conversation about how they all could've kept going for several more miles, that maybe they needed a bigger challenge, like an Iron Man triathlon, or *maybe* they needed to try something even more adventurous. Like climbing Mount Rainier.

"Now you want to climb a mountain?" Brooke asked. "Why, exactly?"

"Because we can," Cade said, matter-of-factly.

"Oh my God, you are such *men*," Addison said.

Simon pointed. "Hold on—if you three are doing this, I want in, too."

Huxley already had his phone out, Googling what time of year was the best to climb. The discussion went on from there, with everyone joking and kidding around long after they'd finished their food.

As the rest of the group was leaving the pub, Simon pulled Vaughn aside. "Let's stay for a beer."

Vaughn was instantly suspicious—presumably, his brother

was supposed to be making a seating chart right then, or practicing his first dance, or doing something else wedding-related. "Why?"

"Do I need a reason to grab a beer with my brother?" Simon asked, looking offended. "I'm getting married in six days. I'm going to have a baby soon. Who knows how many chances we'll get to hang out after this, just the two of us?"

Hmm. Vaughn remained suspicious, but nevertheless followed his brother to the bar.

They grabbed two seats, and Simon waited all of about five seconds after the bartender slid a couple of bottles of beer in front of them before getting down to it.

"So. This thing with Sidney," he led in.

Christ. Vaughn shook his head. "I knew it."

Simon tapped his finger emphatically on the bar. "Hey, I'm your brother. Something's obviously been bothering you these past couple weeks, so we're going to talk about it. That's what we *do.*"

"Oh, right. That's what we do." Vaughn feigned confusion. "Remind me—how long did it take you to tell me Isabelle was pregnant?"

"Okay, that's what we do *now.*" Simon studied him, as if debating where to begin. "I saw the way you were looking at Sidney that night at Rosebud, when we had dinner with Mom and Dad."

Vaughn simply took a sip of his beer.

"See, it's called a *dialogue.* That means you speak, too," Simon explained.

Vaughn merely gave him a look.

"Well, I don't know about you, but I think this is great brotherly heart-to-heart," Simon said.

Knowing that his brother wasn't going to give in, Vaughn finally acquiesced. "What do you want me to say? That I've been thinking about Sidney? Tell me something: what would be the point in admitting that?" He gestured with his beer bottle. "She's dating that Tyler guy now."

"Speaking of that, she came over to Isabelle's the other day to talk. They banished me to the living room, but when

I walked by the bedroom to get something out of the office, I caught a few words."

"I don't want to know," Vaughn said.

Simon gave him a knowing side-eye.

"All right," Vaughn acquiesced. "What'd you hear?"

"I heard Sidney say that she kissed him."

Vaughn said nothing at first, then turned back to his beer. "Well, now I feel so much better. Thanks for the pep talk, bro. We really should do this more often."

"So that's it? You're going to just give up?" Simon snorted. "That's a real bad-ass move."

Now that got Vaughn a little worked up. "Hold on—I think you skipped about five steps in the *dialogue* here. Take this Tyler guy out of the equation for a minute. By saying I'm 'giving up,' you're assuming that I want to pursue a relationship with Sidney. And there's one problem with that—I *like* my life. It's easy, it's fun, and I don't have to deal with any of this . . . confusion and this . . . restlessness and this pit in my stomach every time I think about her being with another guy. 'Cuz let me tell you something I've figured out about those feelings: they suck."

He saw Simon open his mouth, and held up his hand. "Nope, not finished. You wanted me to share, so that's what I'm doing. And let me share something else. *If* we take the Tyler guy out of the equation, *and* we assume—hypothetically—that I'd want to give up my nice, easy, fun life for the confusion and the restlessness and the suck, we still have the small problem that Sidney doesn't want to be with *me*."

"You don't know that," Simon said.

"I heard her say it pretty clearly when you and I were standing outside her window."

"What she said was that she was smart enough not to fall for a guy like you."

Vaughn held out his hands. *Hello?* "Exactly."

"Then maybe what you need to do is convince her that you aren't *you* anymore."

Vaughn leaned in. "And if I'm not me, then who am I supposed to be?" he quipped dryly.

Simon stared him in the eyes. "The man she deserves."

He gave Vaughn a pointed look before turning back to his beer. "You can throw out all the hypotheticals you want. But in the end, I think it comes down to this: do you want to be that man?"

He took a long sip from his bottle, leaving Vaughn to contemplate exactly that.

WHEN VAUGHN GOT back to his loft, he stretched out on the sectional and leaned his head against the cushions. He had Simon's words ringing in his head, and the exertion of the race was finally catching up with him. He closed his eyes, just wanting a few minutes where he didn't have to think.

He woke up to the sound of his cell phone ringing.

He reached over and grabbed the phone off the coffee table, noticing that he'd been asleep for a couple of hours. He didn't recognize the incoming phone number.

"Hello," he answered, his voice gritty.

"Is this Special Agent Vaughn Roberts?" asked a female voice.

"It is." Vaughn sat up, trying to shake off his grogginess as the woman identified herself. It took him a moment to place the name. "Oh, right. I was wondering whether you got my message."

"I apologize for the delay in getting back to you," she said. "My husband and I were on vacation last week. We just got back into town this afternoon."

"It's not a problem. I realize this is a long shot, anyway," he said.

"Unfortunately, I don't have what you're looking for—but I think I know someone who might. That is, assuming you're still interested. I know it's been almost a week since you called."

This was one thing, at least, Vaughn didn't have to think about.

"I'm still interested. Very much so."

Thirty

LATE WEDNESDAY MORNING, Sidney had a video conference call with the customer analytics firm she'd brought on board to help her with the Vitamin Boutique expansion.

"Once we get rolling, the plan is to open one new store each week, and to maintain that pace for two years," she said. "Now I just need you guys to tell me where to put those stores."

The consulting team, made up of market and product research specialists, sat around a conference table taking notes. "And the plan is to start with California and Florida?" asked Brandon, the senior VP of business development.

"Yes." As Sidney knew from working with Brandon and his team in the past, their research would be a two-part process: first, the team members would analyze consumer purchasing preferences and the existing retail density within potential market areas. Then they would travel to the various sites they were eyeing and evaluate those locations for things like proximity to a major highway, the ease with which customers could exit and enter the traffic flow, and the store's visibility and prominence.

Once everyone had their marching orders, Sidney set up

a follow-up call in two weeks to discuss the team's research and their recommendations for the first wave of store openings. After her call ended, she grabbed a sandwich for lunch and decided to treat herself to a brownie from the bakery around the corner from her office—the same bakery from which she'd ordered the desserts for Isabelle's bridal shower.

When she saw the minicakes on display in one of the glass cases, a memory of the first night she'd spent with Vaughn popped into her head.

Any chance you're going to pull something out of there that comes in an extra-large? I feel like a giant.

She turned right around and walked back out of the bakery. Who needed a brownie, anyway?

She'd been doing a good job of not thinking about Vaughn this past week and a half. Mostly. There'd been that one time, when she'd asked Isabelle how he'd done in the triathlon, but that just had been making conversation, really. Fine, maybe she'd been *mildly* interested, knowing that Vaughn had trained for eleven weeks and that he'd wanted to perform well, but it wasn't like she'd been wishing she'd been there to see him cross the finish line or anything. *Pfft*, heck no. Then there'd also been that other time she'd inquired about his undercover investigation—Isabelle's total lack of knowledge about whether he was being careful while hanging out in those dark, sketchy places had been singularly unhelpful—but *obviously* that was just because she didn't want Simon and Isabelle to be down a best man at the wedding. That would . . . throw off the symmetry of the bridal party in the photos.

When Sidney got back to her office, the receptionist stopped her in the lobby.

"You have a visitor, Sidney—a Ms. Ginny Gastel." The receptionist gestured to the waiting area.

Sidney blinked, surprised to hear the name of her mother's friend, who she hadn't seen in over fifteen years. She turned around and saw a blond woman wearing beige pants and a light summer sweater getting up from one of the chairs.

She walked over with a smile. "Oh my gosh, Ginny. I walked right by you."

"Sidney, it's so good to see you. It's been a long time." Ginny set down the large shopping bags she carried and hugged Sidney in greeting. Then she pulled back. "Look at you. The last time I saw you, I think you were fifteen? Sixteen, maybe?"

"Somewhere around there. Here—let's head this way, to my office, where we can catch up."

Ginny cast an admiring eye around the sophisticated office as Sidney led her down the hallway. "I see you followed in your father's footsteps."

"Sort of. There are some differences between hedge funds and private equity funds, but I've found that people tend to get really, really bored whenever I talk about that. So I'll spare you that part."

Ginny laughed as she followed Sidney into her office. "Well, you're obviously doing very well for yourself."

Opting against the formality of her desk, Sidney gestured to the pair of cream leather chairs by the floor-to-ceiling window. "Please, make yourself comfortable. Can I get you something to drink?"

"I'm fine, thank you," Ginny said, resting her bags on the floor by her feet. "I won't be staying long—I need to run a few more errands before heading back out to the suburbs for a house showing."

"You're still in real estate, then?" Sidney shut the door and sat down in the chair opposite Ginny. They chatted and caught up for several minutes, which naturally led into the topic of Isabelle's upcoming wedding.

"Only three days away, I hear," Ginny said. "And you like Simon?"

Sidney was a little surprised that Ginny knew both the wedding date and Simon's name since neither she nor Isabelle had talked to her in years. Presumably, she'd heard the details from a mutual acquaintance. "Simon's great. He makes Isabelle very happy."

"If he's anything like his brother, I can see why."

Sidney cocked her head, completely caught off guard by that. "You know Vaughn?"

"I wouldn't say I *know* him, I suppose. But the couple of phone conversations we've had have certainly left me quite impressed." She looked confused that Sidney seemed confused. "You do realize that the whole idea was his, right?"

Sidney had no clue what that meant. "I'm sorry, I'm missing something here. What was Vaughn's idea?"

Ginny's eyes widened. "Oh, no. Did I screw this up? He didn't say it was a surprise. I'd planned to come downtown today, so I offered to swing by your office and give it to you myself. He gave me your work address and, well, here I am."

Okay . . . still no clue. "To give me what, exactly?"

Ginny chuckled. "Apparently this is a surprise, then." She reached into one of the shopping bags and pulled out a medium-sized box. "See for yourself."

Sidney took the box and set it on her lap. She lifted the lid and unwrapped a layer of tissue paper. When she saw what was inside the box, at first she wasn't sure she knew what she was looking at.

It couldn't be.

Sidney looked up. "Is this . . . ?"

Ginny smiled. "Your mother's wedding purse. Vaughn said you were trying to find something of hers to give Isabelle as her 'something old.' I know everything else was lost, but at least you have this."

Feeling tears spring to her eyes, Sidney gently lifted the purse out of the box.

It was, undoubtedly, the most thoughtful thing anyone had ever done for her.

The purse was simple, made out of white satin that had aged a little and with a gold clasp and delicate gold strap. Sidney smoothed her hand over it and cleared her throat. "How did he know you had this? *I* didn't even know you had it."

"He didn't know, exactly. But from what I understand, you and Vaughn were looking at your parents' wedding albums, and you told him that your mother and I used to be best friends."

Sidney nodded. "I can't believe he remembered that."

"I guess being an FBI agent comes in handy for things like this. He tracked down my home phone number and left a message explaining how all of your mother's wedding things had been thrown away. He'd actually been hoping to locate your mother's 'something borrowed'—he'd asked whether she'd worn or carried something that belonged to me or one of the other bridesmaids that would've been returned to us. It was a good idea—except I have no clue what your mother's 'something borrowed' was. Luckily, I was able to do him one better."

Ginny pointed to the purse. "So here's the story with that: your mother was the first among our friends to get married. That was the purse she carried at her wedding, and then when I got married next, she lent it to me. Then I lent it to another friend of ours, Carol, for her wedding, and then Carol lent it to our other friend, Sandra. So after I heard Vaughn's message, I e-mailed Sandra, and we were in luck. She had the purse packed away in a box with the rest of her wedding things. I picked it up from her earlier this week, and now I happily deliver it to you."

"I don't know what to say, Ginny. Thank you."

"It belongs with you and Isabelle. And truly, Vaughn deserves the credit here. On Sunday, when we talked the first time, I joked that he was taking his best man responsibilities awfully seriously, going to such efforts to track down a 'something old' for Isabelle."

"What did he say?"

"That the FBI agent in him couldn't resist the chance to crack a cold case."

Sidney laughed. "That sounds like him."

"But when I called back to tell him that I'd found the purse, his first response was, 'She'll be so happy to hear it.'" Ginny looked at Sidney pointedly. "Somehow, I don't think he was referring to Isabelle."

They talked for a few minutes longer, and then Ginny collected her bags to leave. She asked Sidney to pass along her best wishes to Isabelle, gave Sidney her business card, and suggested that they keep in touch.

After Ginny left, Sidney walked back over to the chair and

picked up the purse. She peeked inside, saw it was empty, and then leaned against the front of her desk.

She didn't know what to make of the fact that Vaughn had gone through such efforts for her. Part of her was tempted to call him right then, but she was confused and trying not to read too much into the situation, and feeling very uncertain about a lot of things. But Ginny's visit definitely had made one thing clear, something Sidney could no longer deny, no matter how hard she tried.

She missed him.

Thirty-one

THURSDAY EVENING, VAUGHN met with Huxley and the rest of his backup unit to run through the plan for his meeting later that night with Pritchett's crew. He kept things short and sweet—this would be his fourth meeting with the cops, and everyone knew what to expect.

That is, until they got a call from the special operations team that was tailing the suspects.

"We have a situation," said Agent Romero, the team leader of the SOG. "There's a new guy joining the party."

"What do we know?" Vaughn asked.

"He showed up at the cops' rendezvous spot before they got in the vans to drive to Indianapolis. We ran his plate. Name is Mike Mahoney—*Officer* Mike Mahoney, brother of Officer James Mahoney. Just joined CPD last year."

Two dirty cops in one family—how touching. "So James decided to cut his brother in on the action," Vaughn said.

"Looks that way. Although it also looks as though he didn't run that by Pritchett first," Romero said. "There was some kind of argument between Pritchett and the brothers when they first showed up. From the way he got in Pritchett's face,

Mike Mahoney seems to be a bit of a hothead. Maybe Pritchett is worried he's going to be bad for business."

"What's Mahoney carrying?"

"Just his pistol, like the others."

"Did you alert Lyons yet?" Vaughn asked, referring to the undercover agent posing as his gun seller in Indianapolis.

"Not yet. We wanted to tell you first."

"Let's patch him in." Vaughn made the call to Lyons and brought him up to speed. Romero said he would keep them posted on any unusual activity as his team tailed the suspects to Indianapolis, and Lyons agreed to check in as soon as he'd handed the guns off to Pritchett's crew.

After hanging up with them, Vaughn filled in Huxley and the rest of the backup team.

"Do you think this new guy is going to be a problem?" Huxley asked.

"I think we need to be prepared for that possibility." Granted, it was entirely possible that the only thing going on was that Mike Mahoney had heard about his brother making some cash on the side and had decided that he wanted in on the smuggling business. But regardless, Vaughn wanted to be ready for anything.

He opened one of his desk drawers and unlocked the metal case where he stored his Kimber 1911, the handgun he'd chosen to carry during this sting operation since Glocks were known for being law enforcement guns. He loaded the magazine and slid it into place.

LATER, WHEN VAUGHN was at home and changing into one of "Mark Sullivan's" designer suits, Lyons checked in.

"They just left with the guns," the other agent said.

"How's the new guy?" Vaughn asked.

"Young. Built. Big ego. I gave Pritchett crap about bringing in a new guy, and Mahoney didn't care for that much," Lyons said.

"He'll be hearing the same song on my end," Vaughn said. After hanging up with Lyons, he called Romero, who was in one of the cars tailing the cops back to Chicago. "How are we looking?"

"Business as usual," Romero reported. "I'm tailing the van that the Mahoney brothers are in, and they're following the standard route."

"Just wanted to make sure our new guy doesn't get any bright ideas about making off with my guns."

"If that happens, and my team has to rein these jackasses in, please let me be the one to tell them the guns don't even work," Romero said.

"Not a chance. I'm saving that tidbit for when I arrest Pritchett." Vaughn ended the call and put on the Rolex that had been given to him by Stagehand, the internal FBI group that provided the props used in undercover operations. Leaving his own cell phone on the kitchen counter, he slid into his suit-jacket the phone he used while undercover as Sullivan.

It was showtime.

FROM INSIDE THE Hummer, Vaughn saw the headlights of the two vans approaching. He stepped out of the SUV and waited as the vehicles came to a stop in front of him.

Vaughn sized up Mike Mahoney as the young cop exited the second van. Twenty-three or twenty-four years old and built like a tank, he wore his T-shirt tucked into a pair of cargo pants so that his handgun was clearly on display.

Poor form.

"Who the fuck is this?" Vaughn asked Pritchett, nodding in Mike's direction and acting the part of a gun buyer whose smugglers had just showed up with an uninvited guest.

"I'm the fucking muscle, that's who I am," Mike Mahoney shot back.

Clearly, the younger of the Mahoney brothers was going to be a real charmer.

Pritchett, the businessman of the group, was quick to diffuse any potential fireworks. "He's James's brother, Mike. Another cop. James told him about the operation we're running, and he wanted to check it out. I figured with the amount of guns we've been smuggling into the city, it's not a bad idea to have some extra manpower, you know? Just to be safe."

Vaughn knew that Pritchett was lying—according to Romero's intel, the cop was anything but thrilled that Mike had tagged along tonight. But he gave the guy credit for being a fairly decent bullshitter. "Sounds like James needs to work on keeping his mouth shut." Vaughn stepped closer to Pritchett, his tone low. "Next time you think you need extra manpower for a job, you run it by me first. Understood?"

Pritchett swallowed nervously, for once not acting smug. "You're the boss."

"Damn right." Vaughn gestured in the direction of the vans. "Let's see what you've got for me."

Seemingly relieved to have things back on track, Pritchett hustled over to his van and opened up the trunk. Vaughn walked over and saw two large duffle bags, just like the previous two trips. A check of the bags revealed ten AR-15 semi-automatic rifles, which Vaughn once again examined in front of the cops so that it was clear they knew what they were smuggling.

Once he'd accounted for all the rifles, he headed over to the second van. Inside were two more duffle bags, each filled with twenty-five handguns.

"Looks good," Vaughn said. "Let's load them up."

He and the cops grabbed the duffle bags out of the vans and carried them over to his SUV. While loading them inside, he looked back and saw the Mahoney brothers and Howard standing by the back of the second van, where the fourth duffle bag of guns remained. The three men were huddled close together as they spoke.

And that was the moment Vaughn began to suspect that trouble loomed on the horizon.

"Something going on that I need to know about?" he asked Pritchett.

"There'd better not be," Pritchett grumbled.

Buying time, Vaughn kept his pace unhurried as he walked over. Assuming that something was indeed afoot, he scrolled through the various possibilities. He doubted the Mahoney brothers and Howard were planning to steal his guns because three of the duffle bags were already in his SUV. More likely, they planned to shake him down for more money.

Unless they planned to kill him and make off with both the guns *and* the money.

Surrounding the area was Vaughn's backup squad and the eight guys on the special operations team, all of whom were listening in and watching this unfold. Like Vaughn, those twelve men had just identified the Mahoney brothers and Howard as potential problems—problems who were armed, no less. Which meant they all were on high alert right then.

When Vaughn had nearly reached the van, Mike Mahoney stepped forward, blocking the duffle bag. He folded his beefy arms over his chest. "Before you take that bag, Sullivan, I think we need to talk."

Staying in character, Vaughn dismissed this without consideration. "No, we don't. I don't even know you." He stepped forward to grab the bag.

Whether out of anger, bravado, or sheer stupidity, Mahoney reached for his gun.

Fuck. Instinct kicked in and Vaughn immediately grabbed for his own pistol. He had the Kimber out and trained directly on Mike before the cop got his gun out of its holster.

"Easy there, Mahoney," Vaughn said calmly.

Unfortunately, not everyone else stayed quite so calm. The other cops instantly drew their weapons, reacting to the sight of a shady gun buyer pointing a pistol at one of their own.

In the blink of an eye, Vaughn found himself staring down the barrels of five loaded guns.

"Don't fucking move, Sullivan," James Mahoney warned in a low voice.

As Vaughn stood in that dark, sketchy alley surrounded by a group of dirty cops holding him at gunpoint, he knew that trouble no longer loomed on the horizon.

It had arrived.

Thirty-two

VAUGHN'S HEART THUDDED in his chest.

He had mere moments to diffuse the situation before all hell broke loose. First, there was the not-so-small problem of the five guns pointed at his head. But he had another problem to contend with: the FBI backup unit and special operations team who had the area surrounded, unbeknownst to everyone else.

He knew exactly what was happening at that moment. Backup, including Huxley, had seen the cops draw their guns on him and had moved into position to intervene. The SOG snipers were already glassing the six targets, and they had their fingers on the triggers, ready to fire.

As was standard protocol in all undercover operations, Vaughn had a code phrase—in this case, "I don't need this shit today"—that served as a signal to the other agents that he believed he couldn't control the situation and thus needed the cops to be taken down.

He didn't say it. Not yet.

"I'd think carefully about your next move, Pritchett," Vaughn said, purposely addressing the leader of the group.

Mike Mahoney answered instead, his arrogant tone an

indication that he believed he had Vaughn right where he wanted him. "Looks like we're going to have that talk after all, Sullivan. My brother says you're only paying fifteen thousand per run." His eyes fell on Vaughn's Rolex. "I think you can afford more."

"That's your big plan? To shake me down tonight for more money?" Vaughn asked.

"Yep, that about sums it up."

"You might want to think of a new plan," Vaughn advised.

"Why's that?" Mahoney sneered.

"Because I only brought fifteen grand with me, shithead."

That wiped the smile off Mahoney's face right quick.

Having neutralized the idea that the cops could gain from this course of action, Vaughn went back to addressing the leader of the group. "We have a good thing going here, Pritchett. You make nearly four thousand apiece for one night's work. Don't screw it up by listening to this asshole."

"He's bluffing," Mike Mahoney interjected.

Vaughn's tone remained steady. "My seller knows who all of you are. If I go missing tonight—and these guns with me—the people I work with will know that you stole from them. I guarantee you don't want that." He paused to let this sink in. "So here's what we're going to do. I'm going to take my duffle bag, and then I'm going to walk backward until I get to my car. Once I'm inside, I'll drop the cash on the ground and drive away." He surveyed the group. "Anybody have any problems with that plan?"

The cops were all silent. Pritchett finally answered, looking directly at Mike Mahoney. "No."

"Good." Keeping his gun pointed at the younger Mahoney brother, Vaughn grabbed the handles of the duffle bag with his left hand and hoisted it over his shoulder. His body was tense and coiled, ready to act if anyone made a move.

He began backing up, away from the van, as all the cops kept their guns trained on him. Mike Mahoney's jaw twitched, but other than that, everyone remained still. When Vaughn got to the Hummer, he dropped the duffle bag in the back and shut the trunk with his left hand. As soon as he climbed into the car, he started the engine and reached into the glove compartment.

He opened his window and unceremoniously dropped the envelope of money in the dust of his SUV.

He exhaled as he pulled away, knowing that was the moment the FBI snipers finally eased off the triggers of their rifles.

WHEN VAUGHN GOT to the rendezvous spot, a parking lot a few miles away from the warehouse where he'd met Pritchett's crew, Huxley and the rest of the backup squad were already waiting for him.

Huxley walked over to the Hummer, watching as Vaughn got out.

"So, I think we've established that the new guy *is* going to be a problem," Vaughn said.

Shaking his head, Huxley stepped closer and held out his hand, his tone serious. "Well done."

For once, Vaughn didn't respond with a quip or a joke. "Thanks, Seth."

The other squad mates gathered around them, and the SOG team pulled up in their SUVs. "Nice job not getting yourself killed out there," Romero said as he climbed out of the driver's seat.

The comment, Vaughn knew, was intentionally flippant. After the intensity of the situation, they were all coming down from serious adrenaline highs. A little levity was needed right then.

Everyone hung around for a while, the camaraderie thick as the agents rehashed the event from different points of view. After the group finally dispersed, Vaughn stopped at the office to swap out the Hummer for his own car. He and Huxley parted ways in the parking lot of the FBI building.

"So you're good?" Huxley asked.

"I'm good." At this point, Vaughn just wanted to go home so he could unwind and process everything.

"Something like this happens, it kind of gets you thinking, doesn't it?"

Vaughn smiled slightly. Not the subtlest of points, but that didn't make it any less valid. "I'll see you on Monday, Hux."

VAUGHN'S DRIVE HOME was short; it was after two A.M., and there was little traffic on the streets. He let himself into his loft and kept most of the lights off, except for one dim lamp on his nightstand.

He sat on the edge of the bed and slowly exhaled. In his head, he relived the events of the evening several times, and each time he kept coming back to the same thing. There'd been a moment, right as everyone was grabbing for their guns and pointing them at him, when he'd thought, *This could be it*.

And in that moment, he'd thought of Sidney.

It had been just a split-second image, a quick flash of her smiling as she tugged his tie at the restaurant. He'd held back at the time, trying to play it cool, but now all he could think was that he should've said . . . something. Something, that is, other than *cheers* to going out with another guy.

He was a fucking idiot.

He ran his hand through his hair, feeling more restless than ever. He slid off his suit jacket, wanting to get out of his under-cover clothes, and then he realized he still had Mark Sullivan's cell phone in the inside pocket. Remembering that he'd left his own phone on the counter earlier, he walked into the kitchen.

He turned on a light and picked up his phone, noticing that someone had left him a voice mail message.

Sidney.

He immediately hit play.

"Hi, it's me. I was going to wait to say this tomorrow at the rehearsal, but I just . . . wanted to call. I got the purse from Ginny, and she told me what you did. Vaughn, that is the nic-est thing anyone's ever done for me. I've been thinking of you, and . . . I don't know. I guess I wanted to say thank-you. Oh, and I heard you kicked ass in the triathlon and that you're now planning to climb a mountain. Why does this not surprise me, Roberts?"

Vaughn smiled, his chest tightening as he listened to her voice.

"Anyway, thanks again for the purse—I can't wait to show it to Isabelle. I guess I'll see you tomorrow. Good night."

The message ended after that. Vaughn set down his phone and stared at it for a long moment.

She should've been here with him.

After what undoubtedly qualified as a fucked-up day at work, she was the one person he wanted to see. She was the one person he *always* wanted to see.

He knew then what he had to do. No more bullshit. No more playing it cool. Maybe he was about to go down in flames, maybe telling Sidney how he felt wouldn't make any difference.

But there was only one way to find out.

Thirty-three

THE CLOCK WAS ticking. Twenty minutes into the one-hour time slot allotted for Isabelle and Simon's wedding rehearsal, and they were still missing the groom, best man, and two bridesmaids.

Apparently Fate had decided to have a little fun with the opening festivities of the Sinclair-Roberts wedding.

"What are the odds?" Isabelle asked Sidney in disbelief, as they stood near the first row of pews inside the church. They waited with the other people in the wedding party who had made it on time. "Seriously, what are the odds that an *airplane* would make an emergency landing on Lake Shore Drive on the evening of my wedding rehearsal?"

Assuming this was a rhetorical question, Sidney kept her head down as she scrolled through the news reports on her phone—in part because she was interested in the story, and in part to hide her smile, which she guessed wouldn't be particularly appreciated by the stressed-out bride-to-be right then. It was just one of those random, crazy things: a pilot flying a single-engine airplane had been forced to land in the middle of the lakefront expressway after a stabilizing part broke loose

rom the aircraft. The good news was, miraculously, no one
had gotten hurt. The bad news was that everyone who'd been
on the Drive at the time was slowly being funneled off onto
side streets.

"It says here that the pilot timed his landing while traffic
was stopped for a red light. How incredible is that?" Sidney
looked up, caught her sister's glare, and quickly amended that.
"Incredible, but also not so convenient in this particular
circumstance."

Isabelle nervously checked her watch. "We only have until
six o'clock before the next wedding party gets here."

Because Fourth Presbyterian was such a popular wedding
location, the church often booked up to three ceremonies on
Saturdays—as was the case tomorrow. Sidney put her arm
around her sister reassuringly. "And that group will have people who are running late, too. I'm sure, given the circumstances, the church will be accommodating."

"Maybe I'll ask Corinne to talk to the pastor," Isabelle
said, referring to the wedding planner. "See if she can
schmooze him for more time."

As Isabelle hurried off to find the wedding planner, Sidney
walked over to join her father and Jenny, who stood in a group
with Kathleen and Adam Roberts.

"Any word from Vaughn and Simon?" Kathleen asked.

"Simon's last text message to Isabelle said that Vaughn was
going to 'bring the FBI noise' if traffic didn't pickup soon."

Chuckling at that, Kathleen looked around the church. She
took in the striking architecture, which was a combination of
English and French gothic styles. "I was just telling your
father how beautiful your church is." She nodded at the east
window. "That stained glass must be breathtaking on Sunday
mornings, with the sunlight."

Actually, Sidney had no clue what the stained glass looked
like on Sundays, since she hadn't been to church in quite some
time—something for which her heathen ass obviously would
be perishing for all eternity. "It is a gorgeous church," she
said, dodging the question. "I can't wait to see it tomorrow,
with all the flowers for the ceremony."

Kathleen nodded. "Yep, the big day is almost here." She sniffed and suddenly got teary-eyed.

Adam pulled a travel packet of Kleenex out of his pocket and handed it over to his wife. "Figured we'd be needing a few of these."

Kathleen dabbed at her eyes. "I'm going to be a mess tomorrow."

Sidney leaned in affectionately. "If it makes you feel any better, Vaughn's prediction is that I'll be right there with you and those tears during the ceremony." She'd meant it as a joke, but as soon as the words came out of her mouth, she regretted them. It made her and Vaughn's relationship seem so . . . familiar.

A fact that Kathleen, seemingly, did not miss.

There was a sudden gleam of interest in her eyes. "Really? When did you two have this conversation?"

Sidney shrugged, being more careful now. "I think it must've been during the tasting at the Lakeshore Club. Isabelle and Simon asked us to tag along."

"Oh. Of course." Kathleen's shoulders fell.

"Speaking of Vaughn," Sidney's father interjected, "I heard about the purse from Isabelle." He held Sidney's gaze pointedly. "I'm really glad that worked out."

Uh-oh. Probably not the best time for her father to bring up the subject. Yes, Isabelle had been thrilled and very touched when Sidney had given her their mother's purse. But having this conversation in front of Vaughn's parents was likely to invite more questions—questions to which she had no good answers.

"Isabelle told us the whole story," Jenny said. "It's amazing that Vaughn was able to track down the purse after all this time."

"Vaughn hunted down a purse? Sounds like the FBI is a little slow these days," Adam joked.

"I guess we missed this story. Someone needs to catch us up," Kathleen said.

"Sidney had wanted to give Isabelle something their mother had worn on our wedding day. Unfortunately, everything that I'd kept in the attic had gotten lost." Ross held Sidney's gaze, his tone softening. "That was my fault. Something that special can't ever be replaced, I know that."

Sidney stayed silent, surprised by her father's words and the meaningfulness of his tone. Not sure how to respond, she simply nodded.

After a long pause, Jenny jumped in to cover the silence. "But your son saved the day," she told Adam and Kathleen. "Vaughn located a friend of Sidney's mother, and that friend was able to find the purse she had carried on her wedding day."

Ross smiled at Sidney. "I still don't understand how Vaughn even knew Ginny Gastel's name. How would he know that she was your mother's best friend?"

All four pairs of eyes fell on her.

Sidney kept her tone nonchalant. "I . . . guess I must have mentioned Ginny's name to him at some point."

And just like that, Kathleen had that gleam in her eyes again.

Then the doors at the front of the church opened and Simon and Vaughn strode inside. With a grin, Simon led the way up the aisle. "So apparently they've opened a new runway in Chicago."

The group laughed, and Sidney's eyes met Vaughn's as he walked up the aisle alongside his brother. She found herself momentarily holding her breath.

Then he looked away when Isabelle walked up to greet him and Simon.

Sidney exhaled and turned back around, when she saw Kathleen studying her.

"Does he know?" Kathleen asked softly.

Sidney opened her mouth to protest—but before she could say a word, Corinne, the wedding planner, clapped her hands.

"All right, people. We've got a bride, a groom, and a pastor. Anyone who isn't here can get the CliffsNotes later. Let's get this rehearsal started," Corinne said.

Quickly, the scene turned into a flurry of activity as Corinne hustled everyone into place. Simon and the groomsmen lined up at the altar, while the church's wedding coordinator played the processional music through a portable iPod speaker system. The two missing bridesmaids ran into the church just in the nick of time, quickly hugged and apologized to Isabelle. Then Corinne cued Amanda, the first bridesmaid in the lineup, to go.

Sidney waited in the wings for Jayne, the bridesmaid ahead

of her, to hit her mark. When Jayne made it halfway down the aisle, Sidney began walking. She first saw Simon, who gave her an easy smile, and then her eyes drifted over to Vaughn, who stood next to him.

He stared right at her.

So intense and direct was his gaze, Sidney found herself unable to look away—her eyes stayed locked with his the entire way to the altar. Then she walked up the two steps, and took her place next to the other bridesmaids.

"Well. That was interesting," Simon said, standing between her and Vaughn.

The church's wedding coordinator cued the processional music, and Sidney watched as Isabelle came down the aisle on their father's arm. The pastor ran through an abridged dry run of the ceremony, making sure that the two readers and the soloist all knew their cues, and then Simon and Isabelle started off the recessional.

Sidney and Vaughn were up next. He stepped toward her, and she slid her arm through his. They moved down the steps in tandem and began heading up the aisle.

"I got your message last night," Vaughn said. "I wanted to call you back, but it was after two o'clock in the morning by the time I heard it."

"Late night, huh?" Wondering why he'd been occupied until two A.M., she felt her stomach tie in a knot when she realized it was entirely possible that he'd been with another woman. Which he was entitled to do—obviously, she had no claim over him.

"We need to talk," he said, ignoring her question.

"Okay, talk."

"Alone," he said. "Stay back when the rest of the group leaves for the restaurant. I'll drive you."

They were almost at the end of the aisle, where Isabelle and Simon were waiting. Sidney hesitated, suddenly not sure what *anything* meant—the way Vaughn had looked at her while she'd been walking the aisle, her mother's purse, his mysterious late night out, and now his wanting to "talk."

"Please, Sidney," he said, his voice more sincere than she'd ever heard it.

She nodded. "Sure." Then she smiled as they reached Isa-belle and Simon. "Whew. That is one long aisle."

The rest of the bridesmaids and groomsmen filed in behind them. Because they'd started so late, the next wedding party was already waiting in the vestibule as they finished. Things turned chaotic after that, as the wedding planner wrapped things up and tried to hustle everyone out of the incoming group's way. Purses and coats were quickly gathered from the church as people coordinated who was driving with whom to the restaurant for the rehearsal dinner.

Sidney watched as Vaughn spoke with Simon, presumably to explain that he would give her a ride to the restaurant. The brothers exchanged a look, and Simon clasped Vaughn's shoulder before heading off to join the others.

Vaughn returned to Sidney, putting his hand on the small of her back to lead her through the crowd in the direction of a side door. They stepped outside, into an open-air portico with wide stone arches that looked out at a serene garden.

"This way," he said, cutting through the garden. On the far end of the grounds was a bench hidden almost entirely by green shrubbery.

He gestured to the bench. "Why don't you sit down?"

Now he was starting to freak her out a little. He was just act-ing so . . . serious. "All right," she said cautiously, taking a seat.

Vaughn peered down at her. "Just a heads-up, I'm probably going to fumble my way through this. So bear with me."

She wasn't following. "Fumble your way through what?"

He looked at her for another moment, then bent down on one knee.

Sidney's heart leapt out of her chest. "Oh my God, what are you doing?"

"Um . . . getting eye-to-eye so we can talk," he said, as if this were evident.

"Oh. Right."

"And . . . here I'd felt a little awkward before." Vaughn got up and took a seat on the bench. He ran his hand through his hair, as if debating where to begin. "Yesterday, something happened at work. Things got a little hairy during an undercover meeting."

Sidney frowned, not liking the sound of that. "How hairy?"

"One of the guys went for his gun, so I pulled out my gun, and then his five friends all pulled *their* guns on me."

"Oh. So, by 'a little hairy,' you meant that you almost got killed yesterday. Granted, I'm not an FBI agent, so maybe I'm not down with the lingo, but to me that sounds more than a *little* hairy. Like, I'd probably call that *monumentally* hairy. Or *colossally* hairy. And, well . . ." She trailed off, all riled up and feeling relieved and worried at the same time. But more than anything, she wanted to be sure of one thing. "Are you okay?"

He touched her cheek. "I'm okay. You know what helped? When I got home last night and heard your message. Your voice made me smile, just like you always make me smile." He turned to face her. "We're good together, Sidney. And I know you feel it, too. These past couple months I've been fighting the way I feel because this is definitely not what I had planned, but the truth is . . . I'm in love with you."

When her eyes widened in surprise, he kept right on going. "I know you're afraid of getting hurt again. I know you think I'm not the right man for you. You sized me up the moment we met and made up your mind right then. And you're right, the guy who walked up to you that day in the coffee shop wasn't looking for a serious relationship. But that guy is gone." He peered down into her eyes. "He's been replaced by a man who can't imagine his life without you."

She cocked her head, her voice soft. "Vaughn . . . "

"Use the checklist on me," he said intently.

When she paused—her head spinning with everything he'd just said—he continued on with the list himself.

"Not hung up on a prior relationship. Check. Settled in my career. Check. Available whenever you want. Check. I have all the qualifications. The only thing I was missing was the number-one rule: I said I didn't want to be in a serious relationship." He moved closer, linking his fingers through hers. "And now I know that with you, I want that more than anything. Just give me a chance, Sidney. Let me show you that I can be the man you're looking for. I promise you won't regret it."

Sidney sat there for several moments, her throat feeling tight.

He was right—she did know how good they were together. She could so easily picture them laughing over dinner, or breakfast, or while hanging out with friends or spending the holidays up in Wisconsin with Isabelle, Simon, his parents, and a cozy ranch filled with little kids. She could picture the quieter moments, too—when she would be there for him after a tough day at work, or him listening as she talked about some new development in the complex relationship she had with her father.

And with her whole heart, she wanted all of that. She wanted to believe they really could do this.

But there was one thing she needed to know first.

"So, I have a question." She looked Vaughn right in the eyes, for once not trying to hide her vulnerability. "What does it mean when a guy who has spent years avoiding commitment says he's suddenly changed his mind? Is it a fluke thing he's going to regret in a couple of months, or is it the real deal?"

His hand caressed her cheek, his voice husky with emotion. "It means he's found the one woman who makes him want to be a happily-ever-after type. So bring on the damn singing birds and woodland animals."

Sidney smiled, tears filling her eyes. "Good answer." She reached for him and pulled his mouth down to hers. He cupped her face between his hands, kissing her tenderly, and then slowly deepened the kiss. When they finally pulled apart, he gave her a no-nonsense look.

"I think it goes without saying that you will be un-inviting Two-Minute Tyler to this wedding."

"Two-Minute Tyler got nixed two weeks ago," she said.

Vaughn looked unmistakably pleased, hearing this. "Why?"

She slid her arms around his neck. "Because when he kissed me, I pictured you instead."

"Well, I hope you soaked it up, Sinclair. Because that was the last first kiss you'll ever have." He bent his head, his voice low and possessive. "All the rest are mine."

Thirty-four

ADMITTEDLY, HE WASN'T the biggest expert on such things. But from what Vaughn could tell, the Sinclair-Roberts wedding was a huge success.

Standing by the bar in the corner of the room, he surveyed the elegant scene before him. Guests mingled among candlelit ivory-linen-topped tables decorated with centerpieces of roses and orchids. The band played Louis Armstrong's "What a Wonderful World" as couples danced on the ballroom floor, and through the open French doors he saw more guests on the terrace, laughing, talking, and admiring the view of the lake.

Even a few minor blips hadn't dampened the spirits of the evening. Uncle Finn's impromptu—and slightly slurred—toast in which he'd rousingly asked everyone to raise a glass to "Simon and Annabelle." A slightly awkward moment in the receiving line when Vaughn's grandmother got on her pedestal about the high divorce rate among "kids these days" while talking to Isabelle and Sidney's thrice-remarried father. The mild pouting by Cousin Anna, who—after clinking her champagne flute nearly nonstop during the salad course—had returned from the restroom to find her stemware mysteriously replaced by plastic.

Vaughn's gaze drifted to the left, toward the foyer, where he saw Sidney heading up the wide, curving staircase behind her sister. In one hand she held the train of Isabelle's dress—there appeared to be some sort of wardrobe malfunction, although they were both laughing as they walked up the steps. Down on the main level, the photographer scurried into action to capture the moment, while Vaughn tried to decide what was more captivating: Sidney's smile, or the strapless champagne-colored dress that skimmed over her every curve. Between that, the siren-like waves of her auburn hair, the smoky eyeliner, and the strappy heels, he'd barely been able to tear his eyes away from her since she'd walked down the aisle during the wedding ceremony.

Yesterday they'd made the decision to keep the situation between them on the down-low, not wanting to detract anything from Isabelle and Simon's big night. Although there'd certainly been a lot of long, intimate looks during the rehearsal dinner, they'd otherwise proceeded as usual, playing their roles of best man and maid of honor and not doing anything overt to out themselves as a couple.

Then, during last night's toasts, when the two of them had been seated next to each other at a table with their families, Sidney had delivered the bad news.

"I can't wait to get you alone tonight," Vaughn had said in a low voice, speaking in Sidney's ear as everyone laughed while Simon told a funny story about his groomsman Kimo.

"Oh . . . I forgot to mention: I'm not going home tonight," she said. "I'm spending the night in a suite with Isabelle at the Four Seasons. We thought it would make things easier in the morning, since the church is right across the street from the hotel."

No.

"This wedding is starting to become a serious burr up my ass," Vaughn growled.

Sidney laughed, squeezing his thigh reassuringly under the table.

"Not helping the situation here, Sinclair." But he winked at her, clapping along with everyone else in response to Simon's toast, of which he hadn't heard one word.

An hour later, after Simon and Isabelle had been updated on the fact that, yes, Vaughn and Sidney were officially a "we"—the two couples said their good-byes at the Four Seasons hotel. Not wanting to intrude on their siblings' farewell in the lobby, Vaughn stayed outside with Sidney to have a private moment of their own.

The night air was warm as they stood on the sidewalk, surrounded by the twinkling lights of the city. Vaughn bent his head to give Sidney a kiss, struck by how much he didn't want to let her go. "I'll be waiting for you tomorrow, at the end of that aisle."

With one hand resting against his chest, she pressed her lips softly against his in good-bye. "Probably, this would be a really great time to tell you that I love you, too."

VAUGHN SMILED AT the memory, checking his watch after Sidney disappeared from sight at the top of the stairs. Only two more hours left to go with this wedding, and she'd be all his.

"I assume that look means I can skip the lecture on what a fool you'd be to let that one walk away," said a voice to his right.

Yep, nothing quite so awkward as being caught ogling a woman by one's own mother.

"Mom. Hi," he said, turning. "I was just . . . admiring the chandelier."

"I certainly hope you have a better poker face than that when you're working undercover."

Vaughn laughed. "Okay, fine. Yes, you can skip the lecture. As a matter of fact, I planned to talk to you tonight about Sidney. And . . . why are you smiling at me like that, as if you're not surprised by any of this?"

"Surprised?" She smiled cheekily. "No, I'm not surprised. I've had a feeling about you two for a while."

Vaughn pulled back. "Since when?"

"Oh, ever since I found a bunch of my New England Asters smooshed in the clearing that weekend after you kids visited. Almost as if somebody, or two somebodies, had rolled on top of them."

Instantly, Vaughn flashed back to a memory of picking purple wildflowers out of Sidney's hair.

Oops.

"Must've been Simon and Isabelle. Those crazy kids," he said.

His mother snorted. "Please. That poor girl was so sick that weekend, she wasn't rolling around anywhere."

Vaughn shot his mother a look. *Um . . . what?*

She smiled. "Ah, yes. The other big secret I'm not supposed to know anything about." She winked. "Don't tell your brother I know. I've been practicing my surprised face for weeks."

"I . . . have no idea what you're talking about, Mom," he said carefully.

She patted his cheek. "Of course, you don't." Then she went back to the original question. "Now, about Sidney. You said you wanted to talk to me about her tonight. So, let's hear it."

"Do we need to have a Kleenex handy before I answer that?" Vaughn teased.

She cocked her head. "I think that depends on what you're going to say next."

He paused at that, trying to decide how best to put it into words. In the end, it came down to one thing. "I'm crazy about her, Mom."

His mother said nothing at first, then unzipped her purse and pulled out a Kleenex. "Yep. That'll do it."

UPSTAIRS IN THE bride's changing room, Sidney checked out the bustle on Isabelle's gown. "All the hooks are intact. It looks like two of the fastenings just slipped out."

"Someone stepped on my dress when I was dancing,"

Isabelle said, as Sidney made the adjustment. "That's probably when it happened."

After slipping the second fastening onto its hook, Sidney arranged the back of the dress, making sure all the folds fell neatly into place. "There. Good as ever."

She stood next to the mirror, looking her sister over with a slight smile as Isabelle touched up her lipstick.

"Am I showing? It's obvious, isn't it?" Isabelle said.

That wasn't the reason Sidney had smiled. Just . . . memories. "Honestly, you can't tell at all with that dress. You look beautiful, Izz."

Isabelle tucked the lipstick into their mother's purse and snapped it shut. She moved closer to Sidney and put her arm around her. "So do you. You've had this glow about you all day," she said teasingly.

"I'm sure I have. They put about five pounds of bronzer on me at the salon."

"Uh-huh." Isabelle's expression said she wasn't buying that for one second.

They both looked at their reflection in the mirror, and Isabelle rested her head against Sidney's shoulder. "So here's a thought: if you marry Vaughn and take his name, would that make us the *Roberts* sisters?"

Sidney thought about that. "Nah. I say we'll still be the Sinclair sisters."

Isabelle smiled in agreement. "Always."

A FEW MINUTES later, Sidney returned to the ballroom with Isabelle. She spotted Vaughn talking to one of his cousins—there were twenty-three of them; she couldn't keep track of all their names—and made a point to cross the room within his line of sight. She looked over her shoulder, caught his gaze, and then kept going toward the terrace.

Once outside, she took the staircase down to the path that cut across the grounds. The moon sat low in the late-summer sky as she followed the trail of lights along the walkway to the gazebo. Her heels clicked softly against the wood as she stepped inside and headed over to the railing.

She looked out at the clubhouse, watching the guests mingle on the terrace. A light breeze brushed over her shoulders, and she listened as the beginning strains of Etta James's "At Last" drifted down to the gazebo. She heard footsteps, then felt Vaughn's arms circle her waist.

She closed her eyes and leaned back against his chest.

His voice was low in her ear. "Isn't there some tradition that says the best man and maid of honor have to dance together?"

She smiled. "I'm not sure about a tradition. But I like the idea in this case." She turned around and slid her hand into his.

They began moving slowly together to the music, their bodies close.

"I've been thinking about something," Vaughn said, with a teasing look in his eyes.

"I bet you have."

"Not that. Well, yes, that, but something else, too." He studied her. "Your reaction in the church garden, when I got down on one knee . . . When the time comes, is that going to be your answer? A panicked, 'Oh my God, what are you doing?' "

Sidney shifted even closer to him, her thumb stroking over the backs of his fingers. "That wasn't panic, that was shock. Ten minutes before that, I'd been worried you'd spent the night with another woman."

"Hmm."

When he said nothing further, she watched him with a coy smile.

"What?" he asked.

"I'm just waiting for your eye to start twitching after the reference to you getting down on one knee 'when the time comes.' "

Instead of answering, he simply began humming along with the song as they danced. Not an eye twitch in sight.

"You do realize that getting down on one knee generally

refers to a proposal, right?" Sidney continued. "A *marriage* proposal?"

His eyes, a warm green-gold, daringly held hers as he softly sang the next line of the song. " 'You smiled . . . and then the spell was cast.' "

Okay, he pretty much just melted her heart right there.

Still, she'd never been one to back down from a challenge from Vaughn Roberts. "All right, if that doesn't get you all twitchy, how about this? I had a random thought earlier today, that if we have kids, they'll probably look freakishly similar to Isabelle and Simon's."

The song was on its final lyric—*At last*—and Vaughn took her hands and wrapped them around his neck.

"Kids, Roberts," she said, just to be clear. "I have fertile eggs in me, and I'm talking about having *babies*."

She waited for the eye twitch. Or hell, even a tiny twinge.

Instead, with a smile, he pulled her in for a kiss.

Keep reading for a sneak preview of
another irresistible contemporary romance
from Julie James

Practice Makes Perfect

Available now from Berkley Sensation

One

THE ALARM CLOCK went off at 5:30 A.M.

Payton Kendall lifted a sleepy hand to her nightstand and fumbled around to silence the god-awful beeping. She lay there, snuggled in amongst her cozy down pillows, blinking, rousing. Allowing herself these first, and last, few seconds of the day that she could call her own. Then—suddenly remembering—she jumped out of bed.

Today was the day.

Payton had a plan for this morning—she had set her alarm to wake her a half hour earlier than usual. There was a purpose for this: she had observed *his* daily routine and guessed that *he* got to the office every morning by 7:00 A.M. He liked being the first one in the office, she knew. On this morning, however, she would be there when he got in. Waiting.

In her mind she had it all worked out—she would act casual. She would be in her office, and when she heard him walk in, she would just "happen" to stroll by to get something from the printer. "Good morning," she would say with a smile. And without her having to say anything else, he would know exactly what that smile meant.

He'd be wearing one of his designer suits, the ones Payton knew he had hand-tailored to fit him just so. "The man *knows* how to wear a suit," she had overheard one of the secretaries say while gossiping by the coffeemaker in the fifty-third-floor break room. Payton had resisted the urge to follow up the secretary's comment with one of her own, lest she reveal the feelings about him that she had fought to keep so carefully hidden.

Moving with purpose, Payton sped through her morning routine. How much easier it must be to be a man, she reflected not for the first time. No makeup to apply, no hair to straighten, no legs to shave. They didn't even have to sit to pee, the lazy bastards. Just shower, shave, wham-bam, out the door in ten minutes. Although, Payton suspected, *he* put a little more effort into it. That perfectly imperfect, mussed-just-right hair of his certainly required product of some sort. And, from what she had personally observed, he never wore the same shirt/tie combo twice in the same month.

Not that Payton didn't put some effort into her appearance as well. A jury consultant she had worked with during a particularly tricky gender discrimination trial had told her that jurors—both men and women—responded more favorably to female lawyers who were attractive. While Payton found this to be sadly sexist, she accepted it as a fact nonetheless and thus made it a general rule to always put her best face forward, literally, at work. Besides, she'd rather hang herself by a pinky toe than ever let *him* see her looking anything but her best.

The "L" ride into the office was quiet, with far fewer passengers riding this early in the morning. The city seemed to be just waking up as Payton walked along the Chicago River the three blocks to her law firm's offices. The early morning sun glinted off the river, casting it in a soft golden glow. Payton smiled to herself as she cut through the lobby of her building; she was in that good of a mood.

Her excitement grew as the elevator rose to the fifty-third floor. Her floor. *His* floor. The door opened, revealing a dark office hallway. The secretaries wouldn't be in for at least two hours, which was good. If all went as planned, she had a few things to say to him and now she would be able to speak freely, without fear of the two of them being overheard.

Payton strode with confidence down the corridor, her briefcase swinging at her side. His office was closer to the elevator bank; she would pass it en route to hers. Eight years it had been since they had moved into their respective offices across the floor from each other. She could picture perfectly the letters on the nameplate outside his office.

J. D. JAMESON.

My, how the mere mention of that name made her pulse quicken . . .

Payton rounded the corner, grinning in anticipation as she thought about what he would say when—

She stopped cold.

His office light was on.

But—how? This couldn't be. She had gotten up at this ridiculous hour to get in first. What about her plans, her big plans? The casual stroll by the printer, the way she was supposed to smile knowingly and say, *Good morning, J.D.*?

She heard a familiar rich baritone voice behind her.

"Good morning, Payton."

Payton's pulse skyrocketed. She couldn't help it, merely hearing his voice had that effect on her. She turned around and there he stood.

J. D. Jameson.

Payton paused to look him over. He looked so quintessentially *J.D.* right then, with his suit jacket already off and his classically cut navy pinstripe pants and yes, that perfectly styled rakish light brown hair of his. He looked tan—probably out playing tennis or golf over the weekend—and he gave her one of his perfect-white-teeth smiles as he leaned casually against the credenza behind him.

"I said, 'Good morning,'" he repeated. And so Payton did what she always did when she saw J. D. Jameson.

She scowled.

The shithead had beaten her into work.

Again.

"Good morning, J.D.," she replied with that sarcastic tone she reserved just for him.

Noting her arrival, he checked his watch, then glanced up and down the hallway with deliberate exaggeration. "Wow—did I miss the lunch cart? Is it noon already?"

She *really* hated this guy.

I hardly get in at noon, Payton nearly retorted, then bit her tongue. No. She wouldn't stoop to his level and defend herself.

"Perhaps if you spent a little less time keeping track of my comings and goings, J.D., and a little more time working, it wouldn't take you fifteen hours to bill ten."

She watched with satisfaction as her reply wiped the smirk right off of his face. Touché. With a well-practiced cool and calm demeanor, she turned in her heels and headed across the hall to her own office.

Such a silly thing, Payton thought. This endless competition J.D. had with her. The man clearly spent far too much time focusing on what she was up to. It had been that way since . . . well, since as long as she could remember. Thank goodness she was above such petty nonsense.

Payton got to her office and closed her door behind her. She set her briefcase down on top of her desk and took a seat in the well-worn leather chair. How many hours had she logged in that chair? How many all-nighters had she pulled? How many weekends had she sacrificed? All in her quest to show the firm that she was partnership material—that *she* was the top associate in her class.

Through the glass on her door, she could see across the hall to J.D.'s office. He was already back at his own desk, in front of his computer, working. Oh, sure, like he had such important matters to tend to.

Payton pulled her laptop out of her briefcase and turned it on, ready to start her day. After all, she had very important things to focus on, too.

For starters, like how the hell she was ever going to get up at *4:30* tomorrow morning.

Two

"I SEE YOU broke your own record."

Payton peered up from her computer as Irma walked into her office, waving the time sheets Payton had given her earlier that morning.

"I get depressed just logging in these hours," her secretary continued in an exasperated tone. "Seriously, I need to be assigned to a different associate. Someone whose weekly time sheets aren't as long as *Anna Karenina*."

Payton raised an eyebrow as she took the stack of time sheets from her secretary. "Let me guess—another recommendation from Oprah?"

Irma gave Payton a look that said she was treading on seriously dangerous ground. "That sounds like mocking."

"No, never," Payton assured her, trying not to grin. "I'm sure it's a wonderful book."

At least four times a year Irma made the pilgrimage out to the West Loop to sit in the audience at Harpo Studios and be in the presence of Her Holiness the Winfrey. Irma took all recommendations from the TV maven—lifestyle, literary, and otherwise—as gospel. Any comments in the negative by Payton or anyone else were strictly taboo.

Irma took a seat in front of the desk as she waited for Payton to sign off on the completed time sheets. "You'd like it. It's about a woman who's progressive for her time."

"Sounds promising," Payton said distractedly as she skimmed the printout of the hours her secretary had entered.

"Then she falls for the wrong man," Irma continued.

"That's a bit cliché, isn't it? They call this Tolstoy guy a writer?" Payton quickly scrawled her signature across the bottom of the last time sheet and handed them back to Irma.

"This 'Tolstoy guy' knows about relationships. Perhaps you could learn a thing or two from him."

Payton pretended not to hear the comment. After years of working with Irma, the two of them had developed a comfortable, familiar relationship, and she had learned that the best way to handle her secretary's not-so-subtle remarks regarding her personal life was simply to ignore them.

"You've seen the evidence of my lack of free time," Payton said, gesturing to her time sheets. "Until I'm through with this trial, I'm afraid Tolstoy will have to wait." She pointed. "But if Oprah happens to know of a book about responding to subpoenas for corporate documents, *that* I would be interested in."

Seeing Irma's look of warning, Payton held up her hands innocently. "I'm just saying."

"I tell you what," Irma said. "I'll hold on to the book for you. Because after this month, I suspect you'll be able to give yourself a bit of a break." She winked.

Payton turned back to her computer. Despite Irma's repeated attempts to engage her on this subject, she didn't like to talk openly about it. After all, she didn't want to jinx things. So she waved aside the remark, feigning nonchalance.

"Is something happening this month? I'm not aware of it."

Irma snorted. "Please. You've only had this month highlighted in your electronic calendar for eight years."

"I don't know what you're talking about. And stop snooping around in my calendar."

Irma rose to leave. "All right, all right, I know how you are about discussing this stuff." She headed toward the door, then paused and turned back. "I almost forgot—Mr. Gould's secretary called. He wondered if you're free to meet in his office at one thirty."

Payton quickly checked. "Works for me. Tell her that I'll come by his office then." She began entering the appointment in her daily planner when she heard her secretary call to her from the doorway.

"Um, Payton—one last thing?"

Payton looked up distractedly from her computer. "Yes?"

Irma smiled reassuringly. "You're gonna make it, you know. You've earned it. So stop being so paranoid."

Despite herself, Payton grinned. "Thanks, Irma."

Once her secretary was gone, Payton's thoughts lingered for a moment. She glanced over at the calendar on her desk.

Four weeks left. The firm's partnership decisions would be announced at the end of the month. Truth be told, she was feeling fairly hopeful about her chances of making it. She had worked hard for this—long hours, never turning down work—and now she was in the homestretch. The finish line was finally in sight.

Payton felt her heartbeat begin to race as she gave in to the excitement for one teeny-tiny moment. Then, not wanting to get carried away just yet, she calmed herself and, as always, got busy with work.

A FEW MINUTES before 1:30, Payton gathered her notes and her summary trial file folder for her meeting with Ben. She wasn't sure exactly what he wanted to meet about, but she guessed it had something to do with the trial she was about to start next week. As the head of the firm's litigation department, Ben stayed on top of all cases going to trial, even those with which he wasn't directly involved.

As was typical, Payton felt slightly on edge as she prepared for the meeting with her boss. She never knew what to expect with Ben. Despite the fact that he had never given her any indication that he was disappointed in her work—to the contrary, he consistently gave her the highest marks in her annual reviews—she felt that, at times, there was some sort of awkward undercurrent to their interactions. She couldn't quite put her finger on it, she just got a weird vibe now and then. He ran hot and cold with her; sometimes he was fine, other times he seemed a bit . . . stiff. Stilted. At first she had assumed this was just part of his personality, but on other occasions she had seen him joking easily with other associates. Interestingly, all male associates. She had begun to suspect that Ben—while never blatantly unprofessional—had a more difficult time getting along with women. It certainly wasn't an unlikely conclusion to draw. Law firms could be old-fashioned at times and unfortunately, female attorneys still had a bit of an "old boy network" to contend with.

Nevertheless, because Ben was the head of her group—and thus a key player in the decision whether to make her a partner—Payton resolved to keep trying to establish a more congenial rapport between them. After all, she liked to think she was a relatively easygoing person. With one exception (and who really counted *him*, anyway?) she prided herself on getting along well with pretty much everyone she worked with.

Payton grabbed a pen and a legal pad, stuffed them in the file folder she carried, and headed out her office door. Irma's desk was right outside her office, and she turned to let her secretary know she was leaving. In doing so, she nearly ran right into someone coming down the hallway from the other direction.

"Oh, sorry!" Payton exclaimed, scooting aside to avoid a collision. She looked up apologetically and—

—saw J.D.

Her expression changed to one of annoyance. She sighed. She had been having such a nice day until now.

Then Payton realized: oops—they had an audience. With a glance in Irma's direction, she quickly adopted her most charmingly fake smile.

"Well, hello, J.D. How have you been?" she asked.

J.D. also cast an eye in the direction of the secretaries

working nearby. As well practiced in this ruse as Payton, he matched her amiable expression with one of his own.

"My, how nice of you to ask, Payton," he gushed ever so warmly as he gazed down at her. "I'm well, thank you. And yourself?"

As always, Payton found herself annoyed by how damn tall J.D. was. She hated being in a position of—literally—having to look up to him. She had no doubt that J.D., on the other hand, quite enjoyed this.

"Fine, thank you," Payton told him. "I'm heading to Ben's office." She managed to maintain her pleasant grin. Meryl Streep may have her Oscars, but she could learn a thing or two from Payton. Best Pretense of Liking One's Assholic Coworker.

J.D.'s eyes narrowed slightly at Payton's reply, but he too kept up the charade. "What a nice surprise—I'm headed to Ben's office myself," he said as if this was the best thing he'd heard all morning. Then he gestured gallantly to Payton— *after you.*

With a nod, she turned and headed down the back hallway to Ben's corner office. J.D. strode easily alongside her; Payton had to take two steps for every one of his to keep up. Not that she let *him* see that.

After walking together in silence for a few moments, J.D. glanced around for witnesses. Seeing they were safely out of earshot, he folded his arms across his chest with what Payton had come to think of as the trademark J.D. Air of Superiority.

"So I saw your name in the *Chicago Lawyer*," he led in.

Payton smiled, knowing he surely had a thing or two to say about that. She was pleased he'd seen the article the magazine had run in this month's edition. She had been tempted to send him a copy in yesterday's interoffice mail, but thought it would be better if he discovered it on his own.

" 'Forty to Watch Under 40,' " she said, referencing the article's title and proud of her inclusion in its distinction.

" 'Forty *Women* to Watch Under 40,' " J.D. emphasized. "Tell me, Payton—is there a reason your gender finds it necessary to be so separatist? Afraid of a little competition from the opposite sex, perhaps?"

Payton tried not to laugh as she tossed her hair back over her shoulders. Hardly.

"If my gender hesitates to compete with yours, J.D., it's only because we're afraid to lower ourselves to your level," she replied sweetly.

They arrived at the doorway to Ben's office. J.D. leaned against the door casually and folded his arms across his chest. After eight years, Payton recognized this gesture well—it meant he was about to begin another one of his condescending lectures. She gave it 95 percent odds that he'd begin with one of his pompously rhetorical questions that he had absolutely no intention of letting her answer.

"Let me ask you this . . ." he began.

Bingo.

". . . how do you think it would go over if the magazine ran an article called 'Forty *Men* to Watch Under 40'?" He took the liberty of answering for her. "You and your little feminista friends would call that discrimination. But then isn't that, per se, discrimination? Shouldn't we men be entitled to our lists, too?"

J.D. held the door open for her and gestured for her to enter. As she passed by him, Payton noted that Ben wasn't in his office yet, so she took a seat in front of his desk. As J.D. sat in the chair next to her, she turned to him, coolly unperturbed.

"I find it very interesting when a man, a graduate of Princeton University and Harvard Law School, sitting next to me in an Armani suit, has the nerve somehow to claim that *he* is the victim of discrimination."

J.D. opened his mouth to jump in, but Payton cut him off with a finger. Index, not middle. She was a lady after all.

"Notwithstanding that fact," she continued, "I submit that you men *do* have your so-called 'lists.' Several at this firm in fact. They're called the Executive Committee, the Management Committee, the Compensation Committee, the firm' golfing club, the intramural basketball team—"

"You want to be on the basketball team?" J.D. interrupted his blue eyes crinkling in amusement at this.

"It's illustrative," Payton said, sitting back in her chair defensively.

"What's illustrative?"

Payton sat upright at the sound of the voice. She glanced over as Ben Gould, head litigation partner, strode confidently into his office and took a seat at his desk. He fixed Payton with a curious gaze of his dark, probing eyes. She shifted in her chair, trying not to feel as though she was already under interrogation.

J.D. answered Ben before Payton had a chance. "Oh, it's nothing," he said with a dismissive wave. "Payton and I were just discussing the Supreme Court's recent decision in *Ledder v. Arkansas*, and how the opinion is illustrative of the Court's continuing reluctance to embroil itself in state's rights."

Payton glanced at J.D. out of the corner of her eye.

Smart-ass.

Although admittedly, that wasn't too shabby a bit of quick thinking.

The jerk.

Ben laughed at them as he quickly glanced at the messages his secretary had left on his desk. "You two—you never stop."

Payton fought the urge to roll her eyes. He really had no idea.

J.D. seized on Ben's momentary distraction to lean forward in his chair. He held the lapel of his suit out to Payton and whispered. "And by the way, it's not Armani. It's *Zegna*." He winked at her.

Payton glared, tempted to tell him exactly where he could stick that *Zegna* suit.

"Sorry to call you both down here on such short notice," Ben said. "But as you both may be aware, Gibson's Drug Stores chain has just been hit with a class action gender discrimination lawsuit."

Payton had indeed heard about the lawsuit—yesterday's filing of the complaint in a federal court in Florida had made all the national papers and had even been discussed on MSNBC and CNN.

"The complaint was filed yesterday, assigned to Judge

Meyers of the Southern District of Florida," she said, eager to let Ben know she was on top of things.

"The claims were filed under Title VII—one-point-eight million female employees of the company allege they were discriminated against in hiring, pay, and promotion," J.D. added with a sideways glance in Payton's direction. He, too, had done his homework.

Ben smiled at their eagerness. He leaned back, twirling his pen casually. "It's the largest discrimination class action ever filed. That means big bucks to the law firm that defends Gibson's."

Payton saw the glint in Ben's eye. "And who might that be?"

Ben laced his fingers together, drumming them against the back of his hands like a villain in a James Bond movie.

"Funny you should ask, Payton . . . The CEO of Gibson's, Jasper Conroy, hasn't decided yet which law firm will defend his company. He has, however, chosen three of the top firms in the country to meet with."

J.D. grinned. "Let me take a wild stab in the dark here: our firm is one of those three."

Ben nodded, proud as always that his group of litigators was continually ranked as being among the best in the world. "Nice guess. I got the call earlier this morning from Jasper Conroy himself."

He pointed at J.D. and Payton. "And here's where you two come in: Jasper was very clear about the type of trial team he's looking for. He wants a fresher image to represent the face of his company, not a bunch of stodgy old men in suits, like me." Ben chuckled, fully aware that at forty-nine years old he was actually quite young to be the head of litigation at such a prestigious firm. "Personally," he continued, "I think Jasper is just trying to avoid paying partner rates."

Like the good associates they were, Payton and J.D. laughed at the joke.

"Anyhoo . . ." Ben went on, "I told Jasper that this firm just so happens to have the perfect litigators for him. Two very experienced, very savvy senior associates. You two."

Through her surprise, it took Payton a moment to process

what Ben was saying. A large pit was growing in her stomach, because this conversation was headed in a very bad direction.

If someone made her swear an oath under cross-examination—better yet, if Jack Bauer himself subjected her to the full array of interrogation tactics at CTU's disposal—Payton couldn't have said exactly *how* her war with J.D. had started. Frankly, it had been going on for so long that it simply seemed to be the way things always were.

Without ever saying a word, however, she and J.D. had implicitly agreed to keep their mutual dislike to themselves. Both wanting more than anything to be successful at work, they understood that law firms were like kindergarten: it wasn't good to get a "needs improvement" in "plays well with others."

Luckily, it had been relatively easy to maintain their charade. Even though they were in the same group, it had been years since they had worked together on a case. There were a few reasons for this: First, as a general rule, cases in the litigation group were staffed with one partner, one senior associate, and one or two junior associates. As members of the same class, there was little reason for both Payton and J.D. to work on the same matter.

Second, and perhaps more important, the two of them had developed specialties in very different areas of the law. J.D. was a class action lawyer. He handled large multi-plaintiff, multi-district cases. Payton, on the other hand, specialized in employment law, particularly single-plaintiff race and gender discrimination lawsuits. Her cases were typically smaller in terms of damages at stake but higher profile in terms of the publicity they garnered.

Thus far—whether by fluke chance or luck—there had been very little overlap in the niche practice areas she and J.D. had carved out for themselves.

Apparently until now, that is.

Payton remained silent as Ben continued his pitch, trying to refrain from displaying the growing apprehension she felt. She snuck a quick peek at J.D. and saw him shift edgily in his chair. From what she could tell, he appeared just as displeased as she by this development.

"Combined, your skills are perfect for this case," Ben was saying. "Jasper sounded very excited to meet you both."

"This is wonderful news, Ben," Payton said, trying not to choke on her words.

"Yes . . . wonderful." J.D. looked as though he had just swallowed a bug. "What is it you need us to do?"

"Jasper and Gibson's general counsel, and a few of their in-house attorneys, will all be coming to Chicago on Thursday," Ben said. "I want you two to work together and I want you to *bring them in*," he emphasized, tapping his finger on his desk. "Think you're up to it?"

Payton and J.D. eyed each other carefully, both thinking the same thing. Could they really do this?

Knowing what was at stake, in mutual understanding of how the game was played, they turned to Ben.

"Absolutely," they said in unison.

Ben smiled at them, the future of his firm. He leaned back in his chair, getting sentimental. Undoubtedly at the thought of the big bucks they would bring in.

"Ah . . . eight years," he said affectionately. "For eight years I have watched you two grow up at this firm, into the great lawyers you are. I'm excited by this chance to see you work together—you'll make quite a team. And it's perfect timing, too, because soon you'll both be p—"

He abruptly stopped speaking.

J.D. and Payton sat on the edge of their seats, nearly falling off their chairs as they hung on to Ben's last word.

Apparently realizing he had said too much, Ben waved this off with a coy grin. "Well, one thing at a time. Right now, you guys have a pitch to prepare for."